Laying
by Beve

"You don't know me, Trent." Kate practically screamed the words at him. "I'm not sure you ever did."

"That's not fair, Kate. I did know you once. And you knew me. We knew each other inside out." He reached out and lifted her hand, then placed it over his heart. "There was a time when I thought—" He dropped his hold on her as if her hand had suddenly become red-hot. "Sorry. Old habits die hard. Being with you brings back a lot of memories. Good memories."

Don't look back, she told herself. *Don't get sucked in by those good memories.*

It would be so easy to fall into Trent's arms, to fall into his bed in an effort to recapture what they'd once shared. But no matter what happened, even if they found their child, they couldn't go back. It was too late for them.

It was too late for *all* of them.

Miss Pruitt's Private Life
by Barbara McCauley

ᗡᗣᴥᗣᑕ

Miss Marcy Pruitt's Private To Do List:

1) *Get away from demanding fans.*

2) *Take three weeks away from the crazy world to enjoy best friend's wedding.*

3) *Indulge in light flirtation with sexy-as-sin brother of the groom.*

4) *Change look so as not to be recognised.*

5) *Fall into bed with Evan Carter.*
   (Note: Do <u>not</u> fall in love with him!).

6) *Rethink this affair before someone gets hurt.*

Available in June 2005 from Silhouette Desire

Laying His Claim
by Beverly Barton
(The Protectors)
and
Miss Pruitt's Private Life
by Barbara McCauley
(Secrets)

ᕽᔭᔕ

The Last Good Man in Texas
and
Sins of a Tanner
by Peggy Moreland
(The Tanners)

ᕽᔭᔕ

Hot Contact
by Susan Crosby
(Behind Closed Doors)
and
Stone Cold Surrender
by Brenda Jackson

Laying His Claim
BEVERLY BARTON
USA TODAY Bestselling Author

Miss Pruitt's Private Life
BARBARA McCAULEY

SILHOUETTE®
Desire™

*First published in Great Britain 2005
Silhouette Books, Eton House, 18-24 Paradise Road,
Richmond, Surrey TW9 1SR*

The publisher acknowledges the copyright holders of the
individual works as follows:

Laying His Claim © Beverly Beaver 2004
Miss Pruitt's Private Life © Barbara Joel 2004

ISBN 0 373 60202 2

51-0605

*Printed and bound in Spain
by Litografia Rosés S.A., Barcelona*

LAYING HIS CLAIM

by

USA TODAY Bestselling Author

Beverly Barton

BEVERLY BARTON

has been in love with romance since her grandfather gave her an illustrated book of *Beauty and the Beast*. After marriage to her own "hero" and the births of her daughter and son, Beverly chose to be a full-time homemaker, aka wife, mother, friend and volunteer. The author of over thirty-five books, Beverly is a member of Romance Writers of America and helped found the Heart of Dixie chapter in Alabama. She has won numerous awards and has made the *USA TODAY* bestseller list.

To my children and grandchilden:
Badiema, Roger, Brant, Jana, Braden and Bryce.
And to my husband, Billy.
Life gives us no greater treasure
than the blessing of a family.

Prologue

The springtime sunshine shimmered through the stained-glass windows in the old Congregational church. Built in 1834 by Prospect, Alabama's wealthiest families, the magnificent brick structure had withstood the ravages of time, even the War Between the States, and with loving care and several restorations, stood today as not only a house of worship, but a historical treasure. Although she often felt out of place in the church her husband's family had helped establish, Kate attended services every Sunday with Trent and his aunt Mary Belle, Prospect's social grande dame and the bane of Kate's existence. It wasn't that Aunt Mary Belle was ever openly rude to Kate; the exact opposite was true. She smiled at her nephew's wife, patted her affectionately on the back and sung her praises to everyone within earshot. But in subtle ways the woman never let Kate forget that she wasn't quite worthy of Trenton

Bayard Winston IV and took it upon herself to continuously tutor Kate on the proper way to do absolutely everything.

Kate refused to allow Aunt Mary Belle to ruin this glorious Easter Sunday—Mary Kate's first Easter. She wanted the day to be perfect for her two-month-old daughter, the joy of her life. Despite the fact that Aunt Mary Belle had chosen both Kate's and Mary Kate's Easter frocks and decided on the luncheon menu, at least Kate had been allowed to put together her child's first Easter basket. Whenever she complained to Trent, asking him why they couldn't move out of the family mansion—another Prospect historical landmark that dated to the early part of the nineteenth century—he'd kiss and hug her and plead with her to be patient and understanding with his aunt.

"I know Aunt Mary Belle can be overbearing, but she means well," Trent had said numerous times. "This is my home—our home—as well as hers. She's like a mother to me. How could I ask her to leave? After all, she was born in this house and has lived here all her life. I grew up here and want to raise my children here, too."

So for nearly two years Kate had endured Aunt Mary Belle's overbearing guidance, but since Mary Kate's birth, the situation had grown worse. Although she never came right out and said as much, it was obvious that Aunt Mary Belle believed she and she alone should have the last word on how her great-niece was raised. For over two months now, Kate had smiled when she wanted to cry. She'd bitten her tongue to keep from lashing out and she'd agreed to things she hated, in order to keep peace in the family. But she had decided things simply had to change—and soon. She wanted a home of her own and this time when she told Trent she wanted them to move, she wouldn't let him sweet-talk her into staying. As much as she loved Trent—and she all but worshiped the ground he walked on—she could not live the rest of her life being treated at best like an ignorant child and at worst like a servant.

"Why don't we walk home from church today?" Kate suggested to Trent. "It's only a few blocks and it's such a beautiful day." She wanted time alone with her husband this afternoon so she could lead him by the cottage on Madison Avenue. The house had been empty for several years and although it needed some repairs, it was still a lovely home. The place consisted of a huge lot and the house itself was probably a good three-thousand square feet, large by most standards, although much smaller than Winston Hall, which boasted over ten-thousand square feet.

"Not today, Kate. You know Aunt Mary Belle has invited the minister and his family to dinner with us and—"

"Please, Trent. We won't be late for dinner. I promise."

"But we have the car here, today. Remember, you didn't want to ride with Aunt Mary Belle today, so we—"

"Send Guthrie back later this afternoon for your car. Please. This is important to me."

Trent grinned at her—his sexy smile always turned her inside out—then he slipped his arm around her waist. "Here, let me take Mary Kate. She'll get too heavy for you on the walk home."

Smiling, laughter bubbling up inside her, Kate snuggled close to Trent. Keeping Mary Kate secure on her hip, she stood on tiptoe and kissed her husband's cheek. If only talking him into purchasing the old Kirkendall

House on Madison proved half as easy as persuading him to walk home from church, all her dreams just might come true. Dreams of having a home of her own, a place that didn't make her feel as if she were living in a museum.

Just as Kate turned to hand Mary Kate to Trent, Aunt Mary Belle cleared her throat. "Public displays of affection aren't in good taste," she said quietly so only Trent and Kate could hear her.

Ignoring his aunt's comment, Trent turned to her and said, "Kate and I thought we'd walk home from church today. And you needn't worry about our being late for lunch. We won't keep Reverend and Mrs. Faulkner waiting."

"If you intend to walk, then how do you plan for me to get home. I have no desire to walk." Mary Belle laid her ring-adorned left hand over her heart and sighed dramatically.

"Why would you have to walk?" Kate asked. "Guthrie can—"

"I told Guthrie not to bother picking me up, that I'd ride home with y'all." Mary Belle smiled triumphantly.

Trent squeezed Kate around the waist. "We can't ask Aunt Mary Belle to walk, can we? She doesn't approve of ladies perspiring."

"I do not perspire," his aunt corrected him. "Ladies glow or glisten. They never perspire."

"Give Aunt Mary Belle the keys to your car," Kate suggested. "She can drive—"

"I'm unaccustomed to Trent's car and I do so hate to drive any vehicle, but when I'm forced to drive myself I prefer my own Lincoln."

"You could make an exception, just this once, couldn't you?" Kate had no intention of losing this battle. She had lost far too many during her marriage. Maybe she was being silly to make such a big deal out of this, but damn it—*oh, yes, excuse me, ladies don't curse, either, do they?*—she was sick and tired of Aunt Mary Belle running every aspect of her life.

"My dear Kate, is it so much to ask that an old lady, wearing high heels, not be forced to walk endless blocks on a warm Sunday afternoon? Or to be made uncomfortable by driving an unfamiliar car?"

Kate cringed. Trent chuckled. He adored his stuffy, snobby aunt and accepted everything she said and did with good humor. He'd once told Kate that he knew Aunt Mary Belle's many faults only too well and never took her too seriously. But he loved her. She had been both mother and father to him since his parents' untimely deaths when he was twelve.

Trent took his aunt's gloved hand. "Come along. We'll all ride home together. No need to fret." He glanced at Kate, who glared at him. "You and I will find time later today for a walk."

No we won't, Kate wanted to shout. *I will not compromise this time. Just this once, take my side. Please, Trent, don't let her win. Not again.*

"By all means, you go ahead and drive Aunt Mary Belle home. We certainly don't want to do anything that might displease her." Kate looked her husband square in the eyes, tilted her chin and gave him a tense smile. "Mary Kate and I are going to walk home." With that said, she turned and headed down the sidewalk.

"Kate," Trent called to her.

Ignoring him, she increased her pace and hurried away from him.

"Kate!"

Don't shout, dear, it's so unbecoming, Kate could al-

most hear Aunt Mary Belle scolding Trent. But she was
too far away from them to actually hear their conversation. Various church members spoke to her, some nodded, and several, who had probably heard Trent calling
her name, looked at her peculiarly. She nodded and
smiled and kept on walking. Faster and faster.

Mary Kate whimpered. Kate slowed her pace, then
halted to check on her daughter. "What's the matter,
sweetheart?" Her baby girl looked up at her with big
brown eyes identical to Trent's. "Is Mommy walking
too fast? Or do you realize I'm upset?"

Mary Kate gurgled and cooed. Kate adjusted her child's
hand-smocked pink bonnet. A large blond curl popped out
from under the brim to lay against her forehead.

Kate walked down Third Street. Only two blocks
until Madison. If she couldn't show her husband her
dream house, at least she could show her daughter. And
they'd take as long as they liked. She didn't care if they
were late for lunch. Let Aunt Mary Belle gripe and
grumble. Let Reverend and Mrs. Faulkner wait. And if
Trent was upset with her, she didn't care.

The Kirkendall house was on a corner lot at the end
of the four-hundred block of Madison. According to the
Realtor Kate had spoken to about the property, the
house was a Sears Roebuck structure built in 1924.
Painted white, with green shutters, a gabled roof and a
wide, wraparound porch, it wasn't anything fancy, just
homey. A white picket fence encased the front yard.
This was the kind of house Kate had always wanted.

"Look at that big front porch," Kate said to her baby.
"We'll put a swing on that end and a couple of big rocking chairs. We can come out here and I'll rock you to
sleep for your afternoon naps." Kate reached down, un-
latched the front gate and walked down the brick side-

walk. "Look, sweetheart, there's a huge backyard. We'll get you a swing set and a playhouse and—"

"How'd do, ma'am," a woman's voice called out behind her.

Gasping at the sound of the unexpected voice, Kate whirled around and stared wide-eyed at the tall, rather gangly young woman not more than fifteen feet behind her. "Who—who are you?"

"Oh, dear, I'm sorry. I didn't mean to frighten you. But I'm new to Prospect. My husband and I are moving here from Birmingham and I happened to notice the For Sale sign."

Kate let out a relieved sigh. How silly of her to have overreacted, to have been momentarily frightened. Then the woman's comment registered in Kate's mind. This person was interested in the Kirkendall house. *No, please, this is my house. My husband and daughter and I are going to live here and be so very happy. You'll have to find yourself another house.*

"This house is really old and needs a lot of repairs. I'm sure you can find something you'd like much better," Kate said.

The woman wore jeans, a nondescript white blouse and white sneakers. Her hair was short and dark. And she wore sunglasses, which she didn't remove even when she walked into the shade as she approached Kate.

"Perhaps you're right. My husband would prefer something that we can move into without having to do any work." The woman reached out and touched Mary Kate's cheek. "She's beautiful. How old is she?"

"She'll be three months old the fourth of next month.."

"We're trying to have a baby, but…" The woman paused, then swallowed as if trying not to cry. "Would you mind if I hold her?"

Kate felt so sorry for this poor woman. What would it be like, she wondered, to want a child and be unable to have one? She'd gotten pregnant immediately as soon as she and Trent started trying.

"She's a bit of a mommy's girl," Kate said as she handed her daughter to the friendly stranger. "I'm Kate Winston and this is Mary Kate."

The woman took Mary Kate into her arms. "Sweet baby. Your mommy is so lucky to have you." She smiled at Kate. "I'm Ann Smith." She glanced at the house. "Are you the owner?"

"No, I'm not, but I have to admit that I'm interested in buying this house." Kate surveyed the house from the flight of concrete steps leading up to the porch, to the welcoming front door flanked by window panels and all the way up to the dormer roofline. "I'd hoped to show this house to my husband today and—"

Mary Kate whimpered loudly. Kate turned. The stranger was walking down the brick sidewalk toward the street. What did she think she was doing? Where was she going?

"Hey, you, come back here." Kate ran down the sidewalk. "Stop! Stop right this minute!" Was this poor woman trying to steal Mary Kate?

With her heart pounding like mad, Kate caught up with the woman just as she walked through the gateway. When she clamped her hand down on the woman's shoulder and reached out for Mary Kate, a large, strong hand grabbed her from behind and jerked her backward, away from the woman. Fighting fiercely, Kate was no match for the man who shoved her to the ground, then kicked her in the ribs. Kate balled up in pain and screamed.

"Get the kid in the car," the man shouted.

Yelling for help, crying out for her baby, Kate tried to stand, but the man knotted his hand into a fist and hit her several times, knocking her to her knees with the final punch. Her mouth and nose bled profusely. Pain radiated through her body, but she crawled up the sidewalk and watched helplessly as the woman got in the car with Mary Kate and the man jumped behind the wheel and sped off. Unable to maintain her balance, she fell over on her side.

"Oh, God, help me! Please, please!"

It didn't happen, she told herself. It couldn't possibly have happened. Not in Prospect, Alabama. And not to her. She was Mrs. Trenton Bayard Winston IV.

"Mary Kate..." Tears poured down her cheeks as she struggled to stand.

She heard people running, coming toward her. Then she heard voices. As she looked up from where she lay, unable to do more than lift her hand in a plea for help, she recognized Portia and Robert Meyer, who lived two houses down from the Kirkendall place.

"Mary Kate!" Kate called out her daughter's name. "They—they took my baby!"

One

"How long will you be staying, ma'am?" the hotel clerk, whose name tag read B. Walding, asked, a wide smile on his boyish face.

"I'm not sure," Kate replied. "A few days, possibly longer. I'm sorry I can't be more specific. Will it be a problem?"

"We aren't overbooked by any means," Mr. Walding told her. "We have more vacancies here at Magnolia House during the winter months and this being January, we're practically empty. Of course we fill up pretty quick over the holidays and in May, during Pilgrimage Week, we're always booked solid."

Oh, yes, she remembered Pilgrimage Week, one of Mary Belle Winston's favorite times, when Prospect's Junior League and the various garden clubs joined forces with the historical society to act as hostesses at the historical places in the little town and surrounding

county. Aunt Mary Belle opened up Winston Hall to
tourists and excelled in her role as mistress of the grand
old estate. During her two-year marriage to Trent, Kate
had been allowed to dress in costume, too, and assist
Trent's aunt as a hostess. Kate had always felt out of
place in the pantaloons and hoop skirt. Since she knew
for a fact that her family had been poor dirt farmers for
generations, she doubted any of her ancestresses had
ever owned anything half so fine.

Kate shook off the memories, unsnapped her shoulder bag and removed her wallet. "I don't suppose y'all
have room service, do you?"

The freckle-faced clerk grinned and shook his head.
"No, ma'am, we don't. But if you want a plate lunch or
a sandwich, I can run over to McGuire's and get something for you."

McGuire's. Best barbecue and ribs in southeast Alabama. She and Trent had often eaten at McGuire's
when they'd been dating. "Is that place still open?"

"Sure is." Mr. Walding studied her closely. "You
been to Prospect before, have you?"

"Yes. Years ago."

"Well, we're glad to have you back, Miss—?"

"Ms. Malone." Kate handed him her credit card.
"Kate Malone."

"Ms. Malone, we're glad you're back in Prospect for
a visit. You got folks hereabouts?"

"No, I— No I don't have any relatives here in
Prospect." Not unless you counted an ex-husband and
his aunt. Or a few of her stepfather's distant cousins.

"I can run over to McGuire's for you, if you'd like."

"Thanks, Mr. Walding, but I'll just pick up something later."

"Please, call me Brian." He zipped her credit card

quickly and returned it to her, then handed her a key. A real key. "Room one-oh-four. Want me to carry your bag for you?"

"No, thanks," Kate told him. "I travel light." She hoisted the vinyl carryall over her shoulder and glanced around the lobby.

"One-oh-four is to your right."

Kate smiled at the clerk. "Oh, by the way, Brian, does the Winston family still live at Winston Hall?"

"Do you know the family?"

"I knew Trent Winston."

Brian grinned. "I guess that Trent Winston knows every pretty girl who's ever lived in Prospect and at least half who've just passed through."

"Is that right?"

"Well, Ms. Malone, if you ever knew him...of course that depends on how long ago you knew him. But for the past ten years, he's been quite the man about town, if you know what I mean. Ever since his wife up and left him..." Brian leaned over the reception desk and lowered his voice. "Do you know about his wife and daughter?"

Kate's stomach knotted painfully. She shook her head, falsely denying any knowledge.

"I wasn't living here, then, mind you. I came here from Dothan about seven years ago. But it seems Trent Winston's baby daughter was kidnapped and his wife left him. Folks say his wife went kind of funny in the head after—"

"That's terrible about his wife and child," Kate said, not wanting to hear the local gossip about how she went crazy after Mary Kate was abducted. She knew only too well how close she came to a complete nervous breakdown. "Does Trent...does Mr. Winston and his aunt still live at Winston Hall?"

"Yes, ma'am. Miss Mary Belle still lives there and despite the stroke she had last year, she manages to oversee what little real society there is left in Prospect. And Mr. Trent's a circuit court judge now. Got elected by a landslide. Heck, every female in the county voted for him."

Keeping her smile in place, Kate quickly escaped from the chatty Mr. Walding and hurried down the corridor toward one-oh-four. After unlocking the door, she entered the small but rather elegant room. Magnolia House had been built at the turn of the century, and except for a dozen years in the early sixties to mid-seventies, had been open for business. Over thirty years ago the town had purchased the building and statewide investors, with a penchant for preserving history, had restored the old place. Most buildings and houses in Prospect were steeped in history, and keeping the past alive was important to a lot of people, but the only part of the past that mattered to Kate was eleven years and nine months ago. One particular Easter Sunday when Mary Kate Winston had been stolen from her mother's arms.

After laying her handbag and suitcase on the bed, Kate shed her black wool coat and hung it in the antique armoire which served as a closet. After all these years, it seemed odd to be back in the sleepy little Southern town where she'd been born and raised. Her father had been killed in Vietnam, leaving her mother a young widow with a child. When Kate was five, her mother had remarried a likable man named Dewayne Harrelson and Kate's childhood, though poverty-stricken, had been relatively carefree and happy. She'd loved growing up on her stepfather's farm and hadn't minded helping her mother with the never-ending chores. She'd

graduated from Prospect High at seventeen, as the vale-
dictorian, and earned a scholarship to the University of
Alabama. For a high school graduation gift, her parents
had given her an older-model car—a blue Chevy Im-
pala—that she knew they hadn't been able to afford.

During her junior year in college her mother had
died from pneumonia and six months later, her stepfather succumbed to congestive heart failure. Discov-
ering that her parents' farm was mortgaged to the hilt,
Kate had had little choice but to let the bank foreclose.
That last year at the University of Alabama had been a
lean one. She'd lived practically hand to mouth, worked
two part-time jobs and somehow managed to maintain
a grade point average that allowed her to graduate
summa cum laude.

At Christmas time of her senior year, her stepfather's elderly aunt Opal had invited her to spend the holidays with her family in Prospect. Kate made it more
than halfway home before her old car laid down and
died. She'd been on a lonely stretch of Highway 82, between Montgomery and Prospect, and almost in tears
when a sleek gunmetal-gray Jaguar pulled in behind her.
The minute Trenton Bayard Winston IV emerged from
the sports car, Kate's heart had stopped for a millisecond and then began beating ninety-to-nothing. Of
course she'd known who Trent Winston was. Everyone
in Prospect knew him. He was the heir to the Winston
fortune, a descendant of Prospect's founding fathers,
and a student at the University of Alabama's School of
Law. And everyone knew that when he graduated from
college that coming spring and passed the bar, he would
begin work at the local law firm of Winston, Cotten and
Dickerson. Trent's father, grandfather and great-grand-
father had been lawyers.

Trent had given her a ride home that cold December day, and not in her wildest dreams had she ever imagined that before the next Christmas, she would be Mrs. Trenton Bayard Winston IV.

The Congregational church chimes ringing the hour jerked Kate back from her distant past to her present. She walked across the room, pulled back the sheers and looked out the window. The view, although limited, allowed her to see directly across the street at the town square where the county courthouse presided over downtown Prospect. Looking left along Main Street, she saw Corner Drugs and to her right was the office that housed the *Prospect Reporter,* the weekly newspaper. And next door was the building, over a century old, that housed the Winston, Cotten and Dickerson law firm.

Mr. Trent's a circuit court judge now. Every woman in the county voted for him. The hotel clerk's comments echoed inside her head.

She supposed that after their divorce Trent had reverted back into the ladies' man he'd been before they married. And why shouldn't he have done just that? Every unmarried woman in Prospect and half the women at the university had nearly died of broken hearts when Trent married her. Looking back now, she wondered why he'd married her when he could have had any woman he'd wanted. She'd been crazy in love with him. So much so that even now, she was probably still halfway in love with him…despite everything that had happened between them. But she could not allow any leftover feelings for Trent to resurface. She wasn't there to rekindle their fiery romance. After all, apparently Trent hadn't loved her as much as he'd told her he did. Otherwise, Mary Kate's kidnapping wouldn't have ripped them apart the way it did.

Kate let the sheers fall back into place, then she turned and walked into the bathroom. She needed to freshen up before driving over to Winston Hall. Maybe the polite thing to do was telephone first, but she preferred a surprise attack. As she washed her hands, Kate chuckled. Even after all these years, she still thought of facing Mary Belle Winston as engaging in battle with the enemy. *That old woman isn't your enemy anymore,* she told herself. *She has no power over you.* But Aunt Mary Belle wouldn't be happy to see Kate, that she knew for certain. After drying her hands, she looked into the mirror. When she'd left Prospect eleven years ago, she'd been barely twenty-four; now she was thirty-five and no longer the young beauty Trent had proclaimed her to be. But she was attractive. And she was tough. She had the guts to face not only Aunt Mary Belle, but to look Trent in the eye and tell him she'd been right and he'd been wrong. Mary Kate wasn't dead. Their daughter was alive.

You can't tell him she's alive, Kate warned herself. Kate had no proof that Mary Kate was one of the three little girls who were abducted from southeast Alabama around the same time Mary Kate was. But all three baby girls had been sold to adoptive parents within one month of that fateful Easter Sunday. And all three had been approximately three to four months old when adopted.

Kate drank a glass of water. Her hand quivered ever so slightly. *Stay calm. Stay in control.* She retrieved her purse from the bed, removed her lipstick and compact, put on a fresh coat of hot-pink gloss and then powdered her face.

Perhaps she should eat supper first and fortify her body with some of McGuire's ribs. She hadn't eaten a bite since breakfast in Memphis early this morning. *Stop looking for excuses to delay the inevitable,* an inner voice chided.

She took her coat from the armoire, slipped into it and draped the straps of her handbag over her shoulder. Squaring her shoulders she marched out of her room, down the corridor and out the hotel's back entrance. Magnolia House's guests parked in the rear. When she got into the rental car—a white Mercury—she suddenly wished she could drive up to Winston Hall in her own car, her very expensive Mercedes. The purchase of that car had been Kate's one and only extravagance. She lived in a small duplex in Smyrna, outside of Atlanta. She bought her clothes off the rack and the only jewelry she owned consisted of a watch, a pair of small gold hoop earrings and a single gold bracelet. For the past ten years, most of the money she'd earned, first as an Atlanta policewoman and later an agent for the prestigious Dundee Private Security and Investigation firm, had been spent searching for Mary Kate. Even with all of the Dundee Agency's resources, she'd run into one dead end after another. It appeared that her daughter had disappeared off the face of the earth. But Kate had never given up hope, never allowed herself to think that her child might be dead.

Although the Deep South often had very mild winters, this winter wasn't one of them. Today's temperature had dropped into the low forties and the clouds had a look of rain about them. Cold winter rain, perhaps even sleet or ice. Kate turned up the heat in her rental car as she headed down Main Street. Before she realized what she was doing, she turned off on Madison and drove slowly by the old Kirkendall house. The house had been fully restored, with fresh paint on the exterior

and a new white picket fence had replaced the dilapi-
dated one. Heavy white wooden rockers and a large
swing graced the front porch. A decorative Christmas
wreath still hung on the front door, nearly three weeks
after the holiday. Some lucky family had purchased
Kate's dream house. Apparently whoever lived here
loved the old place as much as she had and had restored
it with tender care. Whatever family lived there, Kate
hoped they were very happy. As happy as she had believed Trent and Mary Kate and she would have been.

Emotion lodged in her throat. She willed herself not
to cry. Now was not the time for tears. When she saw
Trent again, she had to be in full control of her emotions. And when she faced Aunt Mary Belle, she had to
show the old biddy that she wasn't in the least bit in-
timidated by her.

"Goodbye, dream house," Kate whispered as she
drove away from four-ten Madison.

In no time at all, she pulled up in front of Winston
Hall, a magnificent Federal-style mansion that presided
over almost a whole city block. The black iron fencing
circled the estate and the massive black iron gates always stayed open, welcoming the elite of Prospect to
come calling. And at holiday open houses and during
Pilgrimage Week, even the lowly were allowed admit-
tance. She'd forgotten how much she hated this house
and how miserable her ex- husband's aunt had made her
life for the two years of her marriage.

Don't look back, Kate reminded herself. *Nothing
can change the past.*

She drove her rental car up and around the circular
driveway, stopped directly in front of the mansion and
killed the engine. After taking several deep breaths, she
got out and walked up the steps and onto the porch. She

checked her watch. Four-ten p.m. Too early for dinner. Kate smiled at the thought of her being invited to dine with the family.

She hesitated at the door, then garnered up all her courage and rang the bell. She barely recognized the elderly man who came to the door. His once-gray hair had turned white and his broad shoulders stooped just a little.

"Guthrie?"

"Yes, ma'am." His faded gray eyes focused on her face, studying her intently. "Miss Kate! That is you, isn't it? Lord have mercy, it's good to see you."

"Hello, Guthrie. How are you?"

"Tolerable," he replied. "You look mighty fine, Miss Kate. Hardly a day older than when you left here."

Kate laughed. She'd always been quite fond of Guthrie, who had worked for the Winston family since he'd been a boy. He served the household as a butler and a chauffeur and oversaw the other household staff, which when she'd lived there had consisted of a cook and a live-in maid for Mary Belle, and two daily maids who didn't live on the premises.

"I'm much older," Kate told him. "Ten years older."

"Been that long, has it?" As if suddenly realizing he'd kept her standing on the porch, Guthrie snapped to attention and said, "Come on in out of the cold, Miss Kate."

"Thank you." She entered the massive marble-floored foyer. When she glanced around, she noted that very little had changed. A spiral staircase took center stage in the room filled with antiques that had belonged to the family for generations.

"I never thought you'd come back," Guthrie said. "But Lord, have I prayed that you would. Mr. Trent, he's—"

"I've come to see Trent. Is he here?"

"Yes, ma'am, he's here. In his study." Guthrie looked up the stairs. "Miss Mary Belle's taking her Saturday afternoon nap."

Kate grinned. "Then perhaps I'll be fortunate enough to conduct my business with Trent and leave before she wakes."

Guthrie chuckled. "Shall I announce you to Mr. Trent or—"

"Since I no longer answer to the Good Manners Society—" Kate rolled her eyes toward the stairs "—why don't I just barge in on Trent without being announced?"

Guthrie chuckled again and gave Kate a wide, approving smile. "We've missed you, Miss Kate. We have missed you a great deal."

"Why thank you. I don't know what to say." And she truly didn't know how to respond to Guthrie's comment. *We have missed you,* he'd said. We? Surely he didn't mean Trent. Of course not. Trent was too busy being the man about town, wasn't he? Too busy charming all the ladies. But what if there's a special lady? What if he's found someone else? For all she knew, he could have remarried. But Mr. Walding at the Magnolia House hadn't mentioned anything about a new Mrs. Winston.

"Guthrie, Trent isn't…that is, has he remarried?"

"No, ma'am."

"Is he engaged?"

"No, ma'am. And you, Miss Kate?"

She shook her head. "No. Not married or engaged or anything."

Guthrie glanced down the hall in the direction of the library. "You know the way to Mr. Trent's study, don't you?"

She nodded.

"I do wish you were staying, ma'am."

He turned and walked away from her, down the hallway toward the kitchen, saving Kate from having to respond. The study, as Guthrie referred to the library at Winston Hall, was on the first floor, on the opposite side from the double parlors. When she reached the study, she found the door closed. Would the door be locked? she wondered. The only time Trent had ever locked the door was when the two of them had been alone in the study, making love. On the rug before the fireplace. On the massive Jacobean desk. On the leather sofa.

Don't do this to yourself. Stop remembering what it was like when you two were in love. But the memories washed over her like a tidal wave, sweeping away a decade of loneliness. And she had been lonely. So very lonely. She had dated a little in the past five or six years, a few really nice men, but try as she might, she hadn't come close to falling in love again. God knows she'd wanted to love someone, had prayed she'd find the courage to trust her heart to another man.

She lifted her arm, curled her right hand into a fist and knocked soundly on the closed door. Her heart fluttered maddeningly.

"Yes, come in," Trent said.

The sound of his deep, distinctive voice sent shock waves through her body. He had a slow, lazy, south Alabama drawl that had always seemed so sexy. But then again, everything about Trent Winston had been sexy. And probably still was.

Kate opened the door and took a hesitant step over the threshold. Trent sat in one of the massive oxblood leather armchairs in front of the fireplace so she could see only his left arm. He wore a cream sweater. Despite being modernized with central heat and air conditioning, Winston Hall kept a chill all winter. Old houses tended to be drafty.

"Hello, Trent." Her heartbeat thundered in her ears. He didn't move, didn't speak.

"I apologize for not calling first, but I—I—"

Trent jumped to his feet abruptly and turned to face her. "Kate? Good God, it is you."

"Yes, it's me."

She stared at him. Blatantly. He had changed. Matured. His shoulders appeared broader. And there were lines around his eyes and mouth. A touch of gray mingled with the dark brown strands of his thick hair, mostly in his sideburns. He was still as handsome as ever, maybe even more so. Maturity certainly agreed with him. But then she'd always known he'd be a good-looking man in his forties and fifties, probably even in his eighties.

"What—when…it's been a long time," he finally managed to say.

"It's been ten years since our divorce became final."

"What brings you back to Prospect?" He hadn't moved an inch from where he stood by the leather chair.

"Personal business."

"I didn't realize you had any family still living here."

"I don't."

He studied her curiously, his dark, pensive brown eyes surveying her from head to toe. "You look—" He cleared his throat. "You look well. The years have been good to you."

"To you, too."

He took a tentative step toward her, then paused. "Please, come in. Would you care for a drink?" He indicated the bar set up on a serving cart stationed beneath one of the two massive floor-to-ceiling windows on the side wall.

"No, thanks." She ordered her feet into action and managed to walk toward him.

With their gazes locked, they met in the middle of the room, each stopping when less than three feet separated them. She could barely suppress the urge to reach out and touch him. They stood there for an endless moment, neither moving nor speaking.

"You said you're in Prospect on personal business. Since you've come to Winston Hall, am I to assume that business concerns me in some way?"

"Yes, it concerns you." *Don't drag this out. Dammit, just tell him.* "I work for the Dundee Agency. It's a private security and investigation firm based in Atlanta."

"You're a private investigator?"

Trent grinned and her stomach did a crazy flip-flop.

"Yes. And before I worked at Dundee's, I was an Atlanta police officer."

Trent shook his head. "You must have changed a great deal. I can't imagine my sweet Kate as either a policewoman or a P.I."

His sweet Kate? *Dammit, Trent, I haven't been your sweet Kate in a long, long time.*

"Recently, a colleague and I were sent to Maysville, Mississippi, a town about an hour's drive from Memphis," she told him. "A two-month-old baby boy had been kidnapped and my colleague was the child's father."

Trent's face paled. "You work on child abduction cases?"

"On this one, yes. I went to Maysville with the kidnapped baby's father and helped him and the child's mother through some difficult days."

"What happened to the baby?" Trent's jaw tightened.

"He was rescued," Kate said. "And returned to his parents."

"That's good." Trent turned away from her. "I'm happy for them."

"The FBI agent working on the case was the head of a sting operation that the bureau had in the works for several years," Kate explained. "You see, there was an infant abduction ring working in the southeast and these people had been stealing babies for the past twelve years."

Trent whirled around and glared at her. "Damn, Kate, don't tell me you've somehow convinced yourself that Mary Kate was taken by the same abduction ring." He came toward her, fury in his eyes. He grabbed her by the shoulders and shook her gently. "I had hoped that after all this time you would have accepted the fact that our little girl is lost to us forever."

Kate gritted her teeth in an effort to stem the tide of tears gathering in her eyes. "Dante Moran was the FBI agent in charge of the operation. He's an objective professional, someone without any connection to Mary Kate. He—he believes that there's a very good possibility that our daughter could be one of three baby girls stolen from southeast Alabama the same month and year that Mary Kate was taken."

After loosening his tenacious hold on her shoulders, Trent narrowed his gaze and glowered at Kate.

"There are hundreds of children who were sold to desperate adoptive parents during the past twelve years," Kate said. "These people, the ones in charge of the abduction ring, kept a file on each infant. The state and sometimes even the city where the child was abducted was noted on records, as was the month the child was supposedly given up for adoption. The FBI is in the process of notifying the adoptive parents of every stolen child, and they're searching for all possible birth parents, too."

"And this FBI agent, this Mr. Moran, believes Mary Kate is one of these children?" Trent gripped Kate's shoulders with gentle force.

She nodded. "There are three eleven-year-old girls who were taken by this abduction ring as infants from this area of Alabama, and given to adoptive parents within a month after Mary Kate was taken. The FBI has already pulled a copy of Mary Kate's birth certificate and the next step is to give the FBI lab a DNA sample. Then they'll compare it to a sample they will take from each of these girls."

Trent caressed Kate's shoulders. "And if none of these little girls turn out to be Mary Kate, what will you do then? Will you finally give up and let her go?"

"Please, Trent, try to believe in the possibility that Mary Kate is alive and we could find her and—"

"And what? Even if by some miracle one of these girls is Mary Kate, what would we do? Rip her away from two loving parents, perhaps from brothers and sisters? And if we did, what do we have to give her— divorced parents fighting over custody?" Trent released Kate and stomped across the room. "No. I don't want to hear this. My daughter is dead. She's been dead for eleven years."

"Don't say that. Mary Kate is alive. And I'm going to find her. I came here hoping you'd want to go with me to find our little girl. But I see now what a terrible mistake I made. I'm sorry I bothered you."

Kate ran from the study and down the hall, not stop-

ping when Trent called her name. Tears blurred her vision as she rushed outside and hurried to her rental car.
She got in, started the engine and headed down the
driveway. When she reached the street, she glanced in
her rearview mirror and saw Trent standing on the
porch, his arms crossed over his chest.

Two

Kate prepared herself a cup of hot tea. She always carried a box of Earl Grey with her whenever she traveled, which in her line of business was most of the time. Wearing her raspberry-pink cotton flannel robe over matching pajamas, she walked out of the bathroom and over to one of two lounge chairs flanking the small table near the windows. After placing the white mug with the Magnolia House emblem—appropriately a magnolia blossom—on the table, she picked up the TV remote control and flipped on the one local station. She hit the Mute button to silence the commercial's chatter, then eased down into the chair and propped her feet on the edge of the nearby bed. Her stomach growled, reminding her that she hadn't eaten any supper. But she'd been so upset, so damn angry when she left Winston Hall, that she wouldn't have been able to keep a bite of food down if she had eaten.

My daughter is dead. She's been dead for eleven years. Trent's words echoed inside her head…inside her heart.

His firm conviction that Mary Kate was dead and her equally resolute certainty that their child was still alive had been the single major issue that finally ended their marriage. Of course it hadn't helped that they'd both blamed themselves for their child's abduction or that she'd suffered a nervous breakdown at the time. And Mary Belle Winston's constant interference had only added fuel to the fire that destroyed any hope of them being able to salvage their relationship.

Why had she bothered coming back to Prospect? What had she been thinking? She should have known that even bringing Trent news of what she considered a miracle wouldn't sway him from his stubborn stand. *How could he not want to find Mary Kate?* She didn't understand his reasoning. But then, she never had.

Dante Moran had given her the basic facts which led her to believe that Mary Kate was one of the girls who'd been adopted over eleven years ago. Even Moran thought it was highly likely. And his was an objective opinion. *So why couldn't Trent believe? Why couldn't he open up his heart to the possibility?*

A fierce ache gripped Kate's chest, emotion so deep and powerful that it took her breath away. Mary Kate *was* alive. She'd always know in her heart of hearts that her baby girl wasn't dead. Now, within a few weeks, she might see Mary Kate, touch her, hold her, tell her that she loved her.

Once again Trent's words tormented Kate. *Even if by some miracle one of these girls is Mary Kate, what would we do? Rip her away from two loving parents, perhaps from brothers and sisters? And if we did, what do we have to give her—divorced parents fighting over custody?*

Needing to comfort herself, Kate lifted her feet off the bed and drew her knees up toward her chest, then hugged her arms around her legs in a fetal gesture. Since the moment Dante Moran had shared the FBI's information with her about the abduction ring's confidential files, she'd dreamed of the moment she would hold her child in her arms again. And she had pushed every negative thought to the back of her mind. But Trent had reminded her of the reality of the situation. Mary Kate wouldn't know her, wouldn't think of Kate as her mother. Her daughter would have been raised by other people. She might already have a mother and father she loved. Where would Kate fit into Mary Kate's life?

Kate keened mournfully, the sound little more than a whimper. Oh, God, her little Mary Kate wouldn't be Mary Kate. Her adoptive parents would have given her another name.

What do we have to give her—divorced parents fighting over custody?

Get out of my mind, damn you, Trent, she screamed silently.

Wouldn't it be enough to know that her daughter was alive? Wouldn't it be enough to see her? she asked herself. *It should be enough. But would it be?*

Special Agent Moran had pointed out that this case would turn into a legal nightmare once all the adoptive parents were informed their children had been stolen from their biological parents and not given up freely. Both sets of parents would have rights. Lawyers would be hired. Court battles would be fought, won and lost.

What would she do if she found that Mary Kate was

a happy child, living with loving parents and perhaps even had siblings? *Stop it! Don't keep torturing yourself this way.* She could make those kinds of decisions later, after she knew for sure that one of the little girls actually was her daughter. First things first..

Sighing, Kate picked up her mug and took several swallows of the delicious tea. Ah, how soothing, how warming. Odd that although she'd never drank anything except iced tea until she married Trent, once Aunt Mary Belle had introduced her to the delicate, distinct taste of Earl Grey, she'd become a lifelong convert. Looking back, she had to admit that all her memories of her ex-husband's overbearing aunt weren't bad. And as much as she had resented the woman's constant tutelage, she had learned a great deal from the old biddy.

Why waste time thinking about that woman? Kate wouldn't have to see her or speak to her. At least she'd been spared that much on this trip. She would leave Prospect first thing in the morning and go straight back to Memphis, where the investigation into finding the birth parents of hundreds of kidnapped children was in full swing. Trent could do as he pleased. She'd done her duty—she'd informed him about the situation.

Just as she began to relax—the aftereffects of the hot bath she'd taken a few minutes ago, the soothing tea and the comfy clothes—someone knocked at her hotel door. Trent? Damn, why was he the first thing that popped into her mind. Wishful thinking?

Kate stood, walked across the room and peered through the peephole. Mary Belle Winston! The last person on earth she ever wanted to see again. Damn. Double damn.

Go away, old woman, and leave me the hell alone. I don't want to talk to you.

Kate hesitated. Mary Belle knocked on the door repeatedly. Good grief, why wouldn't she go away?

"Katherine, I know you're in there," Mary Belle said. "I spoke to the desk clerk and he informed me that Ms. Malone was definitely in her room."

Blast! She'd have to speak to Brian Walding! How dare he give out any information about her, least of all her room number. But then considering who Mary Belle was in this town, he'd probably felt he had little choice. Either kowtow to the grande dame or risk losing his job.

After breathing in deeply and exhaling slowly, she squared her shoulders, stood straight and tall, and then said a please-God-help-me prayer before opening the door. "Hello, Miss Mary Belle."

"May I come in?"

Kate looked at Trent's aunt, really looked at her and was surprised by how much she had aged in the past eleven years. She no longer colored her hair so it was now a stunning snow-white. Delicate wrinkles lined her face, especially around her eyes and mouth. Never a beautiful woman, but always extremely well-groomed and attractive, Mary Belle still maintained that air of old south elegance few women could pull off in this day and time. Kate's gaze traveled from the older but familiar face to the ever present pearls that had belonged to Mary Belle's grandmother. And then Kate saw the cane.

"All right, come on in." Kate stepped aside to allow the woman entrance.

When Mary Belle entered the room, Kate noticed how heavily she braced herself on the cane, her steps slow and precise. What was it that Mr. Walding had said? Something about Mary Belle still presiding over Prospect society despite the stroke she'd had this past year?

"Not a very gracious response," Mary Belle said as she walked over and sat down in one of the two lounge chairs. "Your reply should have been 'yes, Miss Mary Belle, please come in.' And then you should have said—"

"Don't lecture me!" Kate slammed the door.

"I see you haven't changed," Mary Belle said.

Kate faced her nemesis. "And neither have you." Kate stomped across the room, acid churning in her stomach.

"That's where you're wrong, my dear." Mary Belle looked up, focusing her keen dark eyes on Kate. "Perhaps superficially I'm unchanged. I still do my best to rule Prospect society and I'm still an opinionated, domineering old maid who meddles in her nephew's life. But I'm now capable of admitting when I'm wrong and—" she took a deep breath "—I was wrong about you, Kate."

Kate stared at Trent's aunt, wary of her solicitous comment, suspicious of Mary Belle saying she was wrong about anything, especially Kate. "Why are you here? What do you want?"

Mary Belle sighed. *Still dramatic, too,* Kate thought.

"Those are my questions precisely," Mary Belle said. "Why are you here in Prospect, after so many years? And what do you want with Trent?"

"Didn't he tell you?" Kate flopped down in the other lounge chair and crossed her arms over her chest. She wanted to get this visit over with as quickly as possible.

"Trent told me nothing. I wouldn't have known you'd paid him a visit had I not been looking out my bedroom window when you left. I recognized you immediately, of course, and summoned Guthrie. He said you'd visited Trent, but stayed only a few minutes and that Trent stormed out of the house and drove off somewhere directly after you left. So, I assumed that he—"

"Followed me?" Kate laughed sarcastically. "Were you afraid he'd come after me and I might manage to get my hooks back into him?"

"You're terribly bitter, aren't you?" Mary Belle shook her head sadly. "Of course I don't blame you. But I had hoped that after all these years your anger at us— at me in particular—might have lessened."

Utterly confused by Mary Belle's comment, Kate glared at the old woman. "Look, Trent didn't follow me. He's not here. And I have no intention of seeing him again before I leave Prospect in the morning."

"That's a pity."

Kate shook her head in bewilderment. "Am I supposed to know what you mean by that?"

"No, probably not." Mary Belle leaned forward toward Kate. "I can think of only one reason you'd ever come back to Prospect—you've learned something about our precious Mary Kate's fate, haven't you?"

Kate swallowed the knot of emotion threatening to choke her. Despite all her faults, Trent's aunt had, as far as Kate was concerned, possessed one redeeming quality—she had loved Mary Kate and been devoted to the child. Selflessly devoted.

"I came here to give Trent some information about the possibility that it's only a matter of a few days before Mary Kate's whereabouts are known."

Mary Belle gasped. "Then she—she is alive?"

"Yes, I believe she is. I've never thought she was dead."

"Please, my dear, tell me everything."

Kate relayed the information to Trent's aunt, who sat there spellbound while Kate talked. Tears glistened in

Mary Belle's brown eyes. She blinked several times, then reached inside her coat pocket and retrieved a lace handkerchief. After lowering her glasses, she wiped her eyes.

"If I know my nephew—and I do—he stubbornly refused to believe there's a chance one of these little girls is our Mary Kate. And he probably even said that even if one of them was his child, it was too late to make her a part of his life again."

Kate nodded. "You do know him well, don't you?"

"He'll change his mind."

"I doubt it. Trent never changes his mind. Once he decides on something, he—"

"He's still stubborn, but not quite as bullheaded as he used to be. And he's no longer as arrogant and self-centered as he once was." Mary Belle reached across the table and grasped Kate's hand. "Losing Mary Kate… and losing you changed him. In some ways for the better, but in other ways, for the worse. But take my word for it, he will change his mind about wanting to find out if one of these girls is his daughter."

Kate snatched her hand away, then before she thought through her response, she said, "I'll give you my cell phone number, so if Trent wants to get in touch with me, he can." *How stupid was that?* her inner voice asked. *You don't want to see him again, don't want to feel physically or emotionally drawn to a man who hates you.* The last thing she needed was Trent Winston back in her life under any circumstances. She'd done what she thought was right—given him the information. If he chose to continue believing their daughter was dead…

"I'll go now," Mary Belle said. "I appreciate your talking to me. I would have understood if you'd slammed the door in my face."

When Mary Belle rose to her feet, slowly and awkwardly, Kate stopped herself from offering to help the old woman. Bearing her weight on the cane, Mary Belle walked toward the door. Kate stood and followed her.

When Mary Belle reached the door, she turned to face Kate. "Regardless of what Trent does…if it turns out that I'm wrong about him getting involved—would you…please…let me know what happens. If Mary Kate is alive, I'd very much like to know."

Willing herself not to cry, Kate nodded as unshed tears stung her eyes and nose. "You do understand that you have no legal right to interfere in any decisions I make about my daughter, don't you?"

"Kate, all I want is to know if she's alive. Even if I never see her—" Mary Belle's voice cracked. "Just a phone call…one phone call. That's all I ask. You don't have to give me any details."

"All right. If one of these girls is Mary Kate, I'll let you know."

"Thank you, my dear."

Kate opened the door. Mary Belle walked out and into the corridor and kept going, not once looking back. Her steps were very slow. Just as the old woman neared the end of the short hallway, Kate caught a glimpse of Guthrie taking her arm and leading her away. With a heavy sigh, Kate went back into her room and closed the door.

What the hell had just happened?

Had Mary Belle actually mellowed with age? Had she changed so much that Kate thought she might actually like Trent's aunt? Or had she been putting on an act, playing nice-nice in order to get what she wanted? What difference did it make? Mary Belle had no control over her. Kate didn't have to jump through hoops to please her, not ever again.

Kate turned off all the lights in the room, except the one on the nightstand, then she slipped out of her robe, tossed it into one of the lounge chairs and spread out sideways across the bed. She rested there, out from under the covers, her gaze riveted to the ten-foot ceiling. With her eyes wide open memories flashed through her mind. Memories she wanted to forget.

The first time Trent and she made love. Her expensive, elaborate wedding, coordinated by Aunt Mary Belle. Her pleas with Trent to move out of Winston Hall and into a home of their own. The day Mary Kate was born. Love. Happiness. Frustration. So many emotions swirled about inside her. The day her daughter was kidnapped. Fear. Anger. Anguish.

She lay there, mired in self-pity, her mind filled with memories, her heart breaking as if only today her world had fallen apart and she had lost her child and the only man she'd ever loved. She seldom allowed herself to have a case of poor-old-Kate, but just this once, she thought she was due—maybe overdue.

Trent drove his old Jaguar at demonic speed along the back roads of Bayard County. He seldom got behind the wheel of this classic car because it brought back too many memories of his life with Kate. Damn her for returning to Prospect. He'd spent over ten years trying to wipe her memory from his mind and had halfway convinced himself that he'd done just that. It had taken him a long time to forgive her and even longer to forget her and move on with his life. Only recently had he even considered the possibility of remarrying. He had avoided serious relationships as if they were a plague. But after dating Molly Stoddard for the past year, he'd convinced himself that she was the type of woman he needed. A woman from a well-to-do old Eufala family, a lawyer who had relocated to Prospect with her two children after her husband's untimely death three years ago and who now worked in Trent's family's firm. They had a great deal in common, knew all the same people, enjoyed many of the same things. And he liked her children, eight-year-old Seth and ten-year-old Lindy.

But you aren't in love with Molly, he reminded himself tonight, as he'd done repeatedly during the past few weeks, every time he thought about proposing to her. As far as he was concerned it was better for Molly and him that they weren't in love. They cared for each other, respected each other and shared a true friendship. He'd been so crazy in love with Kate that she had consumed him completely. He'd never felt about another woman the way he'd felt about her. And look how badly that had ended. They had hurt each other unbearably. He had disappointed her, had let her down and she'd ripped the heart right out of him when she left.

God help him, it still hurt. Hurt like hell. He wanted to think he was indifferent to Kate, that she meant nothing to him now. But the memories wouldn't hurt so damn bad unless he still felt something for her. So what did he feel for Kate? Anger. Distrust. Most definitely. But the sexual attraction that had once been so powerful between them was still there, at least on his part. He'd like to deny it, but he couldn't. Okay, so part of what he was feeling was just good old-fashioned lust. He could deal with that, couldn't he? Yeah, sure. All he had to do was avoid Kate.

But what about your daughter? What about Mary Kate? a tormenting inner voice asked. She's dead, he told himself. He shouldn't let Kate's enthusiasm affect him. Just because she believed a little girl who'd been kidnapped by some child abduction ring as an infant was Mary Kate, didn't make it so. Let Kate believe in miracles, let her cling to the dream that their child was still alive and they'd someday be reunited with her. He couldn't share that dream. For him that dream was a nightmare. He'd realized a few months after Mary Kate was stolen from them that the only way he could function, the only way he could survive and not fall apart completely was to let go of his daughter. Everyone involved in Mary Kate's kidnapping case—from local and state law enforcement to the FBI—had told them the odds were that they'd never see their child again, that if she hadn't been found within a month or less, they had to stop hoping, consider her lost to them forever and move on. He'd done that. Kate hadn't. In a way, his ex-wife had been far stronger than he, even if she had suffered an emotional breakdown. Even now, after all this time, she clung to the hope that she would find their daughter.

Trent hadn't been able to tell Kate eleven years ago that the reason he chose not to hope, chose to relinquish the dream of being reunited with Mary Kate, was because he didn't have the courage to face each new day with the agonizing questions of where their child was, what was happening to her, if she was being taken care of or being abused. He'd chosen the easiest route to recovery by convincing himself that their baby girl was dead.

What if Kate's right? What if the FBI locates Mary Kate? Didn't he want to see his daughter? Didn't he want to know firsthand that she was well and happy and loved?

Trent's cell phone rang. He slowed the Jag, removed the phone from its holder and punched the On button. "Trenton Winston."

"She's at the Magnolia House," his aunt Mary Belle said. "I made some inquiries to find out if she was still in town. She is. But I suggest you go see her tonight. My guess is she'll be gone by morning."

Before he could reply, his aunt hung up on him. Damn infuriating woman! How did she even know Kate was in Prospect? Had Guthrie told her that Kate had come to Winston Hall? Or had she seen Kate when she arrived or when she left? Aunt Mary Belle knows, he told himself, she knows Mary Kate may be alive. If she knew, that meant she'd talked to Kate. God help us all. What had it been like when those two had met again face-to-face?

Trent realized what he wanted to do, what he had to do. Deny it all he liked, the bottom line was that if his daughter was still alive, he had to know. He was older now, maybe a little wiser and a heck of a lot tougher than he'd been eleven years ago. Whatever happened, he could handle it and maybe this time he could actually help his wife—make that his ex-wife—through whatever lay ahead for them. He owed her that much, didn't he? He'd failed her miserably in the past.

Twenty minutes later, Trent parked his Jag in the rear parking area, got out, locked his car and headed for the Magnolia House's back entrance. When the cold night wind chilled his face, he flipped up the collar on his suede jacket. He swung open the hotel's back door, then walked down the hall and into the lobby area. He didn't know the clerk by name, although his face looked familiar.

"Good evening," Trent said.

"Good evening, Judge Winston," the man replied.

"I believe you have a Ms. Kate Malone staying here."

"Yes, we do. She's in room one-oh-four."

Trent eyed the man whose name tag read B. Walding. "I thought y'all weren't allowed to give out guests' room numbers."

"Ordinarily we're not," Mr. Walding said. "But since Ms. Malone is your ex-wife and you're who you are and all…well, it's like Miss Mary Belle said—"

"So my aunt has been here to see Kate…to see Ms. Malone?"

"Yes, sir. She left about thirty minutes ago and she did mention on her way out that you'd probably be stopping by to see your wife…your ex-wife.'"

Trent nodded, offered Mr. Walding a weak smile and glanced around trying to decide which corridor led to one-oh-four.

"To your right," the clerk told him.

"Thanks."

Nervous and unsure of how Kate would react to him just showing up, Trent marched down the hall. When he stood outside the door to one-oh-four, he hesitated. Once he knocked on the door, there would be no turning back.

He knocked several times. No response. He knocked again, harder this time.

He heard the sound of movement from inside the room, then footsteps. The door flew open and Kate stood there in a pair of baggy, bright pink pajamas, her long blond hair disheveled and her face void of makeup. And heaven help him, she was the sexiest thing he'd ever seen.

She stared up at him with those big, sky blue eyes of hers and his stomach knotted painfully. He remembered only too well how he'd felt the first time she'd zeroed those baby blues in on him. He'd gotten an instant hardon. If he'd been honest with himself at that moment, he'd have known he was a goner. He'd never wanted anything as much as he'd wanted Kate Malone.

"I want to go with you to find Mary Kate," he told her.

She stared at him, an incredulous expression on her face. "You want to…are you telling me that you now believe there's a good chance our daughter is still alive?"

"I don't know what I believe," he admitted. All he knew was that he didn't want Kate to go through this alone. But he could hardly tell her that. She might read more into a statement like that than he intended. "We can be civil to each other, can't we? We can do this together as Mary Kate's parents and not as…" Trent shuffled his feet. "There's no need for us to hurt each other any more than we already have."

"I agree." As if suddenly realizing she'd been staring at him, Kate cleared her throat, glanced away and then said, "Meet me here in the morning at eight o'clock. If we can take your car, I'll turn my rental in and we can ride to Memphis together."

He nodded, then turned to leave. Sensing her watching him, he glanced over his shoulder. She stood in the doorway, temptation personified. Spending days, perhaps weeks with her was going to be pure torture for him. "Thanks, Kate," he said before walking away hurriedly, knowing that if he'd stayed another minute, he would have pulled her into his arms and kissed her.

Three

Kate hadn't slept much and felt the effects of a rest-less night. Knowing she needed some fortification to be at her best this morning, she'd eaten a substantial break-fast and downed three cups of regular coffee at the Prospect Café. When she paid the bill and left, she breathed a sigh of relief. Lucky for her, no one had rec-ognized her. Apparently the local gossip mill hadn't processed the news that Trent Winston's ex-wife was in town. The café was a block from the hotel, so she'd walked the distance, despite the frigid temperature. The clouds that had falsely predicted a cold rain late yester-day had dissipated overnight and today promised to be sunny. The early morning sun shining brightly did lit-tle to warm things up. When she stepped out of the café, Kate slipped-on her red leather gloves and tight-ened the red wool scarf around her neck.

As she approached the Magnolia House, she checked

her watch. It was 7:53 a.m. Would Trent show up? Of course he would. If he hadn't already been certain of what he planned to do, he'd never have come to see her last night. While she'd tossed and turned during the long, seemingly endless night, she had been unable to turn off her mind, to stop a hundred and one thoughts from bombarding her. Memories of the past mixed and mingled with the present and unrealistic dreams for the future. If dreams came true, what would she want? She'd want to be a mother to Mary Kate. That was a given. But what about being a wife to Trent? Perhaps, in the deepest recesses of her heart, that dream existed.

Dreams were well and good. In their place. But she had to face reality. The odds were against her. Even if they found Mary Kate, Trent was right—it was too late to be the child's parents. Could she accept that fact? She really had no other choice. She had to accept the hard, cold facts in order to protect her daughter. One thing she knew for certain—the only thing that mattered was Mary Kate.

A late-model black Bentley pulled up at the front of the Magnolia House just as Kate crossed the street. She instantly recognized the driver. Right on time. Actually a few minutes early. Trent emerged from the car, looked in her direction and threw up his hand. She waved back at him, but forced herself not to increase her pace. She had run to him, into his open arms, countless times in the past, always striving to please him. But no longer. She wasn't the girl she'd once been. Time and circumstances had changed her dramatically.

When she drew closer, Trent came toward her, and they both stopped in the middle of the sidewalk. She offered him a cordial, halfhearted smile. "I've already checked out and put my bag in the rental car," she told him. "If you'll follow me to—"

"That won't be necessary," Trent said. "Guthrie will take care of your rental car later. We'll leave the keys with the clerk at the hotel." He cupped her elbow. "Why don't you give me the keys and I'll get your bag and give the keys to the clerk? You can wait here for me." He opened the front passenger door of his car.

Mr. Take-charge. Trent's trademark. During their brief marriage, he'd made all the decisions and she'd allowed him to, with very little protest. *Do not pick a fight with Trent first thing. Choose your battles. This issue is not worth arguing about and you know it.*

She unzipped her leather purse, retrieved the car keys and handed them to Trent. "Thanks." Avoiding direct eye contact with him, she got in the Bentley and closed the door.

The car had a luxurious feel. Real tan leather and real wood. It seemed odd that Trent, who loved his sports cars dearly, would be driving this sedate sedan. This was a family car, not a bachelor's wheels. Maybe this was Aunt Mary Belle's car. No, probably not. She doubted that his aunt was driving these days, not after her stroke. Besides, she'd always preferred to be chauffeured around by Guthrie.

A few minutes later, Trent returned, opened the trunk and placed her suitcase inside, then he got into the Bentley and glanced at Kate. "Ready?"

"Yes."

"You've had breakfast?" he asked.

"Yes. At the Prospect Café."

"Then we're set until lunchtime." He inserted the key and started the engine. "Do you have a route preference?" he asked. "It's close to an eight-hour trip whether we go through Tupelo or Decatur."

She laughed spontaneously, surprised that he'd asked her opinion. The man was certainly a contradiction these days. Part old Trent, part new Trent.

He eyed her quizzically.

"You're driving," she said. "You choose."

He nodded, then pulled the Bentley into the flow of the sparse morning traffic. "If at anytime during the next few days—or however long this takes—I become over-bearing and insufferable, feel free to hit me between the eyes with a two-by-four."

Kate smiled. At least this new Trent had retained the old Trent's sense of humor. "I'll keep that in mind. And don't be surprised if I do as you suggested. You see, I'm not the easily manipulated, naive, love-sick fool I was when we got married."

"You might have been naive and in love, but you were never a fool." Trent kept his gaze focused on the road. "And as I recall there were times when neither I nor Aunt Mary Belle could bring you around to our way of thinking."

Kate's smile vanished as she remembered how trag-ically her Easter Sunday rebellion nearly twelve years ago had ended.

"Don't go there," he told her. "I was not referring to that Easter Sunday. I seem to recall more than one oc-casion when you balked at being bossed around."

"I'm sure you and I remember the past differently."

"Some things, perhaps, but…"

"But what?"

"Nothing. I think we're better off not discussing the past. We're less likely to argue if we stick to the pres-ent. Don't you agree?"

"If that's what you want. Believe me, dredging up the past isn't something I enjoy."

While he kept his gaze focused directly ahead and both of them stayed quiet, Kate studied Trent. He was remarkably handsome. He came close to being a pretty boy, but wasn't. Not quite. His nose was a little too prominent, his mouth a little too wide. Age had given him an air of distinction, the kind old money and privilege could give a man approaching forty.

"How long have you been a circuit court judge?" she asked, breaking the silence.

"Five years."

"Do you like being a judge?"

"Yes, I do."

"Wasn't it a problem for you to take time off from work to come with me?"

"I arranged for another judge to take my cases for the time being. I consider this a family emergency." Trent cast her a sidelong glance. "What about you? Can you afford to take time off from work? If not, I can help you financially."

"Don't do me any favors." The words were out of her mouth before she realized it. "Sorry. I didn't mean to snap. Looks like I'm still sensitive about money issues. Your aunt Mary Belle often intimated that I'd married you for your money."

"She knows better," Trent said. "She knew better at the time. Any idiot could see how much in love we were. It wasn't a one-sided thing and everyone knew it. Even Aunt Mary Belle."

A zinging warmth spread quickly through Kate. Hearing Trent say in such a matter-of-fact way that he'd been very much in love affected her deeply. She had believed he loved her—up until the day Mary Kate was abducted. From that time on, he'd given her numerous reasons to doubt his love.

"I don't need any financial help, but thank you for offering."

"Then your job as an investigator pays well?"

"Yes, it pays very well."

Silence.

Kate's heartbeat drummed softly in her ears. The well-insulated Bentley kept the outside noises to a minimum. How was it that this man she had once loved beyond all reason, who'd been her husband, her lover and her friend, now seemed like a stranger? Because that's what he is, she reminded herself. *Just as I'm a stranger to him. I'm no more the same person I was than he is.* Losing not only Mary Kate, but each other, both Trent and she had come through the ordeal with numerous battle scars. And in the years in between, they'd gone their separate ways and built new lives.

"You use your maiden name. Does that mean you haven't married again?" Trent said.

"No, I…no, I haven't remarried."

"You should have married again, Kate, and had other children."

"It's not too late," she told him. "I still could. But what about you? I halfway expected to find you married and…" She cleared her throat. "I heard you were the man about town and it was the lady voters who got you elected to the judgeship."

Trent chuckled. "You listened to local gossip while you were in town."

"Only to Mr. Walding, the clerk at the Magnolia House."

"Did he mention my dating a lady named Molly Stoddard?"

Tension tightened Kate's muscles. "No, he didn't."

"Molly is a widow with two children. We've been

dating for about a year. Steadily these past three months."

"Then it's a serious relationship?" Kate asked, although she already knew it was; otherwise he'd have never mentioned the woman.

"It's been heading that way." Trent gripped the steering wheel with white-knuckled strength. "What about you? Anyone special in your life?"

"Hmm." *No, there's no one special, but I wish there was.* She didn't want him to think she'd been pining away for him all these years. "As a matter of fact, I've been seeing a great deal of another Dundee agent. We're very close" *Damn, Kate, that's it—just lie to the man.* But she wasn't really lying. She and Lucie Evans did see a great deal of each other. They were close—the best of friends. Girlfriends, that is. There was nothing romantic in their relationship.

"I'm glad you have someone. Are you and—what did you say his name was?"

"His name? Uh, er, Evans. Lu-Luke Evans." *Now you've really lied and you can't deny it,* she told herself. *There is no Luke Evans!*

"Are you and Luke planning on getting married?"

"No, marriage isn't in our immediate plans." That much was true—neither she nor Lucie had any wedding plans. As a matter of fact neither of them were even dating anybody seriously.

"I've been thinking about asking Molly to marry me."

"What?" She hadn't meant to react by practically screaming her response, but his statement had surprised her. No, it had more than surprised her. It had struck a nerve. Even after being divorced for over ten years, she supposed she still thought of Trent as her husband. "I'm happy for you and…I wish you the very best."

"I haven't asked her, yet. I've just been thinking about it. But I'm not getting any younger. I'm going on forty. And Molly's a wonderful person and I adore her kids."

Molly was wonderful. He adored her kids. Was that any reason to marry a person? Once she wouldn't have thought so. Now, she wasn't sure. Maybe the second time around, a person should look for something other than mad, passionate love. Maybe that's what she should do. Find a wonderful man and settle for contentment instead of passion.

Get real, Kate, you'd never settle for anything less than being in love and you know it.

"Did you tell Molly that you were leaving town with your ex-wife?" Kate asked.

"Yes, of course. I phoned her last night and explained the situation. She was very understanding. That's the way Molly is. Understanding and kind and—"

"Do you love her?" Oh, God, why had she asked him that?

Silence.

"Okay, don't answer," Kate said. "It's none of my business. Sorry I asked."

A long silence followed, then minutes later, Trent spoke. "Do you love Luke?"

"Ah…yes, I do." At least that wasn't a lie. Not entirely. Since there was no Luke, her reply was a half-lie. She did love Lucie, like a sister. That was the truth.

Trent chuckled nervously. "How did we ever get on the subject of love? It's an odd topic for us to be discussing, all things considered."

"I'll choose a safer topic," she said. "How is Aunt—Miss Mary Belle doing since she had a stroke last year?"

"Better than anyone, including the doctors, predicted she would. She's a stubborn, determined woman. Luckily, her mind wasn't affected, just her body. She couldn't walk or use her left arm for days afterward, but with intense physical therapy she came around. She worked like the devil, pushed herself hard to recover."

"She looked well."

"You noticed the cane, of course. That's probably permanent."

"She seemed very much the same and yet different somehow. The minute she entered my hotel room, she corrected me because I'd been less than mannerly when I invited her in."

Trent grinned. "That's just who she is, and who she was raised to be. You never understood that for Aunt Mary Belle there is nothing more important than good manners."

"Oh, I understood all right. Good manners was— is—a religion to her."

"You said you noticed a change in Aunt Mary Belle." As Trent turned north on US Highway 82, he hazarded a quick glance at Kate. "What sort of change?"

"I don't know exactly. It was just that she said something odd."

"What did she say?"

"She said she was capable of admitting when she was wrong and that she'd been wrong about me."

Trent glanced at Kate and smiled. "She said that, did she?"

"Yes, she did. What did she mean?"

"Why didn't you ask her?"

"I think I was too stunned to hear Mary Belle Winston admit she could be wrong about anything."

"She was never as bad as you thought she was,"

Trent said, and before Kate could respond, he added, "And never as blameless as I thought she was."

Kate sat there quietly, absorbing Trent's words, letting them play over in her mind. He was right. Mary Belle wasn't the monster Kate had thought her to be. If only Trent had been able to realize, years ago, how his aunt had manipulated him, how she'd made Kate feel unworthy of being his wife. Hindsight is, as they say, twenty-twenty. For everyone. For her. For Trent. And maybe for Aunt Mary Belle, too.

"I suppose there's more than enough blame to go around, isn't there?" Instinctively Kate reached out to touch Trent's arm in a gesture of comfort, but stopped when she realized what she'd been about to do. Physical contact between them was a bad idea. She had to keep things cordial, but not too friendly. She and Trent could never be just friends, even if they both wanted it that way. They could be Mary Kate's parents. Nothing more.

"What happened to Mary Kate wasn't your fault," Trent said.

"I know that now." But it would have been nice to have heard her husband tell her that right after their child was taken from them. Instead, every time he had looked at her in the days and weeks following their baby's abduction, there had been accusation in his eyes. And when Aunt Mary Belle had come right out and said, "If only you hadn't stormed off on your own the way you did, this wouldn't have happened," Trent had remained silent, hadn't uttered one word in his wife's defense.

A heavy silence hung between them. Kate assumed Trent was lost in the past, as she was, reliving painful memories.

Nearly an hour later, Trent broke the silence. "Do you want to stop for an early lunch in Birmingham or would your rather stop somewhere between Birmingham and Tupelo?"

"It doesn't matter," she replied. "I could wait until we get to Memphis. I ate a big breakfast."

He wondered how many times Kate missed meals. She looked a little underweight to him, but not as thin and unhealthy as she'd looked the last time he saw her. After their daughter's kidnapping, Kate had stopped eating, stopped sleeping, stopped living.

"We'll stop and get a bite along the way," he said. "Maybe we'll run across an old-fashioned burger joint somewhere. Do you still love greasy cheeseburgers with the works?" He remembered how on their first date, she had attacked a huge cheeseburger—with onions—and eaten every bite. She was the first girl he'd dated who wasn't on a diet. He'd liked that about her—that she had a passion for life.

"Oh, yes, I still love cheeseburgers smothered in onions." She smiled at him. "Some things don't change."

Her thousand-watt smile had always turned him inside out—that sure hadn't changed. The basic male animal in him wanted to pull the Bentley off to the side of the road, undo their seat belts and drag Kate into his arms. The powerful physical attraction that had overwhelmed them when they first met, when he'd helped a damsel in distress, was still as potent as ever. He wanted her now, as he'd wanted her then; but he didn't dare act on instinct. He had no rights where Kate was concerned. He'd let her go over ten years ago and now she had a new life and a new love.

Why did that bother him so damn much? It wasn't as if he was still in love with her. And it wasn't as if he didn't have someone special in his life. But he wasn't in love with Molly, either. Being in love was highly overrated, wasn't it? He could have a good life with Molly and he could be a loving and caring stepfather to her children. After all, it wasn't as if he could turn back the clock and make things right with Kate again.

If you could, would you? that damn irritating inner voice asked. It was a moot question.

He could no more have Kate back than the infant Mary Kate could be returned to them.

"Kate?"

"Hmm?"

"Have you actually thought all this through?" he asked. "I mean do you know how you'll deal with whatever we find out, be it good news or bad?"

"I'll deal with the news—good or bad—the way I have for the past eleven and a half years. If none of the little girls turn out to be Mary Kate, I'll keep on searching." She paused briefly. "For the rest of my life."

"Is that what you've been doing all these years, searching for our little girl?"

She nodded. "Except for money to pay for life's necessities, I've spent every penny I've made searching for Mary Kate. One of the reasons I left the Atlanta police department and joined Dundee's is because I knew as one of their agents I would get a discount on services and I'd have all their vast resources at my disposal."

"What if one of these little girls is Mary Kate? What will you do then?"

Crossing her arms at the waist and gripping her elbows, Kate hugged herself as if she'd had a sudden chill. "If we find our daughter, I want to see her. And I want to know all about her life. Who her parents are. If she has brothers and sisters. Is she healthy and happy."

"And if she is happy and healthy and part of a loving family, then what?"

Kate clenched her jaw and shut her eyes. Trent caught a glimpse of the pain on her face, but looked away quickly, unable to bear seeing her suffer. But this time, whatever the outcome, he intended to stand by her and help her deal with the fallout.

"I'd like to believe I'll be able to walk away and not disrupt her life," Kate said. "But I don't know if I'm that strong."

"You are," he told her. "We have to be. Both of us."

"It'll have to be enough, won't it? To see her. Once. And then go away and leave her to her happy life with people she thinks of as her parents."

"You should have another child," Trent said. "You were born to be a mother."

"No other child could ever replace Mary Kate."

"I know that only too well. I don't think I ever want to father another child," he admitted, surprised that he'd actually said the words aloud. He'd never told another living soul that he was afraid to love another child as he had loved Mary Kate, that the fear of losing another child was too great.

Kate turned sideways in her seat and stared at him. "I feel the same way. I can't bear the thought of ever again going through the hell we went through when we lost Mary Kate. I'm afraid to have another baby, so you see I understand the way you feel, only too well."

He glanced at her hurriedly, then just as he looked back at the long stretch of Interstate 65 ahead of them, Kate touched his arm. A tender, caressing squeeze that sent shock waves through his entire body.

Oh, God, why had she touched him?

Trent gritted his teeth in an effort to ward off the

emotional demons that plagued him whenever he thought about all that he'd lost. First his daughter. And then his wife. But his wife—his ex-wife—had come back into his life and she was leading him into the unknown, into dangerous waters. It had taken him ten years to put his life back together and to begin thinking about a future with another woman. And damn it all, here he was heading toward Memphis with Kate—the love of his life—on a journey that might well lead them straight to a hell even more horrible than the one they'd barely survived eleven years ago.

Four

Kate didn't put up a fuss when Trent drove straight into downtown Memphis to the Peabody Hotel. She could have told him it would have been nice if he'd asked her where she wanted to stay, but what was the point? After all, he hadn't considered paying for a two-bedroom suite at a prestigious Memphis landmark hotel as anything out of the ordinary. Having been born with the proverbial silver spoon in his mouth, Trent always traveled first class.

"I phoned last night to make reservations," he'd told her when they came through Germantown on the outskirts of the city. "I booked the two-bedroom suite for a week, with the understanding I might need it longer."

Kate had nodded and smiled as if she were accustomed to having someone else make her decisions for her. But why should she complain? Staying at the most elegant hotel in town sure beat staying at a fifty-dollar-a-night motel, which was what she could afford on her budget.

Her bedroom was luxurious, as was her bath. And the large bed looked inviting. The bellman placed her bag on the suitcase rack and returned to the sitting room. She watched as Trent tipped the man. From the smile on the bellman's face, she figured it was more money than most people gave him.

"Would you like to have supper at *Chez Philippe* or the *Capriccio* Restaurant here at the hotel? Of if you prefer, we can go out to a nearby restaurant." Trent removed his overcoat and tossed it across a nearby chair in the lounge. "Our other choice is to eat in. I could order room service."

She debated her possible replies. She really didn't want to go out, but would eating dinner alone with Trent in their suite be too intimate?

"I'm tired. I'd rather eat in and get to bed early," she told him. "So, if you'd order for me, anything will do. I'm not particular. Just no regular coffee this late in the day. While you do that, I'll use my cell phone to contact Special Agent Moran."

"Steak, pork, chicken or seafood?" Trent called out as he sat down at the desk and picked up the room service menu.

"I'm not really all that hungry," she told him. "Not after the burgers we ate in Tupelo. A salad would do fine for me."

Kate shrugged off her coat, then hung it in the closet. She wasn't exactly a neat-freak, but she had an orderly mind and liked everything in its place. She'd been that way all her life. It had been one of the few things about her that Aunt Mary Belle had approved of during her brief marriage to Trent. Kate removed her scarf and gloves, placed them on the shelf at the top of the closet, and then kicked off her shoes and lined them side-by-side in the closet floor.

When she walked to the door, she heard Trent on the phone, ordering their dinner. After studying him closely, she closed the door and tried to blot out his image. Now was the time to take control of any lingering sexual feelings she had for her ex-husband. They were going to be together for days, perhaps weeks, and she couldn't go around mooning over a guy who was practically engaged to another woman. No matter what happened with the search for Mary Kate, there was no future for Trent and her. Her mind understood; her heart didn't. And she wasn't even going to think about how her libido reacted every time Trent came near her.

After sitting down on the edge of the bed, she removed her cell phone from her purse and hit the button that instantly dialed Dante Moran's number. As she waited while the phone rang, she wriggled her sock-covered toes. On the job for Dundee's she wore slacks all the time and preferred socks to knee-highs. It had been ages since she's put on a dress. Actually she owned two dresses and one suit. Everything else in her closet was slacks, tops and jackets. She almost wished she had brought along one of her two dresses, just in case she needed it.

She shouldn't do this to herself—shouldn't think about pleasing Trent. He'd always preferred her in dresses, telling her numerous times that it was a shame to cover up a great pair of legs.

"Special Agent Moran," the deep male voice said.

"Yes, Moran, it's Kate Malone."

"Are you still in Prospect?"

"No, I'm back in Memphis. Trent came with me. We're at the Peabody. In a suite. A two-bedroom suite."

Moran whistled. "Putting on the Ritz, huh? But I guess your ex-hubby can afford it, can't he?"

"Oh, yes, he can easily afford it." Kate nervously bounced her knees up and down until she realized what she was doing, then stopped abruptly. "So, what's the latest? Has there been any word on—"

"We've found three sets of other parents who lost infant daughters around the same time Mary Kate was taken. Similar circumstances. All the babies were blond and under six months old. We've contacted these people and if everybody makes it to Memphis by eleven o'clock tomorrow, we'll have a general meeting to go over the situation."

"Did you say three sets of parents?" she asked. "But…there are only three little girls. That means—"

"It means we've got four sets of biological parents and only three children who might belong to them."

Kate swallowed hard. She didn't wish heartbreak for anyone else, but she couldn't help praying that Mary Kate was one of those three little girls. "What do you know about these people?"

"All I can tell you is that out of those three sets, only one couple is still married. They're eager to find out if one of the little girls is theirs. They have two other children now. One couple is divorced, like you and Trent, and both of them are interested in finding out if one of the children is theirs. And then there's a father whose wife died three years ago. He's hoping one child is his."

"Is the method of positive ID still going to be DNA tests?" Kate asked. Moran had said that although they could match up blood types and infant footprints, the most reliable testing was DNA. Each little girl's DNA would be compared to the possible birth parents.

"Yeah. And we will speed up that process. Your boss

man, MacNamara, has called in some favors, as has Sam Dundee, to get a rush job for you."

Thank you, Sawyer MacNamara, Kate said silently. Although her best friend and fellow Dundee agent, Lucie Evans, absolutely despised the CEO of Dundee's, Kate had always liked the man. Now she positively loved him. But she wouldn't tell Lucie. Kate smiled to herself.

Sam Dundee was a man everyone liked and admired. Being a father himself, he no doubt understood how important this was to her. Once this was all over, she'd have to phone both Sawyer and Mr. Dundee to thank them.

"Have the adoptive parents been notified?" she asked.

"That process has already begun. And we're starting with the older children first, so since Mary Kate would be nearly twelve years old now, she'll be in the first set."

Kate's chest tightened. *Please, dear God, please, let her be one of these little girls.*

"How soon do you think—?" Kate breathed deeply, then sighed. "How long before we give samples for the DNA tests?"

"Hopefully we'll take samples tomorrow. And within a couple of days, we should be able to set up a meeting with the adoptive parents." Moran paused. "We're asking each of the adoptive parents to bring pictures of their child."

"You'd think a mother would be able to know her own child from a photograph, wouldn't you?" Fear and uncertainty welled up inside Kate. What if she looked at those pictures and didn't recognize Mary Kate? "What if—" her voice cracked. "I may not know my own daughter."

Tears stung her eyes. Dammit, she didn't cry. Not anymore. She'd shed all her tears years ago. Or at least she thought she had.

"Look, Kate, don't do this to yourself," Moran said. "Once we get the DNA results, you'll know for sure."

"Yes, you're right. Sorry about getting all female and emotional on you. I know how you G-men hate emotion." She forced a laugh.

"Lady, if anyone is entitled to get a little emotional about this, you are. If I were in your shoes, I'd be emotional."

Kate really laughed then. "You're kidding me, right? Dante Moran is a man of steel."

He chuckled. "Yeah, I do have that reputation, don't I? But truth be told, we're all emotional when it comes to personal things, even if we don't outwardly show that emotion."

"You know what, Special Agent Moran? I think I like you."

"And you know what, Kate Malone? I know I like you."

"Friends?" she asked.

"Yeah," he said. "I'll call you in the morning if the meeting at eleven o'clock is a go."

"Okay. Thanks."

Kate hit the Off button and laid her phone on the nightstand, then spread out across the bed and tried to relax. If things were different, she just might pursue a personal relationship with Moran. From certain things he'd said, she figured he had some romantic tragedy in his past and that's why he was still single. Most of the good ones were taken by the time they were thirty-five. And Moran had told her himself that he'd never been married.

Oh, we'd make a fine pair, both of us still halfway in love with other people. Dante with the mystery lady from his past, she with Trent. Yes, she was still partly hung up on Trent. She probably always would be. When you loved someone the way she'd loved Trent, it never completely went away. A part of her would always love him.

A soft knock sounded on the door. She sat straight up in the middle of the bed.

"Yes?"

"Dinner will be here in about thirty-five minutes," Trent said through the closed door.

"Fine. Thanks. That'll give me time for a quick nap."

"I'll let you know when dinner arrives."

"Okay."

"Kate, are you all right? Is something wrong?"

Go away, she thought. *Yes, something's wrong. I'm still hung up on you and there doesn't seem to be anything I can do about it.*

"I talked to Moran," Kate said.

"May I come in?" Trent asked.

Oh, great. Just great. "I…uh…okay, sure." She scooted to the edge of the bed and was halfway standing when Trent opened the door.

He looked at her. She looked at him. He frowned.

"Have you been crying?" He came toward her slowly, as if uncertain whether he should.

"No. I don't cry. Not anymore."

He paused when he was within a couple of feet of her. "What did Moran say to upset you?"

"I'm not upset."

"Okay, so what is it? Something's bothering you. I know how you are when—"

"No, Trent, you do not know me," she practically

screamed at him. "You don't have the slightest idea who I am. I'm not sure you ever did."

His shoulders slumped. His frown deepened. "That's not fair, Kate. You could be right about my not knowing the person you are now, but I did know you once. And you knew me. We knew each other inside out." He moved closer, reached out and lifted her hand, then placed it over his heart. "There was a time when I thought—" He dropped his hold on her as if her hand had suddenly become red-hot. "Sorry. Old habits die hard, I guess. Being with you brings back a lot of memories. Good memories."

Don't look back, she told herself. *Don't get sucked in by all those good memories.* She needed to take charge of this situation. Set a precedent here and now. Their past relationship was off-limits. It was in the past and should stay there.

"Moran will call tomorrow if a meeting he's trying to set up works out," Kate said, deliberately changing the subject. "They've found three other sets of people who may be the parents of those three little girls. With us that makes four, so one set of parents is going to be disappointed after the DNA tests results come back."

"You're afraid we'll be those parents, aren't you? That's what's wrong." He gazed at her, kindness and concern in his dark eyes. And true understanding. "You have to know how much I want one of those little girls to be Mary Kate. I want it as much as you do."

She knew he was telling her the truth. As Mary Kate's father, he wanted what Kate wanted. But she also knew that he hadn't dreamed of the day, hoped and prayed for the day, lived for the day that Mary Kate would be found. But she had. Not one single day had passed in the eleven years and nine months since their child had been stolen from them that Kate hadn't longed for the moment she would see her daughter again. No, Trent had chosen a different path—he had believed Mary Kate was dead, that she was lost to them forever.

"I'd like to be alone for a while," she told him, her voice deadly calm. "Please, let me know when dinner is ready."

With a hurt expression on his face, he turned around and walked out of her bedroom. When he closed the door, Kate rushed into the bathroom, turned on the faucets and gathered water in her hands. After splashing her face with cool water several times, she dried her face and hands, then clenched her teeth together tightly, trying her best not to cry.

Things weren't going to get any better between Trent and her. Not only did the past stand between them, a painful reminder of how much they had lost, but the sexual tension smoldering just below the surface frightened her. It would be so easy to fall into Trent's arm, to fall into his bed, in an effort to recapture what they'd once shared. No matter what happened, even if one of those three little girls turned out to be their daughter, Mary Kate would never be her child again. And even if she succumbed to her feelings for Trent, they couldn't go back. It was too late for them. Too late for all of them.

Trent poured himself another cup of decaf coffee, then relaxed across the table from Kate where they'd shared a delicious meal in the suite's spacious lounge. They'd also shared some mundane conversation while they dined—Kate on her Caesar salad and he on his salmon fillet.

"I ordered dessert." With his free hand, Trent lifted the silver lid covering the plate containing a huge chocolate brownie smothered in whipped cream and pecans. "I hope brownies are still your favorite dessert. Brownies aren't a specialty of either hotel restaurant, but they aim to please their guests, so they actually sent out to a bakery."

"My food preferences haven't changed much," she admitted. "At lunch you remembered about the cheeseburgers and tonight you went to a great deal of trouble to see that I got my all-time favorite dessert. You're being very nice to me. And I'm afraid I haven't been all that nice to you. I'm sorry. It's just—"

"You've been nice enough," Trent said. "Besides, why should you be nice to me? I wasn't exactly the ideal husband at a time when you needed me most. I was too wrapped up in my own grief and guilt to help you."

She stared at him, her expression telling him that she was uncertain she'd heard him correctly. "Was that some sort of apology?"

"If an apology will do you any good now, then I'll apologize until I'm blue in the face. I'm sorry, Kate." He set the cup and saucer on the table, shoved back his chair and stood. "God, how you must have hated me." He walked across the room to the windows and looked out over downtown Memphis. Dressed in brilliant lights more sparkling than diamonds, the River City came alive at night, like a beautiful woman decked out in all her finery. A part of him wished he could walk out into the night and disappear. He'd managed to keep his demons at bay for so many years, pretending he didn't care, telling himself over and over again that Mary Kate was dead and that he'd never see either his daughter or his wife ever again. But reality had made a lie of all the beliefs he'd clung to for the past eleven years, ever since Kate had walked out on him. Now Kate was back in his life, even if for only a few weeks. And if fate was on their side, they'd see their daughter soon.

Damn, why hadn't he listened to Kate all those years ago when she'd insisted she was going to find their baby? He should have helped her hunt for Mary Kate. Instead, he'd crawled into a dark, emotionally barren hole and cut himself off from hope and from love.

He felt her presence directly behind him, even before she laid her hand on his shoulder. The minute she touched him, he tensed. God, how he wanted to hold her. Hold her and never let her go.

"Trent?"

He clenched his jaw.

"It's all right," she told him.

"No, it's not all right. I failed you. And I'm sorry about that."

"Neither of us was equipped to handle losing our baby. We each dealt with it the best we could. But what hurt me the most was your agreeing with Aunt Mary Belle that it was all my fault."

What had she said? Trent snapped around and glared at Kate. "Aunt Mary Belle never said it was all your fault. God, Kate, she never—"

"She said that if I hadn't run off angry that Sunday after church and taken Mary Kate with me, none of it would have happened. Don't you dare deny that she said it."

"Yes, she did say that, but she also said that if only she had agreed to walk with us, the way she should have, it wouldn't have happened. Don't you remember her saying—?"

"You're lying!"

"No, you don't remember, do you? By the time Aunt Mary Belle told me she blamed herself, you'd already run out of the room."

Kate stared at him in disbelief.

"Are you telling me that all these years you've thought I blamed you for what happened?" he asked.

"You did blame me. You and Aunt Mary Belle both blamed me."

He stared at her, hurt and anger mixing with love and understanding inside him. "Kate, honey, no one blamed you but you. You were so consumed with guilt that nobody could get through to you, not even the doctors."

When he reached out to touch her, she backed away from him.

"I can't deal with this right now," she told him. "I don't know if I believe you or not."

"Why would I lie to you? What would I have to gain?"

"I don't know, but…if you didn't blame me for what happened, then what were you apologizing for a few minutes ago?"

"For everything," he told her. "For letting what happened, happen. For not being able to make things right. For not taking better care of you. For not being able to give you what you needed to see you through the rough times. God, Kate, if I hadn't made so many mistakes, you wouldn't have left me. I failed you miserably."

"All these years, I thought I'd failed you."

Before he could pull her into his arms the way he wanted to do, she turned and fled. He hurried after her, but halted when she slammed the door in his face. He stood there for several minutes staring at the door, trying to decide if he should storm into her bedroom or leave her alone. When he heard the click of the door lock, the question was answered for him. Kate didn't want or need him. Not anymore.

Five

Kate and Trent had been the first to arrive, but within thirty minutes, everyone was assembled at the local FBI headquarters in Memphis. Dante Moran, looking every inch the federal agent in his black suit, pale gray shirt and striped tie, surveyed the group before his dark gaze settled on Kate. She offered him a hesitant smile. He understood, as she did, that when all was said and done, at least one set out of the four groups of parents here today would be gravely disappointed. There were only three adopted girls who had been stolen around Easter twelve years ago by the infant abduction ring, only three babies taken at that time who could possibly belong to them.

Avoiding eye-contact with Trent, Kate scanned the room. At breakfast earlier this morning, neither she nor Trent had brought up anything about the night before, about the blame-game that Kate didn't understand. She had truly believed that both Trent and his aunt held her responsible for Mary Kate's kidnapping. Was it possible she'd been wrong? After some major soul searching during the night, she still didn't know for sure if Trent had told her the truth. But why would he lie?

How could you have been so wrong all these years? she asked herself. *You were so sure he blamed you for Mary Kate's abduction.*

As Kate glanced from person to person, she noted a similar expression on each parent's face—that odd mixture of hope and fear. No doubt her features conveyed those same emotions. Jayne and Clay Perkins were the only couple still married. They were in their late thirties, he tall and thin, she short and plump. They had a ten-year-old son and a seven-year-old daughter. Their eldest child, Megan, who'd be almost twelve now, had been snatched from her stroller in a downtown Birmingham department store when she was three months old. A week before Easter.

Exotically dark and beautiful Jessica Previn and blond and equally attractive Dave Blankenship were divorced. His second wife, Mindy, accompanied him today, as did Jessica's fiancé, Cory. Dave had a three-year-old son by Mindy and he'd proudly shown-off his child's photos to the other parents. Jessica and Dave's daughter, Charity, had been stolen from her infant swing in the couple's Prattville backyard the day after Easter, nearly twelve years ago.

Muscularly built and sporting a military short haircut, Dennis Copeland, a widower for two years, had been left alone to raise his younger daughter, seven-year-old Brooke. His wife Stacy and he had been students at Auburn University when their first child was born. Two-month-old Heather Copeland had been abducted by a friendly stranger who'd sweet-talked the babysitter into letting her hold the child. The Copeland's babysitter had taken Heather for a stroller ride in a small park near her parents' apartment on the Thursday before Easter.

Kate couldn't help wondering how the loss of their child had affected each couple. The horrific event had no doubt proven as devastating to each of them as it had to Trent and her. Had the Blankenships' marriage disintegrated the same way her marriage had? Had they blamed each other? Or had they simply fallen out of love? What about the other two couples? How had the Perkinses and the Copelands managed to stay together? *What did it matter?* she asked herself. Although the others shared the same tragedy, they were all individuals who had their own unique relationships that had either stayed intact or had fallen apart for reasons only the two people involved knew. And maybe even they didn't know. There were times when she questioned her reasons for leaving Trent. But there was one thing everyone here today shared—a desire to know the truth about their lost child. Apparently the others were as anxious as Trent and she to find out if their daughter was still alive, if by some miracle one of these stolen baby girls might be theirs.

As Dante Moran explained in detail what the FBI knew about the infant abduction ring that had operated in the deep south for the past dozen years, Trent reached over and grasped Kate's hand. Instinctively she started to jerk away, not wanting comfort from anyone, least of all her ex-husband. She hadn't been able to trust another person completely, had chosen to go it alone, to take care of herself and not lean on any man. But common sense stopped her from rejecting Trent's touch.

Common sense and admitting to herself that an emotional bond still existed between them. After years of being apart, of now having very little in common, they still shared one of the most important links any two people can share. A child. And in their case, a missing child.

Kate found herself clasping Trent's hand tightly and inching ever so slightly toward him. She glanced at him and saw her own thoughts and feelings reflected in his eyes. He leaned over and said quietly, "Meeting these other parents makes me wish the FBI had found four little girls."

Kate nodded. "Someone's daughter is still missing, her fate unknown." She gulped down her fear. "Mary Kate may not be one of the these children. We could be the parents whose hearts are broken all over again."

Trent slipped his arm around Kate's shoulders. Understanding his intention, she realized she welcomed the comfort he offered. Truth be told, she was glad she wasn't facing this traumatic experience alone. None of this would be easy whether or not they found Mary Kate.

"The bureau is in the process of notifying all the adoptive parents. They number in the hundreds. We have begun with the oldest children. The three baby girls we believe were taken from within a two-hundred-mile radius in Alabama on or around Easter Sunday twelve years ago this coming April are among the first to be processed. We're asking the adoptive parents of these three young girls to cooperate by allowing us to take DNA samples of their adopted child," Moran said. "Here today we'll try to answer any questions y'all have. Then we want the birth parents to give us DNA samples. These tests will take top priority. One of the birth parents has agreed to pay the expenses to have these four tests done by an independent lab to expedite the matter, so we should know something in a week or less. The DNA tests will confirm paternity. We'll also use blood types and any footprints or fingerprints available for each child."

Kate turned to Trent. "Did you—?"

"Yes."

"Thank you."

"I offered to cover the cost of the DNA tests so we wouldn't have to wait any longer than absolutely necessary," he said softly, for her ears only. "I'd pay ten times that much to find out the truth for us…and for these other parents." He inclined his head toward the others.

"Even if these girls belong to any three couples here, that doesn't mean you'll be able to walk in and claim your child," Moran explained. "We're dealing with a legal nightmare. The adoptive parents of these three girls are already hiring lawyers, as I'm sure will countless hundreds of other adoptive parents in the weeks and months ahead."

"What rights do we have?" Dennis Copeland asked.

"That's probably going to be a decision the courts have to make."

"Are all these girls in good homes?" Jessica Previn asked. "Do they all have loving parents?"

"I don't have that kind of detailed information at this time," Moran told her.

"When do we get to meet the adoptive parents?" Jayne Perkins asked.

"Will we be shown pictures of the girls?" Jessica Previn questioned. "I'm sure I could pick out Charity if I saw her."

"I agree," Jayne said. "I feel certain I'd know Megan the minute I laid eyes on her."

"We plan to try to set up a meeting with the adoptive parents of these three girls, hopefully very soon, within a day or two," Moran said. "We'll ask each to bring pictures of their child. But I caution y'all not to get your hopes up, even if you see photographs of these girls. Your infant daughters were all blond. Two were blue-eyed and two brown-eyed. As we all know hair and eye colors can change over the years. Blondes can become brunettes. And blue eyes can turn green or even brown. And it's been known for children with chocolate brown eyes as babies to have hazel eyes as teenagers."

"Should we birth parents hire our own lawyers?" Dave Blankenship asked.

"I can't advise you on that," Moran replied.

"If you were one of us, what would you do?" Trent asked, then answered his own question, "You'd hire a lawyer, wouldn't you?" Trent looked from parent to parent as he spoke. "I've already contacted my lawyer about this matter and I'd recommend that y'all do the same. I'm sure all of you, like Kate and I, want only what's best for your child—if it turns out one of these girls is your child. What's best may well mean leaving our daughters with their adoptive parents, but even in that case, we'll still want our rights, as the biological parents, protected."

A loud murmur rose from the other parents as they discussed their options amongst themselves. To a person, they all agreed that each couple would hire a lawyer of their own.

"I'll be in touch with y'all when I receive any more pertinent information," Moran told them. "And as soon as we can work something out for a meeting with the adoptive parents, we'll let you know. In the meantime, a technician from O'Steen Labs is here to take your DNA samples. Special Agent Clark will escort y'all, couple by couple, into his office where the technician is waiting. And I want to assure everyone that these DNA samples will be properly collected and will be under FBI protection from here to the lab, as will the results."

As the other couples exited the room, Moran motioned to Kate. Leaving Trent standing by the door, she made her way to the FBI agent.

"Do you know your blood type and your hus—your ex-husband's?" Moran asked.

Kate's heart fluttered with anticipation. "Yes, I know. Why do you ask?"

"What are the blood types?"

"Mine is A-positive and Trent's is O-positive."

"Two of the three girls have O-positive blood type."

Kate swallowed hard. Warmth flushed her face and neck. "Mary Kate has O-positive, the same as Trent."

Moran glanced at Trent, then back at Kate. "I thought you should know. But don't get your hopes up. More people have O-positive than any other blood type. Could be one out of each set of parents has type O."

"I realize that. But at least, it puts us in the running, doesn't it?"

Moran gave her a tender look, one that told her he sympathized. But he didn't touch her or say anything else before he turned and walked away. Strange man, she thought. A mixture of toughness and kindness.

"What was that all about?" Trent approached Kate. "From the way he was looking at you, I'd say Special Agent Moran has a personal interest in you."

"Dante Moran and I are colleagues of a sort. And oddly enough, I think we understand each other. But there is nothing romantic between us." Why had she felt compelled to explain her relationship with Moran to Trent?

"If Luke wasn't in the picture, things might be different, right?"

Oh, God, she'd forgotten about that stupid lie—the one about Luke being the man in her life. There was no Luke. Only Lucie, her best friend. "Look, Trent, I think you should know that Luke is—"

Kate's cell phone rang. Saved by the bell? she wondered.

She flipped open the phone and said, "Malone here."

"Kate, it's Lucie. How are you? What's going on? Where are you?"

"Speak of the devil." Kate chuckled. "Now, how about slowing down. You're shooting questions at me ninety-to-nothing."

"Sorry. It's just that I haven't heard from you in a couple of days, not since you were headed out to Prospect to talk to your ex."

"Trent and I are in Memphis, at FBI headquarters. We just sat in on a general meeting with three other pairs of biological parents. Everyone is submitting samples for DNA testing and the Feds should be able to match up the three girls to their biological parents within a week. Dante Moran is doing his best to help me, although his hands are somewhat tied by the system."

"From all I hear, Moran's a good guy, if a bit unfriendly," Lucie said. "And considering the fact that he supposedly has some difficulty with rules and regulations, I figure it's only a matter of time before he jumps ship and joins Dundee's."

"You're kidding? Is there word around the office about—"

"Daisy let it slip that our fearless leader has made the offer to Moran, and you know Sawyer wouldn't do that unless he was damn sure Moran is interested."

"Moran hasn't said a word to me about it."

"Why should he?" Lucie laughed. "Don't tell me that you and Moran are—"

"No, we are not. We like and respect each other, but that's all there is to it." Kate eyed Trent, who was listening quite intensely to her end of the conversation.

"Okay. So how's the chemistry between you and your ex? You've still got feelings for him and don't deny it. I'm your best buddy and I know you. Does he still have a thing for you?"

"Can't say."

"Is he with you right now?"

"Yes."

"Mmm, hmm. So, call me later with details, okay? I just got back to Atlanta last night and I've told Sawyer that I need a little downtime before he sends me out again. The man's being a real ass about my assignments lately. Ever since our last big brouhaha, he's been putting me on wuss jobs because he knows how I hate being put on lightweight assignments simply because I'm a woman. I swear, Kate, one of these days I'm going to cut that guy down to size."

Kate laughed. "If anybody can do it, you can. But be prepared for a battle royal. We both know that nothing would please Sawyer more than for you to give him a legitimate reason to fire you. You're the thorn in his side, honey, and the only reason you're still with Dundee's is because Sawyer has worked hard to not let his personal feelings dictate his business decisions."

"Let's face facts—neither Sawyer nor I can be impersonal about anything that goes on between us. We can't stand each other and nothing will change that fact." Lucie groaned. "Would you listen to me belly-aching about my stupid feud with the black knight when you've got a major deal going on in your life right now."

Kate's gaze met Trent's and she realized he was curious about her caller. Was now the time to come clean and tell him that Luke was really Lucie? Should she or shouldn't she be honest with him? Having a boyfriend, albeit a fictional one, provided her with a barrier between Trent and her. If she removed that obstacle, would Trent make a move on her or would he remain true to his lady friend, Molly? The God's honest truth was that Kate still had it bad for her ex and it wouldn't take much for her to fall into his arms—or into his bed, for that matter.

"I need a favor," Kate said.

"You name it, you got it."

"I need you to go over to my apartment and water my plants."

"You do, do you?"

Kate didn't have any houseplants and Lucie knew it. The catch phrase she'd just repeated had been a code that Lucie used whenever she found herself in a situation with a guy that she couldn't handle. If Lucie was in danger of giving in to lust and knew she'd regret it in the morning, she'd call Kate with a spiel about watering her plants, which was actually a cry for immediate help. Lucie had a notorious black thumb. She could kill any plant within ten days without even trying.

"It could be a week or two before I get back to Atlanta and I wouldn't want anything to happen to my plants," Kate said.

"Want me to come to Memphis or just be available in case things get dicey?"

"The latter."

"I'll be available." Pause. "Kate, I hope one of those kids turns out to be Mary Kate."

"Yeah, me, too."

"Take care, huh."

"You, too."

Kate closed her phone and returned it to her jacket pocket.

Trent clutched her shoulder. "Was that Luke?"

"Yes and no," Kate admitted.

Trent stared at her, a puzzled expression on his face.

"I was talking to my best friend, Lucie Evans, who is a former FBI agent and now a fellow Dundee employee." Kate sighed loudly. "There is no Luke. Just Lucie. I do love her. She's practically like a sister to me. So I only partly lied to you."

Trent grinned. "Why did you lie about having a boyfriend?"

"Want me to be totally honest?"

He nodded.

"I still have feelings for you and I sense you have some for me, too. It's probably just some leftover lust, but… I thought having a boyfriend might keep you at arm's length."

Trent eased his hand down her shoulder and circled her waist. Looking her square in the eyes, he told her, "If I wanted you and you wanted me, too, a hundred boyfriends wouldn't stop me from making love to you."

Excitement shot through Kate like Fourth of July fireworks. "Trent…I…we—"

He pulled her up against him and lowered his head. His lips came down, down, down.

"The lab technician is ready for you two," Dante Moran called from the doorway.

Kate froze. Trent lifted his head and reluctantly released her.

That was a close call, she thought. The next time it happens—and it would—what if there was nobody around to interrupt them?

Six

Kate sat across the table from Dante Moran in a back booth at the River City Café, an old-fashioned fifties diner not far from the FBI field office. After she and Trent gave the lab technician their DNA samples, she'd insisted that Trent go back to the hotel without her.

"I need to put some space between us," she'd admitted. "I think you need that, too. Why don't you go back to the Peabody and find something to do to pass the time? I want to stay here and go over any records belonging to the abduction ring that Moran will let me look at. I can't handle more than one major problem at a time and dealing with you—with all the old feelings we once had for each other—is posing a big problem for me."

Trent hadn't said much in response; he'd just agreed with her and left. A part of her had been disappointed that he hadn't put up a fight, that he hadn't proclaimed his feelings for her weren't just remnants of a past love.

"Shouldn't you call your ex-husband and let him know you're okay and won't be back to the hotel until later?" Moran glanced over the edge of the menu he held as he questioned Kate.

"I don't have to report in to Trent. We are divorced and the only reason we're together now is because of Mary Kate."

"What did the guy do to you to make you hate him?"

"I don't hate—"

The waitress came to their booth, placed glasses of water in front of them and asked, "So, what'll it be?"

"I'll take the chicken and dressing special," Moran said. "And coffee. Black."

The waitress, a gum-smacking twenty-year-old with spiked white hair, turned to Kate. "And you, ma'am?"

That "ma'am" made Kate feel old. She was only thirty-five. But a world-weary thirty-five. Looking up at the young girl, she replied, "I want the grilled chicken salad and coffee. And I'll need creamer for my coffee."

As soon as the waitress left, Moran rephrased his earlier question. "What's with you and your ex?"

"You're being awfully nosey."

Moran grinned, his teeth pearly-white against his bronze complexion. "I thought maybe you needed to talk about it. If I'm wrong, I apologize."

Kate sighed. "There's nothing to talk about. Trent and I have been divorced for ten years. He's practically engaged to someone else." She looked right at Moran. "And I do not hate Trent. That's the problem. It would be much easier if I did hate him."

"Mmm, hmm."

"Hey, I appreciate your letting me hang around the office all day. And I really have to thank you for giving me access to those files. Will you get in trouble for doing that?"

"Not unless somebody tells on me." He grinned. "To be honest, I'm not greatly concerned about my career with the bureau. I've been giving a great deal of thought to changing jobs."

"Why would you do that?" *So, Lucie's info about Moran leaving the FBI and coming to work for Dundee's was true,* Kate thought.

"My career with the bureau is at a standstill and I'm not likely to move on up, not with my reputation as a rebel."

The waitress brought their coffee and small containers of creamer for Kate. Moran lifted the mug to his lips and sipped the hot brew. After emptying two tiny cartons of creamer into her coffee, Kate stirred it until the black turned a luscious café au lait color.

"Is that a rebel with or without a cause?" she asked.

Moran chuckled. "That depends on who you ask. As far as I'm concerned, I always have a cause. Sometimes I don't play by the rules, but there's always logic behind the madness."

"Do you think this infant abduction ring case will be your last?"

"Yeah, it could be. We should wrap up my part of things within a month, then I'm thinking about moving back south."

"To Atlanta?"

Moran lifted an eyebrow inquisitively. "Who at Dundee's has been talking?"

"Our office manager, Daisy Holbrook, told my buddy Lucie and Lucie told me when we spoke earlier today." Kate smiled at Moran. "If you want my opinion…?"

"Fire away."

"I think Dundee's would be damn lucky to get a man like you."

"Why thank you, ma'am."

"I guess you already know that the pay is very good, as are the benefits. Some assignments are dangerous, some are heartbreaking, some are routine and a few are just downright boring. But Sawyer MacNamara is a top-notch boss. Smart, savvy, fair-minded. Except when it comes to Lucie Evans. With those two, it's tit for tat. Don't listen to anything Lucie says about Sawyer or vice versa. They hate each other with a passion."

"How is it that they're able to work together? Why hasn't Lucie quit or MacNamara fired her if the animosity between them is that bad?"

Kate shrugged. "Lucie would never quit and give Sawyer the satisfaction. He won't fire her because everybody would know he'd done it for personal reasons."

"What about Dundee himself? If MacNamara runs the show on a day-to-day basis, how much input does the owner have?"

"Sam Dundee comes to town at least once a year, occasionally more often if a particular case intrigues him. He's kept informed and if there's ever a conflict for Sawyer, Sam steps in. You'll like Sam. Everybody does. And you won't find a better bunch of professionals anywhere than at Dundee's."

"Tell me something, Kate Malone—are all the female agents as good-looking as you?"

"Humph." Kate couldn't help smiling. "That could be considered a chauvinist statement."

"It wasn't meant to be. Take it as it was meant—as a compliment."

"In that case, yes, all the female agents are attractive,

in their own way. Right now there are only two other female agents. The office manager is female and three of the four office staff are, too. Lucie Evans, my dear friend, is former FBI, as is Sawyer. Their feud goes back to the time they worked for the bureau and neither will talk about it. Lucie's gorgeous. Nearly six feet tall. I'd describe her as a modern-day, brown-eyed, redheaded amazon."

Moran let out a long, low whistle. "Maybe the problem between MacNamara and her is that she's too much woman for him to handle."

Kate laughed out loud. "Don't ever let Sawyer hear you say that."

"I'm looking forward to meeting Lucie."

"J.J. is our other female agent. She's one of the most beautiful women I've ever seen. Picture a young Elizabeth Taylor. Black hair, violet-blue eyes and a petite hourglass figure."

"And she's a Dundee agent?"

"When you meet her, don't let her looks fool you. She's a black belt in karate, is proficient in every weapon imaginable and she rides a Harley."

"I can't wait to meet Lucie and J.J. Are there any rules that say Dundee agents can't date each other?"

"Not that I know of. And it has happened…agents forming personal relationships, but mostly friendships and seldom romances."

"What about you, Kate, are you interested in romance?"

Taken aback by his question, Kate gaped at him, her eyes wide and round. "Are you…" She motioned back and forth between them with her hand. "You and me?"

"Sure. Why not? Unless you patch things up with your ex."

"That's not going to happen."

"Why not? You're still hung up on the guy, aren't you?"

"Maybe I am, but that doesn't mean we'll ever patch things up. Besides, why would you be interested in a romance with me, if you think I still care about Trent?"

"I said romance, not love and marriage." Moran's sly smile gave her the impression he was only halfway joking with her.

"In your language romance translates to sex, right?"

The waitress cleared her throat as she approached with a tray of food. She placed the dishes down in front of Kate and Moran, then asked, "Will there be anything else?"

Kate shook her head.

"No, thanks. We're fine," Moran replied.

"Under different circumstances, you and I might be perfect for each other," Kate told him once the waitress was out of earshot. "Perfect on a temporary basis that is. We're both in the same predicament, romantically speaking."

"How do you figure that?" Moran spread his paper napkin across one knee and picked up his fork.

"Anything we had between us would be friendship and maybe sex, but we're both in love with ghosts from the past, aren't we?"

Moran's hand grasping the fork stopped midair and for the longest moment he didn't move or speak, then finally he laid his fork down and looked at Kate. "I take that to mean you're still in love with your ex or at least with the memory of him. But don't jump to any conclusions where I'm concerned."

"I know you big, strong tough guys don't like to talk about feelings, but it's plain to me that you're pining away for a lost love. It's a matter of it takes-one-to-know-one. I've never loved anyone except Trent and seeing him again, being with him, has gotten me confused. I don't know if I'm in love with the man or with the memory."

"Don't you think you owe it to yourself to find out? You're here with me when you'd rather be with him. Stop running away. Sooner or later, you're going to have to face whatever it is that's happening between you two. And if one of the abduction ring girls turns out to be your daughter, you two won't be able to walk away from each other and never look back."

"You're a very smart man, Dante Moran. So why is it that you can give me such good advice and apparently aren't able to solve your own problems?"

"Look, Kate, I know you mean well and I appreciate your concern, but you don't know anything about me…or about my past."

"So tell me."

"It's not in my nature to open a vein and emotionally bleed all over the place."

"Just tell me one thing and I'll stop badgering you. I promise."

"What do you want to know?" he asked.

"Am I right—is there someone from your past that you can't forget, someone you're still in love with?"

"No more questions if I give you an answer?"

She nodded.

"Yes."

"Yes, what?"

"Yes, there's someone from my past."

Curiosity almost got the best of her, but Kate somehow managed not to pursue the matter. After all, she had promised him, hadn't she? Besides, digging into Moran's past could only temporarily divert her from her own situation with Trent. Moran had been right when he'd said that sooner or later she had to face whatever was happening between Trent and her.

Kate lifted her fork, stirred her salad to equally distribute the honey-mustard dressing, and speared a sizable chunk of mixed greens and sliced grilled chicken. Moran dug into his chicken and dressing, eating heartily. Neither said much while they ate, just a comment now and again on the food and how surprisingly good the coffee was considering the restaurant was an inexpensive diner.

As they finished off their meal and worked on their third cups of coffee, Kate glanced at her watch. Eight forty-five. She really should have called Trent. He was probably wondering about her, maybe even worrying about her. *He has your cell number,* she told herself. *He could call you.* But why should he? Hadn't she all but told him she wanted him out of her sight?

"You're awfully quiet," Moran said.

"Just thinking."

"About your ex?"

A denial was on the tip of her tongue, but why lie to Moran? She nodded. "Man to woman, what would you do if you were in my shoes?"

"My feet wouldn't fit in your shoes." Moran's lips curved into a smirking grin.

"Dammit, will you be serious."

His smile vanished. He reached across the table and clasped her hand, then focused on her face. "If I were in your shoes, I'd go to the guy, tell him how I felt and then drag him off to the nearest bed and make love all night."

Mouth agape, eyes wide, Kate stared at Moran, ut-

terly surprised by his reply. Of all the things she'd expected him to say, that hadn't been one of them. "If
that's how you feel, then why haven't you done just
that? Why haven't you—"

"I can't. She's dead."

Kate felt as if she'd been slapped. Hit hard with the
painful truth. "Oh, God, I'm sorry. I had no idea. I
mean…" *Shut up before you dig yourself in deeper,* an
inner voice warned.

Moran picked up the check, then scooted out of the
booth and said, "Are you ready?"

She nodded, then got up and followed him. She
didn't even protest when he paid for her dinner. They
walked in silence to his car.

After they got in the car , he asked, "Where to?"

"Drop me off at the Peabody."

"Going to take my advice?"

"Maybe."

Moran started the engine and backed out of the
parking space. And all the while Kate thought about
how she'd feel if Trent was dead. She'd be devastated.
Even though she hadn't seen him in ten years, in all
that time apart, she'd known he was alive and well and
possibly even happy. Had she, in her heart of hearts,
always believed that someday they might get a second
chance? Just as she never gave up hope that Mary
Kate was alive and eventually they'd be reunited, had
she secretly hoped that she and Trent would get back
together?

Trent paced the floor in his suite. It was nearly
nine-thirty. Where the hell was she? Why hadn't she
had the common courtesy to call him? After they'd
given their DNA samples, Kate had all but told him to

get out of her sight and leave her the hell alone. He could have protested, could have told her that he wasn't leaving her side, but what good would that have done? They'd have wound up in an argument and he didn't want that. Those last few months when their marriage had been dying, that's all they'd done—argue. Day and night. About everything. About anything. It had been easier to stay angry and fight and fume than to face the agonizing pain that had been eating them both alive.

When Kate had suffered a nervous breakdown right after Mary Kate's abduction, he'd done all he could to take care of her, to comfort her, but she'd rejected him time and time again. After a while it became too difficult to endure yet one more rejection. She'd turned away from him, neither wanting nor needing him. At least that was the way it had seemed to him. Instead of clinging to each other, sharing their sorrow, they'd each retreated into their own private hell. When Kate had asked him for a divorce, he'd agreed without a word of protest. His gut instincts had told him he would regret his decision not to fight for his marriage. At the time not only had he been numb with grief over Mary Kate's disappearance, but his damn masculine pride had gotten in the way. A man doesn't hold on to a woman who no longer wants him.

The only problem was that he'd still wanted his wife. He'd wanted her on the day their divorce became final. He'd wanted her a year later. And two years later.

What about ten years later? he asked himself.

The door opened and Kate walked in, her cheeks flushed from the nighttime chill. "It's freezing out there. It's already twenty-eight degrees and feels more like eighteen."

She shrugged out of her coat, then removed her knit gloves and hat and stuffed them into her coat pocket. "Ooh, it's toasty warm in here."

He wanted to rant at her, to demand to know where she'd been, what she'd been doing, and who she'd been with all this time. Moran? Had she been with the sleek, handsome FBI agent since this morning?

"Have you had dinner?" he asked. He'd grabbed a quick lunch in the *Capriccio* Restaurant there in the hotel. He hadn't eaten a bite since.

"Yes, thanks. Moran and I—"

"You had dinner with Moran?"

"At the River City Café." Kate moved slowly toward her bedroom. "It's not far from the FBI field office."

"You and Moran seem to be awfully friendly." *That's it, act like a jealous husband! Remember, you do not want to get into an argument with her.*

"He's a nice guy." Kate halted by her bedroom door. "He has bent some rules and regulations for me because—"

"Because he's got the hots for you." Trent stomped across the room toward her. "God, Kate, I thought you were smarter than you used to be about people, that you weren't as naive. Moran's being nice and helpful because he wants to get in your pants."

Kate slapped him. Her open palm hit squarely against his left cheek. He wasn't sure who was the most startled by her action—him or her. She stared at him in shock. He rubbed his stinging cheek.

"I—I'm sorry, Trent. I didn't mean to do that. It was a knee-jerk reaction."

He rubbed his cheek for a couple more seconds, then eased his hand to his side. "It's okay. I deserved it. That was jealousy you heard talking."

She tilted her head to one side and stared at him. "You're jealous?"

Trent grimaced. "Yeah. It's those old feelings we talked about. That leftover lust."

"Moran and I had dinner together. That's all."

"I don't have a right to be jealous and I know it, but—"

Kate dropped her coat to the floor and moved toward Trent, closing the three-foot gap between them. He held his breath as she came near. "What are we going to do about it? About those old feelings? About that leftover lust?"

Using every ounce of willpower he possessed he balled his hands into fists and managed to stop himself from grabbing her. "What do you think we should do?"

She lifted her arms up and around his neck, then pressed her body intimately against his. "I think we should diffuse the ticking time bomb."

His sex grew hard and heavy. He tightened and released his balled fists. Sweat popped out on his upper lip. "Having sex could turn out to be a big mistake."

"Yes, it could, but it might also relieve all this tension between us. Afterward, we could find out that the only thing left between us really was just some unresolved feelings from the past. We have to do something. We can't go on this way. I'm willing to risk making a big mistake, if you are."

His willpower vanished. With his body fast taking control, his rational thoughts became fewer and fewer. Trent reached down, cupped her buttocks and lifted her up and against his erection. When she whimpered, he lowered his head and claimed her mouth. She clung to him, her breasts crushed against his chest, her mound pressing into his pulsing sex.

"If you're having any second thoughts, you'd better tell me now." He swept her up into his arms and carried her through the lounge and into his bedroom. Without missing a beat, he laid her on the bed and came down over her, his mouth still devouring hers, his hands ripping at her clothes.

Seven

Kate couldn't remember the last time she'd felt this way—on fire, burning with an all-consuming desire. She'd known other men, had enjoyed the sex and the friendship they'd shared, but only with Trent had she experienced true passion. A passion of the senses, of the heart, of the very soul. Swept away by an unexplainable hunger, by a need so strong that it overpowered everything else, she surrendered herself to her primeval needs. Her body instantly recognized Trent's touch, his smell, his taste. And aroused beyond all reason, she responded instinctively. It had always been like this for them—no holding back, giving and taking with every breath, no rational thought, only an overwhelming desire for appeasement.

She could stop him. It wasn't too late. Not yet. She should call a halt, shouldn't she? This was madness. But heaven help them both, it was such sweet madness.

She had managed to unbutton his shirt while he'd yanked her sweater over her head. As they kissed, they tossed and tumbled on the bed. When she was breathless, Trent ended the kiss and lifted his head. Panting, her heart racing, she stared up into his brown eyes, shimmering with dark, uncontrollable desire. She reached out and touched his face. The light beard stubble scraped her fingertips like a fine sandpaper. Trent rose to his knees, drawing her up with him so that they faced each other. Gripping her shoulders, he let his gaze travel over her face, down her throat, and across her breasts. He reached behind her and unhooked her bra, then eased the straps down her arms and slipped the beige-satin garment off. His hot gaze and the cool air attacked her skin, tightening her nipples to pebble-hard points.

She rubbed her fingers over his chest, her nails raking his tiny male nipples and inching through the vee of curly dark hair. She loved the feel of him. The hardness of his muscular body and the softness of his chest hair. Touching him titillated her, bringing long-dormant emotions to the surface.

After cupping both of her breasts, he flicked his thumbs over her nipples. A tingling, clenching sensation shot through her, sensitizing her breasts and moistening her femininity. The achiness between her thighs grew more intense by the moment. Her body tightened and released. The process repeated itself, preparing her, moistening her.

Wanting, needing, hungry for all of him, Kate undid his belt and unbuttoned his slacks, then lowered the zipper. Her movements eager, yet patiently deliberate, she tugged on his trousers, bringing them down over his hips. He pulled away from her and stood so that he could shrug out of his pants. She scooted to the edge of the bed, reached out and jerked down his black briefs, but they caught on his impressive erection. Gently she eased the material over his sex and down his legs. He kicked the briefs aside, sending them to join his discarded slacks.

An unbearable yearning urged her into action. Still on her knees at the edge of the bed, she grasped his hips and pulled him closer. Her right hand circled him. Caressed. Pumped. Trent groaned. Kate smiled.

He reached down and eased her hand away, then dragged her off the bed and onto her feet to stand in front of him. With less finesse and more urgency than she had displayed in disrobing him, he removed her slacks and panties, leaving her completely naked. With labored breaths, sexual hunger raging inside them, they came together. Bare breasts to hairy chest. Flat belly to hard, pulsating sex. They kissed, tender need soon turning to heated passion. They touched each other, hands petting, clutching, exploring.

He rubbed her buttocks as if he was feeling and appreciating the finest silk. While she deposited damp, adoring kisses on his chest, he forked his fingers through her hair and grasped tightly. Yanking her head up so that she faced him, he stared at her for a millisecond. After releasing his tenacious hold on her head, he pushed her back onto the bed. Before she had a chance to catch her breath, he positioned her hips on the edge, then dropped to his knees, parted her thighs and placed her legs on either side of his hips.

"Trent?"

"Shh."

He kissed first one inner thigh and then the other, repeating the back and forth process from just above her knees to the apex of her legs. Trent was the only man who'd ever realized that her inner thighs were an extremely sexually sensitive area of her body. He added long, wet licks to the kisses, interchanging the two actions until Kate thought she'd climax on the spot. But when she came close to losing it, Trent changed tactics. He kissed her intimately. She shivered. When his tongue touched her throbbing nub, she cried out, pleasure rippling through every nerve in her body.

As he continued loving her with his mouth and tongue, he reached up over her stomach and tweaked her nipples, adding pressure to the pulsating tension drumming through her body. Minutes later, she came. Crying out, undulating her hips, she went wild. And Trent continued, not letting up until she was totally spent, until he'd drained every ounce of satisfaction from her release. As tiny aftershocks fluttered through her, Trent swung her around into the bed and joined her, coming down over her, straddling her hips.

She reached out for him, touching his sex. He shuddered. She longed to give him the kind of pleasure he'd given her. Without asking his permission, she shoved him over onto his back. He flopped over and without protest, let her take charge.

"You don't have to—"

"I want to," she told him.

She kissed his lips, his chin and his throat. Then she licked a moist line from shoulder to shoulder, across his chest and down his belly. With tender caresses and long, all-day-sucker licks, she put her desire into action. He threaded his fingers through her hair and urged her to take him into her mouth. She gave him exactly what he wanted. The taste of him excited her. Giving herself over completely to mindless, exhilarating wantonness, she brought him to an earth-shattering release.

Trent roared, the sound loud and animalistic. As ful-fillment wound itself around him, shaking him from the inside out, he pulled her up and over his damp, hot body, until their lips met once again. When they kissed deeply and their tongues mated, they tasted themselves as well as each other. He wrapped his arms around her and held her close. Neither of them spoke, just lay there for endless moments. Finally, Kate shivered.

"Are you cold?" he asked.

"A little chilly," she replied.

He slipped off the bed and pulled down the cover, al-lowing her to crawl beneath the sheet, blanket and spread before he slid in beside her. She snuggled close to him. He eased one arm under her neck so that her head rested on his shoulder.

"Trent?"

"Mmm, hmm?"

What should she say? Should she admit that she still cared about him? Or should she act as if their having sex was no big deal? While she was trying to form the right sentence, to put together the correct words, the telephone rang. Kate tensed. Trent grunted.

"Any chance that's Moran?" Trent asked as he reached toward the phone on the bedside table.

"Not unless there's been a major new development in the case."

Trent yanked the receiver from the hook. "Yeah?"

Kate felt an instant change in Trent. He eased his arm away, leaving her head resting on his pillow, and then he rose to a sitting position.

"No, I'm sorry. I forgot about calling. It's been a long day and—"

"Who is it?" Kate spoke quietly, more mouthing the question than uttering it out loud.

Trent shook his head.

"No, we don't know much more than we did. We gave DNA samples for testing that will compare our DNA to the three little girls. Look, would you hold on a minute? I want to change phones." Trent laid the phone down on the table, slipped out of bed, walked over to the closet and removed a robe.

Kate watched him as he put on the robe and walked into the lounge, not once looking back at her or speaking to her. Had Aunt Mary Belle called him? Probably. But why did he need privacy to talk to his aunt? What could he have to say to her that he couldn't say in front of Kate?

It's not Aunt Mary Belle, an inner voice told her. *It's Molly Stoddard, his almost fiancé.* And Trent's feeling guilty because he just made love with his ex-wife. She eyed the phone lying on the bedside table. The temptation to pick up the receiver and listen nearly got the best of her.

Don't do it, she warned herself. She reached out, lifted the receiver and set it down on the base. Temptation resisted. She breathed a sigh of relief.

Kate got out of bed, gathered up her clothes and marched through the lounge, not even acknowledging Trent's presence as she rushed to her bedroom. She slammed the door as loud as she could. There, let him think whatever he wants to about that.

Well, hell, what had she expected to happen? Even if Trent's lady love hadn't called tonight, where'd she think that sexual interlude she'd shared with him would lead? Trent has built a new life for himself back in Prospect. He has a career he loves and a woman he wants to build a future with, a woman his aunt knows is good enough for him. Kate didn't even know Molly Stoddard, but right this minute, she hated the woman.

* * *

"Yes, Kate and I are getting along all right," Trent said, realizing that was the understatement of the decade. They were getting along better than all right. Hell, they'd just shared some really great oral sex. And he didn't have a doubt in his mind that Kate had enjoyed it as much as he had.

"I know this must be terribly difficult for you, darling, but once you learn if one of those poor children is or is not Mary Kate, then you can move on," Molly said. "After all, before this happened, you'd been certain your daughter was dead. And if she isn't one of the little girls, then your assumption has probably been right all along. On the other hand, if she is one of the girls, then you and your ex-wife can hardly take her away from the only parents she's ever known."

"Yes, of course, you're right." He didn't want to discuss this with Molly. Not tonight. Maybe not ever. Although she was a parent—a good parent—she couldn't begin to understand how he felt. Only Kate understood. Only Kate felt the same anguish.

Trent eyed the closed door to Kate's bedroom. Only halfway listening to Molly, he thought about his ex-wife, about what had just happened between them. He could still see her, totally naked and toting her discarded clothes, tromping angrily through the lounge, ignoring him completely. And he could still hear the door slamming. She was mad as hell and wanted him to know it.

Damn! She had every right to be upset with him. Why had he acted like an idiot?

"Trent? Trent!"

"Huh?"

"Have you heard a word I've said?"

"Sorry, Molly, my mind wandered."

"Something's wrong. What is it? Tell me. If I can help you, I want to—"

"If you really want to help…" Damn, damn, damn! He was torn between Molly and the truth. He wanted to hold on to Molly, on to the plans he'd been making for a peaceful, contented future with her and her children. But how could he do that to her—keep her dangling on a string while he sorted out his feelings for Kate? And God knew those feelings were about as complicated and confusing as feelings could get.

He wanted Kate now as much as ever. The lust factor between them hadn't diminished one iota. But did he love Kate? Maybe. A part of him would always love her. The real question was did they have a future together, with or without Mary Kate?

"Molly, I owe you honesty," Trent said.

"I'm not sure I like the sound of that."

"Kate and I…that is, we—"

"The ghost of marriage past has risen its alluring head," Molly said. "Is that it?"

"In a way."

"It was bound to happen. Kate was the love of your life, just as Peter was the love of my life. I can't say that I'm not disappointed. I'd hoped we could build a good, solid life together. But in all honesty, if it were possible for Peter to walk back into my life this very minute, I'd run into his arms and never let him go."

"It's not quite the same for Kate and me. When Peter died, you two were still very much in love. Kate and I could barely look at each other by the time our divorce became final."

"Oh, Trent, don't you think I've always known, even without Miss Mary Belle telling me?"

"What are you talking about? What did my aunt tell you?"

"She told me that you'd be in love with Kate Malone to the day you die."

Why was it that Molly's statement hit him like a sledgehammer? Because he was afraid it might be true? "Aunt Mary Belle over-romanticized the situation."

"Look, Trent, I'm not going anywhere," Molly told him. "There isn't anyone else in my life. If you can't renew things with Kate or find out you don't want to, then I'll still be here in Prospect waiting for you. And if you two wind up getting back together, I'll understand. Who knows, I might even like Kate."

"You're a remarkable woman," Trent said.

"Not really. I'm just envious that you might get a second chance with the love of your life."

Trent didn't know how to respond to that, so he said nothing.

"Take care of yourself," Molly told him. "Call me when you get back to Prospect."

"I will. I promise."

Trent hung up, tightened the belt on his robe and marched to Kate's door. He knocked. No response. He knocked again, several times.

"Kate?"

"Go away."

"Kate, we need to talk."

"No, we don't."

"Yes, we do." Trent tried the knob and found the door locked. "Dammit, Kate, don't be this way."

"I do not want to see you or talk to you. Not tonight. Just leave me alone. If we have to talk, we can do it in the morning. I'm tired and I want to go to sleep."

"Look, I'm sorry. Is that what you want to hear? I

handled Molly's call all wrong. I should have told you she was the caller and I should have told her I'd call her back later. It's just that she caught me off guard and I felt odd talking to her while I was lying in bed with you."

"You felt guilty. Admit it. You'd just cheated on her and—"

"Dammit, Kate, don't put it that way. Molly isn't my wife. She's not even my fiancé."

Silence.

Trent lifted his fist to the door, but stopped himself just short of knocking again. He leaned his head against the door and groaned quietly. "Molly knows that you and I have issues we need to work through. She's very understanding. She's not jealous or anything like that."

The door swung open so quickly that Trent almost lost his balance. Hands on hips, Kate stood there and glared at him. "Did you tell her that we'd—"

"No, I did not tell her. But it wouldn't have mattered if I had. She's not the type to—"

"Be jealous? Throw a fit? Come to Memphis and rip my hair out by the roots?" Kate lifted one hand and pointed her index finger in Trent's face. "If she isn't jealous, then she doesn't love you. If I were *practically* your fiancé and you went away with your ex-wife for any reason whatsoever, I'd be jealous as hell. And if I even suspected that you'd made love with her, I'd want to scratch her eyes out."

"That's the difference between you and Molly," Trent admitted. "If you were *practically* my fiancé, you'd be madly in love with me. Molly isn't. Unless you've changed a great deal, loving with all your heart is the only way you know how to love. It was always all or nothing for you."

"Molly isn't in love with you and you want to marry her?" Kate stared at him quizzically as she eased her hands off her hips. "Forget I asked. It's none of my business." Kate turned around and started to close the door.

Trent stuck his foot over the threshold to prevent her from shutting the door. Kate glanced over her shoulder, her eyes questioning his intentions. "I'm going on forty. I want a normal, ordinary existence, a family, someone with whom I can share my life. I like and admire Molly. She feels the same about me."

"In other words, you're willing to settle." Kate pivoted around slowly.

Their gazes met and locked.

"Yes, I suppose I am."

"Well, good for you. When we find out what we need to know about Mary Kate, you can go right back to Prospect and marry Molly Stoddard and live the rest of your lives in peaceful, uneventful mediocrity. No disagreeing, no arguing, no ups and down, just smooth sailing on smooth waters. No waves." Kate indicated an even line with the movement of her hand gliding through the air. "But the downside of that is no passion, no to-die-for love and no blow-the-top-of-your-head-off sex that touches not just your body, but your heart, too. And even your soul."

Kate turned her back on him again and tried to close the door. He remained unmoving.

"To have that kind of love once in a lifetime is more than most of us can expect," Trent said. "And when you've had it and lost it, the best you can do is settle for less."

She stood there, her back to him. He wanted to grab her tense shoulders, drag her into his arms and carry her back to his bed for a repeat performance, but he managed—just barely—to keep his hands off her.

"I'll never settle for less. I still want it all. And if I can't have it all, I'll take nothing."

She tried again to close the door. This time Trent moved his foot and allowed her to accomplish her goal. He stood there staring at the door for quite some time, his mind reeling with a jumble of thoughts. About Kate. About Molly. About the future.

Eight

Dante Moran called at seven-thirty. Kate had been awake since six o'clock, but she hadn't ventured from her room. She'd called herself a coward, a fool and a hussy, not necessarily in that order. A coward for not wanting to face Trent this morning. A hussy and a fool for allowing herself to give in to temptation last night.

Maybe she should add judgmental bitch to that list. After all, what right did she have to judge Trent? If he wanted to settle for a marriage without passion, was that so wrong? For her—definitely yes. But maybe not for Trent. The old Trent, the man she'd fallen in love with and married would never have been satisfied with less than everything. The new Trent—she didn't really know him, did she?

"Kate are you there?" Moran asked.

"Sorry, just gathering wool."

"Did I wake you?"

"No, I've been up for quite a while. But it is early, so why are you calling?"

"To let you know that it doesn't look as if we'll be able to set up a meeting between the adoptive parents and the biological parents."

"What? Why not?"

"None of the adoptive parents are willing to attend a meeting."

"I see." A gut-tightening sense of disappointment hit Kate.

"You can't blame them. Not really," Moran said. "They're all scared to death, afraid they might lose their child. Right or wrong, they see the biological parents as enemies."

"I can understand why they'd feel that way. After all, they're as much victims in this horrific situation as we are. And if the shoe was on the other foot, I'd probably feel the way they do."

"I called you first," Moran told her. "We'll be letting the others know later today."

"Thanks."

"Not all my news is bad."

"How's that?" she asked.

"The adoptive parents did agree to send recent photographs of the girls via e-mail attachments. And one is even sending several photos of their child, dating from infancy."

Kate's heart skipped a beat as her hopes shot sky-high. "From infancy? If we saw a picture of our child as an infant, we'd recognize her immediately."

"I don't know why I told you about that. Dammit, Kate, she's not one of the two with type O-positive blood."

Her sky-high hopes nosedived. "But we will see photos of the other two girls, right?"

Would she know her own daughter from a photograph? Or would her eager heart see something that wasn't there—a resemblance to her or to Trent that would be only in her imagination?

"Absolutely. All of you will get copies. We're expecting those photos this morning. I'll phone you the minute we get all three sets."

"Hey, Moran, you know where all three girls live, don't you?"

"Yeah, we know." A slight hesitation. A deep breath. "But don't ask me to give you the addresses. I can't bend the rules that much."

"Could you tell me if they're close?" she asked. "Just tell me the states they're in."

"The two with type O-positive blood are within three hours of Memphis," he told her. "One's in Mississippi and the other in Alabama. And that's all I can tell you at this point. I'm sorry, Kate, I'd tell you everything I know, but—"

"It's okay. Really. I wouldn't want to get you fired before you have a chance to resign."

He chuckled. "I'll let you know the minute the pictures come in."

"I'll be right here waiting."

She'd no sooner hung up the phone than Trent knocked at her bedroom door. She knew it was Trent. Who else would it be? She had showered and dressed when she first got up, then made coffee and downed every drop the four-cup pot held.

Bracing herself to see Trent, she flung open the door. He stood there looking much too handsome, his dark hair neatly combed, his face freshly saved and wearing jeans and a cable-knit navy-blue sweater over a light blue button-down shirt.

"I ordered breakfast," he said, his voice neutral, neither warm nor cold. Not friendly. Not hostile. "It just arrived. I hope a ham and cheese omelette with whole wheat toast and coffee suits you."

"It suits me just fine. Thank you." It touched her heart that he'd remembered the only way she would eat eggs when she was pregnant with Mary Kate was in an omelette. And her favorite had been ham and cheese.

Before she entered the lounge, he turned away from her and walked over to the table. Whatever tension their lovemaking had diffused had now been replaced with even more friction—sexual tension, a touch of anger and a hint of awkwardness.

When she approached, he held her chair for her and assisted her in sitting. She looked up over her shoulder and offered him a smile. He nodded, but didn't return the smile. After he sat across from her and removed the covers from their plates, she took a deep breath, in an effort to bolster her courage, and looked right at him.

"About last night," she said.

"What about last night? Are you referring to our lovemaking or Molly's phone call or my stupidity or your overreacting to—"

"All of the above."

With his gaze glued to hers, he nodded.

"Look, Trent, I'm the one who should apologize. I shouldn't have said some of the things I did. You have every right to marry whomever you please for whatever reason."

"I'm not going to marry Molly."

Her heart fluttered like a captive butterfly. "You're not?"

"No, I'm not. I thought a great deal about what you said and I realized you were right. I'd tried so hard to forget what it was like between us when we first got married that I'd actually halfway convinced myself that I could live without passion in my marriage. But I can't. Making love with you last night proved that to me. You and I may no longer be in love, but God help us, the passion hasn't faded one bit, has it?"

Her breath caught in her throat and for a moment she couldn't speak. She desperately wanted to touch him, to feel his flesh beneath her fingertips. *But I do love you, Trent. I always have and always will. Why couldn't she tell him? If she admitted her true feelings, maybe he would, too. But what if he doesn't love you? What if passion really is all he feels?*

"The passion certainly was there last night," she said. "In spades."

He smiled then. A warm, genuine smile that showed in his eyes. "May I ask who called you a few minutes ago or is that none of my business?"

"It was Special Agent Moran." Kate poured coffee into her cup, then added a generous amount of cream. "None of the adoptive parents will meet with us, but they are e-mailing photographs of the girls."

Trent lifted his cup and sipped the coffee. "I suppose I can understand why they don't want to meet with us. If I were in their place, I'd be out of my mind with fear. I feel sorry for everyone involved—the adoptive parents as well as us birth parents. We're all in a no-win situation."

"If one of the girls is Mary Kate, we aren't going to take her away from the people who've raised her, are we?" Kate needed him to be strong for both of them because she wasn't sure if once she found out one of the girls was her daughter, she'd be able to do the right thing for Mary Kate. "We can't do that to her, no matter how difficult it is for us."

When Kate lifted her cup, she had to set it back down immediately because her hand trembled so badly. Damn! She swallowed the tears lodged in her throat.

Trent set his cup on the table. "No, we can't do that to her, no matter how much we'd like to take her with us, shower her with love and never let her go."

"I have to see her. I have to believe in my heart that leaving her with her adoptive family is the right thing to do."

"We both need that. Whatever happens, it's going to be difficult for us."

She looked down at her lap, avoiding direct eye contact with Trent as she spoke. "Moran has the addresses for all three girls. I hope to sneak a peek at them when we go to his office this morning. If I manage to get those addresses, will you go with me to see the girls? Like the other birth mothers, I keep thinking that if I saw her, I'd recognize her."

"Call me a fool, but yes, I'll go with you," Trent said. "We'll have to be very discreet. We can't let any one of the three girls or their parents see us and realize why we're there. We're in agreement on that, right? Even if you think you recognize Mary Kate, you won't—"

"There are only two girls we need to see. Only two have type O-positive blood." She lifted her gaze to meet Trent's. "Moran told me yesterday and I'm sorry I didn't share that information with you immediately."

Trent glanced away, a sad look in his eyes. "Even if you're sure one of the two girls is our daughter, you won't speak to her or alert her to our presence, will you?"

"I promise that no matter how much I want to grab her and hug her and kiss her, I won't do anything to make our presence known. We can watch her from a distance. But I have to see these girls. I can't wait. I've been waiting nearly twelve years. I feel as if I'm on the verge of shattering into a million pieces."

"I know how you feel. Believe me, I know."

"Let's not wait for Moran to call back," Kate said. "As soon as we finish breakfast, let's go on over to the field office. Okay?"

"Sure thing. But you have to eat first. You're too thin, Kate. You've skipped too many meals lately, haven't you? You've always been that way, unable to eat when you're upset and worried."

"You know me too well." She offered him a half-hearted smile, then lifted her cup to her lips.

Robin Elliott lived in Corinth, Mississippi, with her parents, Susan and Neal Elliott, and her younger brother, Scottie, who was also adopted. Christa Farrell lived in Sheffield, Alabama, with her paternal grand-mother, Brenda Farrell. She'd been adopted by Brenda's son, Rick, and his wife, Jean, who'd been killed in a plane crash when they'd flown to Barbados for their anniversary six years ago.

While Trent kept the Bentley humming at sixty-five miles an hour along Highway 72, which would take them all the way from Memphis to Corinth, Kate continuously looked at the copies of the two photographs Moran had issued to the four sets of biological parents. While Trent had kept Moran busy with questions, Kate had rifled through the paperwork on Moran's desk until she found the information on the adoptive parents and their daughters, including their addresses. She'd had easy access to the info, leading her to believe that Moran had known what she'd do and had purposely left that specific file folder on his desk for her to find.

Kate studied the first photograph, a school picture of Robin Elliott. The child was lovely, her features perfect. A pink satin clasp held the bangs of her short blond hair to one side. It was difficult to make out the exact color of her eyes, but they appeared to be a light brown, flecked with green. Hazel brown. Trent's aunt Mary Belle had hazel-brown eyes.

The information attached to the picture stated that Robin would celebrate her twelfth birthday in three weeks. She was in the sixth grade, an average student, who excelled at gymnastics and was a mini-midget football cheerleader. From all reports, she was happy, healthy and well-adjusted.

Kate flipped that photo over and stared at the picture of the second little girl with type-O blood. A pair of large brown eyes looked up at Kate. Eyes as dark as Trent's. She wore her long brown hair in dog ears, green bows attached to each in a shade that perfectly matched her sweater. Christa Farrell was a pretty child, but her features weren't perfect. Her lips were too full and her nose just a tad too big. And a smattering of freckles dotted her nose and cheekbones. Kate had been cursed with freckles as a child, but makeup and staying out of the sun kept her few remaining freckles under control.

Christa, who would celebrate her twelfth birthday in two weeks, was a straight-A student, a real little bookworm, but she wasn't social by nature and had very few friends. A quiet, introverted child, she preferred the company of her grandmother and other adults to children her own age. The girl was healthy and exceptionally bright, but had been emotionally fragile since her parents' deaths when she was only six.

Kate laid the pictures side by side in her lap. *Is one of you Mary Kate? If so, why don't I know you? Why can't I look at your face and instantly recognize you as mine?* She found herself drawn first to Robin and then to Christa, for different reasons. She saw herself and Trent in both girls. Christa had Mary Kate's brown eyes, but Robin had her blond hair.

"You're going to wear those photos out before we get to Corinth." Trent gave her a quick sidelong glance.

"I know, but I can't seem to stop looking at them." Kate sighed heavily. "One of these girls could very easily be our Mary Kate. Why don't I recognize my own child? Maybe neither of them is Mary Kate."

"You're driving yourself crazy and that's not doing either of us any good. The DNA test results will be back soon and we'll know for sure."

"I suppose we should have waited for those test results and not gone off on some wild-goose chase, but I swear I think I'd have lost my mind if we'd stayed in Memphis."

"Make that both of us," Trent told her. "Even if turns out that neither of these girls is Mary Kate, we're no worse off than we were before, except for getting our hopes up. I was getting antsy myself just waiting around."

"How long until we get to Corinth?"

"We're less than twenty miles away."

Kate sucked in a deep breath, then let it out in a long, relieved rush. "1212 Oak Hill Drive." She checked her wristwatch. "Robin should be coming home from school in about thirty minutes. Maybe we can catch a glimpse of her then."

"Remember, we aren't going to do anything to alert her or her family of our presence."

"I remember."

* * *

Trent did his best to stay calm, to remain in control, for Kate's sake as well as his own. They had parked the Bentley in the driveway of a house with a For Sale sign in the yard, only one house down and across the street from 1212 Oak Hill Drive. If anyone became suspicious of them, they could say they were shopping for a new home and stopped to check out the place at 1215. The frigid winter wind chilled him to the bone, making him glad he'd worn his heavy wool coat and leather gloves.

Feigning interest in the house and grounds, they tromped around in the yard and peeked in the windows, all the while keeping an eye out for any action at 1212 Oak Hill Drive.

Minutes ticked by. The longer they stayed outside, the more wicked the wind and colder the temperature seemed.

"Why don't we get back in the car for a few minutes and warm ourselves," Trent suggested. "I don't known about you, but I'm freezing."

Hugging herself in an effort to get warm, Kate nodded. "Let's go. I think my feet and hands are frostbitten, and I know my nose is."

Just as they reached the Bentley, Trent noticed a late-model Buick pull into the driveway at 1212. "Look, Kate."

She halted at his side and looked across the street. Gasping, she grabbed his hand. His heartbeat drummed loudly inside his head. Was it possible that he was on the verge of seeing his daughter?

A tall, blond woman emerged from the Buick, quickly followed by two children. A boy who looked to be about eight hopped out of the back seat, a book bag hanging loosely off one shoulder. The passenger side door opened and a thin, willowy young girl in jeans and a brown leather jacket emerged.

Kate squeezed his hand. They moved in unison to the end of the driveway and onto the sidewalk. Trying as best they could to act nonchalantly, they stared at Robin Elliott. She was a beguilingly beautiful child. When she laughed at something her brother said to her as they ran toward the front door, Trent's heart skipped a beat. Her smile reminded him of Kate's smile. And with her blond hair and willowy build, she looked a bit like the pictures of Kate when she was a kid. Was it possible that Robin was really Mary Kate?

"She looks so happy," Kate said.

"She is happy. That's obvious."

"Do you think…could you tell if she's anything like Mary Kate was as an infant?"

"She's got blond hair, although it's a honey blond now. And her smile reminds me of yours. But maybe I'm grasping at straws, wanting her to be ours."

"I don't know if she's Mary Kate," Kate admitted. "I want her to be, but I don't feel it." She laid her left hand over her heart. "I don't sense it, in here."

They continued staring at Robin until she disappeared inside her house. Then they stood on the sidewalk for quite some time, unable to speak or move. Oddly enough it was Kate who finally put an end to their senseless vigil.

"Let's go," Kate said. "It's highly unlikely she'll come back outside in weather like this."

"You're right. There's no sense waiting around for another glimpse, is there?"

They hurried to the Bentley. Once inside, Trent started the engine to warm the interior, then turned to Kate. "We can be in Sheffield in a little over an hour. It's only about fifty or sixty miles from here."

Kate checked her watch. "Christa Farrell goes to the

public library every day after school. Her grandmother works there. We should be able to make it to Sheffield before the library closes."

Trent reached over and ran the back of his gloved hand down Kate's pink cheek. "Are you all right?"

"Yeah, I'm okay."

"Have you thought ahead?" he asked. "Have you thought about what you'll do if neither Robin nor Christa turns out to be Mary Kate?"

"I'll handle it if it happens." Her gaze met his. "You have to know that I'll never give up looking for our child."

He sat there quietly for a few minutes. *Tell her how you feel,* an inner voice advised. *Let her know she isn't alone in her quest.* "If it turns out that way—that neither girl is Mary Kate—I want to help you to continue searching. I want us to keep looking for our daughter together."

Kate clenched her teeth and turned her head. He sensed that she was struggling with her emotions, making a valiant effort not to cry. Damn! He knew exactly how she felt.

Kate's nerves were raw by the time they pulled into the parking place in front of the Sheffield library in the middle of the downtown area. A small town, with many buildings empty, Sheffield looked forlorn, but there was evidence of revitalization here and there. All the way up Highway 72 as they bypassed Iuka, zoomed through Cherokee and hit every red light in Tuscumbia, Kate kept studying Robin Elliott's photo. Images of the laughing child flashed through Kate's mind. If Robin was Mary Kate, then why didn't she feel it in her mother's heart? *Maybe she's not yours,* an inner voice said. *Maybe Christa Farrell is Mary Kate. But what if you see her and don't recognize her as yours?*

"So, do we wait here for the library to close or do we go in?" Trent asked.

Go inside? Oh, God, could she do that? Could she be that close to Christa and remain at a distance? Wouldn't she be tempted to speak to the child, to study her like a bug under a microscope?

"Let's go inside," Kate said.

"Are you sure?"

Kate nodded.

"We can't stare and we can't talk to her. Understood?"

"Yes, I understand."

They exited the Bentley and went inside the library, which was small enough that they could scan the entire interior in one sweeping glance. Kate opened her purse and slid the photos inside, then searched again for any sign of Christa. In her second scan, she saw the little girl sitting alone at a table, a book satchel in the chair beside her, an open notebook in front of her and a pencil in her hand.

"There she is," Kate whispered.

Trent followed her line of vision.

"I wish she'd look up so we could see her face better."

"We've got to stop staring at her," Trent said. "Let's pick out a few magazines and take them over to the table next to her."

Kate followed Trent and after they'd chosen several magazines, they headed for the table nearest Christa. When they sat down across from each other, the child lifted her head and looked right at Kate. Christa smiled, but didn't speak. Kate returned the smile. Her stomach muscles tightened when she noted what a deep, chocolate brown the little girl's eyes were. The same color as Trent's.

That doesn't mean she's Mary Kate.

What was probably Christa's homework once again gained her full attention, so Kate and Trent were able to occasionally glance at the child while they pretended interest in the magazines they'd laid out on the table. The more she studied the little girl, the more similarities Kate recognized. She had eyes like Trent. Same color, same intense expression when she worked. And her mouth was generously full—like Trent's. The shape of her face—like a valentine—and the light dusting of freckles were traits inherited from Kate. She had Kate's mother's nose—a tad too big for her little face, but she'd grow into it as her grandmother had.

Damn, Kate, don't do this to yourself. She was looking for things that would make this girl hers. What about her hair? It wasn't blond like Kate's or dark brown like Trent's. No, but it was a light brown, which could well be the blending of their two hair colors. And Christa was slightly plump. She and Trent had both been skinny as kids, as Robin Elliott was. But Kate knew for a fact that Mary Belle Winston had been a plump child.

There you go again, trying to convince yourself that this child is your daughter, Kate told herself. Was she seeing similarities that weren't there? Or was this little girl really Mary Kate? Something deep inside Kate was drawn to this child, but did that mean the girl belonged to her?

"You're staring," Trent whispered as he reached across the table and clasped Kate's trembling hands.

She forced herself to look away from Christa. "Do you see it? Or am I imagining all the similarities?" Kate kept her voice low and soft.

"My eyes and mouth. Your shape face and freckles."

Realizing Trent had recognized the resemblance, too, Kate couldn't stop herself from glancing toward Christa again. Just in time to see the child chewing on her pencil. Kate's heart stopped. Her mother had scolded her throughout her childhood and teens for chewing on her pencil. Sometimes she still caught herself doing it.

Kate swallowed the lump in her throat. Tears gathered in the corners of her eyes.

"We'd better get out of here," Trent said.

Kate nodded. They gathered up their magazines. Nervously clumsy, she accidentally dropped one on the floor. Before she could get it, Christa jumped out of her seat, bent over, picked up the magazine and handed it to Kate. Their gazes met. Kate looked at the child through the tears misting her eyes. Christa smiled again and it was all Kate could do to stop herself from grabbing the little girl and hugging her for dear life.

"Thank you." Kate accepted the magazine.

Trent slipped his arm around Kate's waist to give her much-needed support. She felt as if her knees were going to give way at any minute.

"You're welcome," Christa said.

Before she embarrassed herself by reaching out and touching the child's angelic little face, Trent urged her into motion and all but forced her to walk away. He took her magazines from her once they were near the magazine rack. Within minutes he escorted her out of the library and straight to the car. He opened the passenger door. Kate turned to him, tears trickling down her cheeks.

Trent grabbed her and pulled her into his arms. She clung to him, weeping quietly. He stroked her back. "Don't do this, honey. You'll make yourself sick."

"I know it's crazy, but I think—I feel—that she's Mary Kate."

"Yeah, I know. I know."

"Did you—" Kate gulped down tears. "Did you feel it, too?"

Trent kissed her. Sweet and comforting. Slightly edged with passion.

"Yeah, I felt it, too. But it could be nothing more than wishful thinking on our parts."

"Maybe, but my heart tells me that that little girl in there—" Kate inclined her head toward the library "—is our Mary Kate."

Nine

The next three days were sheer agony for Kate. And she knew they were for Trent, too, although they didn't talk about it much. The waiting was unbearable. Both of them were on edge, their nerves frayed. They alternated between clinging to each other and arguing over nothing. Kate often left the hotel alone during the day and walked for an hour or two, despite the frigid temperatures. All the pent-up energy inside her kept her on the verge of either crying or screaming. And she knew that if she didn't get away from Trent when the tension reached a fever pitch, she'd wind up dragging him off to bed. The sexual tension between them was palpable, pulsating just below the surface twenty-four/seven. Having sex might give them momentary release, but what would the long-term effects be? She couldn't have a temporary sexual relationship with Trent. Leaving him ten years ago had nearly killed her. She would not put herself through that agony a second time.

This morning Trent had been the one to leave their suite, telling her she could reach him by cell phone if she needed him. If she needed him? Heaven help her, she needed him now. Needed him every minute of every day. And that was bad news for her. She'd already allowed herself to become too accustomed to leaning on Trent, depending on him.

This morning had dragged by, as had the previous days, even though she'd done numerous things to keep busy. She'd put a deep-conditioner on her hair, a thirty-minute treatment. She'd tried to watch a TV talk show, had flipped through several magazines and read a couple of chapters in a paperback novel she'd picked up a couple of days ago at a downtown bookstore. She'd even painted her fingernails and toenails. And she'd drunk four cups of Earl Grey!

What now? It was barely noon and she'd already run out of things to do. As she paced around in the lounge, doing her best not to think about the DNA tests or her gut-level reaction to Christa Farrell at the Sheffield library, Kate mulled over her options. She could take another walk, but the truth of the matter was, she didn't know where Trent had gone and didn't want to run into him. The way she felt right now, she might pull him into the nearest dark alley and have her way with him.

Kate laughed. God, she was losing it.

She needed someone to talk to, someone other than Trent. Lucie! That's it, she thought, who better to commiserate with than her best buddy? Kate dialed Lucie's cell phone. She answered on the third ring.

"Evans here."

"Lucie, it's me. Are you busy? In the middle of something?"

"Hey, girl, what's up? Any news?"

"Nothing yet. I'm losing my mind waiting. And on the verge of attacking my ex-husband."

"Attack as in killing him or jumping his bones?"

"The latter."

"Mmm, hmm. So, why don't you?"

Kate wondered how she should reply.

"Oh, don't tell me," Lucie said. "You've already done that, haven't you?"

"Yes," Kate admitted. "And I can't let it happen again."

"Why not? You're both consenting adults."

"Becoming lovers would complicate things too much and the situation is already complicated enough as it is."

"Why don't you just admit that you're still nuts about the guy? Even if he has a fiancé, I'll bet if he knew how you felt—"

"He's not going to marry her. He's not going to propose."

"Hooray and hallelujah. Grab that man while you can."

"Can't risk it. I may be in love, but I'm not so sure about him. It could be just lust for him. And I'm too emotionally fragile right now to lose both Trent and Mary Kate for a second time."

"Ah, hon, what a situation to be in."

"Lucie?"

"Mmm, hmm?"

"I stole the addresses for the two girls with type O-positive blood and Trent and I went to see them." When Lucie let out a long, exaggerated ooh, Kate quickly added, "We saw them, but they didn't know who we were or that we were looking them over. We were very careful. Very discreet."

"And?"

"And we both got similar vibes from the same child. Her name is Christa. I swear, Lucie, I just know she's Mary Kate."

"That had to have been rough on you. On both of you. You must have wanted to grab her and squeeze the life out of her."

"You have no idea. Dammit, what am I going to do if the DNA test proves me right? How can I not claim her?"

"Did you see her with her adoptive parents? I mean, did you get a glimpse of how their relationship is?"

"Christa's adoptive parents died nearly six years ago," Kate said. "She lives with her grandmother."

"Won't that simplify matters? Doesn't that make it easier for you and Trent to get custody of her?"

"It might, but how do we in good conscience take that child away from the only person who has remained a constant in her young life?"

Lucie groaned. "Yeah, I see the problem."

Kate heard another phone ringing and quickly realized that it was her cell phone, which she'd left in the bedroom. "Lucie, my cell phone is ringing. Hold on, will you?"

"Sure."

Kate laid the phone down on the desk, ran into the bedroom and grabbed her cell phone up off the bedside table. She flipped it open.

"Kate Malone."

"Kate, it's Dante Moran."

Kate gasped, her breath caught in her throat.

"The DNA test results just arrived."

"And?"

"Christa Farrell is your and Trent's child."

"Oh, my God!" Tears clouded Kate's vision. Her heart swelled with happiness.

"Would you like for me to try to set up a meeting for you and Trent to meet with Christa's grandmother, Brenda Farrell?"

"Yes, yes. Please. Tell her we'll do whatever she wants, handle it anyway she wants to, just as long as she'll meet with us and give us a chance to—" Kate's voice cracked.

"Go tell Trent the good news," Moran said. "I'll get back in touch with you when I work something out with Mrs. Farrell."

"Thank you. Thank you so much."

"Kate?"

"Huh?"

"Don't expect too much."

"Yeah, I know. I'll try not to, but...oh, mercy. Mary Kate is alive. And I—I saw her. She's—damn, Moran, I shouldn't have admitted that to you."

Moran chuckled. "It's okay. Don't you think I knew you'd find those addresses?"

"Yeah, I halfway figured out that you'd left them where I could find them."

"I've got to run, but I'll talk to you again very soon."

"Bye."

Kate closed her cell phone, then flew into the lounge and picked up the telephone receiver from the desk. "Lucie! That was Moran. I was right. The DNA test proved that Christa Farrell is Mary Kate."

"Wow! That's great, hon."

"Moran will try to set up a meeting with Christa's grandmother. Keep your fingers crossed for us."

"So how's Trent taking the news?'

"Oh, Lord, he doesn't know. He's not here. I've got to hang up now, Lucie, and call him."

"Keep me posted. And good luck."

"Thanks. Bye."

Hurriedly Kate dialed Trent's cell phone number. He answered on the fifth ring.

"Trent, come back to the hotel immediately," Kate told him.

"What's wrong?"

"Nothing's wrong. Moran just called. The DNA test results are back."

"And?"

"And Christa Farrell is Mary Kate."

Brenda Farrell's home, situated in an area of Sheffield known as the Village, was a neat cream stucco with rust-red shutters and a red-tile roof. Large old trees graced the lawn and neat shrubbery lined the brick walkway leading from the street to the fancy wood and glass front door.

Trent pulled the Bentley into the driveway at the side of the house, then got out and hurried to open the passenger door. Kate couldn't remember ever being so nervous. She'd had to ask Trent to stop twice on the drive from Memphis because she'd been sick to her stomach. Ever since yesterday when Dante Moran had phoned her with the good news, that Mrs. Farrell had reluctantly agreed to meet with them, Kate had been a bundle of nerves.

"Are you okay?" Trent asked, a worried frown wrinkling his forehead.

Kate nodded nervously and offered him a frail smile. "I want this meeting to go well. I'm so thankful Dante was able to persuade Mrs. Farrell to see us. I want her to like us." She grasped Trent's hand. "Oh, Trent, I don't know if I can bear it if anything goes wrong."

"Nothing is going to go wrong." He squeezed her hand. "But we can't expect too much too soon. Mrs. Farrell agreeing to allow us to meet Christa today is more than I expected."

"You're right. I never dreamed she'd be so generous."

Trent put his arm around Kate's shoulders and hugged her. "Come on. Take a deep breath. We're going to meet our daughter."

Kate took that deep breath as she and Trent headed toward the front entrance. Before they had a chance to ring the bell, the door opened. A petite, plump woman with short salt-and-pepper hair and striking blue eyes inspected them from head to toe, then smiled uneasily.

"You must be Kate and Trent," she said in a soft Southern drawl. "Please, won't y'all come in. I'm Christa's nana, Brenda Farrell." She stepped aside and swept her hand through the air in a gracious, inviting gesture.

Trent nudged Kate into action. They went inside, into a sunroom-type foyer filled with a variety of green plants.

"Thank you for seeing us so soon, Mrs. Farrell," Trent said.

"Yes, we appreciate this so much," Kate added.

"Come on into the living room. I've put on coffee and I can fix hot tea, if you'd like."

They followed her into the neat, country-style living room, filled with large comfy-looking chairs, an over-stuffed sofa and an oak armoire used as an entertainment center.

"Please, don't go to any trouble," Kate said.

"Take off your coats and sit down." Brenda motioned with her hand. "Christa isn't here. She's next door with our neighbors, the Kimbroughs."

Kate and Trent removed their coats, laid them across the arm of a nearby chair, and then sat side by side on the sofa. Brenda remained standing.

"We understood from Special Agent Moran that we might get to meet Christa today," Trent said.

"I thought it best for the three of us to talk first, then if…" Brenda cleared her throat. "You must realize that I've been devastated by this whole thing. Learning that Christa was stolen from her birth parents, that she wasn't willingly given up for adoption. I'm simply brokenhearted. For both of you and for me. But mostly for Christa. That sweet child hasn't fully recovered from losing her parents—my son Rick and his wife Jean. I can't bear the thought of her suffering more than she already has."

"Please believe us, Mrs. Farrell, the last thing we want to do is hurt Christa in any way." Kate's voice quavered every so slightly. "She's our daughter, our little Mary Kate. We want only what's best for her."

Trent grabbed Kate's hand and held it tightly. "Mrs. Farrell, we're not here to demand our parental rights. And we're not here to take Christa away from you. First and foremost, we want our child—your granddaughter—to be happy and well and safe."

Tears glimmered in Brenda Farrell's azure blue eyes. "Call me Brenda."

"Brenda, we're so grateful to your son and his wife and to you for taking such good care of Mary—of Christa," Kate said. "All these years, we didn't know where our daughter was or what had happened to her. We're so thankful she's all right."

"Christa is a dear child and I love her more than anything on earth. She's all I have. My son was an only child and—" Brenda sucked in her breath and released it through clenched teeth. "When Rick and Jean died, I brought Christa to live with me. She had terrible night-mares every night for months on end. I saw to it that she got professional help and eventually the nightmares went away. For the most part. Occasionally, when she's under stress, she still has a terrible dream. But basically she's mentally healthy."

"I'm sure we owe you so much," Kate said.

Brenda glanced away. "Let me get that coffee now. How do y'all take it?"

"Black," Trent replied.

"May I help you?" Kate asked.

"No, please, I need a few minutes alone. I'll prepare the coffee and afterward, I'll call next door and asked Edna to send Christa home."

Trent and Kate exchanged hopeful glances, but nei-ther spoke. Brenda walked out of the living room and into the dining room. She paused at the swinging door leading into the kitchen. With her back still to them, she said, "I've told Christa about y'all. She knows she's going to meet her biological parents today."

Kate came halfway up off the sofa before Trent grabbed her and dragged her back down. When she glared at him, he shook his head. Brenda Farrell disap-peared into the kitchen.

"She told Christa about us." Kate planted her hands on Trent's chest. "What if she didn't explain every-thing? What if Christa thinks we gave her away? No, dammit, no, Trent, I won't have my child believing I willingly gave her up."

Trent laid his hands over hers and pulled them down from his chest. "Stay calm, honey. We don't know what Mrs. Farrell…Brenda…told Christa. But I'm sure what-ever she told her, she didn't say anything negative about us. Stop and think, will you? Brenda seems to be a very intelligent lady. She wouldn't do something that might antagonize us anymore than we'd do something to antagonize her. We're all in the same boat here. She wants to protect Christa and so do we. We all love her."

Realizing she was on the edge, tilting precariously close to diving headfirst into calamity, Kate willed herself under control. She reminded herself that Trent was right. Christa's grandmother was hardly likely to do anything that would harm the child.

The child? God, Kate, the child is Mary Kate. Your little Mary Kate.

Fidgety and partially nauseated because she'd been unable to eat a bite since breakfast, Kate rose from the sofa and moved around the living room. Pictures on the mantel caught her eye immediately. She moved closer to get a better look. Her mouth opened on a silent gasp when she realized the line of frames adorning the mantel were filled with photographs of Christa at various ages. Several showed her with a couple Kate assumed were Rick and Jean Farrell. One picture in particular drew Kate's attention. A baby picture of Christa. And from the decorative background and the red velvet dress she wore, Kate figured it was Christa's first Christmas. Big brown eyes sparkled. A small red velvet bow nested in her golden blond curls. This was the child Kate remembered, the child she'd carried in her heart for nearly twelve years.

Trent came up behind her and wrapped his arms around her, then nuzzled the side of her face. "It's going to be all right," he whispered. "Somehow, someway, we'll make it all right. We'll see it through together this time."

Kate clutched Trent's arms that held her and snuggled backward into his embrace. "Do you think there's a solution that will work for everyone involved? Is it possible that Brenda Farrell would be willing to—"

"Coffee." Brenda returned to the living room, a small serving tray in her hands.

Kate and Trent accepted the cups of coffee and returned to the sofa. Brenda placed the tray on the dining room table, then lifted her cup and came back into the living room. She sat across from them in a large, floral wing chair.

"I know that as Christa's biological parents, you two have certain legal rights," Brenda said, gripping her cup in a shaky hand. "But I'm counting on y'all being good people who won't take Christa away from me. It would destroy her if she lost me. We're very close."

"We have no intention of taking Christa away from you," Trent assured her. "If her adoptive parents were still alive, we'd ask only to see Christa and over the years maintain contact so that when she became an adult she could chose whether she wanted to get to know us. But since your son and his wife died six years ago, leaving Christa without parents, I'd like for us to find a way where we can share Christa."

"Share her?" Brenda set her cup on a coaster atop the coffee table. "I don't understand. Are you suggesting an arrangement where she lives with you two part of the time and me part of the time? I was told you two are divorced. Is that right?"

"What I'm suggesting is that you and Christa come to Prospect for a visit," Trent said. "I have a large home with more than enough room for all of us. And yes, Kate and I are divorced, but at least for the initial visit, I'm sure Kate would be perfectly willing to stay in Prospect and live at Winston Hall with us."

Kate sipped on the coffee, hoping it wouldn't hit her stomach like a lead weight. Why hadn't Trent mentioned his great idea to her—his plans to bring Christa and her grandmother to Prospect?

"How long a visit are we talking about?" Brenda inquired.

"That would be up to you. I suggest at least a week the first time."

"I see. Well, I suppose it's something I can consider."

"You don't need to decide tonight," Trent told her. "Take a few days. Talk it over with Christa. You have the opportunity to give her a mother and a father, as well as a great aunt. And you and she wouldn't lose each other. If things worked out, you might consider moving to Prospect."

Wait just a damn minute, Kate wanted to shout. *What about me? I live in Atlanta. Am I suppose to visit Prospect when I want to see my child?*

"I'll think seriously about a visit…soon." Brenda rose from the chair. "I'll go get Christa. Please, remember that y'all are strangers to her. Don't expect her to be happy to see you."

"We understand." Trent looked at Kate. "Don't we, honey?"

Kate nodded.

The minute Brenda left, Kate turned on Trent. "When did you come up with your brilliant idea for Brenda and Christa to visit Winston Hall?"

"You're angry. Why?"

"Why? Because you took charge, made decisions about our child's future without so much as mentioning anything to me. You could have—no!—you should have discussed this with me before you—"

"Hell, Kate, the idea just hit me while we were sitting here. I thought you'd be thrilled if I could get Brenda to agree to bring Christa to Prospect for a week. It would give us a chance to get to know her and for her to get to know her family."

"And what family would that be? You and Aunt Mary Belle and a legion of Winston cousins?"

Trent shot to his feet and stomped around the room, grumbling under his breath. After several minutes of letting off steam, he stopped and looked right at Kate. "Get this through your head right now, so there won't be any misunderstandings later—you and I were Mary Kate's parents so that means you and I are Christa's parents. She's ours. Not mine. Not yours. Ours."

Her nerves raw, her emotions barely kept in check, Kate shivered. "Ours," she said hoarsely.

"If Brenda agrees, she'll bring Christa to Winston Hall for a visit with you and me. And yes, with Aunt Mary Belle, too. We'll spend time together, getting acquainted. Later on, we might try a two-week or even monthlong visit. Or it could be that things will work out so well the first visit that we can make it a permanent arrangement."

"What about me? About my job? My life in Atlanta?"

Trent's expression hardened. "I had thought you'd…" He cleared his throat. "If you don't want to come home to Prospect on a permanent basis, then I could bring Mary Kate—I mean Christa—to Atlanta. Or if you prefer, Brenda could bring her to see you."

The kitchen door opened. Brenda walked in, Christa beside her, clutching Brenda's hand. Kate felt as if her heart stopped, as if the whole world had stopped, as she and Trent turned to meet their daughter.

"Christa, this is Kate and Trent. They're the people I told you about. Your birth parents."

Zeroing in on Kate first and then Trent, the child studied them closely. "You're the man and woman I saw at the library the other day."

"What?" Brenda gasped.

"We came to Sheffield to take a look at Christa," Trent said. "We couldn't wait to see her and we also went by Corinth to see another little girl who might have been our Mary Kate."

"I was the one who couldn't wait," Kate admitted. "I was so anxious to find out if…I wanted Christa to be my daughter."

"I'm not your daughter," Christa said. "Rick and Jean Farrell were my parents. I belong to Nana now. She and I have each other and we don't need anyone else, do we, Nana?" Christa looked pleadingly at her grandmother.

"We'll always have each other." Brenda put her arm around Christa and hugged her close. "Kate and Trent aren't here to take you away from me. I told you they're just here to meet you." When Christa buried her face against her grandmother's chest, Brenda stroked her back lovingly.

"Where are your manners, Christa?" Brenda eased her granddaughter away from her and turned her to face their company. "Say hello to Kate and Trent, then go sit down and we'll have a nice visit."

Tears swimming in her chocolate brown eyes—eyes identical to her father's—Christa glared at her parents. Kate felt as if her heart would break in two. Here was her baby girl, her precious Mary Kate, and the child wanted nothing to do with her.

"Hello," Christa said, her voice a mere whisper.

"Hello," Trent replied.

Christa glanced at Kate, who managed a wavering smile.

"Hello, Christa. I'm so very glad to meet you."

"Why don't you tell Kate and Trent about school," Brenda said. "Tell them what grade you're in and who your teacher is and—"

"No! I won't tell them anything." Christa burst into tears. "Go away. Both of you. I don't know you. You aren't my parents. I'll never leave my nana. Not ever!" Christa ran out of the room.

"Oh, dear." Brenda clasped her hand over her mouth.

"Shouldn't you go after her?" Kate asked, wanting nothing more than to rush after Christa and wrap the child in her arms.

Brenda sighed. "No. When she throws one of her temper tantrums, I've found it best to leave her alone for a while until she calms down."

"That's exactly the way Aunt Mary Belle handled me when I acted like that," Trent said.

Brenda faced them. "I'm so sorry. I thought I had prepared her for this meeting. Apparently I didn't do such a good job."

"It's not your fault," Kate told her. "It's not anyone's fault."

"I think we'd better go." Trent placed his hand beneath Kate's elbow. "We'll stay in town overnight, so if you think it's all right, Kate and I will come back tomorrow."

"I have your cell phone number." Brenda came over and put her hand on Kate's shoulder. "I can only imagine what you must be feeling right now. I am so sorry, my dear."

"Maybe she'll be willing to see us tomorrow." Kate clenched her teeth to keep herself from crying.

She turned and all but ran through the sunroom and out the front door. She was almost to the Bentley when Trent caught up with her. He whirled her around and pulled her into his arms. She melted against him. And cried.

Ten

Trent had gotten them a suite at the Holiday Inn, which was the best Sheffield, Alabama, had to offer. She doubted the employees had ever catered to a guest who drove a Bentley. And from the fact that the manager himself escorted them to their suite, Kate figured the entire staff was duly impressed with Trenton Bayard Winston IV. Odd how most people admired and respected money in a way they did little else.

While the manager kowtowed to Trent, Kate went into the bathroom to escape. She had cried almost the whole way from the Village to the hotel and she now had a killer headache. She turned on the sink faucets, cupped her hands to catch the water and splashed her face, then grabbed a hand towel from the nearby stack and patted her skin dry. Sighing, she flipped the commode lid closed and slumped down on the seat. She felt like a balloon with all the air let out, deflated by a slow, painful leak that had left her flat and lifeless.

Mary Kate wanted nothing to do with them.

No, not Mary Kate—Christa.

She had to get the fact straight in her mind that although Mary Kate was Christa, Christa was not Mary Kate. The baby she and Trent had brought into this world, nurtured and loved for over two months, no longer existed. That child had ceased to exist the day she'd been stolen from Kate. Christa Farrell had no memories of her previous life, no emotional connection to Trent and Kate. They were, as Brenda had pointed out to them, strangers to their own child.

What were they going to do? What if Christa never came around? What if she never wanted them to be a part of her life? *Oh, God, how will I be able to bear it?* Kate's heart wept. Bowing her head, she covered her face with her hands and moaned, the grief welling up inside her, ripping her apart in its wake.

The bathroom door opened. She glanced up to see Trent enter. He came to her, knelt in front of her and clasped her hands, completely covering them with his. She looked at him and saw her own pain reflected in his eyes.

"Oh, Trent…"

"Let it go, honey. Rant and rave and cry some more, if that's what you need to do."

She shook her head. "What good will that do? Besides, I'm not the ranting and raving type. And I've already cried an ocean of tears."

"Yeah, I'm the one with the temper. Believe me, I really need about an hour working out at the gym, preferably with a punching bag."

Kate reached out and caressed his face. "What are we going to do?"

"We're going to wait until tomorrow and hope that Christa will be willing to see us then." Trent took Kate's hands and urged her to stand, which she did. "But for tonight, we're going to try to put today's events behind us. I've arranged for room service, so our dinner should be here within the hour. In the meantime, I'll draw you a warm bath and you can soak in the tub while I make a few phone calls."

"Who are you going to call?"

"Aunt Mary Belle, Dante Moran and my lawyer. I've got the name of a top man in the field of child custody cases. I want to put him on a retainer."

Kate nodded. She didn't know for sure why he would call Moran, but she didn't really care. Not at this precise moment. And as for hiring a lawyer, she'd leave that up to Trent. At least for now. "A warm bath sounds good. I'll get my pajamas and robe—"

"You aren't going to do anything except relax and allow me to take care of you." He went over and turned on the faucets, then unwrapped the guest soap and laid it atop a washcloth on the edge of the tub. After that he set the small bottles of shampoo and conditioner alongside the cloth. "Undress and get in. I'll bring your robe and slippers in here shortly."

"Thank you."

"My pleasure."

As soon as he exited the bathroom, Kate removed her clothes and stepped into the tub. She slid down into the delicious warm water and sighed with contentment. The water level rose higher and higher and when it covered her almost to her neck, she turned off the faucets and laid her head against the back of the tub. She rested in that position for a good five minutes, doing her best to clear her mind of all unpleasant thoughts. Her headache didn't go away, but the throbbing eased up considerably. She soaped the washcloth and scrubbed herself from face to feet. After shampooing, rinsing, conditioning and rinsing again, she let out some of the cooling water and refilled with fresh warm water.

She stayed in the tub for quite some time, soaking away the stress of the day and her body's minor aches and pains. Not until Trent entered the bathroom again did she realize she'd practically dosed off. Glancing up at him, she smiled when she saw he held a small glass in his hands.

"That looks like wine," she said.

"It is wine." Trent grinned. "Compliments of the manager."

"How long have I been in here?" she asked. "I seem to have lost track of time."

"About twenty minutes." He walked over to the tub and held the glass out to her.

She didn't feel the least bit awkward being naked in front of Trent. She supposed she should, but she didn't. He had been her first lover, her husband for more than two years and he had once known every inch of her body better than she had.

Kate took the glass from him, sipped the wine and sighed. "Not bad."

"Finish that off while I get your robe and slippers."

She sipped the red wine, savoring the taste and appreciating its ability, if she drank enough, to partially anesthetize her. Just as she finished drinking the wine, Trent returned carrying her robe. He hung it on the back of the door, then snapped open a large towel and came toward the tub. She understood that he was holding it for her, waiting to wrap her in it when she emerged from her watery bed.

If you allow him to take care of you, things can and probably will get out of control, she told herself. *Is that what you want?*

Kate set the empty glass in the floor, then rose from the water and stepped out of the tub and right into Trent's waiting arms. He wrapped the towel around her and led her over to the commode, the lid still down. After seating her, he took another towel and rubbed her hair until all the excess moisture was absorbed. Using another towel, he dried her feet and calves, dropped that towel to the floor, and then opened the towel draped around her and gently patted her stomach, breasts and neck. Kate drew in a quivering breath.

"You're even more beautiful now than you were when we first got married." He whipped the towel off her and gazed appreciatively at her body.

Her nipples peaked. "You're a skillful liar," she told him. "And I thank you. I suppose I'm in pretty good shape to be thirty-five, but—"

He placed his index finger over her lips to silence her. "You're in great shape." He reached out tentatively, bringing the tips of his fingers to one breast.

She sucked in her breath. He grazed the nipple softly.

"You can't imagine how much I want you," he admitted, his gaze hungry as it moved from her breasts, down her belly to the downy apex between her thighs.

"Maybe I can," she told him, "if it's half as much as I want you."

"Kate?"

"A little comfort to soothe our battle scars?" she asked.

"Label it whatever suits you. Comfort. Lust. Mutual need."

She leaned forward, placed her hands on his cheeks

and cupped his face. "Just for tonight." She wouldn't ask him for any promises, wouldn't expect a commitment just because they had sex again.

"Yeah, honey, just for tonight."

He lifted her up and into his arms. She cuddled close as he carried her from the bathroom to the bedroom. After laying her on the turned-down bed, he stripped out of his clothes. She expected him to join her, but instead he went back in the bathroom. Within seconds he returned, a small bottle of lotion in his hand.

"Roll over," he told her.

Without questioning him, she did as he'd asked. He sat on the bed, screwed off the bottle lid and poured lotion into his hand, then he spread the cool, lightly scented cream across her back and shoulders. She relaxed as he massaged and caressed her. He worked his way down each arm, then along her spine and over her buttocks. A tingling sensation spread through her, like minuscule currents of electricity bringing her body to life.

Trent rubbed the back of her thighs, her calves and even her feet. When they were married, he'd often given her this type of sensual massage and it always ended with sweet and tender lovemaking. The kind of lovemaking that lingered in the body and on the mind for hours afterward.

"Turn over," he said, his voice husky with desire.

She turned slowly, languidly, an odd combination of relaxation and excitement controlling her movements. Her breasts felt heavy and achy. Her nipples were spiked points, begging for attention. Her femininity clutched and released, creating tension between her legs. Moisture gathered between her intimate lips and sexual heat warmed her from head to toe.

Trent used what little was left of the lotion on Kate's belly and hips, his big hands amazingly gentle as they stroked her flesh. When she thought she couldn't bear his ardent attention another minute, he came down over her, his erection pressing against her stomach.

His mouth covered hers and they shared a long, lingering kiss. His lips moved across her cheek to moisten her earlobe. "I want to be inside you. Deep." He licked a path down her neck, then lifted his head and looked right into her eyes. "I want to take you and take you and take you." He flicked the tip of his tongue over one pouting nipple and then the other, eliciting a cry of pleasure-pain from her lips. "Once isn't going to be enough."

She gave herself over to the moment, to Trent and to the love that had never died. While he suckled her breasts, she ran her hands over his broad shoulders and across his back, loving the feel of him. His sex throbbed against her, arousing her even more.

"Trent, please…"

"Not yet, honey."

His hands, lips and tongue explored her body, each little nook and cranny, turning every inch of her into a quivering mass of sexual need. Just when she thought he was going to enter her, he withdrew from her and leaned over to pick up something off the nightstand.

She whimpered.

"I had the hotel manager send out for some condoms," Trent said, a wicked grin on his face.

"You didn't?" Kate giggled.

"I did."

"What must he think?"

"Who cares? But he probably thinks that I wanted to make love to my wife."

"Your wife?"

"That's how I registered. Mr. and Mrs. Winston."

The former Mrs. Winston sighed, then held open her arms, issuing Mr. Winston an invitation.

Hurriedly he undid the foil packet, sheathed his sex and returned to her. When he slid his hands beneath her hips and lifted her up, she wrapped her arms around his neck. He slipped into her with one slick, even stroke. And she was in heaven. Back in Trent's arms. Their bodies intimately joined. Their loving was as natural as breathing to each of them, as if they had been created for only each other. They kissed and touched without rushing, no urgency fueling their desire. She sensed that he was being intentionally gentle, drawing out each precious moment, making it last as long as possible. He did all the giving, showering her with attention.

Kate had never felt so cherished, so completely adored, as she did tonight. Trent's every touch, every move, every word was a form of worship. After he had brought her near fulfillment several times, then held back to intensify her satisfaction, he finally allowed her to do more than enjoy the pleasure he gave her. Their loving became a mutual giving and taking, the passion growing stronger and hotter by the moment. As her body tightened, the end close, Trent quickened the pace, pumping into her hard and fast.

This was right. This was so right.

Her climax hit her with the force of an explosion. Although he was buried deep inside her, hammering her repeatedly, she bucked up, seeking to gain the last ounce of release. And just as the waves of completion washed over her, Trent groaned. He came with a fury, his hard, hot body trembling with fulfillment.

I love you. The words were on the tip of her tongue.

It would be the most natural thing in the world to tell him how she felt. But she couldn't. Not unless he said the words first.

When he rolled off onto his back, she snuggled against him. He shoved his arm beneath her and hugged her to his side, then he stroked her naked hip. The aftershocks of her climax rippled through her as she kissed his chest.

"God, Kate, I've missed you."

And she had missed him, more than she'd realized. "It was always so good…so right with us, wasn't it?"

He kissed her temple. "Always."

She lay there in the semidarkness of their hotel suite, waiting for him to say those three magic words. Moments ticked by. Neither of them spoke again until a loud knock on the door roused them.

"Room service," a feminine voice called.

"Damn! I'd forgotten about ordering supper." Trent jumped out of bed. "Be there in a minute," he yelled. He found his slacks on the floor, picked them up and rushed into the bathroom. When he reentered the bedroom, he grinned at Kate. "You stay right there. I'll go to the door and bring the serving cart in myself."

By the time Trent wheeled in their evening meal, Kate had slipped on her house shoes and robe. Despite the fact that her ex-husband had not mentioned love before, during or after their lovemaking, Kate appreciated the efforts he'd gone to for her sake.

"Dinner is served," Trent said.

"Good. I'm starving."

"Save room for dessert," he told her and winked.

"Don't tell me—whipped cream and strawberries?" They had indulged in those items during their honeymoon, putting more of the cream on each other than on the berries.

"No strawberries," he said, then lifted the cover from a large, round bowl. "But lots of whipped cream."

Kate laughed. Only Trent could have worked this miracle. Only Trent could have taken her mind off their problems and given her such pleasure.

Trent's cell phone rang at eight o'clock the next morning, just as Kate and he were dressing after the shower they'd taken together. They had made love again the night before, using the whipped cream to full advantage. And then he'd awakened her before six this morning and they'd made love for a third time. He couldn't get enough of her. But that wasn't something new. It had always been that way with them. The passion had never faded, even when the love and trust had wavered.

How could he have ever let her leave him? Why hadn't he done more to save their marriage? Hurt pride and his own feelings of guilt had paralyzed him when she'd asked him for a divorce. Kate had been the best thing that ever happened to him, but he hadn't been able to hold on to her after they'd lost their child.

Wearing only a towel around his waist, Trent came out of the bathroom and removed his cell phone from his coat pocket. He flipped it open and said hello.

"Trent, this is Brenda Farrell." His heartbeat accelerated.

"Yes, Brenda, how are you this morning?"

"I'm all right, considering the fact that I slept very little last night." She paused and when Trent didn't say anything, she continued. "I've done a great deal of thinking and soul searching and I've decided that the best thing for Christa is to get to know you and Kate. She deserves to have two loving parents again and I'd be selfish to keep y'all away from each other."

Kate came up to Trent and draped her arm around his waist, then mouthed the question, "Who is it?"

"You can't imagine how glad I am to hear you say that, Brenda." He emphasized her name for Kate's benefit.

"Brenda." Kate whispered the name.

Trent nodded. Kate stood on tiptoes and dragged Trent down enough so that she could put her ear against the phone in order to hear the telephone conversation.

"Christa isn't being cooperative," Brenda said. "I need some time to bring her around. I don't think it's a good idea for y'all to see her today."

Trent's heart sank. "How much time do you need?"

"Just until her birthday. That's not long."

"Mary Kate's birthday is February the fourth."

"We've always celebrated Christa's birthday on the seventh. That's the date on her birth certificate, the one the adoption agency provided Rick and Jean."

"Are you saying we can see Christa again on February seventh?"

"I'm saying that I want to bring Christa to Prospect the day before her birthday for a weeklong stay with you and Kate. I'll make arrangements with her school so that she can make up any work she misses. And you do understand that I'll want to stay with her in Prospect. I can't leave her there. She would feel totally abandoned."

"Of course, you'll come with her," Trent said. "And we'll have a birthday party for Christa, if that's all right with you."

"Yes, that would be very nice. I'd thought perhaps y'all would enjoy giving her a small party."

"We'd love it. Thank you for doing this."

"I realize it won't be easy for you and Kate to wait for a while longer, but please, trust me. I want what's best for my granddaughter and if we can all be a part of her life, then no one has to lose, most of all Christa. If we can work things out to everyone's satisfaction, Christa will be the real winner."

"I agree completely."

"I'll contact you again later on to get driving directions and—"

"I can send someone to get you and Christa, if you'd like."

"Thank you, but that won't be necessary."

"All right. Whatever you want."

"If you'd like to call me to check on Christa, I won't mind. Tell Kate she can call me everyday if she wants to."

"I'll tell her. We appreciate the way you're handling this situation."

"I don't want any of us to suffer more than we already have."

"We feel the same."

"Goodbye, Trent."

The phone went dead. Brenda had hung up. He tossed the phone into a nearby chair, turned and lifted Kate off her feet.

"Brenda is bringing Christa to Prospect to spend a week with us, beginning on the sixth of February."

Trent swung Kate around and around, then stopped and slid her down his body, effectively knocking the towel from his hips. He pulled her into his arms and kissed her soundly.

"You and I are going to give our daughter a birthday party for her twelfth birthday."

"Oh, Trent, this is too good to be true."

"It's true, honey. It's true."

He kissed her again and before either of them knew what was happening, they were back in bed and making love again.

Eleven

Kate arrived at Winston Hall around twelve-thirty on the sixth of February. Guthrie met her at the door, welcomed her home and told her that Mr. Trent was in court until three o'clock this afternoon and Miss Mary Belle, who was having lunch in the breakfast room, would be delighted if Kate joined her. She sucked it up, stiffened her spine and marched into the lion's den. To her great surprise, Kate was met with open arms and a warm smile. Mary Belle hugged her with great affection, then took her hand and led her to the table where two places had been set for the noon meal.

"The minute you telephoned to let us know you'd be here by lunchtime, I had Cook prepare salmon croquettes," Mary Belle said. "As I recall, they were one of your favorites."

"Yes, thank you."

Kate sat down across from Mary Belle, in a semi-state of shock. Cook brought in their salads first and smiled at Kate. "Good to have you back, Miss Kate."

"Iced tea—no sugar," Mary Belle said. "That is right, isn't it? And we'll have our Earl Grey with dessert. A delicious raspberry torte."

"Miss Mary Belle, you've gone to a great deal of trouble just for me," Kate said. "I'm not sure I understand why."

"It's Aunt Mary Belle. You're family, dear girl. And seeing that you have a nice lunch was no trouble at all. As to not understanding my motives for being nice to you—I'd think that would be apparent. I very much want to make it up to you for anything I did wrong in the past. I never meant to hurt you or add to the problems you and Trent were having after Mary Kate was kidnapped. I am sorry. Genuinely sorry."

Kate stared at Trent's aunt. A funny thought crossed her mind. Who was this woman and what had happened to the real Mary Belle Winston?

"You're speechless." Mary Belle laughed. "I love Trent more than anyone on earth and his happiness means everything to me. When he returned to Prospect a couple of weeks ago, he was happier than I've ever seen him since you two divorced. All he's talked about is that Kate and Christa were coming to Prospect to spend a week with us."

"Trent and I are eager to see our daughter again and we're praying that we say and do all the right things. I'm sure Trent told you that our first meeting with her didn't turn out very well." After their night together at the Holiday Inn in Sheffield, Kate had flown back to Atlanta to put her house in order, so to speak, and Trent had returned to Prospect to his job as a circuit court judge. During this period of waiting, they had spoken on the phone almost every day. They had been preparing for the upcoming week when Christa and her nana would stay at Winston Hall for seven whole days.

"I understand completely and I, too, want to do all I can to make sure nothing goes wrong." Mary Belle looked at Kate beseechingly. "I've made some arrangements that I want to discuss with you. And if there's anything you want changed, anything you disapprove of, just let me know and we'll—"

"Aunt Mary Belle, have you actually changed so much that I hardly recognize you, or did I not ever really know you?"

Mary Belle's eyes widened. "Perhaps a bit of both. I'd like to think that I'm not only older, but wiser. And in the past, I spent so much time trying to tutor you, to help you adjust to being a Winston, that I didn't let you know how terribly fond of you I was."

"You were fond of me? I thought you disliked me, that you disapproved of me, that you thought I was unworthy of being Trent's wife."

Mary Belle frowned, deepening the faint wrinkles around her mouth and eyes. "It's true that at first, I had certain reservations. You weren't one of us and...forgive me. You know what a snob I can be. I simply can't help it." She laughed nervously. "But it didn't take me long to see what a good person you were and to realize how much you and Trent loved each other. I suppose I tried too hard to make you over into what I thought Trent's wife should be. But I assure you, I believed I was doing the right thing, for Trent and for you."

"And what about now? I'm not Trent's wife any longer."

"You should be and we both know it. He's never

gotten over you and I suspect you're still in love with him, too, aren't you?"

"How much does your solicitous attitude have to do with Christa Farrell?"

"I won't deny that I hope you and Trent will remarry and make a home for Mary Kate. Yes, yes, I know. I'll have to make myself call her Christa."

Kate sighed. For once she and Aunt Mary Belle wanted exactly the same thing. "Don't forget that Christa has a grandmother who has raised her single-handedly since she was six."

"Winston Hall is a large house," Mary Belle said. "There is room for all of us, including Brenda Farrell."

"You'd be willing to let Brenda live here, too?"

"I'm willing to do whatever it takes to make all of us a family again."

"I see." Kate thought things over for a couple of minutes, then said, "Tell me about the arrangements you've made for Christa and her nana's visit."

Trent arrived home less than ten minutes before Brenda Farrell drove up in her older-model Chevrolet. He'd barely had time to give Kate a hug and a kiss, discard his briefcase and ask her how her trip from Atlanta had gone before their much anticipated guests arrived.

With Trent, Kate and Mary Belle lined up in the foyer, Guthrie opened the door and invited their visitors to come inside. Brenda all but shoved a reluctant Christa over the threshold. Both grandmother and child gawked at the massive foyer, the winding staircase, the impressive grandeur of the old family home. Christa clung to her grandmother's hand, an expression of uncertainty on her face.

"Welcome to Winston Hall," Trent said. "I hope y'all had a pleasant trip down from Sheffield."

"Very pleasant," Brenda replied. "Christa, don't you have something to say to Trent and Kate?"

Kate sought and found Trent's hand, then squeezed tightly. He suspected she was as nervous as he and needed moral support, just as he did.

"Thank you very much for inviting us for a visit," Christa said, but there was little sincerity in her words.

"You're quite welcome," Trent replied. "Would y'all care for some refreshments?"

"No, thank you," Christa said.

"Perhaps you'd like for your mother—for Kate to show you up to your room," Mary Belle suggested, a slight quiver to her voice and tears misting her eyes.

Christa stared at Mary Belle.

"I'm your great-aunt Mary Belle. I was born in this house and have lived here all my life. This is your home, too, you know. You lived here with us for the first two months of your life and we all loved you very much."

"I don't remember," Christa said. "Nana has told me that my birth mother didn't give me away." She looked right at Kate. "Somebody stole me from you, didn't they?"

Kate nodded. Tears glistened in her eyes. When she opened her mouth, but no sound came out, Trent realized she was too overcome with emotion to speak.

"Kate and I loved you so," Trent said. "You were our precious little Mary Kate. You were the joy of our lives."

"I'm not Mary Kate anymore. I'm sorry your baby was stolen and I'm sorry I don't remember either of you." She glanced at Mary Belle. "Or you."

"It's all right, Christa," Kate said. "It doesn't matter. All that matters is that you're here for a visit and we're going to get to know each other all over again."

"Nana told me that y'all have promised you won't take me away from her."

"No, we will never take you away from your grand-mother," Kate vowed. "Isn't that right, Trent?"

"That's right. We want your nana to be a part of our family, too."

Christa's expression changed instantly, all wariness disappeared, replaced with curiosity. "I've never seen a house this big. It's very old, isn't it?"

"Yes, it's very old," Mary Belle said. "Would you like for Trent and Kate to give you a grand tour while your grandmother and I have tea in the parlor so she and I can become better acquainted?"

"Is that all right, Nana?"

"Certainly," Brenda said.

"What would you like to see first?" Trent gave Kate's hand a it's-going-to-be-all-right squeeze.

"I don't know." Christa thought for a couple of mi-nutes. "Did I have a room of my own when I lived here?"

"You had a beautiful nursery," Kate said.

"I don't guess it's still a nursery, is it?"

Kate looked to Trent for an answer. When she'd left Winston Hall over ten years ago, Mary Kate's nursery had been untouched, looking just as it had that Easter Sunday when she'd been abducted.

"Your nursery is just as it was," Trent said. "But Aunt Mary Belle had a new, larger room decorated just for you—for twelve-year-old Christa Farrell."

"Really?"

"Really," Trent said.

"May I see both—my old nursery and my new room?"

"You most certainly may."

Trent held his hand out to his daughter. She accepted without hesitation and went with him up the long, wind-ing staircase, Kate keeping in step on Christa's other side.

* * *

Kate now wished she had listened to her gut instincts and insisted that Aunt Mary Belle pare down the extravagant birthday party she'd planned for Christa. But she'd told herself she was being silly to think that just because all the Winston hoopla had scared the bejesus out of her when she'd been dating Trent, Christa would be overwhelmed by a guest list of fifty, a live band, a clown, a magician, hot-and-cold running servants, a birthday cake five feet high and a pile of presents that could have been for ten little girls instead of just one.

Trent walked up beside Kate and whispered, "I'm not sure the Queen of England has parties this elaborate. Do you think maybe Aunt Mary Belle over-did it just a tad?"

"You think?" Kate uttered a nervous chuckle. "Oh, Trent, look at Christa's face. She's out of her league, just the way I always was."

Trent put his arm around Kate's shoulders. "She reminds me so much of you. Her mannerisms are so like yours and the way she laughs and that sweet shyness."

"She's trying valiantly to put on a happy face, but she's simply overwhelmed." Kate shook her head sadly.

"Maybe we should rescue her."

"Could we, Trent? Would it be terribly rude if we got her out of this mausoleum and away from this three-ring circus?"

"To hell with being rude. Let Aunt Mary Belle explain to all these children and their mothers why Christa's parents stole her away before the party was over."

"How do we accomplish this?" Kate asked.

"You go get Christa. Ask her if she'd like to take a ride with us and get away for a while. I'll speak to Brenda to get her permission."

"Let's do it."

Kate mowed her way through hordes of children devouring cake, ice cream and countless bakery delights. Christa sat in a chair that looked somewhat like a small throne in the middle of the room, surrounded by presents, half of which were still gaily wrapped.

Kate leaned down and whispered to her daughter, "Want to get out of here? Trent and I are going for a ride and we thought you might like to go with us."

Christa shot up out of the chair and grabbed Kate's hand. "I'm ready."

Kate led her child from the room, not responding when Aunt Mary Belle called out their names. When they escaped onto the front veranda, Trent followed a moment later and the three of them rushed toward the garage. After hopping inside the front seat of Trent's Bentley, Christa snuggled close to Kate and didn't protest when Kate put her arm around her shoulders. Trent started the engine and backed the car out of the five-car garage, then within minutes they were headed down the road.

"Where are we going?" Christa asked.

"I have something I want to show you and Kate," Trent said. "It's not far from here."

"Is it another birthday surprise?" Christa frowned.

"Not exactly," Trent told her. "It's something for all of us, but especially for Kate."

Christa smiled. "Really?"

"For me?" Kate stared quizzically at Trent.

"Oh, Kate, I forgot to tell Nana that I was going with you and Trent."

"I asked her permission and it's fine with her," Trent said. "She'll be waiting at Winston Hall for us when we return."

Christa's smile widened. "Are you going to give us a hint about what the surprise is?"

"Let's just say that it's something Kate always wanted."

He'd piqued Kate's curiosity by that last statement, but for the life of her she couldn't imagine what it could be. What had she always wanted? All she could think about was Mary Kate, her baby girl. It seemed that being reunited with her child was everything she'd ever wanted.

"Is it bigger than a bread box?" Christa asked.

"Yes," Trent replied.

Joining in the game, Kate asked, "Is it animal, vegetable or mineral?"

Trent laughed. "It's definitely not animal."

"Ah, gee, it's not a horse or a dog or a cat." Christa tapped her index finger on her mouth. "Mmm, hmm, what could it be? You know, I like this guessing game." She turned and looked up at Kate. "Can't you think of anything you always wanted?"

"I always wanted you." The words were out of Kate's mouth before she could stop them.

Christa studied Kate, a curious glint in her brown eyes. "I really am sorry your baby was stolen. I mean, I'm sorry somebody took me away from you. I guess you've missed me a lot, huh? That's what Nana said. She said you and Trent have missed me and want me to be your daughter again."

"Your nana is right," Trent said as he turned onto Third Street. "There's nothing Kate and I want more than a chance to be your parents again."

"You won't expect me to call you Mama and Daddy, will you?"

"No, honey. You can call us anything you'd like. Trent and Kate is just fine with us, isn't it, Kate?"

"Absolutely."

Kate wondered where on earth they were going. She'd thought Trent was taking them into town, but the direction in which they were traveling now took them away from downtown and along the tree-lined streets of the residential section. When Trent turned the corner onto Madison, Kate held her breath. *It can't be. It's just a coincidence that the house I once thought of as my dream home is on Madison.*

"Oh, look, Kate, isn't that a pretty house?" Christa pointed out the old Kirkendall house on the corner at the end of the four-hundred block. She glanced over at Trent. "It's not that Winston Hall isn't beautiful, but it's so big. It doesn't seem like a home at all. It reminds me of a museum."

Trent laughed heartily. "Where have I heard that statement before? Mmm, hmm." He shot Kate a quick glance as he pulled the Bentley into the driveway at the old Kirkendall house. "Your mother—that is Kate—once said the very same thing to me."

Christa bobbed around and looked up at Kate, her lips curved in a big smile. "Did you really tell him that?"

"I sure did." Kate's heart raced wildly.

"We're here," Trent announced. "Let's get out and go inside."

"What?" Kate and Christa cried in unison.

"This is your surprise, Kate."

"I don't understand."

"You mean the house is Kate's surprise?" Christa bounced up and down, all smiles and happy laughter. "You bought Kate a house?"

"Trent, what have you done?"

Christa tugged on Kate's arm. "Come on, let's go see it."

Halfway in a trance, Kate opened the car door and got out, Christa on her heels. Trent rushed around the Bentley's hood and escorted them up the brick walkway to the front porch.

Trent inserted a key in the lock, then opened the front door. "Come on inside."

"This was someone's home," Kate said. "You didn't force some family to move out just so you could give me this house, did you?"

"Christa, see if you can get Kate to come inside and take a look." Trent stepped back to allow them room to enter. "And for your information, Ms. Malone, I bought this house nine years ago, had it completely remodeled at that time and have since completely furnished it."

Christa pulled Kate into the foyer. Shiny wooden floors, polished to a rich gloss spread out from the foyer into the living room and dining room on the left, then went into the paneled den on the right. Kate's mouth dropped open when she saw a glowing fire blazing in the living room fireplace.

Christa danced around and around as she explored the downstairs. "I love this house. It's just perfect. If I come to live with y'all, are we going to live here?"

Trent draped his arm around Kate's shoulders. "What's the answer to that, Kate? Will you come back to Prospect and live in this house with our daughter?"

"Trent…." Tears pooled in Kate's eyes. Not in her wildest dreams had she imagined Trent would have bought the old Kirkendall house, remodeled it and kept it—for her. "You bought this house nine years ago, after we were divorced, after I'd left Prospect. I don't understand."

"It was a crazy thing to do," he admitted. "But I thought that maybe someday…" He raked his hand through his hair and chuckled. "Hell, I don't know what

I thought. That by buying this house I was holding on to a little piece of you, I guess."

"How many rooms are there upstairs?" Christa asked.

"Four bedrooms and three baths."

"That's more than enough rooms for all of us. When you and Kate get married again, you'll share a room, of course. And I'll have my own room. And Nana will have her room. And there will be a guest bedroom. Or heck, maybe we'll have a baby. I always wanted a little brother or sister."

Kate and Trent stared at each other, totally amazed by Christa's exuberance.

"What if Trent and I don't remarry?" Kate asked. "What if I come back to Prospect and you and I and Brenda live here?"

Christa looked at Trent. "But if we're going to be a family, Trent has to live here, too. Right?"

"Are you saying that you want to come to Prospect to live?" Trent asked. "Do you want us to be your parents?"

"I guess. I mean, yes, I think that's what I want. But not if we have to live at Winston Hall."

"This can be your home," Trent told her. "And you can redo your room anyway you'd like. But it'll be up to Kate whether I live here with y'all or just visit every day."

Christa grabbed Kate's hand. "Please, Kate, tell him he can live here, too."

"Christa, honey…"

Christa reached out for Trent's hand. "I have a great idea, why don't we go get Nana and we all stay here for our visit."

"Would that make you happy?" Kate asked.

"Yes, it would be the very best birthday present."

"Then that's what we'll do." Kate looked to Trent. "Right?"

"Nothing would please me more." He wrapped one arm around Kate and the other around Christa. Both of them looked up at him and smiled.

Twelve

Winter turned into early spring. The days Christa spent with Kate in Prospect flew by, but the days Kate was on Dundee assignments and Christa in school in Sheffield seemed endless. Kate and Christa kept in touch by daily telephone conversations and she and Trent spoke often, too, their main topic of conversation always their daughter. She felt certain Trent wanted to ask her to remarry him, but she'd done everything to put him off, short of telling him she wouldn't go into a marriage only for the sake of their child. A part of her wanted to believe that Trent loved her and would want to remarry her regardless of whether Mary Kate had come back into their lives. But the insecure girl-from-the-wrong-side-of-the-tracks, who'd always felt so unworthy, had her doubts.

With Christa's spring break from school beginning, Brenda Farrell had arranged for them to arrive in

Prospect this Friday evening and stay for nine whole days. Kate could hardly wait. She had come into town the day before and spent the entire day today preparing the house on Madison for their guests' arrival. Trent had joined her for dinner last night and they'd ended the evening by making love. Each time they were together it became harder and harder to stop herself from telling him how much she loved him.

Before he'd left that morning, he'd made a request. "I'd like to stay here with you and Christa during this visit."

"You're welcome to stay, but you can't sleep with me," she'd told him, only halfway joking. "I don't think Brenda would approve. She's the old-fashioned type."

"I'll sleep on the porch if I have to," he said. "I just want to be here with you and our daughter. We've lost so many years. I don't want to lose another minute."

"Oh, Trent. Brenda told me that if this extended visit goes as well as the short weekend visits have gone, she thinks Christa will soon be ready for them to move here permanently."

When he'd hugged her, she'd sensed he didn't want to let her go, as if he was afraid he'd lose her. "If that's the case, don't you think we should make some decisions about our future."

"Not now, Trent. Let's wait and see how it goes."

She had put him off once again. But sooner or later she'd have to face the inevitable. It was only a matter of time before Trent proposed. And then she would have to decide if she could trust him completely, if she could believe he truly loved her.

"Where shall I put these, dear?" Aunt Mary Belle held a large floral arrangement, flowers from the Winston Hall spring garden.

"Those go in Brenda's room," Kate said.

"I think I'll suggest to Brenda that she should come over to Winston Hall and stay with me so that you and Trent can have some time alone with Christa."

Kate groaned. "I know you mean well, but please don't do that."

Mary Belle harrumphed. "Brenda needs to start letting go, just a little. You're the child's mother and unless Brenda allows Christa to bond with you—"

"Let's face it—my daughter may never think of me as her mother. She may always see Brenda in that role."

Mary Belle sighed, then turned to take the flowers into the guest bedroom Brenda Farrell would occupy. Kate returned to her chore—making Christa's bed with the new pale yellow bed linens she'd purchased in Atlanta. She'd found out recently that yellow was Christa's favorite color, so she'd made plans to add more of that color to this room.

"Where is everybody?" Trent called from downstairs.

"We're up here," she told him.

"I'll be on up as soon as I put the groceries away."

"Did you remember the Turtle Tracks ice cream?" Kate asked. "It's her favorite, you know."

"I got it. And the cereal she likes and the strawberry-flavored milk she prefers. You gave me specific instructions, honey. Stop worrying. Everything will be perfect."

"Everything will not be perfect until you two get married again," Mary Belle called out loud and clear.

Silence.

Say something, Trent. Please.

"I'll thank you to stay out of my business," Trent told his aunt.

Kate released her pent-up breath.

Mary Belle came into Christa's room and zeroed in on Kate. "Why won't you marry him?"

"I beg your pardon." Kate rearranged the decorative pillows on the four-poster bed.

"Don't play dumb with me. I know my nephew has been walking around with your engagement ring in his pocket for over a month now. Why haven't you said yes?"

"Trent has my engagement ring? Do you mean he kept my original ring, the one he gave me years ago?"

"That very ring. Half of Prospect is aware of the fact that Trent took your engagement ring and wedding band out of his safety-deposit box this past month."

Kate laughed spontaneously, finding great humor in the fact that a bank employee had spread the word about Trent's withdrawal from his safety-deposit box and that within a few days afterward half the town had known what he'd done. And wasn't it strange, Kate thought, that she didn't seem to mind at all. Once she had hated small-town gossip and the busybodies who generated it. Now she liked everything about Prospect, absolutely everything.

"Trent has not proposed," Kate told Mary Belle.

"He hasn't?"

"No, he hasn't."

"I find that odd."

"Why should you find—"

"Have you been discouraging him?"

Kate gave Mary Belle a withering glare.

"You have, haven't you?" Mary Belle huffed indignantly. "Why on earth would you do such a thing?"

"Why would Kate do what?" Trent asked from where he stood in the doorway to Christa's room.

Kate and Mary Beth gasped and jumped simultaneously.

"I'm going to hang a bell around your neck," his aunt told him.

"Pardon me. Did I interrupt private woman talk?"

"Yes, you did," Mary Belle said. "Kate, I'd very much like for y'all to come to lunch on Sunday, right after church."

"We'd be delighted, Aunt Mary Belle," Kate replied.

Trent looked from his aunt to Kate, his brow wrinkled, his gaze narrowed. "Aren't you two awfully chummy these days?"

"Kate, we'll finish our conversation at a later date. I must run. I have a dinner engagement with the other members of the museum's board of trustees and I shall need a good two hours to bathe and dress." She walked over to Kate, kissed her on the cheek, then did the same to Trent. "Give Christa my love and tell Brenda that there's a room at Winston Hall for her any time she'd like to take me up on my offer."

When his aunt walked out of the room, Trent eyed Kate questioningly. "What's that about—Brenda has a room at Winston Hall?"

"Oh, it's nothing. Just Aunt Mary Belle being Aunt Mary Belle."

Trent came up to Kate and slipped his arm around her, then kissed her on the mouth. When he lifted his head and smiled dreamily, she grinned back at him.

"Before Christa and Brenda arrive, there's something I want to ask you." He took her hands in his and led her out of the bedroom and into the hallway.

Don't propose to me now, she cried silently. I'm not sure if I can say yes. Not yet.

She gave him a pleading look.

He stuck his hand in his jacket pocket. Kate's heart stopped. He knelt on one knee.

"Oh, Trent."

"Kate…" He held up her engagement ring—a three-carat emerald cut stone. "You accepted this ring from me once before." He gazed up at her longingly. "I'm hoping you'll wear my ring again."

"I want—"

"Shh. Let me finish." He took her hand in his. "Kate, will you marry me. Again?"

Before she could utter a word, he slipped the ring on the third finger of her left hand. Kate stared at the sparkling diamond. She loved Trent with all her heart and soul and wanted to be his wife. Besides, remarrying him would be the best thing for Christa. It would make them a family. But that was the very reason she hesitated. She didn't want Trent to marry her because he thought it was the right thing to do for their daughter.

"Trent, why do you want to marry me?"

He stared at her, a puzzled expression darkening his face.

"Yoo-hoo," Brenda Farrell called out from downstairs. "We're here. Mary Belle let us in as she was leaving."

"Oh, God, it's Christa and Brenda," Kate said. "They're early."

"We're upstairs," Trent called. "We'll be right down."

When Kate headed toward the stairs, Trent grabbed her wrist to halt her. "Say yes now."

"Later."

She offered him an encouraging smile, then pulled free of his hold and raced down the stairs to greet Christa and Brenda. Trent came down only a second behind her. Kate skidded to a halt in the foyer, stopping herself only seconds before reaching out to Christa. More than anything she wanted to wrap her daughter in her arms and hug her for dear life. Although she and Trent had made amazing progress with Christa, a barrier still existed between them and their child. And they had agreed not to push her, to give her all the time she needed, to let her come to them when she was ready.

"Hi." Christa had Trent's wide-mouthed smile. "We left Sheffield early. School let out at noon and Nana had us all packed and ready to leave."

"Well, we're delighted y'all arrived early." Trent grinned at Christa, then turned to Brenda. "I'll bring in your bags."

"Just get Christa's bags," Brenda said.

Kate and Trent stared questioningly at her.

"I'm going to stay at Winston Hall with Mary Belle," Brenda explained. "I'll be close by and be able to see Christa every day."

Kate looked directly at her daughter. "Are you all right with those arrangements?"

"Oh, sure. Nana and I talked it over last night. She thinks I need to spend time with you two without her and I'm okay with it."

"Did Aunt Mary Belle have something to do with this?" Trent asked.

Brenda's lips curved into a how-ever-did-you-guess grin. "Don't be upset with her. She telephoned me earlier this week and made the suggestion. And she's right. I'm Christa's grandmother and nothing will change that fact. I'll always be close by when she needs me, but she has a mother and father now and y'all need to form a family bond."

Trent nodded. "Why don't y'all go on in while I get Christa's bags."

"I'm not staying," Brenda said. "Come on, Trent, I'll walk back to the car with you."

She leaned over and hugged Christa. "Behave yourself, young lady." She looked at Kate. "Do not let her get away with anything. She's a smart little cookie. She knows you and Trent will jump through hoops to pacify her."

"Ah, Nana, you're giving away all my secrets." Christa laughed.

"Are you hungry? Would you like a snack?" Kate asked her daughter as Trent opened the front door for Brenda and the two disappeared onto the front porch.

"Do you have any of those homemade oatmeal cookies?" Christa asked.

"I made a fresh batch this morning."

"Oh, Kate, thanks. I knew you would. You're the best."

Christa's smile warmed Kate's heart.

When Kate shoved open the kitchen door, Christa gasped. "Oh, my heavens, Kate, what is that on your finger?"

"What?" Damn, she was still wearing the three-carat diamond Trent had slipped on her finger. "Oh, that's the ring your father gave me when he asked me to marry him the first time."

"Are you two going to get married again?"

"Would you like that?"

"You know I would."

"We're talking about it," Kate said. "We haven't made a definite decision."

"If you do get married again, I could be the maid of honor, couldn't I?"

"Yes, of course, you could."

Oh, Trent, what am I going to do? I love you and

want to marry you. Nothing would please our daugh-
ter more. But you haven't said one word about loving
me. I need the words, Trent, I need the words.

The evening had been perfect, the kind Kate had once
dreamed of having with her husband and daughter. With
Trent and Mary Kate. And despite the years of separa-
tion and the fact that Christa was now their daughter's
name, the three of them had shared a true family
evening. Dinner together in the kitchen. Mother and
daughter doing the dishes. Sitting on the front porch at
sunset, despite it being slightly chilly. Watching
Christa's favorite Friday night TV program while the
three of them shared the sofa, Christa sitting between
them.

When the mantel clock struck ten, Kate rose from the
sofa and Trent used the remote control to turn off the
television.

"Bedtime," Kate announced.

"You're going to follow Nana's instructions to the
letter, aren't you?" Christa sighed dramatically.

"Nana knows best," Trent told her.

"Go on up and change into your new pajamas," Kate
said. "I bought them in Atlanta and put them in the top
drawer of your dresser this morning."

Christa jumped up and down. "Are they those yellow silk pajamas I wanted?"

"Could be."

"Oh, Kate, you *are* the very best." Christa came bar-
reling toward Kate and threw her arms around her.

Kate thought she'd die from joy when her daughter
hugged her fiercely, then released her and ran up the
stairs. Trent came up behind Kate and pulled her back
against his chest, then nuzzled her cheek with his.

"Good feeling, huh?"

"Great feeling." Kate turned around, right into Trent's arms. "Oh, Trent, I'm so happy."

"Me, too, honey. Me, too."

"I know we need to talk." She held up her ring finger. "About this. But could it wait until morning? I want to go up now and see Christa in her new pajamas and then I hope she'll let me stay with her so we can have some girl talk before she goes to sleep."

Trent kissed Kate quickly, then turned her and gave her a shove toward the stairs. She raced halfway up the steps, then paused, looked over her shoulder and blew her former husband a kiss.

"I love you," she mouthed the words and waited for his response.

He shut his eyes for a brief moment, an odd expression on his face. When he opened his eyes again, he smiled at her, but didn't say anything. *Did that mean he didn't love her? Dammit Trent, am I supposed to be able to read your mind?*

Kate lay awake, torn between wanting to go to Trent and wishing he would come to her. She'd been the one who had decided they shouldn't share a bedroom while Christa and Brenda were in the house with them. But tonight was different. First of all, Brenda wasn't here. And secondly, Trent had proposed. She was wearing an engagement ring.

But you haven't said yes, she reminded herself.

Was she allowing three little words to keep her from accepting, from grabbing everything she'd ever wanted and holding on tight? What did it matter that Trent hadn't told her he loved her. He'd shown her in countless ways. Not only did he make her feel loved and cherished every time they made love, but he'd done everything in his power to give her whatever she wanted. He'd let her have her way about their relationship and about dealing with Christa and Brenda and even Aunt Mary Belle.

And don't forget that he bought this house nine years ago—bought it in the hopes you'd come back to him. And he kept it, remodeled it and held on to it all this time. And he gave it to you—in writing, putting the deed in your name.

How much more did a man have to do to prove his love?

Kate slipped out of bed, picked up her satin robe and put it on. Just as she headed for the door, she heard a soft rapping.

"Kate," Trent whispered her name.

She opened the door to him. He stood there in the dark hallway, wearing his pajama bottoms and silk robe, loosely belted. He looked as if he'd gotten no more sleep than she had.

"I was coming to you," she told him.

"Christa is sound asleep. I peeked in on her on my way to your room."

"Couldn't you wait till morning to find out my answer?" she said teasingly.

"I can wait for your answer." He shut the door behind him, then reached out and pulled her up against him, enfolding her securely in his embrace. "But I can't wait until morning to make love to you."

"I feel the same way." Rising on tiptoe, she draped her arms around his neck and kissed him.

That was all it took for him to lose control. His mouth devoured hers and his hands went crazy, rubbing, caressing, massaging her back, her hips, her buttocks.

She gripped his wide shoulders as he deepened the kiss and when his sex thumped against her belly, she yanked off his robe and tossed it to the floor. Within minutes, he'd stripped her, then he discarded his pajama bottoms. They tumbled together onto her bed, touching and tasting each other, their bodies eager to join. She took the dominant position, mounting him, bringing him fully inside her, to the hilt. And then she began a fast, frantic pace, wanting him desperately. Needing him. Loving him. Always. He clasped her hips and urged her into a frenetic rhythm. Hard and fast. Hot and wet. They went at each other as if their very lives depended on this single mating.

Trent grunted. Once. Twice. And then he came.

Kate's own climax came on the heels of his, fast and furious. Pleasure almost beyond bearing. She melted into him, their sex-damp bodies sticky and hot. He stroked her buttocks as she kissed his neck.

"Kate. Kate…"

"I love you, Trent."

"I—"

The scream filled the entire house, as if the child's voice was magnified a thousand-fold. Kate shot straight up, her heart racing maddeningly. Oh my God, it was Christa!

"It's Christa," Kate told him as she got up, found her robe on the floor and slipped into it.

"She's crying. Listen." Trent followed Kate's lead and put on his robe, too.

"She must be having a nightmare."

Kate ran out into the hall and straight to Christa's bedroom. Trent came in right behind her. She rushed over to the bed where Christa thrashed about, moaning and groaning and clawing at the air. Acting purely on instinct, Kate crawled into bed with her child, pulled her into her arms and held her close.

"It's okay, baby, Mama's here," Kate said as she caressed Christa's head and neck and back. "You're safe my darling. No one can hurt you."

Trent stood beside the bed. Springtime moonlight poured through the windows, filtered only by the delicate white lace curtains. His gaze connected with Kate's and they exchanged concerned looks.

The more Kate petted Christa, the tighter she clung to Kate and the calmer she became until finally she quieted. Her eyelids fluttered. Kate kissed her forehead.

"That's it my sweet baby, rest. Mama's here and I'll never let anything or anyone hurt you ever again."

Christa opened her eyes and looked right at Kate. "I had a terrible dream."

"That's all it was, sweetheart. Just a dream. You're fine now."

"I dreamed that we were all together, living here in this house and we were so happy." Christa looked over Kate's shoulder and reached her hand out toward Trent. "Daddy?"

Kate's heart caught in her throat.

"Daddy, this terrible person tried to take me away, but you and Mama stopped him." Christa laid her head on Kate's shoulder. "Daddy fought him and saved me. And you grabbed me and held me, Mama, and told me you loved me."

Tears poured down Kate's cheeks. The joy bursting inside her hurt with the most intense pleasure-pain she'd ever known. *Thank you, God, thank you.* Christa had called her Mama. And she'd called Trent Daddy.

Trent leaned over the bed and wrapped his arms around Kate and Christa. "We both love you," he said.

"Your mother and I love you more than anything, just like we love each other. One of the reasons I love you so much is because you're half mine and half your mama's. And you're special, Christa, because you're you."

Kate reached up and caressed Trent's cheek. "The answer is yes," she told him.

He kissed Kate's forehead. Christa lifted her head from Kate's shoulder and said, "You can do better than that, can't you, Daddy?"

"Yes, I can, young lady, but not tonight. Tomorrow we'll celebrate properly and I'll give Kate a kiss that will knock her socks off. But for now, we all need to get some sleep. We've just been through quite an ordeal."

Trent turned to leave the bedroom.

"Don't go," Christa cried.

"All right, I'll stay." Trent walked across the room and sat in one of the two floral chintz lounge chairs flanking a small tea table. "I'll keep watch from here the rest of the night. Now, you two girls go to sleep."

Christa tugged on Kate's hands. "Sleep with me tonight, okay?"

"Okay." Kate lay down beside her daughter, then pulled the covers over them up to their shoulders.

Christa snuggled against Kate and whispered, "You're going to marry Daddy again, aren't you, Mama?"

"Yes, I am." Kate hugged Christa.

"And I'm going to be your maid of honor, right?"

"Right?"

"And I'm going to be the luckiest man in the world," Trent called from across the room.

"We're all three lucky," Kate said. "We're a real family again."

At long last.

Epilogue

"**T**hey're here," Christa Winston called out to her nana and aunt Mary Belle, then she rushed off the porch and down the brick sidewalk toward her mother and father who were just getting out of Trent's Bentley.

Kate opened her arms as Christa flew toward her.

After giving her mother a hug, Christa said, "May I carry one of them?"

Trent opened the car's back door and looked inside, then smiled at Christa. "Take your pick. Do you want Bay or Belle?"

"Give me Belle," thirteen-year old Christa said. "She and I will have to stick together, being sisters and all."

Trent removed the infant carrier from the back seat and handed his younger daughter to her big sister. "We think she looks just like you did when you were a baby."

"Which means she's a living doll, right Daddy?" Christa beamed happily as she accepted the carrier and headed up the sidewalk. "You should see your nursery, young lady. Mama and I went all out decorating it. Your side of the room is all pink and white. And I chose all your dolls and stuffed animals myself. We let Daddy pick out things for Bay, since he's a boy. He'll probably play football and baseball. But I'll teach you to play soccer and softball. I'm on both teams, you know."

Trent lifted his son's carrier from the car, then reached out and put his arm around Kate. "Miracles do happen, don't they, honey?"

"Absolutely. We are living proof of that."

"Hurry up, you two," Aunt Mary Belle fussed as she came toward them. "You do not want to keep that baby out in this hot July sun another minute. It's enough to give me a heat stroke. Ninety-five in the shade today. That's what the weather forecaster said."

Christa took Belle inside, then Brenda and Mary Belle followed. Kate held open the door for Trent and went in behind him and Bay. Kate gasped as they entered the foyer. Blue and pink streamers hung from the crown molding and draped the staircase. Baskets of fresh flowers—in pale baby pastels—had been situated in every corner of the foyer. Kate saw plainly Aunt Mary Belle's extravagant hand mixed with Christa's youthful exuberance in the celebratory displays.

The entire assembly treaded upstairs, straight to the nursery. The room, a pale cream, boasted a hand-painted mural, and had been decorated in shades of light pink, blue, yellow and green. The furniture for both babies was a rich mahogany—the baby beds, chests, dressing tables and rocking chairs. Trenton Bayard Winston V's bed was an identical Genny Lind style to his sister's except hers had a white-eyelet-lace canopy. Where Bay had his father's brown hair and mother's blue eyes, Brenda Belle Winston was her older sister's look-alike, with Trent's brown eyes and Kate's blond hair.

After removing both sleeping infants from their carriers and placing them in their beds, Christa and the adults stood watching the little ones, in awe of the miracle before them.

"Babies are so amazing, aren't they?" Brenda said. "I'd hoped to have more children after Rick, but it wasn't meant to be." She put her arm around Christa. "But God blessed me with this young lady."

"And now you have two more grandchildren." Christa looked from her mother to her father. "Isn't that right?"

"Absolutely," Kate said.

"And I'll teach them to call you Nana, just like I do," Christa told her.

"Christa, I'm not sure—"

"Of course, they'll call you Nana." Kate smiled at Brenda. "You and Aunt Mary Belle will share the honor of being their grandmother, just as y'all do with Christa."

"I've got to phone Shelly and Alexa and tell them they can come over and see our babies." Christa galloped out of the nursery, then called back to her parents, "Is it all right for them to come over in about an hour?"

"An hour should be fine," Trent replied, then draped his arm around Kate's shoulders. "Now, Mrs. Winston, I think it's time for you to lie down for a while. You've had a busy day today, not to mention the fact you just gave birth to twins only a few days ago."

"Brenda and I will go downstairs and see to lunch and field any phone calls." Mary Belle ushered Brenda from the nursery.

Trent and Kate heard the two talking like magpies as they went up the hall and down the stairs. Christa's nana and her aunt Mary Belle had become fast friends and both seemed to greatly enjoy living together at Winston Hall. Mary Belle had gotten Brenda involved in all her clubs and civic organizations and you seldom saw one of them without the other.

While the ladies kept busy and happy blocks away at the old family manor, Trent, Kate and Christa lived what Kate thought of as a fairly normal life here on Madison in their homey old house, with a swing on the front porch and a white picket fence. Last year Kate had thought she couldn't be happier, that she had everything her heart desired. That was until she discovered she was pregnant—at thirty-six—with twins.

Trent marched Kate into their bedroom and all but forced her to take off her shoes and lie down. "Rest while you can," he told her. He kissed her forehead, then turned to leave.

"Stay with me."

"You won't rest if I'm here."

"I won't rest if you're not."

"Okay, but no hanky-panky," Trent said jokingly as he got in bed with her and sat, his back against the headboard.

"We'll save the hanky-panky for a few weeks." She snuggled up against him, placing her head in his lap. "For now, I'll settle for some TLC. Lots and lots of TLC."

"Ah, honey, you're going to get plenty of tender loving care. Now and for the rest of our lives." He tenderly stroked her head, threading his fingers through her hair. "I love you, Kate. I love you so much it hurts."

She sighed. "And I love you the very same way."

Life didn't get any better than this. After years of loneliness and heartache, Kate and Trent had been given a precious gift—a second chance for a happy life as husband and wife. And as parents.

* * * * *

Look for a classic novel from Beverly Barton
also out this month in Silhouette Spotlight's
Expecting the Cop's Baby.

MISS PRUITT'S PRIVATE LIFE
by
Barbara McCauley

BARBARA MCCAULEY,

who has written more than twenty novels for Silhouette Books, lives in Southern California with her own handsome hero husband, Frank, who makes it easy to believe in and write about the magic of romance. Barbara's stories have won and been nominated for numerous awards, including the prestigious RITA® Award from the Romance Writers of America, Best Desire of the Year from *Romantic Times* and Best Short Contemporary from the National Reader's Choice Awards.

One

Dear Marcy,
I am taking a train across the country from the
West Coast. I need to travel light, with a wardrobe
that will include casual to dressy. Do you have any
tips on how best to pack for a long trip, yet travel
light?
Angie in Anaheim

Marcy stared out the window of her private sleeper
car, watched the Texas landscape rumble by in a blur
of thick mesquite. July heat shimmered off the sparse
landscape, while cattle, mindless of the passing train,
grazed languidly under the midday sun. In the distance,
a tall metal windmill twirled like a child's toy in the hot,
summer breeze.

It was like looking at a picture postcard, Marcy
thought, resting her head back against the leather-up-
holstered seat. A deep blue sky. White, puffy clouds on

the distant horizon. The gentle rocking of the railroad car—

The shrill ring of her cell phone.

Fifteen hundred miles between herself and Los Angeles and still it wasn't enough.

Marcy glanced at her wristwatch. Eight-thirty L.A. time. She'd been waiting for the call, knew that her manager would be picking up the message she'd left her right about now: *Helen, this is Marcy. I'm taking the next three weeks off. Please cancel my appointments and have Anna reschedule. Thank you.*

Helen Dunbar would not be a happy camper.

At the insistent ringing, Marcy sighed. *Just get it over with,* she told herself. She knew she'd only prolong the inevitable if she didn't. Pulling the phone out of her navy-blue blazer pocket, she took a deep breath, then pushed the green button.

"Hello, Helen."

"Marcy, honey," Helen said, out of breath. "I got your message, and I'm on my way over to your place. We'll have some coffee and talk."

"There's nothing to talk about." Marcy could picture her manager now, dragging a brush through her cropped red hair, meticulously scanning her day planner and mentally reviewing the day's events, all while she talked on her speakerphone. "And there's no point in coming over. I'm not home."

"What do you mean, you're not home? Where are you?"

Marcy stared out the train window again, noticed a

hawk soaring over the plains. The magnificent sight stirred something in her blood, gave her courage. "I'm gone."

"Gone? What do you mean, gone? You can't be gone," Helen insisted. "We have an editorial meeting at one-thirty today to go over the November issue. We still have to discuss the article on creating a vintage table runner from grandma's linens, plus we need a new and creative way to stuff a turkey."

Marcy had a suggestion, but twenty-six years of manners and etiquette kept her from saying it. "Helen, I told you, I'm gone. I've left Los Angeles. In fact, I've left California."

"You what!"

There was a crash at the other end of the line, then Helen's muttered cursing about coffee on a new suit.

"I told you I needed some time off this month." Marcy pulled the bridal-shower party and wedding invitations from her canvas tote bag and laid them on her lap. "I'm taking it."

"Marcy—" Helen sighed patiently "—honey, we talked about this and agreed this isn't the time. You have an interview with *Stylish Homes* on Wednesday, a meeting on Thursday with the topics coordinator for the premiere of your TV show, then a celebrity charity luncheon at the Ritz-Carlton on Friday."

The thought of endless meetings, long hectic days and hurrying from one event to the next had Marcy instinctively reaching into her purse for an antacid.

She stared at the small, tin pillbox in her palm, tossed

it back into her purse, then reached for her emergency bag of chocolate-covered cherries instead. Sugar might not calm her nerves, she realized, but it would certainly make her feel better. "*We* didn't agree this was a bad time, Helen. You agreed."

"Marcy, we need you," Helen said firmly. "We'll find a better time and then I promise you can—"

"No."

There. She'd said it. She'd actually said *no*. Amazingly, the sky didn't spit lightning and the train hadn't derailed. Helen, on the other hand, had apparently been stunned into silence.

"No?" Helen said quietly after a long moment. "What do you mean, 'no'?"

"I mean no." The breath Marcy had been holding rushed out. "I'm not coming back."

After another long pause, Helen said hesitantly, "Marcy, honey, are you feeling okay?"

"Helen." Marcy struggled to keep her voice even and firm. "Last month I asked you not to schedule the next three weeks for me."

"Sweetie, I didn't think you were really serious, and you never were clear why you wanted so much—"

"And the month before that," Marcy interrupted, "I asked you not to schedule the same three weeks."

"But opportunities keep sprouting up like daisies. How can I not pick them?" Helen's voice softened. "Honey, I know it's been a grueling pace for the past four years. But it's paying off now. *Life With Marcy Pru-*

itt has quadrupled subscriptions, your Life and Home how-to column is syndicated, your last book hit the *Times* nonfiction list and your cable show is starting up in five weeks. You're practically a household name. Sweetie, there are a lot of people counting on you. There'll be time later to take off. I promise. Right now, we need you."

Marcy closed her eyes, felt the gentle rocking of the train underneath her. Maybe she was being selfish. Wanting time to herself, especially when everyone around her was working so hard, too. She didn't want to let anyone down. Didn't want to disappoint them.

And three weeks was a long time.

Marcy looked at the invitations again. Clair Beauchamp had been the only person in Marcy's life who had gone out of her way to make friends with the girl who didn't fit in. A painfully shy girl who wore horn-rimmed glasses and a simple, chin-length haircut.

How ironic it was that what had made her so different when she was growing up, was now her trademark.

Clair had asked her to be her maid of honor and she had said yes. She would *not* change her mind. Tucking the invitations back into her bag, Marcy straightened her shoulders. "I've left extensive notes and the project files with Anna. She knows them as well as I do, probably better. She can sit in for me until I get back."

Helen gasped. "You want your personal assistant to run your company! For God's sake, please tell me you aren't serious."

"I'm very serious. Anna has been with us for two

years now. She's more than capable. You'd know that if you'd give her a chance."

Marcy thought it best not to mention that Anna was also the only person who knew where she was going and why. If Helen had known, Marcy knew she'd never have been able to pull this off.

"Marcy, look, I know she's a good kid." Helen's voice turned frantic. "And I admit, she's a hard worker, too, but—"

"Sorry—" Marcy ran her fingertips back and forth over the cell-phone receiver "—you're breaking up. Gotta go."

"Marcy, no, please, listen to me, there's something you don't know. Something I should have told you. We need to talk in person. Just tell me where you—"

As if I'd fall for that, Marcy thought. Still, afraid she might weaken, she turned her phone off and slipped it back into the pocket of her blazer.

For the past four years, every aspect of her life had been carefully orchestrated. Meetings, TV appearances, more meetings, book tours, radio shows, fund-raising events. More meetings. She still loved her work as much as she always had, but in those four years, she hadn't taken one day for herself that wasn't connected to business in some way.

She was taking it now.

Nervous, but excited, Marcy folded her hands neatly on her lap, then looked out the train window and smiled.

* * *

Evan Carver stood in front of the floor-to-ceiling office window and stared down at the Olympic-size swimming pool. The heat had brought out an interesting array of hotel guests today. On the east side of the pool three elderly men in Hawaiian shirts and cowboy hats played pinochle under the shade of a blue-striped umbrella. On the west side, a very pregnant brunette herded two little blond girls toward the shallow end, away from a group of teenage boys playing an enthusiastic game of volleyball in the deep end of the pool.

And finally, stretched out in lounge chairs on the south side of the pool, lay an entire row of sun-kissed, bikini-clad females.

Evan smiled.

He was single, between construction projects for the next three weeks and staying at a hotel with a convention of swimsuit models.

Life couldn't possibly get any better.

"That's odd, she's not answering her cell phone."

"Hmm?" Evan glanced over his shoulder at his brother's fiancé. She sat at her sleek, cherrywood-and-glass desk, looking more like one of the models at the pool than the owner of an upscale hotel. Her suit jacket was the same deep blue as her eyes, her shoulder-length dark hair almost as black as her knee-length skirt. And while he could appreciate her fine, feminine qualities, Evan already thought of Clair Beauchamp as the sister he'd never had. "Who's not answering her phone?"

Frowning, Clair replaced the receiver in its cradle. "Marcy. All I'm getting is her voice mail."

Oh, right. Marcy. Clair had mentioned her maid of honor was coming into town today for the bridal shower tomorrow, then staying until the wedding. "Maybe she turned it off," he suggested.

"Marcy never turns her phone off."

"Out of range?"

"She shouldn't be." Clair glanced at the crystal-framed clock on her desk, then picked up her phone and pushed redial. "She's taking a train in from L.A. and I'd hoped to reach her before she gets to the station. I told her last night I'd be picking her up, but the editor in chief of *Texas Travel* showed up two days early and wants a tour of the hotel by yours truly."

"I'll pick her up for you," Evan said absently as he watched one of the boys in the pool bounce a wet beach ball on the stomach of a well-endowed blonde. *Smart kid,* Evan thought with a smile.

"I appreciate the offer." Sighing, Clair hung up the phone. "But it's really not necessary. I can send a hotel car."

"It's no problem." To the delight of every male within eyesight, the blonde stood and strolled to the edge of the pool, then with great flourish tossed the ball back. "Besides, didn't I tell Jacob I'd watch over things until he gets back from Philadelphia tomorrow?"

"He's in *Boston*." Clair rose from her desk, then moved beside Evan and stared down at the pool. "I'm glad to see you take the job so seriously," she said, arching one eyebrow. "Maybe I *should* send a hotel car."

Turning from the window, he grinned at her. "What time is her train getting in?"

"Eleven-fifteen," Clair said hesitantly. "Are you sure you don't mind?"

"Just tell me what she looks like and I'm on my way."

Clair moved back to her desk, then picked up a magazine and handed it to him. "Here."

Life With Marcy Pruitt?

The cover of the magazine depicted the familiar brunette with black, horn-rimmed glasses sitting in a field of lavender. Her dress was lavender, as was the bouquet of flowers she held. The title read, "Lavender Fields Forever."

When Clair had said her friend's name was Marcy, it had never occurred to Evan she'd meant *that* Marcy. "Marcy Pruitt is your maid of honor?"

"You've heard of her?"

"Sure." Evan flipped through the articles in the magazine: making place cards from scraps of wallpaper; preparing an elegant dinner in less than thirty minutes; a master-bedroom makeover. "Didn't she write a book?"

Clair nodded. "Two books. *The Easy Life With Marcy Pruitt,* and *The Ultimate Easy Life With Marcy Pruitt.* How-to tips for the average homemaker. She's made quite a name for herself since our college days."

"You can say that again." Evan glanced at the cover again. She was kind of cute, he thought, in a quirky, homespun kind of way. "So is she single?"

Clair plucked the magazine away. "Yes, she's single, but trust me, she's not your type."

He winked at her. "Darlin', every woman's my type."

"Maybe I shouldn't trust you with her," Clair said, arching her eyebrow.

"Me?" Evan placed a hand over his heart. "I'm harmless."

"Of all the things you aren't, Evan Carver, it's harmless." But she smiled as she said it. "Also, we're keeping Marcy's trip here as quiet as possible, so she's going to be traveling incognito. Look for a big, white hat."

"That's incognito?"

"For Marcy it is." Clair pulled a card key out of her jacket pocket. "I'm putting her in the suite across from yours. Think you can behave?"

He gave her a crooked smile. "I'll manage to control myself."

"That's what your brother told me when I first met him." Clair waved her engagement ring at Evan. "Now look at us."

"Don't worry." Evan backed up as if the ring was made of kryptonite. "I'll deliver your friend safe and sound."

And right after he did—Evan glanced out the office window again—he intended to hightail it straight down to the pool.

* * *

At precisely eleven-fifteen, Marcy stepped off the train with the other passengers. It felt as presumptuous as it did ridiculous to wear the oversize, wide-brimmed hat and take off her glasses, but she preferred to err on the side of caution. Though the odds of anyone paying her any mind at the train depot were very slim—which was exactly the reason she'd chosen a train instead flying—she wasn't willing to push her luck or jeopardize her newfound freedom.

Suitcase in hand, she skirted a group of giggling adolescent girls wearing bright blue T-shirts that read CAMP WINNEMONKA. Based on all their energy and excitement, Marcy assumed the girls were on their way to camp, not returning.

Stepping to the side, Marcy set her suitcase down. No sign of Clair, but over the heads of the people hurrying through the station, Marcy couldn't help but notice a dark-haired man who stood several inches above most of the people in the depot. Arms folded over his broad chest, he was watching the passengers who were still pouring off the train.

Heavens.

Marcy knew very little—okay, she knew nothing— about men, but her lack of experience certainly didn't prevent her from appreciating a fine male specimen when she saw one. She *was* on a vacation, after all, so why shouldn't she enjoy the scenery? And anyway, it wasn't as if he'd notice her. Men who looked like that rarely gave her more than a cursory glance.

He stood like a rock in the swiftly moving stream of people. Six foot three, she thought, maybe taller. Rugged was the best word to describe the man, though handsome was certainly a close second. Based on his tanned face and muscled arms, she decided he probably worked outdoors. Square jaw. Strong chin. Large hands. Hair dark and thick, slightly wavy on the ends, skimmed the collar of his black T-shirt.

His eyes—brown?—narrowed slightly, and Marcy followed his gaze, noticed an attractive redhead stepping off the train. The woman smiled at the man and when he smiled back, Marcy felt her pulse skip. If she'd thought him handsome before, well, when he smiled, he was downright lethal.

You are one lucky woman, Marcy thought with a sigh.

But then, surprisingly, after the redhead hesitated a moment, she walked the other way. Curious, Marcy couldn't pull her gaze from the man, wanting to know who he was waiting for.

A slender blonde stepped off the train, definitely a possibility, Marcy thought, but she was greeted by two little girls and a man. Then a pretty brunette wearing a halter top and tight capris appeared. That *had* to be the one, and Marcy glanced back at the man to see his reaction.

"Excuse me."

Marcy jumped at the unexpected touch on her arm. Two women, fortyish, both wearing CAMP WINNEMONKA CAMP COUNSELOR T-shirts, stood beside her.

"Aren't you Marcy Pruitt?" the one with short, curly brown hair asked.

Marcy's stomach dropped. "Me?"

Not exactly a lie, but not an admission, either.

"I told you it wasn't her, Alice." The second woman, a pencil-thin platinum blonde, squinted and leaned in closer. "She doesn't look anything like her."

"Oh, for heaven's sake, Betty Lou." Exasperated, Alice shook her head. "She looks exactly like her. Put your glasses on."

"I don't need my glasses," the blonde argued. "It's not her."

"It is so." Alice looked back at Marcy and smiled. "Your article last month on homemade greeting cards was brilliant. Who would have ever thought to use old buttons and scraps of ribbon like that?"

"She's too skinny," Betty Lou insisted. "And too tall."

Alice rolled her eyes, then put a hand beside her mouth and whispered, "Don't mind Betty Lou. She just likes to be contrary."

"I'm not deaf, you know," Betty Lou harrumphed, then folded her arms and looked Marcy up and down. "I'm telling you it's not her."

"Marcy." Alice sighed. "Will you please tell my friend I'm right?"

If there was one thing that Marcy couldn't do well at all, it was lie. But if she told them the truth, she might as well go back to Los Angeles now. Her throat tightened, and she looked from one woman to the other. "I, well—"

"Darling. There you are."

At the sound of a deep male voice, Marcy turned. And froze.

The man she'd been staring at was now standing directly behind her, smiling down at *her.*

Had he just called her *darling?* Obviously he'd mistaken her for someone else, but before she could correct him, he pulled her into his arms. "I've been looking everywhere for you."

Marcy was too shocked to react, let alone speak. When he dropped his mouth down on hers, her heart slammed against her ribs. He tightened his hold on her and the feel of his chest against hers was like pressing against a brick wall.

Then he slid his mouth across her cheek and whispered in her ear, "Clair sent me."

His warm breath sent shivers up her spine. It took a moment for the words to make sense. *Clair sent me.* "Clair?"

"Clair. You know, your friend."

Wondering if he might have made a mistake, Evan lifted his head and stared at the woman. He supposed she did look a little different from the pictures he'd seen in her magazine. Not only because she wasn't wearing her renowned glasses, but something about her face looked softer, and her eyes, though wide as a frightened doe's, were the color of spring sage. He couldn't see her hair because of the ridiculous hat she had on, but based on the light brown bangs skimming the top of her eyebrows, he was fairly certain he had the right woman.

Evan dropped Marcy back to the ground, then slid an arm around her waist. "Who are your friends, darling?"

"They—" Marcy's voice cracked "—they think I'm Marcy Pruitt."

"Alice does," the blonde said. "I don't."

"Be quiet, Betty Lou." Alice narrowed her eyes and stared at Marcy. "She looks just like her."

"My wife gets that all the time." Evan laughed and yanked Marcy closer. "She can't hardly go anywhere someone doesn't ask for her autograph. Isn't that right, sugarplum?"

"I—ah." Marcy nodded. "It happens sometimes."

"What did I tell you?" Betty Lou crossed her arms and smiled at Alice. "Marcy isn't married. So now who's contrary?"

"I swear you could be her twin sister," Alice said, shaking her head. "It's amazing."

"You'll have to excuse us now, ladies." Evan picked up Marcy's suitcase, then winked at the women. "But I'd like to get my wife home and give her a proper hello, if you don't mind."

Betty Lou grinned and took hold of Alice's arm. "We don't mind at all. Sorry we bothered you."

Even as she was being dragged away, Alice kept staring.

For good measure, Evan squeezed Marcy again, then spun her around and headed in the opposite direction through the thinning crowd. "Well, that was close, though I'm not sure we convinced Alice and she just might—"

"Wait." Marcy yanked on his arm. *"Wait!"*

"What?" He stopped so abruptly she had to grab her hat to keep it from flying off her head.

"Who *are* you?"

"Evan." He glanced back to see if anyone was watching them, then pulled her around a corner and into a hallway that led to a lost-baggage claim office. "Evan Carver."

"Carver?" Her forehead furrowed, then lifted with recognition. "Jacob's brother?"

"The one and only." He grinned at her. "Clair tried to call your cell phone to give you a heads up, but you didn't answer."

"I turned it off." Nibbling her bottom lip, she studied him carefully.

"Clair had an unexpected meeting. If you're nervous about me driving you back to the Four Winds, you can call Clair's office and—"

"I'm not nervous." She pulled her arm away and straightened her shoulders. "You just caught me off guard. It's not every day a strange man kisses me and calls me his sugarplum."

"Sorry 'bout that." He grinned at her. "Clair told me you wanted to keep your trip quiet. When I saw those two women with you, I was trying to help."

"Actually, you did help," she said, then shoved her

hands into the pockets of her blazer. "I—I'm sorry. I don't mean to appear ungrateful."

The flush on the woman's cheeks brightened her face and made the green in her eyes appear darker. He realized he'd surprised her, but shoot, that little peck could hardly be considered a kiss.

She *had* tasted good, though, now that he thought about it. Like cherry—and chocolate, too. And her lips had been amazingly soft.

When a man and woman walked around the corner and glanced at Marcy, Evan moved in closer to shield her from their view. He waited until they moved past, then straightened.

"Shall we get the rest of your luggage?" he asked.

She glanced at the bag he already held. "That's all I have."

He furrowed his forehead. "You've only got one suitcase for three weeks?"

"Packing is really about making decisions on what you really do or don't need and sticking to a list." She shifted the canvas tote higher on her shoulder. "Lightweight garments that mix and match and don't wrinkle, two pairs of shoes, one pair of sandals, travel toiletries and a hat."

"Sounds like you wrote the book."

"Just a short article in last month's travel section."

"Really." Apparently, she hadn't realized he'd been teasing her. It seemed that Miss Marcy Pruitt was wound a little tight. "So have you written any articles on how to escape from a crowded train station without being seen?"

"That's scheduled for the January issue. I'm still researching that one."

For a split second, he thought she was being serious, but then he saw the corner of her mouth twitch. So the woman did have a sense of humor, after all. That was good, especially since he'd be spending the next thirty-five minutes in the car with her.

Grinning, he took her arm. "Ready to make a run for it, Miss Pruitt?"

"Ready when you are, Mr. Carver." She pulled her hat lower, then slipped her glasses back on. "Lead the way."

Two

Dear Marcy,
I am one of your biggest fans. (I tried your recipe for chocolate cake in the February issue and loved it!) In your interviews, you say you are shy, but on television, you always appear so confident and relaxed. What is your secret?
Linda from Kansas City

Suitcase in the trunk and hat folded in her canvas tote, Marcy watched Evan pull out of the train station and accelerate the shiny black luxury sedan smoothly onto the open highway. She breathed in the scent of new car, then slid her hand over the butter-soft leather seat. A glance at the digital readout on the rearview mirror told her that the interior of the sedan was a comfortable seventy-four degrees, even though the temperature outside was a scorching one hundred.

Somehow the polished, elegant car didn't quite suit

the man, she thought. With his large, callused hands, broad shoulders and faded blue jeans, she could easily picture Clair's future brother-in-law behind the wheel of a pickup or a Jeep or even a Hummer. Something masculine and tough that could drive off the road and splash through mud, rumble over huge boulders or tear through thick terrain.

"Something wrong?" Evan asked.

"Wrong?" She looked at him, realized that she had leaned forward to run her fingers over the grain of the mahogany dashboard. Self-conscious, she snatched her hand away and straightened. Touching things, needing to know the feel and texture or analyze how it was made had become so second nature to her, she rarely knew when she was doing it.

"No, nothing's wrong." She folded her hands in her lap. "I was just admiring your car."

"Not mine, the hotel's," he said, turning his attention back to the road. "For some strange reason, Clair thought you'd be more comfortable in this than my pickup. You women from California have something against trucks?"

"No, of course not. I wouldn't have minded at all. And I'm not really from California. I was actually born in Burbridge, Ohio, it's just a small town outside of— oh." She saw one corner of his mouth curve. "You're kidding."

He grinned. "Sorry. Couldn't resist. Actually, this car's fun to drive. Even at ninety, she still purrs like a kitten."

Ninety? Marcy swallowed hard. She didn't think she'd ever gotten her little Camry over sixty-five. When Evan suddenly zipped into the left lane to pass a truck and horse trailer, she grabbed onto the seat belt. He sped up, then zipped back into the right lane and slowed down again.

Good heavens! The man certainly liked to drive fast.

It took a moment for her stomach to slide back down from her throat.

"Music?"

"What?" She loosened her grip on the seat belt. "Oh, sure. Whatever you like."

He settled on a Rolling Stones song, and while Mick Jagger sang about moving it to the left and then the right, Marcy watched the passing countryside. The open space amazed her. Big, white farmhouses and tall, red barns. Pastures, horses and cows. A man riding a large green tractor in a field waved as they drove by. They were as blissfully far from the city as a person could get.

"Feels good to play hookey, doesn't it?"

Turning, she looked back at Evan, realized he'd been watching her. He had those kind of eyes. Dark and intense, not just intelligent, but…observant. Eyes that didn't just look *at* you like most people's, but eyes that looked *inside.* Suddenly the car felt smaller, the space between them shorter. "Hookey?"

"You know, sneaking away from work, hiding out from all those exciting meetings."

"Oh. Right." She looked back at the road ahead of them, watched the heat curling up off the asphalt. "I don't think it's quite sunk in just yet. I keep expecting Helen to jump up out of the back seat or suddenly drive alongside of us."

"Helen?"

"My manager. She's not very happy with me right now."

"Because you're taking a few days off?" Evan asked. When he sped up and passed a semi-truck, Marcy held her breath.

"Three weeks is a lot more than a few days." She slowly released her breath when they were back in their own lane again. "To Helen, that's a lifetime. On top of that, I wouldn't tell her where I was going. It will drive her crazy."

"It's good to drive people crazy once in a while. Keeps them on their toes."

Marcy imagined that Evan kept lots of people on their toes, most of them female. Since that kiss he'd given her at the bus station, she'd been more than a little off balance.

Not that she considered it a real *kiss,* in a manwoman sense of the word. But nevertheless, as ridiculous as it was, the unexpected brush of his lips on hers had made it difficult for her to concentrate on anything else.

Good grief, she *really* needed to start dating more. Well, actually, she just needed to start dating, period. Working 24/7 these past four years had definitely taken its toll on her personal life. The fact was, she had no per-

sonal life. And now that she'd decided to get one, conse-
quences be damned, she wasn't sure what to do with it.

What she did know, was that it was time to stop acting like a timid child. In new situations, she had always
been a little nervous. Even now, every time she spoke in
public or did guest spots on TV, her knees shook. And
just thinking about her upcoming television show sent a
shot of adrenaline rushing through the pit of her stomach.

The only way she'd survived these past four years in
the limelight were the techniques she'd learned to calm
her nerves. Looking over at Evan, it seemed as if there
was no time like the present to apply a few of those techniques—although the one about seeing your audience
naked didn't seem like the best one to use at the moment.

Breathe. Slowly…deeply, release. Three times.

Visualize my peaceful place. Toes in the sand, on an
empty beach.

Concentrate. Think about what needs to be done and
how to do it.

"You okay over there?" Evan asked.

"Fine." Calmer now, she slowly released her third
breath and looked at Evan. "Clair told me you own a
construction company. What do you build?"

"Custom homes, mostly." He turned off the highway
onto a picturesque, tree-lined road and slowed the car's
speed. "I buy ten- to fifteen-acre parcels around the
state and build five to seven houses on them."

"Why so few?" In L.A., Marcy thought, there would probably be closer to thirty or forty houses on that amount of land.

"Because I believe in space, for one thing," Evan said. "For another, if I'm in one place or with the same project for more than a few months, I get antsy."

"Antsy to get back home?"

He shook his head. "Antsy to move on. My 'home' is a twenty-eight-foot fifth wheel that goes with me."

"You build houses, but you live in a trailer?" she said in amazement.

"I'm not home enough to mow lawns or clean gutters," he said with a shrug. "What about you? What kind of house does Marcy Pruitt live in? Wait, let me guess—country cottage with a white picket fence and rose gardens?"

"More like Canyon Cottage, picket fence and bare dirt." She'd fallen in love the minute she'd laid eyes on the house nestled beside a creek off the Malibu coast. "I just moved in six months ago and it still needs a lot of work."

"Will it be in 'Marcy's Makeover' column?"

Surprised, she looked at him. Marcy's Makeover was the most popular monthly feature article in her magazine. Sometimes they took a single room in a house, sometimes they took an entire house, then gave it a new look. "You've read my magazine?"

"I glanced through a copy in Clair's office. The one where you're sitting in a field of lavender."

"Oh." She always felt uncomfortable about being on the cover, but her publisher insisted she appear on at least four of the twelve monthly issues. "I've never done a makeover on a trailer. How about you let me do one on yours?"

He shot her a you've-got-to-be-kidding-me look.

"I promise I won't use pink or feathers," she reassured him, but could have sworn he paled at the very thought.

"Thanks, but no thanks. Here we are, Miss Pruitt." He passed a gas station connected to a motor lodge and café, then turned left off the two-lane road. "Welcome to Wolf River."

Small-town America was alive and well, Marcy noted as they drove down Main Street. The storefronts were brick and shiny glass, the stores themselves offered a variety of just about anything a person might need, including a wide range of restaurants. Shoppers strolled along freshly swept sidewalks, in no apparent hurry to get wherever it was they were going.

Clearly, the pace was slower here and the traffic was light. By Los Angeles standards, she thought, it was deserted. There were more pickup trucks than any other vehicle on the streets, and only two stoplights that she could see, but when they drove past a side street, she spotted a multiplex theater and two popular fast-food chains. Based on the construction taking place off the main drive into town, it appeared that Wolf River was growing by leaps and bounds.

But the newest and one of the largest additions to the town, Marcy knew, was the Four Winds Hotel. It sat at the east end of town—not especially large by city standards, but for Wolf River, the twelve-story hotel stood like a skyscraper. Under a wide, spreading portico, beside a pair of tall, glass entry doors, a trio of life-size bronze horses seemed to be racing through a water fountain. Huge brass planters of white and purple petunias, cooled by an overhead mist system, lined the curb where uniformed bellmen greeted guests and handled luggage.

"It's beautiful," she murmured.

The first time he'd seen it, the elegance of the Four Winds had surprised him, too, especially compared to the size of Wolf River. "Wait till you see the inside. It'll knock your socks off."

He pulled the car around to a side entrance with an iron gate and pressed a remote clipped to the visor. The gate opened and he drove through, then parked in an underground area reserved for the hotel guests staying on the top floor.

"There's a private elevator that will take us to the suites." He slid out of the front seat and came around to open Marcy's door. "I'd take you on a tour, but this is Clair's baby and I have the feeling she'd like the honors."

"I can't wait to see it." She followed him to the elevator after he plucked her suitcase out of the trunk. "It's just so hard to believe that only a few months ago she was still in Charleston and was going to marry Oliver and—" She stopped and bit her lip. "Sorry. I shouldn't have mentioned that."

"It's hardly a secret, Marcy." Evan held the elevator door open. A Beatles' instrumental, "Love Me Do," played softly on the overhead speakers. "Did you know him?"

"I met him a few times when he came to see Clair at Radcliffe, but there were no warm fuzzies between us. He didn't approve of Clair's friendship with me."

Frowning, Evan pushed the button for the top floor. "What do you mean, 'he didn't approve'?"

"To help pay my way through school, I not only did some light housekeeping, I started catering for the faculty parties," she said. "One time I overheard Oliver tell Clair it didn't look good for her to be roommates with the girl who cleaned houses and prepared food for the teachers."

"What an ass," Evan muttered under his breath.

Marcy smiled. "I think it was the only time I ever saw Clair angry. She told him if he couldn't be nice to me, then she couldn't marry him. After that, Oliver was so polite and so friendly every time he saw me, it was all I could do not to laugh. I know it killed him, which only made me want to laugh all the more."

"Sounds like we're both happy she didn't marry the jerk," Evan said.

The elevator doors slid open silently and they stepped into a small lobby with a polished black-marble floor and sparkling crystal chandelier. Against one wall sat a

cranberry-colored suede sofa and two tapestry armchairs, and against the opposite wall was an antique
sideboard with coffee-and-tea service, plus fresh-baked
goods.

Her suite was at the end of the hall, and when Evan
opened the door for her, the scent of flowers drifted
from the room. On the entry table, a huge bouquet of
white roses filled a cut-crystal vase.

"Oh, they're beautiful." Marcy rushed to the roses
and stuck her nose in them.

There it was again, Evan thought as he watched her
breathe in the scent of the flowers. That uninhibited rush
of excitement, the softening of her voice. He liked this
side of Marcy Pruitt, he decided as he watched her slide
the tips of her long, slender fingers over the rose petals.

Her skin had felt like that, he remembered. And her lips.

Realizing his thoughts were taking him in an odd direction, he cleared his throat. "Bedroom?"

"Excuse me?" Her head swung around.

"Your suitcase. Shall I put it in the bedroom?"

"Oh. No, thank you." She turned from the flowers
and moved toward him, her hand outstretched. "I'll take
it from here. You've already done more than enough and
I really—"

She stopped suddenly and sniffed the air. Her eyes
widened. "Hamburgers," she said, her voice a bit
breathless.

"What?"

"Hamburgers," she repeated, then spun on the heels

of her navy-blue flats and hurried into the living area of the suite.

Intrigued, he followed her, watched her lift a shiny silver lid off a tray sitting on a food cart. "Oh, look at this," she said with a laugh.

Evan set the suitcase down and moved beside Marcy. "Yep. Hamburgers, all right."

A pile of hamburgers, actually. Surrounded by a moat of thin, tiny French fries. Around the outside edges were little silver bowls of condiments, everything from ketchup to pickles to chili and cheese.

"Now that's room service," he said with admiration. "So what gives?"

"This is Clair's way of saying hello," Marcy said, then laughed again when she lifted the lid off a second plate that contained a huge slice of dark chocolate cake, a small, napkin-lined basket of candy bars and a can of spray whipped cream chilling in a crystal bowl of ice. "In college, Clair was a health nut and always on a diet of some kind, even though she never needed to be. But I, on the other hand, was a food junkie. What you're looking at here was my favorite four-course meal."

"My kind of woman." Evan stared in awe at the feast on the table. "Maybe we should get married."

"I'm a little busy right now." Smiling, she dipped her finger in the chocolate icing. "Ask me again later." Evan swallowed the sudden lump in his throat when Marcy licked the chocolate icing off her finger, then closed her eyes on a soft moan.

"Would you like to join me?" she asked, opening her eyes.

He had to wait a moment for his pulse to steady, reminding himself they were talking about food here and nothing else. There had to be something seriously wrong with his hormones, he decided, mentally shaking his head, and blamed the unexpected jolt of lust on the mouthwatering display of food.

Smiling, he politely pulled a chair out for her and gestured for her to sit. "I thought you'd never ask."

Seated at the table, her napkin neatly on her lap, Marcy watched in fascination while Evan methodically assembled his hamburger. For her own, she'd gone with a little mayonnaise, lettuce and a tomato, while the only condiments Evan seemed to have bypassed were the mustard and pickles.

Everything about the man seemed bigger than life, she thought. His size, his personality, his looks.

And definitely his masculinity.

She decided conversation would distract her from thinking so much. "Clair told me you and Jacob were raised in New Jersey. What brought you to Texas?"

He reached for the mustard and dropped a dollop on his open bun. "U.T."

"University of Texas?"

"Six years." He gave her a goofy grin. "Got me a master's in science."

She raised an eyebrow at that and handed him the pickles. "But you ended up in construction."

"I hated working indoors. Thanks." He took the pickles and spread a layer on his bun. "I spent a summer as a carpenter and found out I not only liked working with my hands, I was good at it."

She studied his hands now as he finished building his mansion of a hamburger. They were large and had a rough appearance. His fingers were long, his nails cut short. It was easy to picture him holding a hammer or a saw, but when her imagination took her further and she pictured him without a shirt, his tanned face and broad chest covered with sweat, she quickly blinked the image out of her mind.

Turning her attention back to his hamburger, she watched him take a bite of his creation, then frown.

"Something wrong?" she asked.

He looked at the condiment bowls. "Needs something."

"More ketchup?"

"Amateur." He dumped a few French fries on his burger and took another bite. "Much better."

"French fries on your hamburger?" She stared at him in amazement. "Really?"

"Bet that's not in any of your recipes." He held out his hamburger to her. "Try it."

"No thanks." Admittedly, she *was* curious, but taking a bite of his food seemed like such a personal thing to do. "I'm fine."

"One little bite." He waved it under her nose. "Come on, sugarplum. I dare you."

Sugarplum. She frowned at him. Well, a dare *was* a dare, she thought. And it *did* smell good. She leaned forward and nipped off a tiny bite.

"You call that a bite?" He shook his head. "Come on, show me the stuff Marcy Pruitt's made of."

With a sigh, she put her hands on his, then took a healthy sample of his concoction. Out of habit, she closed her eyes and focused on identifying every taste.

"Well?" he asked.

"Sweet." She licked her lips. "Definitely salty." She chewed slowly, letting her taste buds explore. "Interesting."

Somewhere between Marcy's murmur of "sweet" and "salty," Evan's mouth turned dry as a midsummer's creek. With her eyes closed and her mouth slightly pursed, Marcy's face had taken on an appearance of sheer pleasure and absolute delight. But it was the slow slide of her tongue over her lips that had pushed him over the line of just messing around to something completely different.

He couldn't take his eyes off her lips.

She had the most amazing mouth. Wide, full, with corners turned upward. When the tip of her tongue swept over her bottom lip again, he felt a jolt of pure, unadulterated lust.

This was Marcy Pruitt, for crying out loud, he told himself. And Clair's friend, on top of it. He had no business thinking what he was thinking.

When she made a small sound of pleasure deep in

her throat, sweat broke out on his forehead. He yanked the hamburger back, then hunkered down in his chair and took a bite, trying not to think about the fact that her mouth had just touched the very spot he'd bite off.

Marcy opened her eyes and smiled. "I like it. Is it your secret recipe, or can I use it in my magazine?"

"It's all yours," he said as casually as he could muster. "Do whatever you like with it."

Her eyes narrowed thoughtfully. "I don't think I've done an article on hamburgers yet. It might be interesting."

He thought it would be a pretty short article. What was there to know? Meat, bun, lots of condiments.

"Knock, knock." Clair stuck her head in the door. "Anybody home?"

Evan watched Marcy's face light up when she saw Clair, who was already hurrying across the room, her arms spread. The women hugged each other and laughed.

"Did Evan find you all right?" Clair's words rushed out. "I guess he did, since you're here. Oh, I've missed you so much!"

Sniffing, Marcy pulled a tissue out of her pocket and dabbed at her eyes. "You look absolutely radiant. Being in love and buying a hotel obviously agrees with you."

"It does. And you—" Clair wiped at her own eyes. "Your own magazine and books and a syndicated column. It makes my head spin."

"I have a great group of people I work with," Marcy said. "I couldn't do any of it without them."

"You always were modest." Clair hugged her again. "But that's one of the reasons I love you. Oh, I can't wait for Jacob to meet you. He'll be back in town tomorrow morning, so you and I are having a slumber party tonight."

"Can I come, too?" Evan asked hopefully.

"Not a chance." Clair moved to Evan and kissed his cheek. "But thank you for picking Marcy up. Did you find her all right?"

"Big white hat." He grinned at Marcy. "And a crowd of adoring fans."

"Two is hardly a crowd," Marcy said, shaking her head. "And Evan managed to throw them off."

"Really?" Clair arched an eyebrow and looked at Evan. "How did you do that?"

He grinned at Marcy, who blushed. "I kissed her and said she was my wife."

Clair gasped. "You did what?"

"I had to do something," he said. "Alice and Betty Lou were closing in."

"Alice and Betty Lou?" Confused, Clair narrowed her eyes.

"Alice, actually. Betty Lou didn't think our girl here looked anything like Marcy Pruitt."

Jaw slack, Clair looked at Marcy. "He's kidding, right?"

"Actually, he's telling the truth," Marcy said. "Betty Lou thought I was too skinny and too tall to be Marcy Pruitt."

Dumbfounded, Clair looked from Evan to Marcy,

then just laughed and hugged Marcy again. "Sounds like we have a lot to catch up on. I've cleared my afternoon schedule so we can start right now."

"I can take a hint." Evan stood. "You guys have fun."

Marcy held out her hand. "Thank you for picking me up."

"No problem." Smiling, he took her fingers in his. "Anytime you need a ride or a husband, just let me know."

Her blush deepened. "I'll do that."

"So you want to tell me what happened?" Clair looked at Marcy after Evan closed the door behind him.

"What do you mean?"

"Did he really kiss you?"

"Only with the best of intentions," Marcy said, annoyed when the memory of that kiss made her lips tingle. "I assure you, he was much more interested in these hamburgers than me, which I haven't even thanked you for yet. A stroke of genius on your part, Miss Beauchamp."

"The kitchen thought it a little odd when I put the order in," Clair said with a grin. "But you've barely eaten anything. Sit down and eat while I talk your ear off about Jacob."

The love shining in Clair's eyes made Marcy's chest tighten. "He must be special. You never glowed when you were with Oliver."

"I came so close to making the worst mistake of my life." Pulling her pumps off, Clair sat cross-legged on the chair Evan had occupied. "If Jacob hadn't found me, I'd be Mrs. Oliver Hollingsworth right now."

When Marcy reached for a handful of fries and placed them neatly on her hamburger, Clair gave her a questioning glance. Marcy smiled. "Evan's idea."

"Watch out for any ideas from Evan," Clair warned. "He's got way too many."

"That's the last thing I need to worry about," she said. "Men don't look at me that way."

"You're a beautiful woman, Marcy," Clair said firmly. "If you weren't hiding behind big glasses and a haircut that covers most of your face, you'd be fighting off the men."

The very thought made her laugh. "I'm not hiding. This is just who I am. And even if I wanted to change, I really couldn't. People expect me to look and behave a certain way."

Clair sighed and shook her head. "Honey, if I can learn not to worry about people's expectations, then anybody can. There's a wild woman inside Marcy Pruitt," Clair said with a grin. "She's just waiting for you to let her loose."

A wild woman! Marcy shook her head at Clair's foolishness. But it felt good to be silly, she thought, to relax and laugh with an old friend.

"Enough about me," she said, still chuckling. "We were talking about you and Jacob, remember? Now start from the very beginning and don't leave out one single detail."

Three

Dear Marcy,
My fiancé and I are planning a summer wedding. We would like to have the ceremony outdoors, but worry about problems with the weather. What is your opinion?
Tiffany and Chris in Woodland Hills

The details of Clair's story, Marcy soon found out, were fascinating.

It would make an incredible movie. A car crash on an icy road outside a small town. A father and mother killed, but their three children survive: two boys, seven and nine, one little girl, barely three. A greedy, hate-driven uncle who separates the children and pays a corrupt lawyer to illegally adopt the children out, none of them knowing their siblings are alive. Twenty-three years later, a cousin learns the truth and hires a private

investigator to find the children and reunite the family.
Jacob was the private investigator. Clair was the little girl.

"And you found all this out two days before your
wedding?" Marcy asked, still trying to absorb the enormity of Clair's story.

"I was having a last-minute fitting on my wedding
dress," Clair said. "Jacob followed me when I came out
of the shop. He told me that I had been born in Wolf
River County, Texas, that my real name—my birth
name—was Elizabeth Marie Blackhawk, and that I had
two older brothers, Rand and Seth."

They'd settled comfortably on the white sectional
sofa in the living room of the suite. Room service had
come and gone with a basket of blueberry scones and
a pot of fragrant peppermint tea. With their shoes off
and their feet tucked under their legs, Marcy listened
while Clair continued.

"It was so absurd, I didn't believe him at first. I thought
he was a crazy person, or he'd made a huge mistake. How
could my parents have lied to me like that?" Clair poured
two cups of tea and handed one to Marcy. "But he had
proof. Pictures, newspaper articles of the accident. A
birth certificate. Even copies of the adoption papers
signed by my parents." Clair stared at the steam rising off
her tea. "It explained so much. I had parents who loved
me, money, the best education. And yet I always had such
a strong sense that something was missing in my life.
That something wasn't quite right and I just didn't fit in."

Now *that* was a feeling Marcy could relate to. After

her own parents had died and she'd gone to live with her Aunt Hattie, Marcy had been the proverbial square peg. Her aunt, an eccentric widow with no children of her own, had never quite known what to do with her eight-year-old niece. On an intellectual level, Marcy understood why she was different from the other kids, but that certainly didn't make it any less painful. Didn't make it any less difficult.

But sitting here with Clair, Marcy thought, sharing tea and scones, this was easy. It didn't matter that they hadn't seen each other in a year or that they didn't even speak that often. The time dissolved and there was only then and only now.

"I'm sorry I wasn't there for you when all this happened," Marcy said with a sigh. "I've spent the past four years listening to other people tell me where to be and what to do for the good of my career. I'm finally learning how to say no."

"Good for you. Here's to that one little, but extremely powerful word." Clair tapped her cup lightly against Marcy's. "But it really was for the best you couldn't make it. I would have felt awful if you'd canceled a European book tour for my wedding, only to watch me run out of the church while the bridal march was playing."

"I actually do wish I could have been there to see that," Marcy said. "I can't imagine myself doing anything that brave."

Clair shook her head. "It certainly didn't feel brave at the time. But when I saw Jacob standing at the back of church and our eyes met, I knew I couldn't marry Oliver and live a lie. I walked right up to Jacob and asked him for a ride, and I haven't looked back since." Tears filled Clair's eyes. "For the first time in my life, everything feels right. Jacob, meeting my brothers, buying the Four Winds. And now having you here. Life is perfect."

"Don't make me cry, too." Swallowing back the thickness in her throat, Marcy squeezed Clair's hand. "I'm just so happy that you're happy. Jacob is lucky to have you."

"I'm the lucky one," Clair said, beaming. "But enough about me and Jacob for now. I want to hear about your magazine. And tell me—" Clair leaned closer "—do you really write all the answers to the questions in your lifestyle advice column yourself?"

Laughing, Marcy sipped her tea and settled back on the sofa. "Every last one."

It was a good morning for a swim. Air still fresh and slightly crisp, and at six-thirty, most of the hotel guests were still sleeping or in their rooms sipping their first cup of coffee. Except for the soft hum of the pool filter and the distant flutter of birds in a nearby tree, it was stone quiet.

Peeling his T-shirt off, Evan dove into the deep end and cut smoothly through the cool water. It seemed like a million years ago he'd been on the swim team in high school, even though it had only been—what? Twelve years. Damn. That *was* a million years ago.

He finished his first lap and moved into his second. He enjoyed the invigorating pump of blood through his system, fell easily into a rhythm and held it.

Out of habit, he always woke early. Working in construction, a man had to start his day at the crack of dawn to get a jump on the hot Texas sun. He enjoyed every aspect of his work, from the design element to swinging a hammer to digging trenches. He loved to start with nothing but a piece of dusty, weed-congested dirt, then build something that would stand the test of time. He'd finished up his last project just last week and already he was impatient for something to keep his hands and mind occupied.

Women, of course, were always his first choice to fill his spare time. While he was on a job, his day started too early and ended too late to give the opposite sex the attention they required. Which meant that he had a lot of time to make up for when he wasn't working.

Last night, he'd met a couple of the swimsuit models, Mandy and Suzanne, in the lounge downstairs. They'd invited him to a party they were throwing tonight in their suite, but with the bridal party for Jacob and Clair, he'd had to turn the women down.

Personally, he didn't think men belonged at a bridal shower, or anywhere near one, for that matter. But Clair had insisted that the party was for the bride *and* the groom, and that it was his sibling responsibility to attend.

With Jacob settling down, Evan figured his greatest sibling responsibility was to pick up the slack with all the single women, starting with Mandy and Suzanne. But since neither Clair nor Jacob would see it that way, he supposed the models would just have to party tonight without him.

A damn shame, he thought.

But Mandy and Suzanne weren't the only women on his mind this morning, Evan realized as he pushed off the side of the pool for his fourth lap. Strangely enough, he'd also been thinking about Marcy.

Before yesterday, he'd never given much thought to the woman one way or the other. Now that he'd met her, it seemed he couldn't quite get her out of his mind.

That funny, oversize hat. Her startled look when he'd kissed her at the train depot. The almost sexual manner in which she'd touched and smelled the roses Clair had sent. The expression of pure pleasure on her face when she'd tasted his hamburger.

He'd wanted to taste her lips at that moment. Wanted to lick the salty sweetness. He was thankful that Clair had walked in, or he just might have. He could only imagine he would have scared Marcy to death if he actually *had* kissed her. Not like the little peck he'd given her at the depot, but a real kiss.

I might still kiss her, he thought. A slow and easy kiss, nothing too suggestive. He didn't want to give her the wrong idea or scare her. He just wanted a little taste, that's all. Enough to satisfy his curiosity.

Or maybe he just needed another fifteen laps in the pool. Some physical exertion to burn up the excess energy he always had when he wasn't working. But then he thought about how soft Marcy's lips were, how smooth her skin had looked.

Better make it twenty-five, he told himself and pushed off the side of the pool again.

If Marcy had thought the outside of the Four Winds Hotel elegant, then the only word for the downstairs lobby was exquisite. Freshly polished black Italian-marble floors shone under huge iron-and-elk-horn chandeliers. Strategically placed antique European tables blended with rugged wood beams and adobe walls. In the main lobby, a giant bouquet of sunflowers and purple delphiniums graced an oval glass table. Sofas and easy chairs in shades of rich browns and deep reds invited guests to relax while strains of classical music mingled with the sound of water bubbling from a stone-wall fountain.

Casual sophistication, Marcy decided, following Clair on her early-morning round of the hotel. They'd already toured the well-equipped gym and spa, a lovely clothes boutique, a luxurious beauty salon and a spotless, state-of-the art kitchen that serviced the two hotel restaurants. From wrapped chocolate mints to fresh coffee service by the registration desk, it appeared that no detail had been overlooked.

"You must be exhausted," Clair said when Marcy stopped to examine a bronze statue of a horse on a side table. "All that traveling, then I keep you up all night talking your ear off."

"I seem to recall doing my fair share of talking." The bronze was wonderful, by an artist she'd never heard of before. Marcy filed the name away. "And one o'clock is hardly all night."

"It is when you get up at five-thirty." Clair waved to a pretty brunette behind the registration desk. "And what good is a vacation if you can't sleep in?"

It was only six-thirty now, and except for staff, the hotel lobby was empty. It seemed to Marcy that it was the best time to see the hotel without needing to wear a hat. "I couldn't sleep anyway," she said truthfully. "I was too anxious to see your hotel. I absolutely love what you've done."

"My cousin Lucas designed and built the hotel as a tourist and conference center." Clair led Marcy down a hallway past the lobby elevators. "I just did some remodeling when I bought it from him. Olivia Cameron is the interior designer I've been working with for the past few months. She owns an antique store in town."

"I'd love to meet her," Marcy said. "Our upcoming January issue is going to be dedicated to small-town antique stores. Maybe we can include her."

"She'll be at the party tonight, you can meet her then." Clair paused to stare at a vase of flowers sitting on a granite-topped rosewood table. She turned the vase a centimeter, then moved on. "I want to show you my office, then we'll have breakfast."

Marcy followed Clair through double glass doors

that led back to the private lobby and set of elevators reserved for the executive staff and guests staying in the suites. The elevator doors opened and a man wearing a charcoal suit and silver tie stepped out. He was tall, his thick, dark hair short and neat. When he smiled at Clair, the corners of his startling deep blue eyes crinkled. "Miss Beauchamp." He nodded, then turned his gaze on Marcy. "Miss Pruitt. Welcome to the Four Winds."

"Sam Prescott is my general manager," Clair explained. "I told him you'd be staying with us. You can trust him and all the staff here to be discreet."

"A pleasure, Mr. Prescott."

"Sam," he said, taking the hand she offered. "And the pleasure is mine. If there's anything at all I can do to make your stay with us more comfortable, please don't hesitate to let me know."

"Thank you."

"Ladies." Sam held the elevator door open. "Enjoy your day."

After the elevator door closed again, Marcy looked at Clair and blurted out, "Good heavens, are *all* the men in this town handsome?"

Laughing, Clair pushed the third-floor button. "Wait till you meet my cousin and brothers. If they weren't taken, I'd fix you up."

Evan's not taken.

The thought popped into her head before Marcy could stop it, and she breathed a silent sigh of relief that she hadn't said it out loud.

She'd thought about him last night, just before she fell asleep. It embarrassed her a little to think about it now in the light of day. She'd never been one to overly engage in sexual fantasies. Not because she was a prude, but simply because she'd never met a man whom she'd been so attracted to, or a man who had...stimulated that line of thinking.

But lying in that big bed alone, on the soft sheets and firm mattress, she'd wondered what it would be like if he'd been there with her. Wondered what his muscles would feel like under her hands. What his skin would feel like. How it would taste.

That thought made her stomach flutter and her pulse quicken.

"You okay?" Clair held the elevator doors open, waiting for Marcy to step off.

"What? Oh, yes. Fine." Flustered, she hurried off the elevator. "It's just that I'm still in awe this is all yours."

"Me, too." Clair smiled and headed down the hallway. The carpet was plush royal-blue, the paintings on the walls nineteenth-century western artists. Clair opened a tall, pale oak door. "I couldn't think of a better way to start a new life and at the same time invest the inheritance I received from the Blackhawk estate. After you."

"Oh, Clair, I love this," Marcy said when she stepped inside the office. The room had a slightly more traditional look to it, with just a touch of vintage china and crystal ware on the mahogany bookshelves and desk. "It's wonderful."

"It's still a work in progress, but I'm getting there." Clair stepped to her desk and picked up the phone. "Just let me check my messages and we'll go down and eat."

Marcy moved to the floor-to-ceiling windows and stared down at the pool, then slipped off her glasses to watch a lone swimmer cut through the light fog rising off the water. A man, she realized. His strokes were sure and even and when he reached the pool's edge, he rose up a moment.

Marcy's pulse jumped.

It was Evan.

When he kicked off the edge again to continue another lap, she couldn't take her eyes off him. He moved across the pool in what seemed like an effortless burst of power, muscles rippling as he sliced through the water. Lord, he was a sight to behold! Long legs. Hard, wet body. It was enough to take a woman's breath away.

He moved across the pool again, paused, then placed his hands on the deck and swung himself out of the water. Water glistened on his tanned skin, and she couldn't help but admire the curves and angles of solid muscle and his flat, hard stomach. He dragged a hand through his wet hair, then reached for a towel. His navy-blue swim trunks clung to his body.

She leaned closer to the window, wishing she had a pair of binoculars.

"Ready?" Clair asked, hanging up the phone.

"What?" Marcy turned quickly on knees that felt loose. "Oh, sure."

But even as she walked away, even as she forced the image of Evan's half-naked, wet body from her mind, she heard a little voice whisper, *"Are you?"*

After he dressed, it took Evan a while to track Clair and Marcy down to a large, private patio off the main ballroom where they were having breakfast outdoors. Leaning against the doorjamb, he watched them drinking coffee and nibbling on pastries.

Women fascinated him. They were impossible to predict. Usually fickle. God knew he'd given up trying to understand them years ago. Now he simply enjoyed them. The way they moved, the way they smelled.

All those wonderful curves.

He looked at Marcy, tried to visualize her curves under the pink long-sleeved shirt and tailored slacks she had on. He knew she was slender, but she seemed to go out of her way to cover up the details.

Which only made him wonder all the more.

She was laughing at something Clair said, and the sound had an almost musical quality to it. He smiled, watched her lean close to Clair and whisper something, then they both laughed.

He knew he should walk away. Leave them to share their secrets and catch up on lost time.

But hey, they'd had all night to do that, hadn't they?

He pushed away from the doorjamb and moved across the patio. "Morning, ladies."

Marcy's smile froze when she looked up and met his gaze. It was almost visible, the defensive shield she raised with strangers. He wasn't certain if she was aware of her own self-defense system, but he certainly understood why she did it. It had to be a bitch, living her life like a mannequin in a store window. She probably couldn't even go out to eat without it being reported the next day what restaurant she'd gone to, who she'd been with, what she'd eaten.

I sure as hell couldn't live like that, Evan thought. But since he didn't have to, he had no reason to be concerned about it, either.

"Evan." Turning, Clair smiled at him. "Come join us."

"I don't want to intrude."

"Yes, you do." Clair poured him a cup of coffee. "You're bored to death with Jacob gone. Admit it."

"I'm never bored around pretty ladies." He looked at Marcy. "Morning, Miss Pruitt."

He felt a sense of accomplishment when the smile on her lips made it to her eyes. "Good morning, Mr. Carver."

"So formal," Clair teased. "And to think it was only yesterday you two were married."

"She left me," Evan said with a sigh, then eyed the basket of pastries on the table. "But one of those Danish and maybe some ham and eggs might ease the pain."

"I'll see what I can do about the latter." Clair lifted the basket and held it out to him. "As to the former, what would you like?"

Before he could decide, Evan was distracted when Marcy lifted her coffee cup to her smiling lips. Once again he found himself entranced with her mouth. *What would he like?* He could think of several things.

But since Clair was referring to breakfast, he decided on an apple Danish, then sat in the chair beside Marcy. "So when will Big Jake be here?"

"Anytime now." Clair glanced at her wristwatch. "But he's mine for the morning. We have an appointment with the photographer. You can have him this afternoon when you go for your tux fittings."

Evan frowned. Damn. He hated those fitting things. Twice before—his high-school prom and his foreman's wedding three years ago—he'd been subjected to what he considered the male equivalent of a nineteenth-century corset. "You know, it's still not too late to fly to Vegas," he suggested. "I hear you can get married now at a drive-up window. Chapel Bell. The ceremony comes with a dozen tacos and a quart of guacamole."

Clair rolled her eyes, but laughed. "I just might consider that. Especially since the church in Wolf River is booked with weddings for the next few weeks. We considered an outdoor service, but with the unpredictable weather, we decided to have the ceremony in one of the ballrooms."

"Chapel Bell, I'm telling you." Evan looked at Marcy. "What do you think?"

"I think it's an interesting idea," Marcy muttered.

"Don't encourage the man." Clair furrowed her forehead when she saw the thoughtful expression on Marcy's face. "You aren't serious, are you?"

"Not the Vegas part," Marcy said with a dismissive wave of her hand. "The chapel part."

Marcy could never explain how ideas came to her, they just did. She'd learned over the years not to squelch them, but to give them free rein and see where they took her. Sometimes an idea, even one that started off as the most ridiculous thought imaginable, could turn into something amazing.

"You could build one right here," Marcy said. "This patio is beautiful, but between the heat and uncertain weather, it's probably not usable a good portion of the year. You could convert it into an enclosed garden chapel and have the feel of the outdoors no matter what the weather is, then offer wedding-reception services all year round."

When Clair and Evan just stared at her without saying anything, Marcy shifted awkwardly, then picked up her coffee cup. "Just a thought."

"It's a *wonderful* thought." Clair looked at Evan, a mixture of excitement and hope in her blue eyes. "Would it be possible to build something like that in three weeks?"

"It's possible." Evan glanced around the patio. "Especially with the right crew. And even if we didn't finish, it seems the worst that could happen is you go back to your original idea with the ceremony in the ballroom."

"A gazebo ceiling would be beautiful." Marcy could picture it now. Blond maple or oak and a white-iron chandelier hanging from the center. "With French doors that can be opened when the weather is nice."

Evan took in the area they had to work with. "French doors would be good around the back and side, but we should enclose the front half with drywall and build a raised platform."

She nodded. "If you use the same stone as the floor, I can create a garden area on both sides of the steps."

"I love it already!" Clair jumped up and hugged Marcy, then kissed her cheek. "You're brilliant."

"Hey, how 'bout me?" Evan stuck his cheek out. "I gave her the idea."

Clair hugged and kissed Evan, too. "Where do we start, what do we do, who should we—" The excitement drained from her face. "Wait. No. Neither one of you is here to work. I can't let you do this."

Evan looked at Marcy and grinned. She smiled back. "Just try and stop us," he said.

"Oh, I love you both!" There were tears in Clair's eyes. "I can't wait to tell Jacob."

"Tell me what?"

Marcy glanced up and saw the man standing in the doorway. There was no mistaking the Carver family resemblance, she thought. Same dark hair and devastating grin, same angular features. He looked a little travel weary, stubbled beard and rumpled white shirt, but it only added to his rough-around-the-edges good looks.

"Jacob!" Clair spun, then ran to Jacob and threw herself in his arms.

When they kissed, Marcy politely looked away. Shaking his head, Evan sighed and sat back in his chair. "This could take a while. You want a warm-up on your coffee, a newspaper to read, maybe a novel?"

But Clair was already pulling Jacob across the patio. "Jacob, this is Marcy. Marcy, Jacob."

Jacob's hand closed over Marcy's. "I've heard a lot about you," he said.

Marcy smiled. "And I, you."

"Sweetheart, you won't believe this." Clair slid her arms around Jacob's waist. "Marcy and Evan are going to build a chapel for us. Right here."

Jacob lifted an eyebrow and looked at Evan. "In three weeks?"

Evan nodded. "We'll need to get some plans and a crew together right away, but that shouldn't take more than a couple of days. We can probably pop this puppy out in two weeks." Evan grinned at his brother. "I might even put a hammer in your soft hands."

"We'll see who's soft," Jacob said with good nature. "Last time I saw you on the site, all you did was stand around and look pretty while you barked orders at everyone else."

"Now can I help it if I'm pretty?" Evan said with a shrug, then looked at Marcy. "He always was jealous 'cause I got the looks."

"Enough of the brotherly love," Clair said, shaking her

head. "Marcy, Evan, you have carte blanche on this. What-ever you want, whatever it costs, you got it." Clair looked up at Jacob. "Now we have to go make that ugly mug of yours presentable so we can have our pictures taken."

Jacob frowned, then shook his head and kissed Clair. "There isn't another woman on this earth I'd do this for," he said against her lips.

"I love you, too," Clair said with a smile and kissed him again. "Maybe we can be a few minutes late."

"You know it, darlin'."

Arm in arm, Clair and Jacob walked back into the hotel. Marcy sighed, then looked at Evan, who was still shaking his head at the lovebirds' retreat.

The enormity of the project ahead of them suddenly sucked the breath out of her. "We can do this, right?"

"No sweat. We'll probably need a lot of this, though," he said, picking up his coffee. "And we'll have to work closely together."

Her pulse skipped at the thought. "It's for a good cause."

"We'll have to put in a lot of hours to get the plans drawn up this quickly and coordinate all the work."

"That's fine."

He leaned in closer. "We'll probably have to work some nights, too."

Her pulse went from skipping to an all-out sprint. "Whatever it takes."

His gaze dropped to her mouth and Marcy held her breath. When he glanced up quickly and looked behind her, she started to turn, but he caught her chin in his hand.

"Don't turn around," he said, lowering his voice. "Someone's looking this way."

"Who?"

"Take off your glasses," he whispered.

Quickly, she slipped them off. "Are they still looking?"

"Yeah. Uh-oh. They're coming this way. Better make this good."

"Make what—"

He answered her question by dropping his mouth on hers.

Four

Dear Marcy,
I've invited my boyfriend's mother and father to dinner and I want my table to look special without spending a lot of money on fancy china or silverware. What do you suggest?
Melissa in Queens

Like the first time Evan had kissed her, Marcy was too stunned to move. Too stunned to breathe.

But this time—unlike the first time—she kissed him back.

She couldn't imagine who was more surprised, herself, or Evan. But when his lips touched hers, she knew she didn't want to pull away. She'd spent half the night fantasizing about this man. How could she let this opportunity pass, even if it wasn't for real?

She couldn't.

Not that she wasn't nervous, of course. Heavens, her

BARBARA McCAULEY   63

heart was slamming in her chest, and her lungs refused
to draw in air. But he'd told her to make it look good,
hadn't he? Even if kissing wasn't in her area of exper-
tise, she could certainly give it her best effort. Whenever she'd put her mind to a project, she always gave it
one hundred and ten per cent.

She leaned into Evan and laid her palms flat on his
chest. His lips were firm against hers; he tasted like cin-
namon and apple. The scent of his aftershave made her
think of thick, dark woods and damp, mossy earth. Sensations rippled through her like satin ribbons of brilliant
color.

Incredible.

She felt his hesitation when she moved her mouth
against his, the momentary flex of his strong muscles
under the palms of her hands. She was certain he was
going to pull away from her, that Evan's idea of making something look good and hers were two entirely different things. Disappointment and embarrassment
flooded through her.

But he didn't pull away. Instead, he slid his hand behind her neck and tugged her closer, slanted his mouth
against hers, then slowly traced her bottom lip with his
tongue.

Amazing.

There were more sensations now. Unfamiliar, yet
exciting. Thrilling. Tiny, intense arrows of pleasure
shooting through her. Even if someone was watching
her and Evan, at this moment, she simply didn't care.

The only thing that mattered in the whole world was the feel of his mouth on hers and the hot, moist slide of his tongue over her lips.

When he slipped inside, she shivered.

Her curiosity became a startling desire, and she curled her fingers into the soft cotton of his T-shirt. She could feel the heat of his body under her hands, the steady thud of his heart. Her own heart was racing. Her skin felt tight, her breasts ached. With every stroke of his tongue, a need she'd never experienced before intensified. It frightened and thrilled her at the same time.

She wasn't sure if it was the sound of a distant lawnmower or the chirping of a bird from a nearby tree, but a noise invaded her muddled brain, bringing reason back.

Blinking her eyes open, she pulled away, then reached for her glasses and slid them back on. Prayed her hands weren't shaking too badly. She couldn't look at him, was afraid if she did, she would see what had just happened didn't mean anything to him, or worse, that he might even find amusement in her inexperience.

"Are they gone?" she asked, struggling to control her emotions.

"Yeah." His voice had a rough edge to it. "You're safe."

Safe? Good Lord, she was anything but "safe" around this man!

"So," he said quietly, "shall we go to my room, or yours?"

Shocked, Marcy looked up, was relieved to see there

was no amusement in his eyes or indifference, either. Anything but. His dark brown gaze held more than a glint of desire.

My room or yours?

She swallowed hard. No man had ever asked her *that* before.

Still, the best she could manage was a mouselike squeak. "What?"

"I've got drafting supplies in my room," he said. "We'll need to sketch some rough plans and have Clair look them over, then I can get exact measurements later and use a computer to draw the blueprints."

"Oh, right." Of course he hadn't been suggesting anything more than work. She felt as ridiculous over her assumption as she did at her disappointment. "Your room is fine."

At least work was one area of her life where she felt completely confident and comfortable. *I'm a professional,* she told herself. As long as she stayed focused on the project, she wouldn't be thinking about Evan in a physical manner.

But even as she followed him to the elevators, even as she turned her mind to the task at hand, her lips still tingled and her skin still burned and she knew the next three weeks were indeed going to be a challenge.

Watching Marcy work was almost as incredible as kissing her, Evan decided two hours later. One minute she was doodling on a pad of paper, the next she was talking to herself.

At the moment, she was doing both while she paced back and forth from the living- to dining-room area.

She hardly seemed to know he was in the room, though every so often she'd look at him, glasses on top of her head, and her eyes would widen with some new idea. Then she'd quickly jot down a note with the pencil she'd stuck behind her ear.

He sat at the dining-room table, scratching out basic designs one after the other, an exploration of different ideas, each sketch building on the one before. He knew they were getting closer to the final design and were down to details now.

He respected the fact that she was a perfectionist, had been accused of the same crime himself. In the building trade, Evan had met far too many people who settled for "good enough," but he had no tolerance for sloppy work or cutting corners. It had taken him years to find the right crew and suppliers, men and women who were as meticulous as he was. Some of them were pain-in-the-butt prima donnas, but he tolerated their idiosyncrasies, just as they tolerated his.

He slid the sketch he'd been working on—his tenth—across the table. "How's this?"

"Almost." Tapping her chin, she studied the drawing. "I think the ceiling should be a little higher for a more cathedral look. A wedding is a spiritual and emotional joining of two people. A promise of forever. The environment we create has to support and give credence to that promise. Not just with our minds, or hearts, but with our souls."

He didn't know what to say to that. Hearts and promises and forever weren't exactly his forte. But he knew she wasn't really looking for an answer, anyway. In the past two hours, he'd learned that was how she operated. She'd ask herself a question or make a comment, roll it around in her brain, pull it apart, then put it back together until all the pieces fit neatly into place.

He'd also learned she really didn't need her glasses except for fine print, she didn't like ice in her water, and she'd never seen a reality show. He felt as if he already knew more about Marcy than most of the women he'd dated.

He watched her pluck a pencil from behind her ear, then sketch a rectangular window on the drawing and slide it back. "How about a stained-glass window right here? The light streaming through will give the room an ethereal look."

He nodded. "Good idea, but we won't have time to have it built, so that gives us two weeks at the most to find one premade."

Marcy's face lit with enthusiasm. "The thrill of the hunt gets the blood pumping, my Aunt Hattie used to say just before we'd go to the local flea market every Saturday."

He thought if she kept looking at him like that, with her cheeks flushed and her green eyes glittering, she was going to get *his* blood pumping right here and now.

He'd kissed her earlier on an impulse, an irresistible urge to wipe that prim look from her face. He'd also figured that if they were going to be working together, he should just get it out of the way, rather than wasting time wondering. He'd intended it to be a simple, friendly kiss.

Then she'd gone and done the unexpected.

She'd kissed him back.

And there'd been nothing simple about it at all. Nothing friendly. It had been *hot*. Arousing.

Disturbing.

He didn't like being off balance like that. He prided himself on control, especially when it came to women and sex. But when she'd pressed those soft, warm lips of hers against his, when she'd laid her hands on his chest and made that small sound in her throat, he'd lost it. All he could think was that he wanted to drag her upstairs, take her to his bed and finish what he'd started.

"Oh, Evan, I think that's a wonderful idea."

Startled, he looked up at her. Good God, could she read minds, too, or had he said out loud what he'd been thinking? "What's a wonderful idea?"

"The arch in the doorway here. I love that." She stood behind him, looking over his shoulder at his sketch. "We could even paint climbing roses and give it the feeling of an arbor."

He'd been so preoccupied thinking about making love to Marcy, he'd barely realized what he'd drawn.

She leaned in and tapped her fingertip to his drawing. "Right here we could arch the area over the French doors and the stained-glass window, too. It will give the room a softer effect."

Evan was used to working closely with his clients in the design stage, but he'd never worked quite this close, or been quite so distracted before. Marcy's scent reminded him of the honeysuckle that had grown wild behind the apartment house he'd lived in when he was a kid. He remembered how sweet the flower tasted if you pulled it off the vine and sucked on it.

That thought stimulated more than a memory.

"Oh, and right here—" oblivious to his discomfort, she reached in closer, absently brushing her arm against his "—this is where the bride will enter, so I think a higher, wider doorway will have a more dramatic impact."

She paused for a moment, deep in thought, and then she was off again, pacing and making notes.

He let out the breath he'd been holding. Good God. He could barely keep up with her. And though he told himself not to, he couldn't help but wonder what all that excess energy of hers would be like in bed.

It was an interesting thought.

He didn't intend to sleep with her, of course. Kissing her was one thing. Taking her to bed was another matter entirely. It would be awkward, at best. Not only because she was Clair's friend, but somehow, he didn't really think Marcy was the let's-have-a-wild-night-of-sex-then-go-our-own-way kind of girl.

She was more the let's-pick-out-rings type.

He shuddered at the thought, then turned his attention back to the sketch he was drawing, adding in the doorway and window she'd suggested and realized she'd been right. She truly had an amazing eye for design and detail. He glanced up at her, watched her touch the pencil to her lips, lightly stroking it back and forth.

Dammit.

If this was any other woman, he might have thought she was intentionally teasing him. But this was Marcy, and he was certain she didn't have a clue that she was driving him crazy.

When she started to nibble on the eraser, his hand tightened and he snapped the lead on his pencil.

"Marcy."

"Hmm?"

"Stop that."

"Stop what?"

"Chewing on your pencil."

She furrowed her forehead. "That bothers you?"

"As a matter of fact, it does," he said. When she looked at him, confused, he frowned. "It's bad for your teeth."

"It is?" She slid her glasses from the top of her head back onto her nose and stared at the pencil.

"Yeah." Well, it *could* be, he thought, then rolled his shoulders and leaned back in his chair. "Why don't we take a break?"

"Okay. I'll go to my room and you can—"

"Sit."

"No, really, I should—"

"Sit." Using his foot, he pushed one of the chairs away from the table.

She hesitated, then sat down, but her back was stiff as a two-by-four and he figured if he put a level to her shoulders, she'd be plumb. Unbidden, the thought came to him and he smiled.

Sugarplumb.

"Tell me about this aunt of yours," he said.

"Aunt Hattie?" Marcy tucked her hair behind her ears. "Well, she was my mother's sister, twelve years her senior. We lived in the same town. After my parents died, she took me in."

He watched her pick up a scrap of paper from the table and fiddle with it. "How did they die?"

"We had an old house, faulty wiring," Marcy said quietly. "My parents' bedroom was in the back of the house and the firemen couldn't reach them in time. All I remember is waking up on my front lawn and my aunt was holding me, crying. I was only eight."

Evan resisted the urge to cover her hands and still those busy fingers of hers. "That's a tough one." Hell, what else was there to say? he thought.

"Everyone used to call Henrietta Thatcher eccentric. She made sculptures out of old iron and odds and ends she found in the junkyard or on the side of the road." Marcy smiled. "Now that I've made a name for myself, they call her a character. She sells her work in galleries across the country."

Marcy set the piece of paper she'd been folding on the palm of her hand. She'd made a tiny bird, Evan realized. Lifting an eyebrow, he looked at her.

"It works with napkins, too," she said. "If you're having a dinner party, it spruces up a table. I'd be happy to teach you."

He could just see himself folding napkins for a dinner party in his trailer—or anywhere, for that matter. That would happen the same day he took up knitting and candle making.

"I'll let you know," he said with a chuckle, then set the bird on the table and took her hands in his. "Marcy, I think we should talk about what happened this morning on the patio."

Her gaze dropped. "You're right, we should. I apologize."

He frowned at her. "What?"

"Well, I know you were just trying to prevent someone from recognizing me, and I, well, I got a little carried away in the moment."

"Marcy—"

"You're a very good kisser," she said in a matter-of-fact tone. "But I'm sure you know that already."

"Marcy—"

"I didn't mean to put you in an awkward situation," she went on. "Especially since we're working together. But I assure you, I won't do that again and if you want, I—"

"Marcy!" In one swift move, he leaned forward and dropped his mouth over hers, a quick kiss, then he sat back down.

Eyes wide, she looked at him.

"Marcy," he said firmly. "I didn't kiss you this morning because anyone was looking at you. I kissed you because I wanted to."

"Because you wanted to?" Her eyes grew wider still. "Why?"

"It's called spontaneity. I felt like kissing you, so I did. Is that so hard to understand?"

"Well," she said, shifting awkwardly. "Actually, it is."

"And why is that?"

"Let's just say I'm not the type who normally motivates spontaneity."

Before he'd met her—certainly before he'd kissed her—he probably would have agreed with her. But definitely not now.

"It's not that I don't appreciate it," she went on when he didn't say anything. "And I certainly enjoyed it. But it's just that, well, I think it's best if it doesn't happen again."

That, he agreed with, but still, he'd like to hear Marcy's reasoning on the subject. "Why is that?"

"Number one, we're going to be working together and it's distracting."

True. It was damn distracting.

"Number two, it can't go anywhere, so it would just be—" she blushed "—frustrating."

Very true, but he couldn't resist asking her, "Where exactly were you thinking 'it' can't go?"

Her blush deepened. "The natural development of a mutual attraction would probably lead to the next step of intimacy."

He couldn't help but grin at her. "Gosh, I like it when a woman talks dirty. I can hardly wait to hear number three."

"Number three," she said softly and raised her gaze to meet his, "is that I like you."

I like you? He lifted an eyebrow. Well now, this was a first. A woman didn't want to be "intimate" with him because she liked him.

"You're going to be my best friend's brother-in-law," she said. "I'm certain that we'll see each other from time to time. If we were to—if we—"

"Slept together?"

Nodding, she lowered her gaze. "I'm sure you'll agree it would be awkward."

He leaned back in his chair. A woman's logic, he thought with a sigh. He knew better than to argue with that.

And besides, she was right, dammit.

"Fine. I won't kiss you again. We'll just concentrate on getting this chapel built. How's that?"

"Great," she said with such a bright, sunny smile that he didn't know whether to be insulted or pleased.

When the phone rang, Evan moved into the living area to answer it, grateful for a reason to not only stretch his legs, but put some distance between himself and Marcy. "May I speak with Marcy Pruitt, please?" a woman said on the other end of the line.

"Marcy Pruitt?"

Marcy's gaze snapped up.

"Tell her it's Anna."

"Anna who?"

Marcy was up on her feet and had the phone out of his hands. "What's wrong?"

He watched Marcy's face turn pale as she listened. Whoever Anna was, and whatever she had to say, didn't appear to be good news.

"Are you sure about this?" Marcy dragged a hand through her hair. "All right. I promise I won't say anything. Call me in the morning, but don't use the office phone."

"Problem?" he asked when she hung up the phone.

"I'm going to kill Helen."

"Your manager?"

"My *ex*-manager," she said tightly. "I can't believe she would do this. Even for Helen, this is extreme."

"What did she do?"

Marcy pressed her lips into a thin line. "She hired a private investigator to find me."

Five

Dear Marcy,
I am in charge of planning my friends' wedding
shower. Do you have any suggestions for games
at a shower that can include men and women?
Arlene from Indianapolis

"She hired a private investigator?"

Marcy stared blankly at the phone. "Anna said she overheard Helen talking on her cell phone. She only caught bits and pieces of the conversation, but from what she could gather, Helen has actually hired someone to find me."

"Whoa." Evan whistled softly. "Isn't that a little extreme?"

"That's Helen's middle name." As the reality of it seeped into her brain, so did the anger. "I'm going to kill her."

"Why don't you just fire her?" Evan asked.

"There'd be no pleasure in that." Hands fisted, Marcy started to pace. "I can't believe this."

"So you're saying you're *not* going to fire her?"

Marcy reached the sofa, then spun on her heels and headed back toward the dining-room table. "I can't do that."

"Surely any contract you have won't hold up under something like this."

Marcy marched back toward the sofa again, shaking her head. "We don't have a contract."

"You're kidding me." He stared at her in disbelief. "How is that possible?"

"I know how incredible that sounds, but we've never needed one. I trust Helen completely."

"What a minute." Frowning, Evan snagged her arm before she could get away again. "You're making me dizzy. Sit."

When she sank down on the chair beside him, he put his hands on both sides of her knees and leaned in. "Are we talking about the same woman here? The one who just hired a P.I. to find you?"

"Our relationship isn't based on lawyers and contracts and legalities," Marcy said. "As foolish as it might seem to you, it's based on faith and friendship. Helen might be controlling and demanding, but she would never do anything to hurt me."

"This doesn't hurt you?"

"No." She pressed her lips firmly together. "But it does make me mad."

He shook his head. "I don't get it."

She tried not to focus on the fact that Evan had moved into her space, or the fact that his hands were a fraction away from touching her legs. And she desperately tried not to think about the fact that he had kissed her—for the second time that day—only a few moments ago.

"You have to understand our history," she said with a sigh. "After college I moved to Los Angeles and started my own catering company. I had steady bookings, but the competition was fierce and I didn't know how to run the financial aspect of a business. After a year I had an Everest-size mountain of bills and was two months late on my rent. I was broke and tired and ready to give up. And then I met Helen."

Marcy remembered how lonely she'd been, living in a tiny apartment in West L.A., working out of an even smaller office and kitchen. "I was catering a birthday party for a Hollywood producer. I thought it would be my last job and I would make just enough to pay my bills and maybe gas to get back to Burbridge. Helen approached me at the party, told me that I made the best chocolate soufflé she'd ever had. She also said I had something, a look, a style, that she could market. She gave me her card and told me that within three years Marcy Pruitt was going to be a household name. I laughed at her, of course, and thought she was a nutcase. I didn't even call her back. But she showed up at my apartment as I was packing my bags, then took me to lunch and laid out her plan. Three hours later, she put me up in a hotel, had six celebrity parties booked for me, and was already working on the layout for my first how-to book."

"That's admirable," Evan said evenly, "but, honey, she made a lot of money on you."

"She earned every penny and still does." No one worked harder or with more dedication than Helen, Marcy thought. "What really mattered was that she believed in me, even when I didn't believe in myself. She never gave up or let up. Everything I have, where I am today, I owe it all to her."

"I can understand you're grateful," Evan said, shaking his head. "What I don't understand is what she hopes to accomplish by hiring a P.I. to track you down, unless she plans on having you tied up and dragged back to Los Angeles."

"If she could get away with it, she might." Marcy smiled at the thought. "But really I think she just wants to know where I am and that I'm all right. On top of being tenacious, she's also a worrier."

"So why don't you just call her up and let her know you're on to her, then tell her to back off?"

"If I'm ever going to have any time to myself, I need Helen to learn to trust Anna to make decisions. If Helen finds out that Anna told me about the P.I., I'm afraid she might not work with her at all. And then I'll *have* to go back."

"Women." Evan sighed, then took Marcy's hand in his and balled her fingers into a fist. "Guys could just duke it out and move on."

When Evan's hand closed over hers, Marcy's heart stuttered. "I'd rather you didn't mention this to Clair just yet. She's got a lot on her mind right now. She doesn't need to worry about me, too."

"She needs to know, Marcy. She can alert her staff and beef up her security here."

"I'll tell her after the party tonight," Marcy said, then pulled her hand from Evan's. "We should get back to work if we're going to finish the final sketch today. Clair and Jacob will be back anytime now, and you've got a fitting this afternoon."

"Fittings and showers." He rolled his head back and groaned. "Las Vegas, I'm telling you. The only way to go."

Lucas and Julianna Blackhawk lived in a two-story blue-gray clapboard a few miles outside of town. Not an especially large house, Evan thought as he pulled into the gravel-lined circular driveway, but it definitely had appeal. White shutters, front porch, beds of blooming roses and colorful flowers. To the west of the house, a stand of trees lined a creek bed. To the east, horses grazed inside a white-fenced pasture. The surrounding land, thousands of acres of Blackhawk ranch, stretched as far as the eye could see.

There were several cars already parked in front of the house and Evan pulled his truck alongside a black SUV, then shut off the engine. "Here we are."

When Marcy didn't respond, he glanced across the seat at her. Deep in thought, she stared out the car window, fiddling with the pearl necklace she wore. The black sheath she had on wasn't exactly sexy, he thought, but it suited her conservative style. Her shoes, also black, had a low heel, nothing intended to stir a man's blood.

And yet, nonetheless, his blood did stir. There was something about this woman. He wasn't sure what it was. Just…something. He wondered if that's what Helen had seen in Marcy—that undefinable "it" that so many celebrities had. Helen had obviously recognized Marcy's universal appeal and packaged it.

The manager might be a female snake, but she was one smart snake.

He came around and opened Marcy's door, then surprised her by wrapping his hands around her waist and lifting her out of the truck.

"Evan!" She laid a hand on his chest to steady herself. "That wasn't necessary."

"It's a long step down." He let his hands linger on her waist even after he set her on the ground. "You look pretty tonight."

"Thank you." She blushed at his compliment. "And you look handsome."

"Thanks." Reluctantly, he let go of her, then tugged at the tie choking him. He'd drawn the line on a suit, but had compromised with a sport coat and slacks. By the time this wedding business was over, he figured his brother was going to owe him big-time.

"After you."

He followed behind her, appreciating the sway of her hips as she moved up the front steps. The scent of Italian spices drifted on the warm, early-evening air, mixing with the sound of animated conversations from inside the house.

"By the way," he said, leaning in close as he knocked on the front door, "you've got great legs."

She looked at him, eyes wide, but didn't have time to respond before Lucas opened the door.

Smiling, he followed her inside. This party just might be fun, after all, he decided.

Marcy decided that walking into Lucas and Julianna's home was a bit like white-water rafting. From the moment Lucas had opened the door with his six-month-old son in his arms, there had been an endless, swiftly moving current of introductions, enthusiastic handshakes and unexpected warm hugs. The Blackhawks were a bit overwhelming, a little wild and definitely noisy.

Marcy liked them immediately.

While she sipped a glass of wine and waited for the guests of honor to arrive, Marcy stepped back from the hubbub and mentally ran through the introductions again.

Rand and Seth, Clair's brothers, were easy to remember. They had Clair's smile and thick, shiny dark hair. Rand's wife, Grace, a lovely redhead, was perhaps the most elegant woman at the party, while Hannah, Seth's wife, had a homespun beauty with dazzling blue eyes and a mop of blond curls. And though Marcy still wasn't sure who belonged to whom, it seemed to her that there were children everywhere. She watched at least a half-dozen youngsters, screaming and giggling, race down the stairs and fly out the front door, while the adults, seemingly oblivious to the ruckus, never missed a beat in their conversations.

There were two other couples at the party Marcy had met, friends that Clair had made since moving to Wolf River. Nick Santos and his wife, Maggie, who were expecting their third child and Clay and Paige Bodine, who were expecting their second.

"I've decided it's something in the water."

Marcy turned. A beautiful woman with shoulder-length auburn hair stood next to her.

"Olivia Cameron."

She held out her hand and Marcy took it, couldn't help but notice the exquisite silver rings and bracelets she wore. "Marcy Pruitt. What's in the water?"

"The wedding-and-baby bug." Olivia looked across the room while she sipped from her wineglass. "At least I hope it's the water. If it's airborne, we're all doomed."

Marcy smiled. "You're the antique dealer and interior designer Clair told me about. I love what you did with the lobby at the hotel."

"Thanks." Pleasure sparkled in Olivia's soft blue eyes. "But I saw the 'Marcy's Makeover' article your magazine did on that turn-of-the-century farmhouse. It was amazing. I'm still drooling over the antiques you pulled out of the basement."

That project had been one of Marcy's favorites. Tourists had bypassed the bed-and-breakfast in northern California's wine country for years and the owners had sent in a plea for help. Since the article, Marcy had heard that business was booming.

"There were some great antiques in the barn you might be interested in," Marcy said. "I can call the owner for you. Oh, and I'd like to come by and see your store, too. If you wouldn't mind, I'd like to include you in a feature we'll be doing on small-town antique stores."

"If I wouldn't mind?" Olivia stared at Marcy. "You're kidding, right?"

"Not at all. I could interview you before I go back to L.A., then after the wedding, I can send a photographer."

"Well, I—" Olivia put a hand to her throat and made a choking sound. "Sure."

"You okay?" Frowning, Julianna came over with a tray of tiny crab cakes. "Can I get you some water?"

When Marcy and Olivia looked at each other and laughed, Julianna furrowed her forehead.

"Olivia thinks all the weddings and babies have something to do with the water," Marcy explained.

"Is that what it is?" Julianna smiled, then looked at her husband, who was tossing their newest child into the air and making the baby laugh hysterically. "I'll have to make sure I drink my eight glasses a day, then."

"She's lost." Olivia rolled her eyes. "But do tell. Who is that gorgeous man standing next to Lucas, and please tell me he's not married or engaged."

When Marcy turned to see who Olivia was referring to, her stomach twisted in a knot.

"That's Evan, Jacob's brother. Would you like to meet him?"

Olivia arched an eyebrow. "Oh, yeah."

"I have to go check on my lasagna first," Julianna said, "then I'll take you over."

"I can introduce you," Marcy said politely.

Olivia frowned, then her eyes widened. "Ohmigod. Are you here with him? I'm so sorry, I didn't—"

"No." Marcy shook her head. "He just drove me here from the hotel, that's all. I'm not here with him. I barely know him."

"Are you sure? Because if there's something—"

"There isn't." Marcy smiled her TV smile. "Really, I'd be happy to introduce you."

"That's not necessary." Olivia locked her gaze on Evan and sipped her wine. "I think I can find my way over there."

"Watch out, boys." Julianna smiled when Olivia walked away. "Here she comes."

"Evan can manage," Marcy said thoughtfully.

"If he's anything like Jacob, I imagine he can," Julianna said with a nod. "Excuse me one minute, will you?"

"Can I help you in the kitchen?" Marcy offered, wanting something, anything, to keep her busy.

"Thank you, but absolutely not. You're here to relax, not work." The children ran in the back door and up the stairs, all of them screaming like banshees. Julianna looked at Marcy, then sighed and walked off, mumbling, "Maybe I should stick to bottled water from now on."

Marcy glanced at Evan, watched him smile at Olivia, then shake her hand. The woman was beautiful, single and obviously not interested in marriage or children. They'd make a perfect match.

The knot in her stomach tightened.

Not quite ready to join back in the party, she wandered outside onto a raised, covered patio. The sun was dipping low on the horizon and though it was still warm, the air had cooled several degrees. Beyond the wide expanse of freshly mowed grass and children's lawn toys were two corrals and a tall, red barn. To the left of the house, on the far edge of the lawn, she could hear a creek running below a white gazebo.

She turned at the sound of laughter from inside the house. The Blackhawks were certainly a lively bunch. Animated conversations, genuine laughter, sincerity in their obvious affection for each other. She'd missed that growing up—family gatherings on holidays, weddings to celebrate, babies to coo over.

It didn't take a rocket scientist to figure out why she'd started her career in catering. Planning parties gave her the connection with people she'd so badly needed. She'd always taken great pleasure watching people enjoy themselves, had never minded standing on the sidelines. Her work had been her greatest joy and she'd thrown herself into it.

She turned and rested her arms on the patio railing, glanced at the children's toys on the lawn, the redwood boxes of tomatoes and squash, the carefully tended beds of flowers. And suddenly she knew all that she had, all that she'd accomplished, wasn't enough anymore. She wanted this in her life, too. This bond of family, the connection of friends. And a home. Not just a house—she had a house—but a *home.*

She knew it was her attraction to Evan that had stoked the home fires in her. She'd never felt anything like this before. This breath-stealing, heart-pounding, flutter-in-the-stomach feeling. It was new and exciting, and while she knew that a relationship with Evan was out of the question, he'd definitely opened her eyes to the possibilities.

By the way, you've got great legs.

Remembering what he'd whispered to her just before Lucas had opened the door made her smile. He'd done that on purpose, she thought. Tried to throw her off-kilter. She supposed he couldn't help himself, saying and doing outrageous things like that. She certainly knew she couldn't take him seriously.

But she'd be lying to herself if she didn't admit that his compliment had felt good.

It had felt great.

"Hiding out?"

Surprised at the sound of Evan's voice, Marcy

glanced over her shoulder, was even more surprised that Olivia wasn't with him.

"Just enjoying the view," she said honestly.

A bottle of beer in his hand, he moved across the patio toward her. He'd already loosened his tie, and the casual gesture only increased his rugged appeal.

"Don't you have views in Los Angeles?" he asked, leaning on the rail beside her.

"Not like this." She watched a horse stroll across one of the corrals. "Have you ever been there?"

"Never had a reason to." He reached out and tucked a loose strand of hair behind her ear. "But you'll be the first to know if I do."

The brush of his fingertips on her ear sent a jolt through her. She stiffened at the contact, watched him lift his beer bottle and tip his head back to drink. Her own throat went dry.

"Marcy Pruitt, when did you plan on telling me what's going on?"

Marcy jumped back at the sound of Clair's voice. When she turned, Clair was standing at the patio door, frowning. Jacob was right behind her, looking very guilty.

Flustered, Marcy stepped away from Evan. "Nothing's going on."

"I know you had an urgent phone call this afternoon from Los Angeles that was forwarded to Evan's room," Clair said. "It seems that everyone, including my future husband, knows what that phone call was about but me." Clair turned her frown on Jacob. "And he's not talking."

Oh, thank goodness. Clair was referring to the private investigator. Marcy breathed a silent sigh of relief. And she'd thought that Clair—well, it didn't matter what she'd thought.

Marcy narrowed her eyes and looked at Evan. "You weren't supposed to say anything."

"Well, actually," he scratched the back of his neck, "you asked me not to say anything to Clair. But I thought Jacob should look into it."

"Look into what?" Clair threw her hands out in exasperation. "Somebody tell me what's going on before I scream."

"My manager hired a private investigator to find me," Marcy said.

"What!" Clair's mouth dropped open. "This is someone who works for you?"

Marcy sighed. "To say the least, she's tenacious."

Clair made a rude sound. "Tenacity is fine in business, but honey, this is your personal life."

That was the problem, Marcy realized. She'd never had a personal life, and Helen didn't know quite what to make of it. *For that matter, I'm not quite sure myself,* she thought. But she really didn't care to admit that in front of Evan and Jacob.

"I'd like to give that woman a piece of my mind," Clair said through clenched teeth. "I'd tell her to—"

"Let's talk about this later, shall we?" Jacob took

hold of Clair's shoulders. "I called a friend of mine in L.A. He's going to ask around, see what he can find out. In the meantime, we'll keep our eyes open for anyone suspicious, either in town, or at the hotel."

Jacob slipped his arms around his bride-to-be and kissed the top of her head. Clair's shoulders relaxed, then she leaned into him, the movement as natural and unconscious as breathing. It was a beautiful thing, Marcy thought, a rare thing, to see two people this much in love.

In spite of her happiness for them both, Marcy couldn't stop the twinge of envy. Ashamed of herself, she quickly shoved the feeling out of her mind. This was not the time to be thinking about her own love life—or lack of one, anyway.

"It's not as if you both don't have enough to do, and now you have to baby-sit me, too?" Marcy shook her head. "I didn't come here to be a bother."

"Watching out for a friend is hardly baby-sitting or a bother," Jacob said. "And besides, you didn't come here to work, either, and here you are, designing a wedding chapel."

"That's not work, that's fun," she said truthfully.

"So how soon can we see what you two have done?" Clair asked, her eyes bright with excitement.

"I'll have the basic plan drawn tomorrow morning," Evan said.

"Not that she's being pushy or anything." Jacob gave Clair a squeeze. "She talked about it all afternoon, and

I had to physically restrain her from going to Evan's room and bothering you two."

"Is that what you call what you were doing?" Clair asked, lifting one eyebrow.

Grinning, Jacob planted a quick kiss on Clair's mouth.

Evan looked at Marcy and shook his head. "Nause-ating, ain't it?" he said.

Marcy thought it was wonderful, but she refrained from commenting.

"We should get back inside." Clair took Jacob's hand. "Julianna says we have to play The Almost-New-lywed Game before we eat dinner. If I win, you have to write a poem for me and recite it in front of everyone."

"Like hell," Jacob said with a snort, then thought for a moment. "So what happens if *I* win?"

"I have to model all the lingerie I get at the shower for you. In private, of course."

"Is that so?" Grinning, he wiggled his eyebrows, then took Clair's hand. "Well, then, let the games begin."

Evan shook his head after Clair and Jacob went back in the house. "Six months ago, if anyone had told me that my brother would be willingly playing a game at his own wedding shower and agreeing to write a poem, I would have said they were drunk or just plain crazy."

"Love can do that," Marcy said softly, staring after the moonstruck couple.

He moved beside her, then leaned against the porch rail and grinned at her. "Make you act stupid?"

She studied him over the rim of her glass. Underneath the teasing smile, she could see he was dead serious. "Apparently, you've never been in love."

"I like to keep my sanity, thank you very much."

There was a certain amount of reason in that, she supposed. "It's exhilarating. Wonderfully, horribly thrilling, and you just know you'll die if that person doesn't love you back."

"Gosh, that sounds like fun." He looked as if he'd just sniffed something that had been forgotten in the back of a refrigerator. "So what was the lucky guy's name?"

"Leo Fitzmeyer."

He arched one eyebrow. "Leo Fitzmeyer?"

"He had the most amazing eyes." Smiling at the memory, she sipped her wine. "Every girl in the fifth grade was madly in love with him."

"Ah." His grin widened. "Lucky Leo."

He moved in closer and Marcy's nerves began jangling like a fire bell. What had she been thinking? Initiating a conversation as to whether he'd ever been in love? Talk about stupid.

"So where is Leo now?" Evan asked.

"In New York." Casually, she inched away. "He bought a hair salon in Manhattan. Very chic."

"Ah." He nodded. "I see."

"Leo has a beautiful wife and three handsome boys, all of them very definitely his." Marcy cocked her head and met Evan's gaze. "Last I heard they were trying for a girl."

"That's the fun part of kids." His grin widened. "Trying."

In spite of her determination to resist his charm, she laughed. "You don't like children?"

"Sure I do. I can't wait for Jacob and Clair to have a bunch of little rugrats. I figure I'll come visit, get them riled up, then I'll leave."

"You really are impossible," she said, shaking her head. But when she turned to leave, he took hold of her arm.

"Hey." He met her gaze, then his tone turned somber. "I just want you to know I'll be watching your back."

"I—" She hesitated, wasn't sure what to say. "Thank you."

His hand lingered for a moment, then dropped away at the sudden burst of laughter from inside the house. Apparently, the game had begun. With a resigned sigh, he gestured toward the doorway. "After you, Miss Pruitt."

Six

Dear Marcy,
I've been living with the same dull, drab walls and carpet in my house for almost twenty years! I'm way past ready for a change. Can you give me a few simple tips to help me "spice up" my life?
Tina in Tulsa

It felt good to swing a hammer again. Working alongside his crew, surrounded by the buzz of saws and the smell of fresh-cut wood, all that gave Evan a sense of satisfaction no office job ever could. At least at the end of the day, he thought, he could take a step back and see what he'd accomplished.

Slipping his hammer into the work belt around his hips, he wiped at the sweat on his forehead and took a step back now. They'd managed to get a rush on the permits, then torn down the old patio cover, poured the foundation and were moving swiftly along on the framing and electrical.

Not bad for a week's work.

He glanced overhead, watched a crane lower one of the ceiling beams onto a brace. Jacob and the site foreman, Tom, were perched on a scaffolding, helping guide a twelve-by-twelve beam into place. Everyone had worked hard in the sweltering heat these past few days, but the extra hours had paid off. They were already ahead of schedule—a rare occurrence in the construction trade.

But his men and Jacob weren't the only ones who had worked hard.

He looked at Marcy, who stood several yards away, absently running one hand over the strap of her overalls while she studied the paint samples she'd taped to a bare stud. She had a habit of losing herself in her work, becoming so completely focused that she was oblivious to the sounds and activity surrounding her.

A little *too* oblivious, he thought, scanning the area for anyone who didn't belong there.

She might not be concerned that her manager had hired a P.I. to find her, Evan thought, but he sure as hell was. Until Jacob's contact in Los Angeles could verify Anna's information and come up with a name or a face, Evan had decided they couldn't be too careful. He'd cordoned off the construction site from any curious hotel guests and made sure she'd stayed close by him all week.

His men had grumbled at first that she was in their way, always asking questions or making suggestions, but it seemed they'd not only gotten used to her being around, they'd even presented her with a hard hat and tool belt of her own. Obviously, she'd been accepted as part of the team.

Some of them had accepted her just a little *too* much, Evan thought as he watched James, one of the younger apprentices, stroll in Marcy's direction with a can of cold soda. The kid all but fell over his own feet as he offered the drink to Marcy. When she smiled and accepted the can, James actually blushed and shoved his hands into his jeans' pockets.

When James happened to glance over, Evan scowled at him. Wisely, the apprentice beat a quick retreat.

It had become apparent in the past couple of days that the kid had developed a crush on Marcy. He'd followed her around like a lovesick puppy until Evan had barked at him yesterday to get his butt back to work. The other guys had teased the apprentice, but he was an easygoing kid who took the ribbing in stride.

Personally, Evan did not see the humor in it.

Evan had spent a lot of time with Marcy this past week, not only on the job site, but in the evenings, too. Every night after the crew went home, she would come up to his room and they'd order dinner, then go over what had been accomplished to date—what would happen the next day, what had been ordered, when deliveries of materials and samples would be made. She'd stayed involved with every step of the construction, and he had to admit, her contributions of ideas and suggestions for changes as they went along had been impressive.

It was easy to see why she'd been so successful in her career. Her enthusiasm infected and inspired everyone around her. She seemed to take delight in every stud nailed into place, every wall that took shape, every window and door that was framed. It should have annoyed him that she was endlessly curious and seemed to be underfoot, but strangely, he hadn't minded. In fact, they'd worked very well together.

Made him wonder how well they might do other things together, too.

She could spout off speeches about just wanting to be friends and she *liked* him, but underneath all that rationalizing, he knew damn well she was doing some wondering herself. He also knew that whenever he moved in too close, or when his hand brushed hers, she wasn't thinking "friend." He could see it in her eyes, could feel the tension between them.

He made her nervous, and that, he decided, was a good thing.

He'd managed to keep his hands off her and maintain a professional distance, but every night when she came to his room, all he could think about was kissing her. And every night when she left, it was all he could do not to ask her to stay. Hell, they were both adults, attracted to each other, unattached. That was easy enough.

So why not?

He watched her raise the can of soda to her mouth and drink, then felt a jolt of lust when she licked her bottom lip.

Swearing, he quickly looked away, then pulled his hammer out of his belt and drove another nail into the door frame he'd been working on.

He knew why not, dammit. Because it wasn't so easy. She was different than any other woman he'd ever dated. Different from any other woman he'd ever been attracted to before. Marcy's whole life was based on hearth and home. Marriage. Kids. He wasn't ready for any of that. Didn't know if he ever would be.

She'd be going back to Los Angeles after the wedding, he'd be moving on to his next job. Marcy Pruitt wasn't the type to have a casual affair. For that matter, unless he'd completely read her wrong, she was a virgin.

A *virgin,* for crying out loud.

That alone was enough for him to keep his distance. The last thing he wanted to do was hurt her. She was delicate. Fragile. Like fine china. She deserved a hell of a lot more than he could offer her.

He drove another nail into a stud, glad that he had the type of job where he could pound some of his frustration away.

But it didn't take long before he found his attention drawn back to Marcy again, couldn't help but think she looked adorable in her hard hat, overalls and work boots. Even that silly tool belt she wore turned him on, dammit.

When James strolled back over to Marcy and started talking to her again, Evan decided he'd had enough.

He jammed his hammer back into his tool belt and stomped over. When James saw him coming, he visibly swallowed, then stumbled over an air hammer in his haste to get back to work.

Oblivious to the exchange between the two men, Marcy turned and smiled when she noticed him walking toward her.

"You're just in time to give me your opinion," she said, looking back at her paint chips.

He had an opinion, all right. She should come up to his room and get naked with him. But he doubted that was an opinion she wanted to hear.

When he noticed the EVAN CARVER CONSTRUCTION logo on the white T-shirt under her overalls, he lifted an eyebrow. "Nice T-shirt."

"Tom gave it to me. He said all the crew members have one, so I should, too. Do you mind?"

He noticed the curve of her breast directly under his logo and felt his pulse quicken. He wanted his hands and mouth there, dammit, and it irritated him that he couldn't even have a conversation with this woman and not want to touch and kiss her all over. "Why would I mind?"

She gave him an odd look, then looked back at her paint chips. "Which do you like for the French doors, Cloud Nine or Vanilla Ice?"

He wondered briefly who the hell came up with these

ridiculous names, then stepped closer and studied the samples. "Buy a quart of both. The light in here will change after the walls are up and we'll see how they look."

Nodding, she placed her hands on the small of her back and stretched. It was an innocent movement on her part, certainly not intended to evoke lust, but somehow that made her all the more appealing. Rather than take her hand and drag her upstairs, he clenched his teeth.

He *really* had to stop this line of thinking.

"Evan, this is all so wonderful," she said, glancing around the site. "I can't believe what you've managed to do in a week."

"Not me. We." She had a smudge of sawdust on her cheek, and though his first inclination was to wipe it off, he looped his thumbs inside his tool belt. "And the overtime Clair is paying the guys hasn't hurt, either. They're highly motivated."

She shook her head. "It's not just the money, it's you. You work right alongside them, never ask anyone to do anything you wouldn't do yourself. Your crew respects that—they respect you. There are things money can't buy, and that's one of them."

Evan stared at Marcy, not sure how to respond. The sincerity in her voice and her big gray-green eyes stunned him. No one had ever said anything like that to him before, except for maybe Jacob. And heck, Jacob was his brother. He had to say stuff like that.

"Thanks." He shrugged, then twisted his head to loosen a knot in his neck. "But I think my men are more concerned about pleasing you than me. In case you haven't noticed, you've got a few fans here, too. I may have to fire James if he doesn't stop staring at you."

Course, then he'd have to fire himself, too, Evan thought.

"James?" Forehead furrowed, Marcy glanced over at the apprentice. Her cheeks turned pink when she saw that the young man was indeed staring at her. "Surely you don't mean that he—"

Her blush deepened, and she looked back at Evan.

"That's exactly what I mean."

"But he's got to be at least five years younger than me," she said, then frowned. "You can't fire him, I'd feel awful if you did and there's no reason to, anyway. Honestly, I assure you, absolutely nothing is going on between us. Nothing at all." She pushed her glasses up her nose. "You wouldn't really fire him, would you? Please tell me you wouldn't."

Well, she was getting awfully worked up worrying about James, Evan thought. Which made him wonder if maybe something might be going on, or maybe she did have a thing for the kid, but was too embarrassed to admit it. Evan cursed his loose tongue. Why the hell did he have to go and put ideas in Marcy's head?

"I won't fire him, okay?" Evan said irritably. "As long as he keeps his mind on his work, his private life, or yours, is none of my business. Now do you think we can get back to work?"

"Of course." Obviously relieved, Marcy picked up a notepad sitting on a stack of two-by-fours. "I made some sketches and a list for the interior-and-exterior garden area. I'll need to order the flowers and plants by tomorrow. Oh, and we'll need to discuss the sprinkler system and the design of the fountain, too. If you want to do that tonight—"

"Fine." When his cell phone rang, he snatched it off his belt and answered it. "Yeah."

Good grief, Marcy thought when Evan practically growled into the phone. What in the world was *his* problem? He'd been moody the past couple of days, and though she realized he'd been working hard, he certainly didn't need to take it out on her.

She watched his expression soften, then his voice lower as he turned away. "Hey, Olivia, what's up?"

Marcy's heart sank. She shouldn't be surprised. At the party last week, the interior designer had certainly made it clear she was interested in Evan. The woman was confident, beautiful and obviously not afraid to go after what she wanted.

And if she hadn't been going after Evan, Marcy might have appreciated all those traits.

"When?" Marcy heard Evan say, then he glanced at his watch. "Okay, I can do that."

When he hung up, he turned back to her, grinning. "Tonight's out. Why don't you spend the evening with

Clair? We can look at your sketches and ideas in the morning."

"Sure." She forced a smile, didn't tell him that she knew Clair had a dinner appointment with the CEO of an oil company who wanted to book a seminar. "Sounds good."

"Great."

Evan looked up at Tom and yelled, "When that beam's in place, knock off for the day. Tom, have the drywallers and brick masons here at six-thirty sharp tomorrow. I want them done and gone in three days."

When he turned back to her, Marcy could see he was anxious to leave.

"Jacob will be around tonight if there's a problem." He plucked the pencil from behind her ear and scribbled on her notepad. "Here's my cell-phone number if you need me."

If she needed him? Hardly! She'd walk naked through the lobby before she'd call him. "I'll be fine."

"I'm sure you will," he said. "But it's probably best if you stay in your room. Take the evening off and relax."

"Sure, I'll do that," she said through gritted teeth. "See you in the morning."

"Right." He tucked the pencil back behind her ear, met her gaze and his grin widened. "See you in the morning."

Clutching her notebook, she watched him walk away, barely holding on to the emotions bubbling under the surface.

Stay in her room? Relax?

Like hell she would.

Enough of being treated like a child, she thought. Enough of hiding out like a frightened kitten.

Enough of the plain, Miss Marcy Pruitt persona.

She'd need help, of course. She was fully aware of her own limitations. And since she couldn't ask Clair for help, that left only one other person she could turn to.

Straightening her shoulders, she headed for the elevators, then pushed the button for the third floor.

Evan came back to his room that night a satisfied man.

Whistling, he stepped off the elevator and headed down the hallway. It was barely ten-thirty and though he should be dog-tired, he was buzzing with energy.

He paused beside Marcy's room, considered knocking to see if she was sleeping. He leaned closer to the door, listening for the sound of female voices or a television.

Nothing.

Just because he was too keyed up to sleep didn't mean he should wake her up. She'd worked tirelessly this past week and had certainly earned a night off.

Still, he did feel a little guilty leaving her tonight. He supposed she had come to rely on him being around, especially after all the time they'd spent together this past week.

Maybe she was still awake, he thought. Reading or watching television. He knocked lightly.

No answer.

Okay, so she probably was asleep. Or maybe she was in the bedroom watching TV and she couldn't hear. He knocked louder.

Still no answer.

He resisted the urge to knock again. If she was sleeping that soundly, he supposed he should just leave her be. There was really no need to wake her up tonight, anyway. He'd see her in the morning.

He glanced at his phone when he went into his room, but the light wasn't blinking. Maybe he should call her. Just to make sure she was all right. She wouldn't even have to get out of bed, he thought, and picked up the phone. She could just say hello, then go right back to sleep.

When Marcy didn't answer, he frowned at the receiver. Good Lord, the woman must sleep like the dead. After five rings, he hung up.

Sighing, he dragged a hand through his hair, then looked around his room. It felt…empty.

Dammit, he missed her.

Well, hell. It was Friday night. A live band played in the Four Winds lounge on the weekends. A little music and a cold beer in an iced mug would be the perfect way to end the day, he decided.

He took a quick shower, pulled on a pair of tan slacks and a black shirt, then was on his way out the door when he stopped and looked at the phone again.

His palms itched, but he shook his head and kept moving.

The lounge was crowded and noisy, the couples on the small dance floor energetic. Evan knew that the weekend live music had been Clair's idea and it had been wildly successful, drawing not only hotel guests, but locals, as well. Clair, who'd been raised to be a Southern socialite and host tea parties and fund-raisers, had proven to be a savvy businesswoman.

Making his way through the throng of people, Evan glanced around the room. A pretty blonde smiled at him and, out of habit, he smiled back, but kept moving. When a cute redhead danced in front of him, gesturing for him to move onto the dance floor with her, he shook his head.

Maybe this hadn't been such a good idea after all, he thought. He really wasn't in the mood for flirting or idle banter tonight. He started to turn around, intending to head back to his room when he spotted Jacob sitting at the bar.

"Hey," Evan yelled over the music as he slid onto the empty bar stool beside his brother. "Does your fiancé know you're hanging out in bars?"

"I'm meeting her here," Jacob yelled back, then signaled the bartender to bring another beer. "She had a meeting that went late."

"A meeting?" Evan stiffened. "Clair wasn't with Marcy tonight?"

Jacob shook his head. "Clair told me Marcy was with you."

He wasn't liking the sound of this at all. "Why did she think that?"

"Marcy left a message on Clair's machine telling her she'd be out all evening. We assumed she was with you."

"She wasn't," Evan said, frowning. "I told her to stay in tonight."

"You *told* her to stay in?"

"Maybe it was more like a strong suggestion." Worried, Evan glanced around the room. He noticed a man sitting with a pretty, shorthaired brunette in a corner booth, tried to remember where he'd seen the man before. "For her own good."

"For *her* own good—" Jacob lifted an eyebrow "—or yours?"

Evan picked up the mug of beer the bartender slid in front of him. "And what the hell is that supposed to mean?"

"You've got it bad for her," Jacob said over the pulsing Latin beat the band had slipped into. "You're the only one who doesn't know it yet. Well, you and James."

Laughing, Evan took a drink of his beer. "Boy, do you have it wrong, I don't have it bad for—" He stopped, then looked sharply at Jacob. "What about James?"

"He's a cute kid, but his light isn't shining all that bright upstairs." Grinning, Jacob sipped his beer. "He told the guys he's going to ask her out."

"Is that so?" He just might be short one crew member tomorrow, Evan thought irritably.

So is that where she was tonight? he wondered. Out

with James? He looked around the room again, but couldn't imagine the kid would bring her here, not only because Marcy wouldn't want to be out where anyone might recognize her, but also because hanging out in bars simply wasn't her style.

For some reason, Evan's attention was drawn back to the man and woman in the booth. Who *was* that guy? Evan watched the man gesture to a cocktail waitress. Whoever he was, he certainly had good taste, Evan thought. The brunette he sat next to was hot, and the little black dress and high heels she wore revealed a pair of legs that went on till Tuesday, not to mention a plunging neckline that showed a generous display of lovely female flesh.

"Hi, guys. Sorry I'm late." Clair slid her hands around Jacob's shoulders, then kissed his cheek and smiled at Evan. "Where's Marcy?"

"Evan lost her," Jacob offered.

"I didn't lose her," Evan said tightly, then stood and gave Clair his stool. "But I will go look for her."

Clair shook her head. "She left a message for me fifteen minutes ago, asking me to meet her in the lounge when I finished my appointment."

"Here?" Evan's gaze shot through the crowd of people again. "Is she crazy? Someone will spot her here, for sure."

"I thought it was a bit odd," Clair said, furrowing her forehead. "There's Sam. Let me go ask him if—ohmigod."

Evan followed the direction of Clair's startled gaze.

She was looking at the man in the corner booth. *Sam.* Her general manager. That's why the guy looked so familiar. And the hottie sitting next to him—

It couldn't be.

Evan stared at the woman in the sexy black dress and high heels. The woman with the wispy, short hair and plunging neckline.

Marcy?

He stared at her, and when her gaze lifted and met his, the corners of her glossy red mouth turned up. He'd know that smile anywhere. And those eyes.

It *was* Marcy.

His heart slammed in his chest.

"Good heavens," Clair breathed. "Well I don't think she has to worry about anyone recognizing her."

"Close your mouth, bro." Jacob slapped a hand on Evan's shoulder. "You're drooling."

"Shut up," Evan growled. But afraid that his brother was right, he snapped his jaw closed.

"Why don't you go say hi?" Jacob suggested.

"I intend to," Clair said. When Jacob grabbed her arm and eased her onto the bar stool, she looked at him. "What?"

"I was talking to Evan," he said, lifting an eyebrow.

"Oh." Clair looked at Evan, then Marcy, then back to Evan. "*Oh.* Right."

"Course, you might not want to bother her." Jacob picked up his beer and slipped an arm around Clair's waist. "Seeing's how she's on a date and all."

Date? A muscle twitched in the corner of Evan's right eye. He leaves her alone for one lousy evening and she not only turns into a sexpot, she's on a date?

He'd see about that.

He slapped his beer back onto the counter, then made his way across the bar.

Seven

Dear Marcy,
I need to replace an arched panel of glass over the
windows in my bedroom, but there are so many
choices! I'd like something that not only lets the
light in, but is romantic and pretty, as well. What
do you think will best set the mood?
Caren in Fairfax

Marcy's heart slammed against her ribs when Evan
moved through the crowded bar toward her. Good heavens! The intensity in his dark, narrowed gaze sucked the
breath right out of her. Her hand tightened on the glass
of merlot Sam had bought her. She knew if she'd have
been standing, her knees would have buckled under her
for certain.

"You okay?" Sam asked.

"Fine," she lied, gulping down a swallow of wine. "Absolutely fine."

"If you're worried about anyone recognizing you, we can—"

"No." If she wasn't so nervous, she'd have laughed. "Even *I* don't recognize me."

"Marcy." Sam smiled and covered her hand with his. "You look incredible. Relax."

It had been awkward at first, asking the Four Winds general manager to help her create a new look for herself. But Sam—and the entire staff at the beauty salon—had been wonderful. For the past five hours, she had been trimmed and polished, waxed and buffed, sculpted and dressed.

Marcy Pruitt was a new woman.

A new, *terrified* woman.

Heart hammering, she watched Evan move closer.

While she'd been sitting in the salon chair, she had told herself it didn't matter what Evan's reaction would be. She told herself she was changing her appearance because *she* wanted to. But she knew that was a lie. She hadn't done this for herself.

She'd done this for Evan.

Maybe it was stupid, maybe it was foolish, but she'd wanted him to look at her exactly the way he was looking at her right now. As if he wanted to consume her.

Sam leaned in and whispered in her ear, "I think it's time for me to go."

"Go?" At the thought of being left alone with Evan,

sheer terror shot up her spine. "But you—we just got here."

Sam glanced at Evan, who was quickly making his way toward their table. "I think we both know who you'd rather have sitting here."

She opened her mouth to protest, but it seemed useless to even attempt to lie. Apparently, Sam hadn't completely bought her story that she'd simply wanted a new look so she wouldn't have to hide in her room the rest of her visit.

With a sigh, she slumped back in her seat. "Am I that obvious?"

"You aren't, but Evan is. And if I want to keep my teeth, I better leave now." Sam looked at Evan again, then grinned. "Oh, what the hell, let's push him to the edge."

It startled Marcy when Sam leaned over and kissed her cheek. When she glanced at Evan, his eyes had narrowed to dark slits.

"Night, Marcy," Sam said, then stood and nodded at Evan. "Mr. Carver."

Evan stopped in front of the table and nodded back. "Sam."

Evan stared bullets at Sam's back when he walked away, then he slid into the booth next to Marcy. "What do you think you're doing?"

"Having a drink with Sam," she said in what she hoped was a casual tone. "At least I was."

"You know what I mean." He frowned at her. "What are you doing, hanging around in a bar, dressed like that? And what did you do to your hair?"

Her heart sank. She'd completely misread him. What a fool she'd been to even hope he might want her if she changed the way she looked. It seemed that even an army of salon technicians couldn't turn plain little Marcy Pruitt into a femme fatale. She was as resistible now as she had been before, only she was killing her feet in the process.

And *that* made her downright grumpy.

"I don't know what your problem is, Evan Carver," Marcy said coolly. "But I happen to like my hair *and* the dress and if I want to hang around in a *bar,* as you so rudely put it, then that is *my* business."

"Did I say I didn't like your hair or the dress?" He stared at her with a look of utter confusion, then sighed heavily. "For God's sake, what's not to like? What I meant was *why* did you do it?"

"I'm sick of hiding in my room, then watching over my shoulder when I do come out." Though the story obviously hadn't worked with Sam, it *was* partially true. "I figured if you and Clair and Jacob didn't recognize me, then I'd be safe."

His frown deepened. "Lady, the last thing you are right now is safe. Come on. We're getting out of here."

"But I haven't finished my—"

He took her by the hand and hauled her from the booth, then pulled her behind him through the crowd. Marcy glanced around the bar, but there was no sign of Clair and Jacob. *Some friends,* she thought, leaving her alone with Evan like this. With no one to rescue her, all she could do was toddle along behind Evan as fast as her ice-pick heels would allow.

Terrific. Her humiliation was complete. He'd probably order cocoa for her and tuck her in bed, although that was one way to get him in her bedroom, she thought.

It surprised her when Evan dragged her not toward the elevators, but outside, where he headed toward the construction site.

"What are you doing?" she managed between breaths.

"I want you to see something."

"Tonight?"

"Tonight."

So much for the new Marcy Pruitt. Apparently, Evan was still more interested in talking business. She might as well be wearing overalls and boots.

He paused at the opening of the heavy plastic liners that enclosed the construction site. "Close your eyes."

"What?"

"Close your eyes."

She sighed, then did as he asked. He took her by the shoulders, then led her through the opening. The air was hot inside, the scent of sawdust heavy. She could hear the sound of rippling water from the nearby fountain, and the faint beat of music coming from a party in one of the ballrooms.

"This is crazy," she muttered, couldn't deny that his hands on her shoulders made her pulse race. She cursed herself for being weak. "You're crazy."

"Yeah." He guided her slowly across the floor. "I think maybe I am. Okay, open your eyes."

She did, then gasped.

Moonlight streamed through the large, beveled and stained-glass window that had been installed high on one wall. The pattern was an intricate diamond cut, with a border of red roses that intertwined with vines of deep green. Over the window, an arched panel continued the diamond cut, with two red roses in the center.

It literally took her breath away.

"How…when…?"

"I had asked Olivia to keep her eyes open for a window," he said. "She found this one at an auction today."

"That's why she called you?" Marcy turned and looked at Evan. "I thought—"

She bit her lip and quickly turned back around.

"What did you think?"

She ignored his question. "Why didn't you tell me what you were doing?"

"I was going to surprise you in the morning."

The moonlight cast a pattern of iridescent diamonds and roses across the walls and stone floor. "It's beautiful."

When his hands slid up her arms and cupped her shoulders, a thrill raced up her back.

"You're beautiful," he said softly.

No man had ever said those words to her before. She

hadn't realized until this moment how badly she'd wanted to hear them. For the first time in her life, she felt like a woman. A desirable, sexy woman.

He'd moved so close their bodies were nearly touching. "What did you think when Olivia called me?" he asked her again.

With his mouth next to her ear, she couldn't even think straight, let alone lie. "I—I assumed you were with—" She hesitated. It was too embarrassing to even say it.

"With Olivia?"

She nodded.

"Marcy, I'm not interested in Olivia."

When his lips brushed her earlobe, her pulse skittered through her veins. "You're not?"

"No." He ran the tip of his finger up her neck. "Your skin feels like rose petals."

His touch sent shivers all the way down to her toes. She closed her eyes and leaned into his chest, felt the warmth of his skin radiate through his shirt.

"I like your hair short," he murmured. "Now I can do this."

He nibbled on the back of her neck and her knees went weak. "That's—" she shuddered when his teeth nipped skin "—nice."

He lifted his head. "Just nice?"

"*Very* nice."

"Marcy," he whispered softly. "I want you."

Her heart leaped. "I—I want you, too."

He turned her in his arms and looked down at her, his gaze somber. "I need you to be sure. If you have any doubts, then just—"

She touched the tips of her fingers to his mouth. "No doubts."

He kissed her fingers, then circled her wrist with his hand and pressed his mouth to her palm. Such a simple touch, yet it made her blood burn. When he bent his head, she slid her hands around his shoulders and pressed closer, parting her lips when his mouth touched hers. His kiss was gentle, but insistent, and when he pulled away, they were both breathing hard.

Desire glinted dark in his eyes. He took her hand and turned. "Let's go."

She hurried after him, struggling to keep up with his long strides. A mix of excitement and nervousness shivered through her, but she wanted this, wanted Evan, with a need she'd never experienced before. Knowing that he wanted her, too, made her heart sing with joy.

His face set with purpose, he led her to the elevators without saying a word. Once they were inside and the doors swished closed, he dragged her into his arms again. His mouth was hungry and hard, and his kisses left her breathless.

"My room." He reached for her hand again when the elevator doors opened.

"Wait." She paused to take off her shoes, then together they hurried down the hall.

She felt giddy and delirious with anticipation. He dropped his room card twice and they were both laughing when he finally managed to get the door open.

He pulled her inside, then dropped his mouth on hers and backed her up against the closed door. She melted against him, returning his kiss, meeting the thrust of his hot tongue with her own.

Her shoes tumbled to the floor.

When his hands slid slowly down her arms and the tips of his thumbs brushed the sides of her breasts, pleasure shot through her like a hot spear.

"You are so damn soft," he said raggedly. "I've wanted to get my hands on you since the minute I met you."

Since the minute I met you? Stunned, she lifted her gaze to his. "You mean before I—before tonight?"

He smiled at her. "Sugarplum, you look sexy as hell, and I'd be lying if I didn't say I love what you've done. But you didn't have to change one little thing for me. Even those overalls you've been wearing all week turned me on."

"My overalls?" She furrowed her forehead. "You're kidding."

"Nope." He ran his lips over hers and nibbled the corner of her mouth. "I couldn't stop thinking about taking them off you."

He meant it, she realized. He really had wanted her before tonight. Had thought about her in her *overalls,* for heaven's sake! His words thrilled and empowered her, brought out the woman in her she hadn't known existed until this moment.

"Well, if you prefer them to this dress," she teased, "I suppose I could go put them on."

"You're not going anywhere, Miss Pruitt," he said, shaking his head. "Except my bed."

She gasped when he swept her up in his arms and headed for the bedroom. She wrapped her arms around his strong shoulders, breathed in the fresh, manly scent of his skin. Salty, she thought, sliding her tongue over a spot directly below his earlobe. Spicy. He sucked in a breath when she explored the area further with her teeth and tongue. It surprised, and pleased her that she could draw that kind of a reaction from him, made her wonder what else she could do…

It would be interesting to find out.

He stopped beside the bed, crushing his mouth to hers as he lowered her to the floor. She wrapped her arms tightly around his neck and clung to him. Sensations spiraled through her, textures, and colors, as brilliant as they were intricate, all swirled together in a vortex of need. This moment, this man; there was nothing else.

Oh, but there *was* something else, she thought dimly when he reached for the zipper on the back of her dress. There was a great deal more.

She shivered with anticipation.

The soft rasp of her zipper mixed with the sounds of their labored breathing. His callused hands skimmed over the sensitive skin on her back; pleasure, intense, shimmering, rippled through her body. Her dress floated slowly down her body, pooled around her bare feet. She stood before him, naked, except for two slivers of black satin.

"I want to see you," he whispered, then inched back and looked down at her.

His gaze seared her, heated her insides, softened her bones. If her knees hadn't locked, she was certain she would have sunk to the floor. She heard Evan's soft hiss as he released a breath, heard him mutter something inaudible. He reached for her, cupped her aching, swollen breasts in his large hands, then caressed the hardened nipples with the pads of his thumbs.

Her head dropped back on a moan, and when he lowered his head and kissed the soft swell of one breast, she bit her bottom lip and sucked in a breath. He took his time, nuzzling, lightly biting her skin. Impatient, eager, she twisted against him, wanting him to hurry. But still he took his time, a lifetime, she thought, until finally his hands moved to the clasp of her bra. It fell away.

His mouth was hot and wet; his tongue stroked. When he drew her nipple in and sucked gently, a sharp arrow of intense pleasure shot from her breast to the V of her legs. She moaned, overpowered by the driving, overwhelming need coursing through her. He took his time, giving equal attention to each breast. With every heated kiss and slide of his hands and tongue, the tension coiled inside her, tighter and tighter, until she thought she could bear it no longer.

"Evan," she gasped, dragging her hands through his thick, dark hair. "Please."

They tumbled to the bed, rolled until he was over her, his hands moving up her thighs, over her hips. The texture of his rough hands on her soft skin was like nothing she'd ever experienced before. She felt wonderfully, gloriously *alive,* as if every nerve ending were exposed, and she shuddered from the intense pleasure rippling over her body.

"Clothes," she murmured, working clumsily at the buttons on his shirt. When the last one opened, he yanked the shirt off, his mouth never leaving hers. Quickly, eagerly, she moved her hands over his solid, broad chest and arms, felt the ripple of sinew and the heat of arousal. She wanted to touch him all over, wanted him to touch her all over. She spread her fingers across his chest, then pressed her lips to his hot skin. His muscles jumped under her touch, and when she slid her hands down his belly to the buckle of his belt and opened it, he drew in a breath.

He moved away from her, quickly tugging off his clothes, and then he was back, his mouth on hers, kissing her hard and deep, until she was dizzy and gasping for breath.

His hand slid to the juncture of her thighs and cupped her; she sank back into the mattress on a moan, and when his finger slipped under the thin sliver of black satin and into the hot, damp glove of her body and stroked her, she writhed under his touch.

She reached for him, closed her hand around the

hard length of his arousal, stunned at the feel of velvet over steel. The longing in her turned to a desperation. She wanted, *needed* him inside her and she stroked him, wanting to pleasure him as he did her.

"Wait." He stilled her hand, then circled her wrist with his fingers. "Not yet."

She wanted to protest, but then his mouth clamped onto her breast and sucked hard. Instinctively, her body bowed upward. His tongue laved her tight, pebbled nipple while his finger continued to stroke between her thighs. She gripped the bedclothes in her fists, felt the cool sheets against her back while fire raced through her blood. And then the sliver of black satin was gone and his mouth moved down her belly. She stilled, shocked at the direction of his roving lips.

"Evan! It's too—I can't—"

But her words were cut off when his lips moved over her, lightly nipping, caressing. When the tip of his tongue found the core of her, she bucked upward, dragging her fingers across his scalp on a gasp.

A person could surely die from pleasure this intense, she thought. Her entire body throbbed, and the pleasure mixed with pain.

"Please," she begged. "Now…"

He lifted his head, blazed kisses across her belly, her hip, then he moved away, left her quivering with need while he dug through the nightstand. And then he was back, lowering himself between her legs, easing himself gently into the heat of her body.

"I don't want to hurt you," he murmured, bracing himself on his forearms.

"You won't." She wound her arms tightly around his shoulders and wrapped her legs over his. "It's wonderful."

Still, he hesitated, and she could see the effort in the tight set of his jaw and narrowed eyes. Sweat beaded on his forehead.

"Just tell me if—"

"Now," she repeated, lifting herself up, moving her hips against his in a sensual rhythm as old as time.

Desire swamped caution, and the need, raw and wild, consumed them both. The urgency built, higher, hotter, tighter, then broke fiercely inside her, his name on her lips when she shattered. His hands on her hips, he held her tightly, his thrusts deep and hard, fast. On a groan, he shuddered violently, again and again.

When he stilled, she slid her arms around his neck to steady herself as much as to draw him closer. The weight of his body pressed her into the mattress. Smiling, she sank into the softness and brought him with her.

"I'm crushing you," Evan said when he could think again, when he could breathe. His heart was still thundering in his head, his lungs burning.

"No." She tightened her hold on him. "Don't move."

He didn't think he had the strength to. No experience had ever left him this spent, this weak, and the best he could manage was to lift his head and gaze down at her.

And feel as if he'd been socked in the gut.

The moonlight played across her face, giving her an ethereal appearance. As he looked at her, he felt something shift in his chest and thicken in his throat.

Beautiful, he thought. She was absolutely beautiful. Her eyes were closed, the corners of her kiss-swollen lips curved into a contented smile. Knowing that he'd put that smile there, he couldn't stop the smug satisfaction sprinting through his veins.

"Are you okay?" he asked quietly.

Her eyes slowly fluttered open. "If you have to ask, I must have done something wrong."

"You know what I mean." He kissed the tip of her nose. "And trust me, you sure as hell didn't do anything wrong. That's about as right as it gets."

"It *was* pretty amazing." Smiling, she ran her fingertips over his shoulders. "Is it always like that?"

It's never been like that, was his first thought, though he couldn't exactly define what was different about making love with Marcy. And some things he simply preferred not to analyze. "You're amazing."

Her smile widened, then she dropped her gaze. "I never thought I'd be any good at it."

"Why on earth would you think that?"

"I always figured there was something wrong with me because I was more interested in my work than in dating or sex. I'd hear other women talk about it, but I never could really understand what all the hoopla was about. And now—" she raked her fingers lightly across his back "—well, now, I do."

The light rake of her fingernails on his skin and the upward thrust of her hips made his heart slam in his chest. He clamped his hands on her hips and rolled to his back, bringing her with him. Eyes wide, she gasped at the unexpected movement.

"I've heard it called many things." He slid his hands up her sides, then cupped her pretty breasts in his hands, watched her gaze darken with desire again. "But never a hoopla."

Chuckling, she covered his hands with her own, then the smile faded from her mouth as she found her rhythm. He'd never seen anything more arousing than the sight of her moving over him, her lips softly parted, her eyes clouded with need.

"You know," she said, her voice breathless, "you called a six-thirty start tomorrow."

"Thinking about work?"

"Just wondering how late I can keep you up." Her eyes widened as she realized what she'd said. "I mean, awake."

Laughing softly, he thrust his hips up to meet hers. "Why don't we find out?"

Eight

Dear Marcy,
I loved your article on diet and nutrition in your
March issue. Do you have any other suggestions
for cutting calories and getting in shape?
Jeannie in Cortland

Every muscle in her body ached when Marcy woke at
5 a.m. She wasn't certain she could move, let alone get
out of bed, get dressed and walk across the hall to her
own room.

She hadn't intended to stay the night, had even tried
to leave at 2 a.m., then again at three. But each time
Evan had dragged her back into his arms, and each time
he'd changed her mind.

Not that she'd put up much of a fight.

She looked at the man sleeping soundly beside her.
He lay on his stomach, one muscled arm wrapped
around a pillow, the other arm draped possessively

across her waist. Even in sleep he looked tough and rugged and absolutely virile.

Even in sleep he made her tingle all over.

After the night they'd spent together, she wouldn't have thought she'd had any tingle left in her. Evan had been an amazing lover. Tender and gentle one moment, then lusty and demanding the next.

What shocked, and delighted her, was that she'd been equally lusty. Equally demanding.

Who would have ever thought?

No one, she thought. Least of all herself. And the wonder of it left her positively in awe. And absolutely thrilled.

There were no regrets. She believed in fate. Believed that whatever happened in life was meant to be. She'd waited for the right moment, for the right man. Last night was the moment; Evan was the man.

She studied his face in the dim light, resisted the urge to run her fingertips over the dark shadow of his morning beard. And it wasn't just his face she wanted to touch. She wanted to explore every inch of solid muscle, every hard plane and sharp angle of masculine physique. Curiosity might have killed the cat, she thought, but she would certainly die one happy cat.

Desperately, she tried not to confuse the physical act of making love with the emotional feeling of love. But lying here, her body still humming from the most incredible night of her life, the line between the two was hazy. In the light of day, perhaps, that line would be more distinct. But there was no future for them; she was certain of that, and it would be very foolish to let herself fall in love with Evan.

She didn't have the experience to know how to act now, or what to say. When she thought about what they'd shared last night, what they'd done, her cheeks burned. Maybe it would be easier if she wasn't here when he woke. Isn't that what men always said they wanted? Space? She could give him that.

Holding her breath, she slowly, quietly, eased herself from under his arm, then sat on the edge of the bed and reached for her dress.

"Get back here."

She jumped at the sound of his raspy voice, didn't have time to respond before his hand snaked out and dragged her back into bed with him.

"It's five o'clock," she argued, then gasped when he rolled and pinned her underneath him.

"Yeah?" He rubbed his lips lightly over hers. "So?"

"You have to be—"

"Right here." He nuzzled the corner of her mouth. "And right here."

When he blazed feather-light kisses across her jaw, then down her neck, she sighed. When he nibbled on her shoulder, she shivered.

"Right there is nice, too," she said breathlessly.

He took his time, moving his mouth over her, gently biting, tasting, until she was floating on a soft cloud of sensual pleasure.

When his mouth moved to her breasts, the cloud

turned thick and heavy, darkening with every brush of his lips and every slide of his tongue. She arched upward when he sucked strongly on her nipple, moved her hips against his. When he kneed her thighs apart, then slid inside her, she groaned.

She murmured his name, met every thrust of his hips, wrapped her arms and legs tightly around him. The urgency grew, higher and hotter, coiling tighter, then tighter still.

The climax rolled through her, then broke apart. She cried out, raking her nails across the rippling muscles of his broad shoulders. He thrust harder, deeper, then moaned, shuddered with the force of his climax.

Her arms slid bonelessly to her sides. She wasn't sure how much time had passed before she was able to think again. If she'd had the strength, she might have glanced at the bedside clock.

As her senses returned, she heard the sound of Evan's harsh breathing and felt the wild beating of his heart. He lay sprawled on top of her, heavy, but not uncomfortable.

"Wow," he murmured, rubbing his lips across her jaw.

She smiled. It was the sweetest, most wonderful thing any man had ever said to her.

"Yeah." She found the strength to slide her hands up his arms. "Wow."

He raised himself on his elbows and gazed down at her. "You are the damnedest woman, Miss Pruitt."

She traced a fingertip over his chin. "I hope that's a compliment."

"Oh, yeah." He kissed her fingertips. "It's a compliment."

"Thank you," she said primly, then drew in a sharp breath when he slid his hands down her sides and cupped her breasts. "By the way—" she struggled to pull air into her lungs "—I agree with your reasoning to go into the construction business instead of the sciences."

"Oh?" He circled her nipples with the pads of his thumbs and she squirmed, was shocked at the rush of desire coursing through her. "And what reason was that?"

"You really are very, very good with your hands."

Evan did his best not to whistle when he walked onto the job site later that morning. The last thing he needed was to draw any unwanted attention from his men, and the fact that he was more than an hour late would already raise a few eyebrows. If he showed up in a good mood, as well, he'd be the subject of intense scrutiny, not to mention a great deal of ribbing.

But hell, he *was* the boss here, he reasoned. As long as the work got done, he could be as late as he wanted—although he might never have shown up at all if he'd done what he wanted.

It was damn hard to leave a sexy, naked woman in his bed.

He'd told Marcy to stay in and get some sleep, that there really wasn't anything she needed to do until after the drywall was up and they looked at paint samples. But his motive for suggesting she sleep in had been entirely selfish. He couldn't wait to get the woman back in bed tonight, and he wanted her well rested when he did.

He'd certainly been right about one thing. Marcy's enthusiasm and creativity had carried over into the bedroom.

He still wasn't sure exactly what had happened last night. Well, other than the fact that they'd made love. Several times, he thought, smiling. But something else had taken place, too. Something that went beyond simple pleasure. He'd hardly been a monk in his life, but he'd never experienced anything like this before. Never experienced anything like Marcy.

The intensity. The near insanity. The overwhelming desperation. It was all new to him. It made him edgy and yet exhilarated at the same time.

"You should probably wipe that grin off your face," Evan heard Jacob say from behind him. "The men are already taking bets as to who the lucky lady was last night."

When Evan turned, Jacob held out a tall, steaming mug of coffee. Frowning, Evan took the mug. "Don't mess with me, bro. It's too damn early."

"I'm not messing with you."

Evan looked at his crew, who were all staring at him. When he scowled at them, they all quickly turned back to their work.

"Nobody looks that happy in the morning unless they got—"

"Shut up." Evan lowered his voice when a few men glanced over. "It wasn't like that."

"So what was it then?"

"None of your damn business," Evan said irritably.

"Normally, I'd agree with you," Jacob said evenly. "But we're talking about a woman's reputation here, and she's one of Clair's best friends, too."

Jacob was right, Evan thought with a sigh. He just wasn't used to explaining himself to anyone. "I like her. That's what this is. She's smart and sweet and there's nothing phony about her. She's...different from any other woman I've ever been with before."

"To say the least," Jacob said with a nod. "She's also more vulnerable."

"You think I don't know that?" Evan shot back, then dragged a hand through his hair. "Why the hell do you think I've kept my hands off her this long? But it happened, and I'm not sorry it did. And I can tell you right now, it's going to happen again."

"You're both adults." Jacob folded his arms. "All I'm asking is for you to be careful."

"I am being careful," he said, letting his temper ease off. "She's the last person I want to see get hurt. But we happen to enjoy each other's company, so until she goes back to Los Angeles, that's the way it is."

"Is that so?"

"That's what I said, didn't I?" Evan didn't like the look in Jacob's eyes. One of those big-brother, I-know-something-you-don't looks. "Now if you're through interrogating me, do you think we can get to work?"

"Uh, boss?"

James stood a few feet away, shifting awkwardly. Evan glared at the young man, hoped he hadn't heard the exchange between Jacob and himself. "What?"

"Uh, do you know where Marcy is?"

Talk about bad timing. Part of Evan wanted to say *yeah, she's in my bed, now buzz off and don't even think about looking at her again.* But the part of his brain that was still managing to operate properly took control. "Why do you want to know?"

"Well, there was an inspector here asking about her a while ago."

"Inspector?" Evan narrowed his gaze. "What inspector?"

"Tall guy, thick glasses, hard hat and clipboard. Said he was from Building and Safety, and that she'd asked him about a code spec."

Evan looked at Jacob, saw the concern in his brother's eyes. "Do you know anything about this?"

Jacob shook his head. "I just got here ten minutes ago."

Evan was as sure as he could be that Marcy hadn't called or even spoken to Building and Safety about a code spec. He wasn't liking the sound of this one little bit. "He asked specifically for Marcy Pruitt?"

"I think so." James scratched his neck. "Or maybe he didn't. Gosh, now I'm not sure."

Evan clenched his jaw. "And what did you tell him?"

James grinned. "I told him I didn't know who he was talking about."

Thank God. Evan released the breath he'd been holding. "All right, but if you see this guy again, let me know."

"Sure thing." James shoved his hands into the front pockets of his jeans. "So, ah, *do* you know where she is?"

Evan narrowed a look at James. "Get your butt back to work or you're fired."

"But—"

"Now," Evan barked.

"Sure, boss."

Evan glared at James's back as he scurried away.

"Well, that was subtle," Jacob said, shaking his head.

"Tell Tom I'll be gone for a while." Evan took off the tool belt he'd just strapped on. "You keep an eye out for anyone hanging around who shouldn't be."

Dammit! Evan turned and headed back toward the elevators. If he hadn't been late, he'd have been here when the guy had shown up. And if he hadn't really been an inspector, Evan thought, he'd have given the man something to look for, all right—his teeth.

But now, Evan was more concerned about Marcy than putting his fist in some jerk's face. He needed to know she was all right. The image of her lying in his bed, those long legs of hers entwined in the rumpled sheets, her hair tousled and her cheeks flushed, quickened more than his pace.

Hopefully—he glanced at his wristwatch as he pushed the elevator button—the woman would be right where he'd left her.

* * *

The Four Winds coffee shop had the same casual finesse as the rest of the hotel. Mirrored walls, soft leather
booths, fresh flowers. In spite of the early hour, several
tables were occupied by hotel guests, but no one seemed
to notice Marcy as she followed a cheerful, gray-haired
hostess to a corner booth where Clair was already
seated. It felt good, Marcy thought, to walk in a public
place and not have people stare at her. Although, as she
glanced around the restaurant, she did notice a nice-
looking man watching her over the newspaper he was
reading.

The attention gave her an extra shot of confidence,
but she wasn't interested in any man other than Evan.
She knew she was walking around with a silly grin on
her face, but she couldn't help herself. It was all she
could do to keep herself from skipping across the restaurant.

Her smile widened when she slipped into the booth
with Clair and gave her a quick hug. "Thank you so
much for meeting me."

"You're kidding, right?" Clair slid a cup of steaming coffee across the table toward Marcy. "Jacob had to
hold me back from calling you at six. Look at you, my
God! You look amazing. And your hair—I love it!"

Smiling, Marcy touched the short ends at the back
of her neck. They were still damp from her rushed
shower, but all the cut required was a quick blow-dry
and a simple finger comb. Her face felt naked without

her glasses, but she'd taken the time to brush on some pink lip gloss and a touch of mascara—something she wouldn't have bothered to do before today.

When she glanced in the mirrored wall, she still didn't recognize the woman staring back.

"It's going to take some getting used to," she said, looking back at Clair. "But I like it, too. Your salon staff are all magicians."

"They're good, granted, but they had a great subject to work with." Clair scooted in closer. "Now you want to tell me what possessed you to take a multimillion-dollar image and change it?"

"My hair will grow back." With what she hoped was a casual shrug, Marcy picked up a menu. "I was just tired of hiding out and looking over my shoulder all the time." She used the exact same words she'd said to Evan last night. "I figured if you and Jacob and Evan couldn't recognize me, then no one else will, either."

Clair gave her the same doubtful look that Evan had. "You're saying you did this because you didn't want anyone to recognize you?"

Without her glasses, Marcy had to bring the menu a little closer than normal. "Of course."

"Marcy." Clair pushed the menu back down with her finger. "Sorry, hon, but you never were a very good liar. And I'm not blind. I saw the look in Evan's eyes when he dragged you out of the lounge last night. You want to tell me what that was all about?"

Marcy tightened her grip on the menu. Why had she thought she could hide the truth from Clair, when even Sam had seen through her? Drawing in a breath to steady her nerves, she closed her menu and met Clair's gaze. "We...slept together."

"Well, duh." Clair rolled her eyes. "I can see that."

Feeling as if all eyes in the restaurant were staring at her, Marcy quickly glanced around, breathed a sigh of relief when she realized no one was watching. Not even the man who'd been reading his newspaper. Now he was staring at a pretty blonde who'd slipped into a booth next to his. Fickle man, she thought with a smile, then looked back at Clair. "What do you mean, you can see?"

"Honey, you're glowing, and when you walked through the restaurant, you looked like you wanted to hug every person here. Trust me, I know that look."

Well, so much for her weak attempt at being nonchalant, Marcy thought. But why was she trying to be casual about the most wonderful night of her life, anyway? Clair was the one person—probably the only person—that Marcy knew she could trust implicitly. Who better to share her joy with?

"Actually," Marcy said quietly, then leaned in closer and smiled slowly, "I felt like skipping."

"Skipping?" Clair arched an eyebrow and picked up a glass of water. "Now *that* sounds serious."

"Oh, not at all," Marcy said, shaking her head. "It's just sex."

"Marcy!" Water sloshed over the sides of Clair's water glass. "I can't believe you just said that."

"Me, either." She laughed at herself, and the look of shock on Clair's face. "But I'm in too good of a mood to be embarrassed. Evan and I might have slept together, but it was just one night, sort of a culmination of all the time we've been spending together."

"That's an understatement." Clair blew out a breath. "So that's it? You're telling me you had a one-night stand with my fiancé's brother and you're fine with that?"

She picked up her coffee and sipped. "Absolutely."

"And you're also saying it's not going to happen again?"

"I really haven't thought that far ahead." Nor could she allow herself to. If making love with Evan was just "one of those crazy, wild nights," then she'd at least have that to take home with her. The last thing she wanted was for Evan to feel awkward around her. And she didn't want him to think that she had any expectations. That would certainly send him running in the opposite direction as fast as his truck and trailer would take him.

"I need to sit down," Clair said, blinking slowly. "Wait. I am sitting down."

Marcy smiled. "I'm still trying to absorb it all myself. But whatever happens, I promise it won't effect Evan's and my working on the chapel. And at the speed Evan's men are moving along, it should be finished in just a few days. You've already got your flowers ordered and I can get the garden area planted easily and, ohmigod, I haven't told you about the stained-glass window yet, you won't believe—"

"Marcy," Clair said quietly, but with emphasis. "Stop already. I'm not worried about the chapel. I'm worried about you."

"Me? Why?"

"Honey, I don't want to see you get hurt."

"Believe me, I've given that a great deal of thought." It was all she could do *not* to think about it. "I'm certain that as long as Evan and I can stay friends, then our relationship doesn't have to be awkward, now or later."

"Friends." Dazed, Clair leaned back in her seat. "You really believe that?"

"I know there are risks," Marcy said softly. "What's life without them? I've been sheltered most of my life, first by my aunt, then by Helen. You of all people know what that's like. But when you ran out of that church, you took a risk. If you had known then that everything between you and Jacob would end badly, would you have done anything differently?"

Clair sighed, then shook her head. "Not one single thing."

"So there you go." Smiling, Marcy covered Clair's hand. "Now can we order food? I'm absolutely starving. Did you know that just kissing for thirty minutes can burn twenty-eight calories? And when you—"

"Dammit, Marcy, where the hell have you been?"

She'd been so engrossed in her conversation with Clair, Marcy hadn't noticed Evan come into the restaurant. Arms folded, he stood beside the table, his eyes narrowed.

"What do you mean, where have I been?" Confused by his behavior, she stared at him. "I've been right here."

"You were supposed to be sleeping," he said tightly. "Why didn't you tell me where you'd be?"

She frowned at him. "I didn't know I needed to."

He slid onto the seat beside her, shocked her when he dropped a kiss on her lips. "Well, you do. Mornin', Clair."

"Morning, Evan." Clair cleared her throat, then pushed her coffee aside. "Ah, maybe I should get to work."

Somber, Evan shook his head. "No, stay."

It struck Marcy that Evan wasn't angry, he was worried. "Is there a problem?" she asked.

"I'm not sure." Evan picked up Marcy's coffee cup and drank from it. "Did you call or speak to anyone at Building and Safety about any code specs?"

She thought about his question. "I know I didn't call, but I suppose it's possible I might have spoken to one of the inspectors at the site. I really wouldn't know if they were with Building and Safety or part of the crew. Why?"

"James said someone was asking about you this morning." He looked at Clair. "Has your staff noticed anyone hanging around who shouldn't be?"

Clair shook her head. "No, but I'll call a staff meeting later and let everyone know to be extra cautious." She glanced at her watch. "I'll also go over all the check-ins for the past few days and see if anyone looks suspicious. If someone knew Marcy was at this hotel, it would make sense they'd stay here, too."

Evan nodded. "Sounds good. And maybe while you're at it, you should change her room. Just in case she's already been spotted. Better yet, she can move her things into my room."

"What!" With great effort, Marcy jumped into a conversation that was already moving at warp speed. "Stop. Both of you. Just stop."

When both Clair and Evan stared at her, waiting, she swallowed, then squared her shoulders. "I don't need to move anywhere. You're both making assumptions, and anyway, even if someone was looking for Marcy Pruitt, do you think he'd recognize me now? The two of you didn't even know who I was last night."

"I suppose that's true," Clair said hesitantly.

Evan frowned. "Maybe, but nevertheless, I'll feel better if you move her into my room."

"*You'll* feel better?" Marcy pressed her lips together and arched an eyebrow. "How about you ask me how *I* feel about that?"

Evan's frown darkened. "Fine. How do you feel about that?"

She took her coffee cup from Evan's hands, then sipped as she looked at Clair. "I'll move my things this morning."

Nine

Dear Marcy,
Help! There are too many choices for wedding hair accessories. Combs and clips, jeweled hair sticks, barrettes, hairpins, tiaras. I know it's a personal choice, but I simply can't decide. What do you suggest?
Arlene in Alabama

With the drywall up and the first coat of mud on, Evan sent his crew home for the day and knocked off early himself. At the rate they were going, the chapel would easily be finished by early next week and that would give them one more week to take their time with the details or any problems that might still arise.

There'd been a camaraderie on this project unlike any he'd ever seen before. Partly because his crew all knew Jacob and liked him, but Evan was sure it was mostly because his men had wanted to please Marcy.

The fact that she hadn't shown up today had caused concern, but Evan had reassured everyone that she was fine and she'd be back tomorrow.

Moving her out of her suite and into his made sense, Evan reassured himself as he rode up the elevator. If this P.I. had managed to track her down to the Four Winds, then it would look as if she'd checked out. Even if the guy was still hanging around, the odds of him recognizing the new Marcy Pruitt were pretty slim. And if he kept her close, Evan reasoned, it would be easier to watch for anyone who might be watching her.

And besides, she'd spent more time in his suite than her own these past few days, anyway. They were both adults, two people mutually attracted to each other. Now that they were sleeping together, why have two rooms when one would do just as well?

Still, it *had* been an impulsive decision. He knew Jacob was right, that Marcy's inexperience with men made her vulnerable. Which was exactly why he probably shouldn't have asked her to move into his room, Evan thought. He cared about Marcy. Probably more than any other woman he'd been with before. He'd chew nails and swallow them before he'd see her hurt.

Damn. He stepped off the elevator and headed for his room. Maybe he hadn't thought this through very well. Maybe it wasn't such a hot idea, after all. He felt a tightening around his throat, then wiped at the fine layer of sawdust on his temple. Maybe he should talk to her. Give her an out now, before things got more—what was the word she'd used herself? Complicated.

He stepped into the room, smiled when he heard the sound of her quietly singing in the bedroom, then moved to the door. The first thing he noticed was the pile of shopping bags on the bed. The second thing he noticed was her.

She stood in front of the closet-door mirrors, wearing a soft pink slip dress. The hem of the dress skimmed her calves, but when she swiveled her hips, the flared skirt danced around her knees.

Damn.

He took in the sight of her long legs, her slender neck and graceful arms. He had to grab hold of the doorjamb to brace himself. There was a lump in his throat, a mixture of lust and fear and something else he couldn't identify. He swallowed hard, and when his brain cleared, managed to catch a few words of what she was singing: …*never gonna get it, never gonna get it*…

"Never gonna get what?"

Clutching her throat, she spun on a gasp. "Evan!"

He stayed where he was, partly because his legs were still locked into place, partly because he was afraid he'd have to touch her if he moved any closer.

"Nice dress."

"Thank you." Her cheeks were a deeper shade of pink than her dress. "I didn't hear you come in."

"Just got here." Lord, she looked pretty in pink. It was all he could do not to put his work-dirty hands on her and gobble her up. "Looks like you went shopping."

"I did. Well, we did." She moved to the bed and picked up a blouse lying there, held it to her chest to cover herself. "Clair has a great boutique here at the hotel, plus we went out to a couple of dress shops in town."

He understood she was modest, but considering the night they'd spent together, it was a little late to hide that lovely body of hers from him. "Looks like you're going to need another suitcase."

"Maybe." She looked at all the clothes. "Or maybe I'll just get rid of what I brought."

"Really?" He leaned against the doorjamb, watched the hem of her skirt flitter around her calves as she shifted awkwardly back and forth. "So you're keeping this new Marcy?"

"I'm thinking about it." She glanced in the mirror at herself, then looked back at him. "What do you think?"

It startled him when his first thought was that *he'd* like to keep her. He shook that thought off and smiled at her. "You looking for a compliment?"

"What if I am?"

When one corner of her mouth curved up and she tossed the blouse back on the bed, his heart jumped into his throat. Another side of her he hadn't see before, he thought—the tease.

He definitely liked it.

He moved toward her and took her hand in his. The texture of her soft, smooth skin against his rough, dust-covered palm absolutely floored him.

"This is what I think." He placed her hand on his chest. "That's what you do to me when I look at you."

His heart was pounding like a bass drum under her fingertips. He watched her catch her bottom lip with her teeth, then smile shyly at him. "Me, too," she said.

"I told you the truth last night, Marcy." He brought her hand to his mouth and pressed his lips to her palm. "You got to me the first time I laid eyes on you. You were so damn cute in that silly hat, so flustered trying not to lie to those women. Makes me laugh every time I think about it."

She stared at him with a mixture of wonder and amazement in her smoky-green eyes. "I—I'm not even going to pretend to know what to say to that."

"You don't have to say anything." When he kissed her wrist, he felt her pulse flutter under his fingertips. "Just stand right there while I go take the world's fastest shower."

"I won't move," she said, her voice breathless.

He started for the bathroom, reached the doorway, then swung around on his heels and came back to her.

"On second thought," he said, grabbing her hand and pulling her to the bathroom with him, "let's make it a nice, long shower. Together."

Sometime later when they were lying in his bed, incapable of movement, Evan realized that he'd completely forgotten about the talk he'd intended to have with Marcy. The one where he would give her an out if she really didn't want to stay in his room. The talk about how maybe they shouldn't complicate their relationship any more than they already had. The talk about how he didn't want her to get hurt.

It was no longer an issue, he decided. She was staying with him and he didn't want to give her an out. And as far as their relationship getting complicated, it was way too late to prevent that.

He still didn't want to hurt her, of course. But who was to say he would? He'd made it clear he wasn't looking to settle down. She was a big girl and they were both adults. They'd tried to deny their attraction and that sure as hell hadn't worked. For the next two weeks, why shouldn't they simply enjoy each other?

Why not indeed? he thought, and tucked her warm body closer to his. With a sigh, she snuggled against him, then drifted off to sleep.

Yeah. He closed his eyes and smiled.

Why not indeed.

"My baby. My beautiful baby." Josephine Beauchamp slipped the last pin into her daughter's veil, then stepped back and clasped her hands to her chest. "Isn't she the most beautiful bride you've ever seen?"

"Mother, please, enough," Clair complained. "You've asked Marcy at least ten times already."

"She does look beautiful," Marcy agreed, and it was true, of course. With her hair pulled back to set off her exotic looks, and the heart-shaped neckline of her beaded gown, Clair was truly a vision in white. "And so do you, Mrs. Beauchamp."

Josephine was a stunning woman, Marcy thought. She looked at least ten years younger than her fifty years and had a figure a thirty-year-old would kill for. Shiny black hair, high cheekbones, deep, blue eyes that matched her designer silk suit—no one would have ever guessed she wasn't Clair's birth mother.

"Thank you, Marcy. And you—" Josephine touched Marcy's cheek and smiled. "Absolutely exquisite."

When Josephine turned back to fuss with Clair's veil, Marcy relaxed. It still made her uncomfortable when anyone complimented her. Not that she hadn't appreciated all the kind words she'd heard over the past few days. She'd enjoyed it immensely. In her entire twenty-six years, she'd never once been whistled at, but when she'd returned to the work site with her new haircut and no glasses, there had been several whistles. When the men realized who she was, the whistles were followed by a long, stunned silence, then a round of applause, then more whistles. Though they'd made her blush, she hadn't minded the attention, but Evan certainly had. He nearly burst a vein when he yelled for everyone to get back to work. At that point, it hadn't taken a genius for everyone—including James—to figure out that she and Evan were sleeping together.

Even to herself, it seemed odd she didn't mind the crew knowing about her and Evan. She wasn't ashamed, and she wasn't embarrassed. She was deliriously happy.

She was hopelessly in love.

It was a mistake, falling in love with Evan. She'd known that from the beginning, had listed all the reasons to remain objective in their relationship, even after they'd shared a bed.

Unfortunately, logic did not exist in the heart. She'd given her feelings flight, and for what felt like a brief, exhilarating moment, she'd soared higher than she could have ever imagined. She wouldn't regret that, not ever.

Tomorrow afternoon she would board a plane for Los Angeles. The day after that, she would be back to work.

Back to reality. Back to the real world.

But if lying in Evan's arms, making love with him, laughing, working, even just sitting on the sofa watching TV—if all that wasn't reality, if that wasn't real, then why did it suddenly hurt so bad?

She wouldn't think about it now. Today was Clair and Jacob's day. Today she would smile and be happy for them. She would enjoy her last day here with her friends and her last evening with Evan. Cherish each and every moment.

A quick knock at the door, then Julianna stuck her head in. "We're good to go out here," she said, smiling at Clair. "You ready?"

"Ready," Clair said, excitement sparkling in her eyes. "Let's do it."

While a string quartet entertained the waiting guests, Evan stood at the front of the crowded chapel, clench-

ing his jaw to distract himself from the bow tie squeez-
ing his throat. How the hell did they expect a guy to even
breathe in this monkey suit? he wondered. He figured
if he turned blue, he'd at least match the color of the
bridesmaids' dresses.

To Evan's left, Rand, Lucas and Seth had assumed
the position of groomsmen, as well, and to Evan's right,
the groom himself stood as rigid as the beam resting fifteen feet over his head, the same beam that Jacob had
helped set in place just two weeks ago.

It amazed Evan that they'd finished with four days
to spare, plenty of time for Marcy to add the finishing
touches: lush ferns, bubbling wall fountain, oak pews
salvaged from an abandoned church and refurbished, a
five-foot bronze statue of an angel. Shoot, even *he*
would want to be married here, he thought, then quickly
frowned.

Figuratively speaking, of course.

Evan stretched his neck to allow more air through his
windpipe, then glanced at the wedding guests. Over the
past couple of weeks, especially since the incident at the
work site, it had become a habit to search the faces
around him to look for anyone who might be watching
Marcy. But considering the way she'd changed her appearance, watching the people watching Marcy had become a full-time job.

He almost wished she'd kept her old look. At least
that way he wouldn't have to walk around with the urge
to start a fight with nearly every male who came within

twenty feet of her. He'd never had an issue with jealousy before. What the hell was happening to him?

She'd gotten under his skin, dammit. He wasn't even sure how it had happened, or exactly when, but it had. On the job site he found himself constantly seeking her out, and when she wasn't there, he wondered what she was doing. She consumed his thoughts, and it was downright irritating.

They hadn't talked about it, but he knew she had a flight back to Los Angeles tomorrow. She hadn't asked him to take her to the airport; he hadn't offered. Not because he didn't want to drive her, but because he didn't want her to go.

He knew she had to leave, knew he had to be on the road himself. His next project was scheduled to break ground on Tuesday. It wasn't as if either one of them had a choice. But somehow that didn't make it any easier, and the persistent tug in his chest worried him. Even if she was different from any other woman, even if he cared about her more than he had any other woman, that didn't mean he couldn't let her go. He could, dammit.

Just not yet.

When the quartet switched to Handel's *Water Music*, Evan straightened. They'd been given instructions at the rehearsal last night as to who went where when, but he'd had a hard time paying attention. Marcy had worn that pretty pink dress, and all he'd been able to think about was the afternoon he'd taken it off her. And then all he'd been able to think about was taking it off her again.

When they'd gotten back to their room last night, that was exactly what he'd done. The memory of what had happened next made him smile. All that silky smooth skin under his hands…the sound of soft laughter when he'd kissed that ticklish spot on her ribs…her sigh when he'd slid into her…

Good grief. He blinked, reminded himself that he was standing in front of one hundred and fifty people— fantasizing about Marcy!

Thankfully, every head in the room had already turned to watch Julianna emerge from the back of the chapel. Grace followed several steps behind, then Hannah. Carrying small bouquets of white roses, they all wore blue satin that flowed to their ankles. No doubt about it, Evan thought as he watched the women walk up the aisle. The Blackhawk family had some fine-looking females.

And then Marcy stepped through the doorway and the other women blurred from his vision.

He went numb.

Her dress was the same color blue, but unlike the others, it was strapless, emphasizing her long neck and lovely shoulders. Diamonds sparkled on her earlobes and at the base of her throat. Her smile lit up the room. When she turned her smoky-green gaze on him, he swore his heart stopped.

He was certain if someone even blew on him, he'd fall straight back.

His pulse pounded as she walked down the aisle, then up the steps toward him. She took her place beside the other women and he slowly released the breath he'd been holding, then waited for the feeling to come back into his body. When the bridal march began, Evan heard the gasps and murmurs of delight, then turned to watch Clair walk down the aisle. She looked beautiful, of course, and happy. Evan glanced at Jacob, saw the moisture in his brother's eyes as he watched his bride glide closer to him. Evan had to clear his throat.

Since they'd been kids, he and Jacob had only had each other to rely on. Now Jacob had Clair, and though Evan knew all their lives would be better, he also knew they'd be different.

He was happy for them both, yet he suddenly felt as if part of him was being torn away, leaving a jagged, empty hole. He shrugged the feeling off, told himself all this hearts-and-flowers stuff was making him soft and he'd be glad when it was over.

He glanced at Marcy, felt the hole in his chest widen and knew there was one thing he wasn't glad about.

When Clair's father handed her to Jacob, Evan squared his shoulders and turned his attention to the reason they were all *really* here, of course.

Free beer and food.

Lights twinkled in every darkened corner of the Four Winds ballroom. Huge floral arrangements, white and blue, graced every table. Silverware clinked against fine china. The food was impeccable, the champagne as expensive as it was endless.

But it was the bride and groom who stole the show, Marcy thought, watching Clair and Jacob gaze into each other's eyes while they danced together on the crowded floor. It was impossible to imagine two people more in love.

Until she'd met Evan, Marcy couldn't have even guessed what it felt like.

She sat at a table, her shoes off, watching Evan as he scooped up Julianna and Lucas's little girl in his arms and danced with her. The child laughed when he dipped her and Marcy found herself laughing, too, even while her heart ached.

I'll get over him, she told herself. Maybe fall in love again. It could happen.

In another lifetime, maybe.

She let herself feel the pain for a moment, then pushed it away. There would be plenty of time for that later, she told herself. Too much time.

"I think there's a law here against not dancing." Rand sat in the chair next to her. "That's what my wife told me, anyway."

Marcy tilted her head. "You're not dancing."

"The boys sent me on a beer run. Can I get you anything?"

"No, thanks." She held up the glass of champagne she'd been sipping. "I'm good."

Apparently in no hurry to complete his beer mission,

Rand settled back in the chair. "I hear you're headed back to L.A. tomorrow."

She nodded. "As it is, I've been gone so long my manager had to double her antianxiety medication."

"Send her out here," Rand said. "Nothing like mucking out a stall or riding fence to reduce stress. I could use another hand."

Just the thought of Helen mucking out a stall or riding a horse made Marcy laugh. With her manicured nails, designer suits and expensive shoes, Helen Dunbar was the last woman in the world to wield a pitchfork or ride a horse. "I'll be sure and extend your offer."

"You do that." Grinning, Rand stretched out his long legs. "So I take it nothing ever came of her hiring a P.I. to find you."

"Jacob's friend in L.A. couldn't find anything, and my assistant, Anna, never heard Helen mention it again. It seems we all overreacted." Marcy smiled when Evan scooped up Hannah's twin girls and somehow managed to dance with all three children. "And even if she did hire someone to find me, it doesn't matter now, anyway. Obviously, they didn't."

"By the way—" Rand glanced at the dance floor, then looked back at Marcy "—that was a nice toast Evan gave."

"It was, wasn't it?" she said with a smile. Evan had made everyone laugh when he'd asked for all of Jacob's old girlfriends to return his house keys and at least a dozen women, including one of the female servers and Clair's mother, stood up and handed over keys. Then he'd made everyone sigh when he'd raised his glass and welcomed Clair Carver to the family.

But Evan hadn't been the only brother-in-law to propose a toast to the newlyweds. Rand had stood up, as well. "Your toast was beautiful, Rand," Marcy said. "You made Clair cry."

"I got a little choked up myself," Rand admitted, then frowned at Marcy. "But if you tell anyone I said that, I'll deny it."

Marcy smiled. In fact, there hadn't been a dry eye in the house after Rand had stood and said that Clair might be Jacob's wife, but she would always be his and Seth's little sister, that he knew their parents' love and their spirit was here with them today, and that the power and strength of that love had brought them all back together.

I want that kind of love, Marcy thought. The kind that endured fire and time and every hardship life had to offer. She looked at Evan, and realized *she* did have it. The problem was, the person she loved, didn't love her back.

"The boys are looking thirsty." Rand leaned over and gave her a friendly kiss on the cheek, then stood. "Sure I can't get you anything?"

Evan, was her first thought, but she simply smiled and shook her head.

She glanced around the room at the people celebrating, imagined what this room would look like if this was *her* wedding. She could see it clearly in her mind: pink roses, hundreds of them; a four-tiered cake with raspberry filling; a live band that played everything from

Glen Miller to contemporary rock. Her dress would be organza, with satin ribbons and a full skirt.

And a tiara, she thought, smiling. What woman could resist a tiara?

A commotion from the corner of the room jolted Marcy out of her daydream. One of the guests, an attractive blonde, had spilled a glass of champagne on the photographer and she was profusely apologizing. Marcy knew that it was rare for any wedding not to have a problem of some kind, but a spilled glass of champagne would hardly be considered a crisis.

Still, years of catering and party planning were in her blood. She started to wave for a member of the staff to help, but suddenly three little girls had hold of her arms and were pulling her out to the dance floor. Grinning, Evan grabbed her shoulders and kissed her square on the mouth.

"Evan Carver!" Marcy gasped, then looked down at the little girls, who were all giggling.

"They dared me to kiss you." Evan winked at the girls. "I can't very well turn down a dare. I'd look like a sissy."

Rolling her eyes, Marcy glanced at the children and with her finger, made a circle by her head. Laughing, the girls ran off.

"I'm crazy, all right." He pulled her into his arms when a slow song started. "Crazy 'bout you."

Her heart jumped, even though she knew he didn't mean it the way she wanted him to mean it. But it sounded wonderful, so she held on to him, bare feet and all, and slowly swayed to the Eagles' "I Can't Tell You Why."

"Let's get out of here," he said, brushing his lips over her ear.

She lifted her head and looked at him, saw the dark desire shining in his eyes. "The party's not over."

"Close enough. We'll see Jacob and Clair tomorrow morning before—" He stopped, then slid his hand down her back. "Come upstairs with me."

She knew he'd almost said "before you leave." It was easier not to talk about tomorrow, she thought. Easier to just be in the moment.

"All right." She glanced at Jacob and Clair, who were saying goodbye to an elderly couple. "I'll meet you in the hallway."

It took her a few moments to gather her purse and the heels she'd left under the table. She was heading for the hallway when she stopped suddenly, then turned and was drawn back to the double doors leading to the chapel.

She needed to see it one more time, at night. Just for a moment, she told herself and stepped inside. She breathed in the lingering scent of roses, touched each pew as she slowly walked down the aisle, felt the cool tile under her feet.

This chapel was her "baby," she thought, smiling softly. Hers and Evan's. She wanted to embrace what they'd done, etch it in her mind and keep it in her heart.

From the back of the chapel, Evan watched her move up the steps to the spot where Clair and Jacob had said their vows earlier. Moonlight streamed through the stained-glass window and caressed her face, flowed like water over her blue dress.

Like the first time he'd seen her stand there, he simply couldn't think.

Couldn't breathe.

Quietly, he turned and walked away. When he was outside, he dragged a long pull of air into his lungs, then went to the hallway and waited for her.

She woke slowly the next morning, drifted in and out of that warm, comfortable place between sleep and consciousness. It was a lovely place to be, and she thought she could stay there forever, floating, half dreaming. She stirred, felt the solid length of Evan's body against hers. Opening her eyes, Marcy realized he was already awake, his elbow bent, resting his head on his hand while he gazed down at her.

"Mornin'," he said softly.

"Morning." It embarrassed her that he'd been watching her, but in an odd way, it pleased her, as well. Smiling, she pulled the sheet up and snuggled under the covers. "What time is it?"

"Six-thirty."

Groaning, she closed her eyes and burrowed deeper into the mattress. They'd had very little sleep last night. But then reality hit her and she realized what day it was: the last day they would wake up together.

Suddenly six-thirty seemed very, very late.

When his hand skimmed the bare curve of her hip, she shivered. He kissed her, soft and slow, with a tenderness that melted her bones. She wrapped her arms around his neck and kissed him back, until they were both breathing hard and more than a little aroused. His lips still on hers, he rolled her to her back.

"By the way," he said, "I ordered room service."

"Already? It's so—" on a moan, she gripped the bedclothes in her fists when his hands slid to her breasts "—early."

"Yeah, but I'm starving."

He nibbled on her neck, then moved lower. Fire skipped through her blood when his tongue found her hardened nipple.

"How much time do we have?" she asked breathlessly.

"Thirty minutes."

"Wonderful," she murmured, then arched upward, awash in the delicious sensations rippling through her. Restless, she stroked her hands over his back and shoulders, murmuring his name. He kissed her breasts, her hip, her stomach, then moved over her and slid inside. She wrapped herself around him, needing him closer still, felt the desperation rage inside him, dark and wild and raw. It shuddered from his body into hers, then ripped through them both, as sharp as it was fierce.

He filled her. Her body. Her heart. Her soul.

I love you, she nearly said, but managed to hold those three precious words back. She couldn't bear it if he turned away from her now.

It was a long moment before either one of them moved, then he gathered her close and kissed her cheek, then her nose.

"I'll go warm up the shower," he said, his voice still ragged. "Join me?"

"Sure." But she wasn't certain her legs could hold her up at the moment. "In a minute."

She watched him walk to the bathroom, felt her heart tighten and twist. *Later,* she told herself. Don't think about it now.

She sat slowly, dragged a hand through her hair, was reaching for her robe when she heard a knock from the other room. *Room service.* She'd completely forgotten about them, and apparently so had Evan. Pulling her robe on, she padded through the living room and opened the door.

When the camera flashed in her face, she froze.

Ten

Dear Marcy,
I'm giving a fiftieth anniversary party for my parents and though I want to make my own invitations, I'm not very creative and don't know where to start. Can you help me?
Kathy in Aurora

Evan had just opened the shower door when he heard Marcy cry out. He grabbed a towel and flew out of the bathroom, kept moving when she wasn't in the bedroom.

"Get out of here!" Evan heard Marcy yell from the living room. "Leave me alone!"

When he raced around the corner, a flash blinded him for a moment, then he saw the short, balding man standing in the suite entry, his foot shoved against the door while he quickly snapped pictures.

Evan saw red. On a roar, he charged the man, who

managed to snap another picture before he spun on his heels and dashed down the hall.

"Evan, no!"

He felt Marcy grab his arm, but it didn't even slow him down. He tore after the guy, wasn't even halfway down the hall before the man was already inside the elevator.

Dammit, dammit, dammit! Evan yelled at the man, who actually had the nerve to grin and wave as the doors were starting to close. Son of a bitch! He'd never catch him now!

Later, Evan would realize that the woman who seemed to appear out of nowhere had actually stepped out of the suite closest to the elevators. But at that moment, the only thing he really noticed was a blonde in gray sweatpants and a white tank top move in front of the elevator and slam her hand on the doors to keep them from closing. The grin on the man's face turned to shock as the blonde stepped onto the elevator and snatched the camera.

"Hey!" the guy hollered and grabbed at the woman. In one fluid move, she had the guy's hand in hers and he was on his knees, moaning in pain.

Smiling, the woman tossed the camera to Evan when he reached the elevator. She flicked her gaze downward and arched an eyebrow. "Nice towel."

Adrenaline still pumping, his chest heaving, Evan caught the camera with one hand and held the towel with his other. "Thanks."

"Evan!" Marcy ran up behind him, clutching her robe tightly together. "Are you all right?"

"Better than this jerk." Evan nodded at the photographer, then looked back at Marcy. Her cheeks were pale, her eyes wide and frightened. "You okay?"

"I'm fine. He just surprised me." Marcy stared first at the man on his knees, then at the blonde. "Who are you?"

"You got no right," the man choked out the words while he tried to stand. "I'm going to sue your—"

The woman tweaked the man's hand a fraction, and he went down again, groaning even louder. "I'll be back up in ten minutes." The blonde gave a toss of her long ponytail and reached for the elevator button. "And if it's not too much trouble, do you think you guys could get me some coffee?"

"My name is Shelby Richards." Sitting at the dining-room table in Evan's suite, the woman opened two sugar packets and dumped them in her coffee. No one could have looked at the slender, pretty blonde and imagined that fifteen minutes ago she'd taken down a man with a mere flick of one slim wrist. "I'm a private investigator from Los Angeles."

Marcy sucked in a breath and glanced at Evan. Arms folded, he stood beside the table, clenching his jaw. They'd managed to drag some clothes on before room service had shown up, but Marcy was still too shook up to eat and Evan was still too angry.

"So it's true then?" The knot in Marcy's stomach tightened. "Helen hired you to find me?"

Shelby lifted her coffee and blew on it. "Not exactly."

"Why don't you tell us *exactly* what *is* true?" Evan said tightly.

"She hired me to keep an eye out for your friend, Arnie Blanchard." Shelby eyed a piece of bacon. "Do you mind? I'm starving."

"Arnie Blanchard?" Marcy's eyes widened, then narrowed with anger as she slid the plate of food closer to Shelby. "I thought he looked familiar."

"Do you ladies care to fill me in?" Evan said, frowning. "Or am I supposed to guess?"

"Arnie calls himself a journalist, but he's nothing more than a sleazeball tabloid paparazzi." Shelby munched on the bacon. "He'd been after Marcy here for some time, looking for something to tarnish her shiny, wholesome image."

"Arnie's been after *me?*" Just the thought of it made Marcy's skin crawl. "How do you know this?"

"Helen has her sources," Shelby said.

Evan lifted an eyebrow. "You mean she has you."

"Let's just say I know who to ask what." Shelby rolled a shoulder and finished off the bacon. "But that's irrelevant for this conversation. What is relevant is that Helen knew Arnie had been trying to dig up dirt on Marcy for the past couple of months, especially because of all the PR her new TV show is getting. It would be a real coup to get a scoop on Miss Marcy Pruitt. He nearly got it this morning. Tomorrow's headline in all the media would have probably been Marcy Pruitt's Secret Love Nest, complete with pictures."

Oh, dear Lord. Marcy closed her eyes and drew in a breath to steady herself. Shelby was right. A story and picture like that *would* make news. And if it had, there was no telling what the producer of her show might do.

"So Arnie's been watching me all the time I've been here in Wolf River?" The thought of it sent a chill slithering up Marcy's spine. "Taking pictures of me?"

Shelby shook her head. "He just got here yesterday, and it took him a while to track you down here. I think your new look threw him off. By the way—" Shelby smiled "—you look fantastic. That haircut is so right for you and I love what you—"

When Evan cleared his throat, Shelby glanced up. "Oh, right. Well, anyway, I followed Arnie to the reception last night and kept an eye on him to make sure he wouldn't bother you."

"That was *you* last night." Marcy remembered the commotion in the corner just before she'd gone out on the dance floor with Evan. "You spilled champagne on the photographer."

Shelby nodded. "I distracted him long enough to stop him from following you up here when you both left the reception, but I knew it wouldn't take him long to figure out what room you were in. I've been waiting for him, but he moved a little quicker this morning than I thought he would."

"Too bad I didn't answer the door." Evan's eyes narrowed to slits. "I would have made that camera part of his lower intestines."

"Now *that* would make a picture," Shelby said with a grin. "The manager here had him hauled off to the sheriff's station. They'll keep him locked up for a while, at least until Marcy's left town."

Until she'd left town. Once again, the reality that she was leaving in a few hours hit her like a two-by-four. She glanced at Evan, saw the grim expression on his face. But she couldn't read his eyes. Couldn't tell if Shelby's statement had any impact on him at all.

A thought suddenly occurred to Marcy that made her back stiffen and her insides turn inside out. She glanced quickly around the room, then looked at Shelby. "Did you…are there any, ah—"

"No bugs, if that's what you're thinking." Shelby tilted her head and batted her thick lashes. "What kind of a girl do you think I am?"

An impressive one, Marcy thought, wondering if the woman might teach her that little move that had put Arnie on the floor.

"Look," Shelby said, the teasing tone gone. "I admit I've been aware of where you've been and with whom, but please believe me, I only came here to watch for Arnie and keep him away from you if he showed up. I didn't come here to snoop on you. Helen very specifically told me *not* to tell her what you were doing. She said if you wanted her to know, you'd tell her yourself."

Marcy sighed heavily, then shook her head. "Helen should have told me about Arnie."

"You'll have to take that up with Helen." Shelby eyed the omelette sitting in front of her. "Are you going to eat that?"

"Why don't you take it on your way out?" Evan suggested. "It seems to me your job here is finished."

"That it is." Shelby picked up the plate, then glanced at Marcy. "By the way, I managed to dig up a little dirt on Arnie myself, so unless he wants his own face on the tabloids, he shouldn't be bothering you anymore."

Marcy didn't even want to know, but it did give her a sense of relief that the man wouldn't be hiding around corners or sneaking around her house or office.

"Thank you," Marcy said when Shelby stood. "In spite of the awkwardness of all this, I do appreciate what you've done."

"Just doing my job." Shelby headed for the door. "You ever need anything, Helen's got my number." She looked over her shoulder at Evan. Her gaze lowered and she grinned. "Nice to meet you, Evan."

Marcy supposed at any other time, with any other woman, she might have felt a little jealous, but considering the circumstances, and the unexpected blush on Evan's cheeks, all she could do was smile. "Looks like you've got a fan," Marcy said after Shelby closed the door behind her.

Frowning, Evan stared at the door. "All the time, she was right under our noses. Damn, I feel like an idiot."

He shook his head, then reached for Marcy and pulled her into his arms. "You okay?"

"I am now." *Now that you're holding me.*

"When I saw that guy with his foot holding the door while he took your picture, I swear I wanted to kill him."

"Most people who come into contact with Arnie say that." Marcy laid her hands on Evan's chest. "I never dreamed my life would have been interesting enough for him to come after me."

"I've played cards with the sheriff a few times," Evan said. "He might look the other way while I pay my respects to the ass—"

She pressed her fingertips to his lips. "Thank you for the gesture," she said, laying her head on his shoulder. "But it doesn't matter. He won't bother us anymore."

Evan stilled the moment she said the words. She hadn't meant to say "us." She knew there was no "us." Not after today. After all they'd been through, she didn't want their goodbye to be awkward or uncomfortable.

"Why don't you go take a shower while I pack?" Lifting her head, she kept the smile on her lips. "I need to give Helen a call."

Something flickered in Evan's dark gaze, and for a moment, she thought he was going to kiss her. Instead, he dropped his arms and nodded. "All right."

She swallowed the thickness in her throat as he walked toward the bedroom. He stopped at the doorway, then turned and met her gaze. "It's not an easy life you live, Miss Pruitt."

I'd give it up for you, she thought, and she knew she would if he wanted her to. But he hadn't asked, and she couldn't offer. All she could do was nod and smile and pray he couldn't see that her heart was shattering into thousands of tiny little pieces.

The growl of bulldozers and the rumble of cement mixers filled the hot Texas afternoon. Clouds of dust kicked up by the heavy machinery lay like a wool blanket over the construction site and the constant *beep-beep-beep* of a tractor grated not only the dirt, but Evan's nerves, as well.

Almost two weeks on the job and already there'd been nothing but problems. A delay with the surveyor's report, two thunderstorms, a misplaced load of foundation forms. All he needed now were the locusts to come through.

Instead, Tom knocked on the trailer door, then stuck his head in. "The generator's down. I sent James into town to pick up a gasket."

Evan swore hotly and slammed down the cup of coffee he'd been drinking, which spilled onto the blueprints he'd been studying—which made him swear all the more.

The locusts have arrived, he thought, then grabbed a napkin to soak up the coffee.

"So—" Ignoring Evan's outburst, Tom stepped inside the trailer "—how's the foot?"

"Fine." Actually, his foot hurt like a son of a bitch,

but he'd be damned if he'd admit it. He'd broken two toes yesterday when he'd kicked a boulder after arguing twenty minutes with an idiot inspector. Bone against stone—stone wins. "Something I can do for you?"

Tom dropped down on an office chair. "Well, my nail gun's broke."

Evan frowned. "And you're telling me this because…?"

Tom tipped his hard hat back from his sweaty face. "I figured I could stuff a box of nails in your mouth and you could spit 'em out for me."

Evan turned to glare at his foreman. "Are you trying to make me mad?"

"Don't have to." Tom stretched out his long legs and crossed one dirt-covered boot over the other. "You're doing that all by yourself."

"I don't know what the hell you're talking about." *Nor do I want to know,* Evan thought and turned back to the blueprints. "We're already behind schedule here, Tom. You of all people should know what that costs us."

"And you of all people should know what happens when a crew walks off a site."

Evan looked up sharply. "Who's walking off?"

"No one," Tom said. "Not yet, anyway. But you keep snarling like a junkyard dog and they will."

Evan's first instinct was to tell Tom to go to hell, but he bit back the words. In his gut, he knew damn well that his foreman was right. He *had* been taking his bad mood out on everyone around him.

And in his gut, he knew damn well why.

Marcy.

He couldn't get the woman out of his mind. Not a day, an hour, barely a *minute* went by he didn't think about her. In two weeks, he hadn't slept one night, hadn't cared about food and didn't give a damn about his work.

He missed her. Missed waking up next to her every morning. Missed her smile, her laugh, the way her lips pursed when she was deep in thought. He missed discussing his day with her, missed hearing about hers.

Nothing like this had ever happened to him before. No woman had ever turned him inside out and upside down. No woman had ever affected his work. No woman had ever made him think that his trailer was too small.

Too lonely.

He hadn't talked to her since the day she'd left for the airport. He hadn't even driven her there—she'd insisted that Shelby was driving there anyway and it was silly for her not to ride with the woman.

He should have argued, dammit. Should have insisted she let him drive her. But she'd almost seemed as if she was in a hurry to get rid of him. In a hurry to leave, to go back to her life in a fishbowl. Her life where fans rushed her in train stations, where her own manager hired a P.I. to keep track of her, where slimy tabloid reporters followed her halfway across the country just to get a damn story that would hurt her.

He wanted no part of that life.

But he wanted Marcy.

He had no indication how she felt about him. She knew his number, and she hadn't called. And he hadn't been able to bring himself to call her, knew that she was getting ready for her TV show. She'd be in meetings, or rehearsals or book signings. The last thing she needed was him bothering her for no other reason than to say hello. To hear her voice.

With a sigh, he dropped down in a chair beside Tom. "Junkyard dog, huh?"

Tom nodded. "With fleas."

Hell. Evan scrubbed a hand over his face, realized he hadn't shaved in a while, though he wasn't certain how long.

He had to do something, that much he knew.

The tough part was figuring out what.

"Ten minutes to air everyone." Sean Monahan, director of *The Real Life With Marcy Pruitt* show, waved a clipboard, then looked at Marcy. "How you doing?"

Marcy smiled and nodded calmly at the director, even though her stomach was fluttering and her hands shaking. Behind her, Helen and Anna were fussing over last-minute changes on the prop table, while the cameramen and soundmen made adjustments with their equipment.

Deep breaths, she reminded herself, then closed her eyes while the makeup artist dusted her face with fresh powder. Today would not only be her maiden show, *live* from Los Angeles, it would also be the national un-veiling of the "new" Marcy Pruitt. Today could very well be the day that would make—or break—her career.

And if all that wasn't difficult enough, the producer had brought in a test audience for Marcy to interact with during the show. If she wasn't afraid she'd ruin her crisp, mint-green blouse and khaki skirt, she just might throw up.

Instead, she concentrated on her breathing, slowly felt herself relax as she imagined herself on a deserted beach. Aqua blue water. Warm sand. The gentle lap of waves on the shore. She was wonderfully, blissfully alone.

But then suddenly she wasn't alone. Evan was with her. Lying on a towel beside her, his skin bronzed and damp from swimming, his dark hair slicked back. She smiled at him, reached out to touch him.

And he vanished.

Fool, she thought, not certain if she meant herself or Evan. Maybe both.

"Don't frown, sweetie," Trixie, the makeup artist warned. "You'll get wrinkles."

What do I care? Marcy thought. What were a few wrinkles compared to a broken heart? When she'd left Wolf River, she hadn't thought she could possibly hurt more than she had that day.

She'd been so wrong.

She hadn't heard from Evan, though idiot that she was, she jumped every time her cell phone rang, eagerly checked her messages at home every night, hoping, wishing…

Apparently, he had moved on easily enough.

"Five minutes!"

Her eyes flew open and her stomach twisted into little knots. But strangely enough, she preferred this piercing arrow of fear to the overwhelming pain she felt when she was alone. The only thing that had saved her since she'd returned home had been her work. Her work gave her a reason to get up in the morning, to force herself to smile and act like nothing was wrong, when inside her heart was aching.

"Marcy." Helen hurried toward her, then slipped an arm around her waist. "Honey, I need to talk with you."

"Now? But we've only got—"

"It's important." Helen pulled her away from Trixie. "I just want you to know how proud I am of you."

"Thank you." Marcy glanced nervously at the director, who didn't seem concerned they had only four minutes till airtime.

"I know I don't always make the best choices for you." Helen took Marcy's hands in hers. "But I promise you I only have the best of intentions."

"Helen, we've already settled all this between us," Marcy said quietly. "I understand why you hired Shelby, and it's fine. We've agreed, you won't do anything like that again, and you won't keep things from me. Right?"

"Right." Helen smiled, then squeezed Marcy's hands. "I only want you to be happy, sweetheart."

The sudden moisture in Helen's eyes stunned Marcy. In four years, she'd never seen Helen cry. Not once.

"Stop that," Marcy said firmly. "This is no time to get emotional on me. I'm going on live television, for heaven's sake."

"That's my girl." Helen blinked back her tears, then quickly composed herself and squeezed Marcy's hands. "Now go knock their socks off."

As the director counted down, Marcy stood on her mark behind the kitchen work counter where most of the show took place. She'd be reading from a teleprompter for the opening, so the most important thing for her to remember was which camera to look at when.

"Ready…" The director held up his hand. "Five, four, three…"

Marcy slowly drew in a breath, slowly released it, and smiled. "…two, one—" the director pointed at her "—and you're *on!*"

"Welcome to *The Real Life With Marcy Pruitt,*" Marcy said after the applause died down. "I'm Marcy Pruitt, your host for the next hour. Now some of you may be shaking your heads and saying, that's not Marcy Pruitt. I know what Marcy Pruitt looks like and that's not her." Marcy picked up her glasses sitting on the counter in front of her and put them on. "Recognize me now?"

She explained that she'd decided it was time for the

"Ultimate Marcy Makeover" on herself, and she hoped everyone liked her new look, then asked everyone to let her know, either by phone or mail or on her Web site.

"On our first show today," she said, "we'll be designing homemade invitations for that special occasion, baking brownie cookies and learning how to extend the vase life of cut flowers. So stay right where you are and we'll be right back."

When they cut to a commercial, Marcy dragged in a big gulp of air, waved at the clapping audience, then moved to her mark for her first segment, which was the handmade invitations.

So far so good.

The director cued her, and once again, she was smiling into a live camera. "Our first project today is handmade invitations," she said, "and I'm going to take you step-by-step through our first sample, a wedding invitation."

Marcy reached for the invitation, realized that while it was handmade, it wasn't the one she'd created for the show. *My first crisis on live TV,* she thought, struggling to remain calm. Smiling, she held the invitation and described the layered effect of lace, torn paper and pearl beads on the outside while the camera zoomed in for a closeup. When she opened the card, her heart stopped.

A tiny paper bird popped up, and underneath the bird, in large letters:

Evan Carver and Marcy Pruitt would like you to
join them in their wedding ceremony, any month,
any day, any time of Marcy's choice.
As long as it's soon.
Evan Carver

Was this a joke? she thought, too dazed to move. No
one would be that cruel. She heard applause, heard the
murmurs of excited voices, but she was still too numb
to respond. She simply stood there, staring at the invitation, until she felt someone—Helen—touch her
shoulder and tell her to look up.

When she did, she saw him.

Heart pounding, Marcy watched a man wearing a suit
and tie stand up from his seat in the back row of the audience. *Evan!* The cameras followed him as he walked
down the steps toward her, carrying a bouquet of red roses.

She couldn't speak, couldn't breathe. He stopped in
front of her and handed her the roses, then took her hand
and pulled her from behind the counter.

When he dropped down on one knee, she thought for
certain she would faint.

"Marcy Pruitt." He looked straight into her eyes,
pulled a small black velvet box out of his pants pocket,
opened it, then held it up. "Will you marry me?"

Will you marry me?

She stared at him, then looked at the audience. Every

woman in the room, including herself, seemed to be holding their breath. Marcy quickly glanced at Helen and Anna, who were hugging each other and smiling.

She'd have to talk to them about this later.

At the moment, though, she was a little busy.

Marcy stared at the diamond solitaire Evan offered her, could feel her heart vibrating through her entire body.

"Marry you?" was the best she could manage.

"Marry me," he repeated softly, then took the ring and slid it on her finger. "Please."

"I—" she swallowed the tears in her throat "—I— yes!" she gasped, then threw her arms around him. "Yes!"

He kissed her then, as if no one else in the world was there. No audience, no cameramen, no two hundred thousand television viewers sitting in their living rooms. And she kissed him back.

The audience was on their feet, clapping and cheering. Over the thunderous applause, Sean, the director, stepped to the camera and said, "*The Real Life With Marcy Pruitt* will be right back after this commercial, folks. Stay with us."

Sean turned to Evan. "We'll have three minutes of commercial here, then five minutes of on-air setup with the producer before we bring Marcy back to the stage. That's eight minutes. Not one second more."

Marcy wrapped her arms around Evan's neck when he lifted her off her feet and carried her behind the set. Before she could speak, his mouth was on hers again, kissing her, driving out every other thought. She couldn't think, but she could feel.

Lord, how she could feel. Her heart swelled in her chest, blossomed like the roses she still held in her hand.

"I love you," he said against her lips.

"I love you, too." She was still reeling, still confused. And incredibly happy. "But how did you…when did you—"

He put a finger to her lips. "I was going crazy without you. And making everyone around me crazy, too. I think if I hadn't come here myself, my crew would have tied me up and mailed me."

"I could have lived with that," Marcy said with a smile.

He grinned at her. "The point is, I can't live without you. I don't want to. And if that means being part of all this—" he nodded toward the set "—then fine."

"Evan, you just proposed to me on television." She touched his cheek, knew that the seconds were flying by before she'd have to be in front of the camera again. "Why—and how?"

"Why, because I decided to face head-on the one thing that I didn't think I could handle, which was being in the spotlight. I figured if I could do this and survive, and if you'd have me, then the rest would be a piece of cake. And the how—" he shrugged "—well, I called Helen and she took care of that."

"Helen?" Marcy looked over her shoulder, was surprised the woman wasn't peeking around the corner. "This was Helen's idea?"

"She ran it by the producer and we all collaborated," Evan said.

So that's why Helen had been acting so odd just before the show, Marcy realized. She wasn't sure whether she should fire her manager or give her a raise.

"You mean conspired," Marcy said, arching an eyebrow.

"Whatever it took to make you say yes." He brushed his lips lightly over hers. "I wasn't sure if you'd have room for me in your life. I didn't want to give you time to think about it."

"You really don't know?" she said softly, touching his cheek. "I'd have walked away from everything for you. I still would, if you asked me to."

"And deprive your fans of brownie recipes and tips on cutting flowers?" He smiled at her. "I'll share you during the day, Miss Pruitt. But at night—" he pulled her closer "—at night, baby, you're all mine."

Just the thought of it made her heart sing. "But what about your business? How will you—"

"Jacob's giving up the P.I. business. He wants to settle down now that he's married. He and Tom will run Carver Construction in Texas, and I'll run a branch here."

"You're going to live here—in L.A.?" She could

barely hear him through the symphony playing in her head. "And work here?"

"Well, of course I am." He frowned at her. "Why wouldn't I live where my wife lives?"

Wife. The reality of it all sank in and she had to blink the tears back. Any minute now, she would have to be on camera again. She didn't dare cry now.

Later, she told herself. Later, she'd need an entire tissue box.

"And anyway," Evan said, "your little canyon cottage is big enough for two, isn't it?"

"Actually," she said a bit sheepishly, "it's not that little. It's more like five thousand square feet."

"Five thousand?" He whistled softly. "Well, then, I suppose we won't have to add on when we have babies, will we?"

Wife. Babies. That did it. She couldn't stop the tears.

He held her close, pressed his mouth to her temple. "Say when and where, sweetheart."

"We'll talk about when later, when I can think straight. As for the where—" She lifted her head and through the blur of her tears met his gaze. "I know this great little chapel in Texas."

Smiling, he kissed the tip of her nose. "I was hoping you'd say that."

"Marcy!" Helen stuck her head around the corner. "The phone lines are jammed and so is your Web site. Everyone loves you!"

If Helen hadn't left as quickly as she'd popped up, Marcy might have told her that she only needed one person to love her.

And that person, Marcy thought as she kissed Evan again, was in her arms.

* * * * *

Narrated with the simplicity and unabashed
honesty of a child's perspective, *Me & Emma*
is a vivid portrayal of the heartbreaking loss
of innocence, an indomitable spirit and
incredible courage.

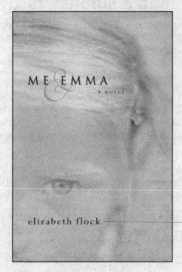

ME EMMA

a novel

elizabeth flock

ISBN 0-7783-0084-6

In many ways, Carrie Parker is like any other eight-year-
old—playing make-believe, dreading school, dreaming of
faraway places. But even her naively hopeful mind can't shut
out the terrible realities of home or help her to protect her
younger sister, Emma. Carrie is determined to keep Emma
safe from a life of neglect and abuse at the hands of their
drunken stepfather, Richard—abuse their momma can't
seem to see, let alone stop.

On sale 15th July 2005

FREE!

2 Books
and a surprise gift!

We would like to take this opportunity to thank you for reading this Silhouette® book by offering you the chance to take TWO more specially selected titles from the Desire™ series absolutely FREE! We're also making this offer to introduce you to the benefits of the Reader Service™—

- ★ FREE home delivery
- ★ FREE gifts and competitions
- ★ FREE monthly Newsletter
- ★ Exclusive Reader Service offers
- ★ Books available before they're in the shops

Accepting these FREE books and gift places you under no obligation to buy. you may cancel at any time, even after receiving your free shipment. Simply complete your details below and return the entire page to the address below. You don't even need a stamp!

YES! Please send me 2 free Desire books and a surprise gift. I understand that unless you hear from me. I will receive 3 superb new titles every month for just £4.99 each, postage and packing free. I am under no obligation to purchase any books and may cancel my subscription at any time. The free books and gift will be mine to keep in any case.

D5ZEF

Ms/Mrs/Miss/Mr ....Initials...........................
BLOCK CAPITALS PLEASE

Surname ....

Address...

....

....Postcode ....

Send this whole page to:
UK: FREEPOST CN81, Croydon, CR9 3WZ